Praise for th

The Shining City

"A fine fantasy that magically charms the audience."
—Paranormal Romance Reviews

"A great book of political intrigue, mystery, evil, and a love that will endure."
—Romance Junkies

"A finely crafted, fascinating story by an author with a fantastic imagination."
—Romance Reviews Today

The Tower of Ravens

"By the time you've finished, I guarantee you will say that this is one of the best fantasy reads ever. . . . A fantasy novel that will transport us into the realms of imagination."
—*Armidale Express* (Australia)

"A rich, enthralling ride across the pages of fantasy."
—Fresh Fiction

"An elaborate and fascinating land with a history of battles between good and evil, and peopled with original beings with Celtic flavor. Magic permeates this world. . . . Exciting, well-written."
—Romance Reviews Today

"Filled with artfully drawn characters and creatures . . . finely detailed and infinitely believable. There's something for everyone here."
—The Romance Reader's Connection

continued . . .

The Witches of Eileanan Series

"A trilogy like the kind that made me fall in love with fantasy in the first place."
—SF Site

"An entertaining, old-fashioned adventure."
—*Locus*

"In the tradition of Anne McCaffrey and Marion Zimmer Bradley . . . a satisfying read."
—*Bundaberg NewsMail* (Australia)

"Kate Forsyth has woven a stirring epic fantasy, a marvelously rambling tale of outlawed witches, ruling-class conspiracy, blossoming occult talent, and strange and wonderful creatures. . . . A worthy first novel from a writer with a sound streak of both imagination and talent."
—*dB Magazine* (Australia)

"Superb! A rich, vividly described world peopled with such complex characters."
—*Australian SF News*

"A rich fantasy novel with a great cast of characters."
—*New Englander-Armidale* (Australia)

"A remarkable fantasy debut . . . it sings with quality."
—*The West Australian*

"Forsyth . . . writes with aplomb and style."
—*The Examiner* (Australia)

THE HEART OF STARS

BOOK THREE OF RHIANNON'S RIDE

Kate Forsyth

A ROC BOOK

ROC
Published by New American Library, a division of
Penguin Group (USA) Inc., 375 Hudson Street,
New York, New York 10014, USA
Penguin Group (Canada), 90 Eglinton Avenue East, Suite 700, Toronto,
Ontario M4P 2Y3, Canada (a division of Pearson Penguin Canada Inc.)
Penguin Books Ltd., 80 Strand, London WC2R 0RL, England
Penguin Ireland, 25 St. Stephen's Green, Dublin 2,
Ireland (a division of Penguin Books Ltd.)
Penguin Group (Australia), 250 Camberwell Road, Camberwell, Victoria 3124,
Australia (a division of Pearson Australia Group Pty. Ltd.)
Penguin Books India Pvt. Ltd., 11 Community Centre, Panchsheel Park,
New Delhi - 110 017, India
Penguin Group (NZ), 67 Apollo Drive, Rosedale, North Shore, Auckland 1311,
New Zealand (a division of Pearson New Zealand Ltd.)
Penguin Books (South Africa) (Pty.) Ltd., 24 Sturdee Avenue,
Rosebank, Johannesburg 2196, South Africa

Penguin Books Ltd., Registered Offices:
80 Strand, London WC2R 0RL, England

First published by Roc, an imprint of New American Library,
a division of Penguin Group (USA) Inc.

First Printing, May 2007
10 9 8 7 6 5 4 3 2 1

PUBLISHER'S NOTE
This is a work of fiction. Names, characters, places, and incidents either are the product of the author's imagination or are used fictitiously, and any resemblance to actual persons, living or dead, business establishments, events, or locales is entirely coincidental.
    The publisher does not have any control over and does not assume any responsibility for author or third-party Web sites or their content.

For Greg
Always

> *"Life itself is but the shadow of death, and souls departed but the shadows of the living: all things fall under this name. The sun itself is but the dark* simulacrum, *and light but the shadow of God."*

—SIR THOMAS BROWNE
The Garden of Cyrus, 1658

The story so far . . .

Onehorn's daughter is not like the other satyricorns of her herd. Born of a human father, she has failed to grow the horns that mark her place within her herd. Soon, she knows, the other satyricorns will kill her. Her only chance is to escape. But how can she possibly outrun the swift hunters of her herd?

One day, a young man, Connor the Just, rides into the satyricorns' territory and is captured. He begs Onehorn's daughter to help him escape, for he is one of the Rìgh's own elite guard and he carries news of dire importance to Lachlan the Winged. She cuts him free—but only because she has escape plans of her own. Onehorn's daughter dreams of capturing one of the fabled black winged horses of Ravenshaw and flying to freedom. To do this she needs Connor's saddle and bridle, and besides, she empathizes with his urgent desire to get free of the brutish satyricorns.

However, when the herd hunts Connor down and he threatens the life of her mother, Onehorn's daughter shoots him in the back, as much to hide her own betrayal as to save the life of her mother. As is the way of satyricorns, she hacks out all of Connor's teeth and cuts off his little finger to add to the necklace of bones she wears about her neck, and claims all his belongings as her own. With their help, she captures a winged horse and so is able to escape her herd.

Exhausted and injured, she and the winged horse are discovered by Lewen MacNiall, son of the treeshifter Lilanthe. He tends her and the horse, and gives her a name—Rhiannon. In the old tales, Rhiannon had been able to ride so swiftly none could catch her.

Lewen is on holiday from his studies at the Theurgia, the school for witches in Lucescere. It is decided he should escort Rhiannon and her winged steed, Blackthorn, through Ravenshaw to Lucescere, in the company of a journey-witch, Nina the Nightingale; her husband, Iven; and son, Roden; and a group of young acolytes wishing to be admitted to the witches' school.

On the way, the body of Connor is discovered in the river. Wanting to carry the news back to the Rìgh as quickly as possible, Nina and Iven decide to take the short-cut through the valley of Fetterness, past the ruined Tower of Ravens, even though they are warned that the old witches' tower is haunted and the valley cursed. For twenty-five years, young boys have gone missing, graves have been robbed, and ghosts and revenants walk the fields and woods. Confident of her powers, Nina ignores the stories and pushes on.

A storm forces the little party to take refuge at Castle Fettercairn, which guards the ruined Tower. The chatelaine of Castle Fettercairn is a strange old woman named Lady Evaline, who is still grieving for the loss of her husband and young son during the reign of Maya the Ensorcellor. The little boy's ghost haunts the castle. Only Rhiannon can see him clearly, though many of the other acolytes are fearful and disturbed by the dark atmosphere of the castle. The ghost of the little boy—who is just the same age as Roden—awakes Rhiannon one night and shows her a room filled with the ghosts of hundreds of murdered boys, begging her to help them. Terrified, Rhiannon flees—and stumbles upon a secret passage to the Tower of Ravens. There she discovers Lord Malvern, the lord of Fettercairn Castle, attempting to raise the spirit of his brother, with the help of a circle of necromancers. Instead, they raise the spirit of a malevolent queen. She promises to help Lord Malvern find the secret spell of resurrection so that he may bring his dead brother and nephew back to life. First, though, Lord Malvern must resurrect her.

Rhiannon's presence is sensed by the ghost, and she flees back to the castle to warn Nina and the others. They do not believe her, though, thinking her ill or dreaming. Then Nina and Lewen overhear Lord Malvern and his sister-in-law planning to kill Rhiannon to stop her revealing what she saw. They also seem to have sinister plans for Roden, who looks very much like Lady Evaline's dead son, Rory. Nina decides they must flee the castle as quickly as possible.

Rhiannon, meanwhile, has escaped on Blackthorn's back, convinced her life is in danger. Lewen pursues her and persuades her to go back, so that they all may leave without arousing suspicion. However, a great storm blows up and Lewen and Rhiannon are forced to take refuge in the Tower of Ravens. Here, they unwittingly drink from the Cup of Confession, an ancient relic that had been given to Connor many years before. Enchanted by the goblet, Lewen and Rhiannon declare their love for each other, and consummate their desire. Lewen then discovers the necklace of bones and teeth, and Rhiannon admits that she killed Connor. Lewen is shocked and horrified, and leaves Rhiannon, who flees.

In the morning, Lewen again drinks from the goblet, and then—when he contacts Nina through the Tower's Scrying Pool—is compelled to tell her what he has discovered, even though he feels as if he is betraying Rhiannon. She tells him to contact the Rìgh and tell him all their news, which he does. The Rìgh is most distressed by the news, and commands Lewen to bring Connor's murderer back to Lucescere to face justice. Unhappily Lewen goes in search of Rhiannon and manages to save her from being shot by Lord Malvern's men. She is bound and locked up in one of the caravans, and the small party set out once more on their journey to Lucescere.

In the next town, they are told an old tale that sheds much light on Lord Malvern's behavior. He had once been an apprentice at the Tower of Ravens, but was expelled. Hating all witches, he had become one of Maya's Seekers, using his extrasensory talent to search out witches and faeries during the time of her reign. One day he arrested a young girl and condemned her to death by burning. She was held in the dungeons at Fettercairn Castle, where his brother Falkner was lord. Then Lachlan the Winged and his band of rebels sneaked into the castle to rescue her. Lachlan fought a duel with Lord Falkner and killed him, not knowing the lord had hidden away his young wife, Evaline, and their son, Rory, in a secret room. For more than a week they were trapped in the secret room, and the little boy eventually died of cold and hunger. Lord Malvern and Lady Evaline were both driven half mad by this tragedy and spent the next twenty-five years seeking to raise their loved ones from the grave and searching for a way to have their revenge on Lachlan, now Rìgh of Eileanan. Nina and the others all realize how lucky they were to escape Fettercairn Castle.

Early the next morning, Lord Malvern and his men kidnap Roden and gallop back with him to the castle. Rhiannon is released so she and Blackthorn can help track him down. There is a desperate chase back to the castle, and Rhiannon manages to find Roden and rescue him, although poor Lady Evaline jumps out the window after him and is killed. The lord of Fettercairn and his followers are arrested, and taken back to Lucescere to face trial for murder, treason, and necromancy. Rhiannon too must face the courts, and though Lewen assures her all will be well, she is a satyricorn, and satyricorns do not believe in happy endings.

Rhiannon has the right of it. As soon as she arrives in Lucescere, she is locked up in Sorrowgate Tower, the city's prison. She is thrown into the Murderers' Gallery, guarded by the sadistic warden, Octavia the Obese. Lewen manages to have her transferred to a private cell the next day, with the help of his friends Owein and Olwynne, the younger children of Lachlan the Winged.

The lord of Fettercairn and his followers are also locked up, all except for his skeelie Dedrie, who manages to gain the support of the Coven's head healer, Johanna, who is Connor the Just's sister.

Rhiannon is haunted by the ghost of the dead queen she saw at the Tower of Ravens, and distressed by her separation from both Lewen and her winged horse, Blackthorn. Her anxiety grows the closer it gets to the date of her trial.

Then, on May Day, Olwynne NicCuinn casts a love spell on Lewen, making him turn away from Rhiannon. Rhiannon, abandoned and forgotten in prison, is in despair.

The night before their trials, Lord Malvern tries to kidnap Rhiannon during a prison breakout, for in order to raise the dead queen from her grave, they must sacrifice a young woman with strong magical powers, and Rhiannon—who knows too much about them—is their first choice. Rhiannon manages to evade them, however, and so they flee the prison without her.

Rhiannon goes to trial the next day for treason and murder and is found guilty and condemned to death by hanging. Even though Lewen believes his earlier love for Rhiannon was false, he is still shaken and upset. He jumps the Midsummer fire with Olwynne, a public declaration of the intention to marry. Nina, meanwhile, begs the Righ to pardon Rhiannon, and he agrees, though he knows Connor's sister, Johanna, will be very angry that her brother's murderer will go free.

Later that night, Isabeau returns to her room and discovers that Johanna has sneaked in to surreptitiously consult *The Book of Shadows*. Isabeau asks the magical book to show her what Johanna had been reading. It takes her to a spell of resurrection, but, to Isabeau's horror, she discovers it is a trap concealing another deadly spell, written by the evil sorcerer Brann the Raven a thousand years before. It is a spell of compulsion that forces whoever reads it to travel back in time to the day of Brann's death and resurrect him from his grave. By reading the spell, Isabeau too is trapped by Brann's compulsion.

The next day is Midsummer's Day, and Lachlan's elder son Donncan is marrying his cousin Bronwen, daughter of Maya the Ensorcellor. The nuptials are marred by the sudden illness of Bronwen's best friend, the Celestine princess Thunderlily, and by the tension between Donncan and Bronwen.

Then Olwynne is greatly upset by the news that Rhiannon is to be pardoned. She leaves the feast so no one will realize her distress and, to her horror, sees her father, Lachlan the Winged, being shot by a poison dart. As she swoons with the shock, a healer comes to her aid—except the healer is really Dedrie, the lord of Fettercairn's skeelie. She drugs Olwynne and kidnaps her, at the very same moment that Roden, Nina's young son, and Olwynne's twin brother, Owein, are also kidnapped.

Meanwhile, Donncan flies to Johanna, the head healer, for help for his father, but to his horror discovers that she is involved in the plot to kill the Rìgh. She has Thunderlily imprisoned, and abducts him too. It is her plan to force Thunderlily to guide her on the Celestines' secret roads back in time to the day of Brann's death, where she will sacrifice Donncan to raise the evil sorcerer from the dead.

Similarly, Lord Malvern intends to sacrifice Olwynne to raise the dead queen, who Isabeau suspects is her old enemy Margrit of Arran. He will then take Owein and Roden back to Fettercairn Castle to resurrect his brother and young nephew. Thus will he have his revenge on Lachlan and his family returned to him at the same time.

In the meantime, Rhiannon escapes from Sorrowgate Tower, not knowing Lachlan had planned to pardon her. When Lachlan's widow, Iseult, hears the news, she immediately suspects Rhiannon to be the one to have murdered the Rìgh. She calls up a dragon and flies in pursuit, her grief and anger finding form in a violent snowstorm that turns midsummer to winter. She finds Rhiannon and drags her back, ordering that she be hanged at the ringing of the dawn bell. Isabeau and Nina protest, but then news of Roden's kidnapping is brought and Nina is so distraught she leaves Rhiannon's salvation in Isabeau's hands. But Isabeau is caught in Brann's web and cannot help.

It is up to Lewen to save Rhiannon, and all he can do is stop the bell from ringing by wrapping his own body about the massive clapper, giving Rhiannon's friends time to convince Bronwen, the new Banrìgh, to pardon her.

For Bronwen, daughter of the Ensorcellor, must rule in her husband's stead, in a court seething with intrigue, betrayal, and suspicion. If Donncan is not found and returned to his own time, she will be a widow before she was ever a wife. The only person who has a chance of stopping Johanna is the Keybearer, Isabeau, but she too is caught in the spell of compulsion.

With the MacCuinn clan rent apart and the court thrown into utter confusion, there is no one to stop Lord Malvern but Rhiannon and her winged mare, Blackthorn. She must risk everything to try to save the woman she hates more than anyone—the Banprionnsa Olwynne, rival for Rhiannon's one true love, Lewen. In her desperate flight to save Olwynne and her twin brother, Owein, Rhiannon must face the possibility of losing all that she holds most dear—Lewen, Blackthorn, her freedom, even her own life . . .

ONE FOR SORROW

"Who never ate his bread in sorrow,
Who never spent the darksome hours
Weeping and watching for the morrow
He knows ye not, ye heavenly powers."

—JOHANN WOLFGANG VON GOETHE
Wilhelm Meisters Wander, 1796

Rescue Flight

❦

Rhiannon flew into the tumultuous darkness, her face lifted so she could feel the sting of rain against her skin and taste it with her tongue. Wild and sleety, the wind dragged at her hair and clothes, so strong it seemed as if invisible arms were dragging at her, seeking to fling her down into the dizzying space beneath her.

Rhiannon laughed. She flung wide her arms, embracing the storm. Between her knees she felt the warm, living architecture of her winged mare's body; the delicate bones, the straining muscles, the laboring heart that worked together to keep the great wings beating. If Blackthorn's wings should falter, there was nothing between Rhiannon and death but one long scream.

Rhiannon was not afraid. She was alive. She was free. She was loved. She could have shouted her exultation to the wind, if there was not such a desperate need to be silent.

It was almost dawn on a bitter-cold storm-wracked midsummer's night, at a time when all the known order of the universe was wrenched awry. The Rìgh was dead, murdered in his own banquet hall. His heirs had disappeared, stolen away by enemies whose purpose could only be evil. Summer was banished, and in its place had come this unnatural winter, the corn and oats rent by wind and hail, the fruit stricken by frost, the lambs perishing in the snow. It was a storm born of a banrìgh's grief, and until her children were found and restored, and her husband's murderer found, there seemed little chance of summer returning.

Although Rhiannon felt a natural sense of awe at the power that could turn the seasons inside out, she otherwise felt little sympathy for Iseult, the Dowager Banrìgh. The Rìgh who had died was not her Rìgh, and if it had been up to his widow, Rhiannon would have swung at the end of a rope for his murder. She had escaped only because of the desperate efforts of her lover, Lewen, who had wrapped himself about the clapper of the giant bell that tolled the change of hours. Iseult had commanded that Rhiannon be hanged at the ringing of the dawn bell, but Lewen's shaken and battered body had rendered the bell mute, giving her friends time to beg for a pardon from the new Banrìgh, and so Rhiannon had been saved.

Rhiannon smiled. Although many cold, dark hours had passed since they had parted, Lewen's farewell kiss still warmed her all through. She wondered how long it would be before she could again lie in his arms, feeling the length of his naked body pressed against hers, his fingers clenched in her hair, his groan in her ear. She had to press her knees tighter into Blackthorn's sides and grip her hands into the wet, bedraggled mane to control her instinctive swoon at the thought of it.

The faster ye find Roden, and the prionnsa and banprionnsa, the faster ye can go home, she told herself.

Below her the forest stretched dark and dense. She could see only dimly, despite the sharp eyesight she had inherited from her satyricorn mother. The rain was in her eyes and there was no moon or stars to shed any light. The dark tossing leaves below her were as impenetrable as the clouds above her. Nonetheless, Rhiannon bent over Blackthorn's shoulder, scanning the forest for any sign of life. They would not have lit a fire in this wild, wet storm, but they might have lanterns to help light their path through the forest, or perhaps she would see the square shape of a carriage or a glint of steel or glass. She could, perhaps, hear the whicker of a horse, or the cry of a small, frightened boy. Rhiannon could only watch and listen and smell the wind, and hope her enemies thought themselves safe.

An hour passed and there was still no sign of them. Blackthorn's vitality was flagging. She was not built for flying so far, against such a wind. Rhiannon searched for a gap in the storm-tossed canopy, somewhere where they could land safely. She was conscious of sharp disappointment. Once daylight came, it would be harder for her and Blackthorn to fly the skies without being seen.

She saw the ragged shape of a large clearing and directed Blackthorn towards it. The mare stumbled as she landed, and although she recovered her footing, her head and wings drooped with weariness. Rhiannon led her into the meager shelter of the trees and unbuckled her halter and saddlebags so the winged mare could scrape aside the snow and graze. They were both wet to the skin, but with the sleet still lashing down, there was little either of them could do but endure.

Soon the sky began to lighten, and Rhiannon's little bluebird popped its head out of her capacious pocket and began to warble. Rhiannon lifted the bird out carefully, and it perched on her finger and ruffled up its vivid feathers against the cold.

"Why are ye complaining, Bluey?" Rhiannon said. "Ye've been snug and warm in my pocket all night long!"

The bluebird chirped in response, shook out its feathers, and took to the air, flashing like a blue-fletched arrow into the trees. Rhiannon watched its flight with acute pleasure, for she saw the bird as a living symbol of Lewen's love for her. He had carved the bird from a piece of wood and somehow, miraculously, brought it to life. Soon after, he had been struck down by the Banprionnsa Olwynne's love spell and had forgotten his feelings for Rhiannon. Later, when Rhiannon had been about to hang, it was the bluebird who had found Lewen and reminded him, to some degree, of what he and Rhiannon had once shared. Without Bluey, Rhiannon was sure, she would now be dead.

A thin ray of light struck down through the trees. Rhiannon rubbed her gloved hands together vigorously, then put back the sodden hood of her cloak and looked about her.

She was sitting on the verge of a rough track through the forest. On one side the forest rose steeply, oak and hemlock towering over thorny sloe-bushes and bracken. Here and there great grey boulders thrust up from the ground. Wisps of clouds hung over the trees, and the sky overhead was heavy with cloud. It was very cold. Rhiannon shivered and wished fervently for dry clothes and a warm fire. When she rose to rummage through her bags for something to eat, her boots squelched. She found oatcakes spread with bellfruit jam, which she shared with Bluey, and a crisp apple, which she shared with Blackthorn, for there was little food here to sustain her animal friends. Rhiannon washed it all down with water, wishing she had the witch-skills to heat it without fire, like her friend Fèlice, to make herself a hot cup of herbal tea.

Deep ruts in the road were filled with water. As Rhiannon ate, she regarded them thoughtfully. She could not help but hope they were the tracks of her enemy, but it was impossible to tell much more than that a heavy vehicle had passed this way. It was not a logger's dray, for the hooves of the horses were too small and it was a team of four, not six, that had pulled the load. There were outriders, she could see, and some way up the road a horse had fallen and slid in the mud. Whoever had passed this way had been traveling too fast for caution.

Rhiannon clicked her tongue at Blackthorn and, when the mare had picked her way daintily through the mud to her side, slung the bags back over her withers. She did not mount, however. The mud was deep and slippery, and Blackthorn was weary. So, walking side by side, they made their slow way up the road, Rhiannon's boots sinking deep into the mud at every step.

The bluebird sang halfheartedly as it flew on ahead, but otherwise there was no sound but the rushing of countless streams of water down the sides of the gully. They crested the hill, went down into a grey misty valley, and climbed another hill. Rhiannon had to suppress her impatience. They climbed higher. Patches of dirty-looking snow lay beneath the trees. The road crossed a rushing burn, and Rhiannon knelt to examine the wheel ruts, which had cut deep into the mud. Her pulse quickened with excitement. It was clear the carriage had passed along this road only a day or so ago, since the storm had broken. The horses were struggling to pull it in the muddy conditions and were only moving slowly. For the first time Rhiannon began to feel sure she could catch up.

They came to a clearing and there were signs of horses having been tethered to an iron post driven deep into the ground. There was a muddle of footprints. Rhiannon found a number that could only have been made by a lady's high-heeled shoe, and felt her pulse quicken. How many fine ladies would be traveling through the highlands of Rionnagan in this weather? It had to be the Banprionnsa Olwynne NicCuinn, who had disappeared the same night her father the Righ was murdered.

Rhiannon had to resist the urge to leap on Blackthorn's back and soar in pursuit. They were no fools, these enemies of hers, and their stakes were high. They would be watching for any sign of pursuit.

Slowly, carefully, she went on studying the footprints. Olwynne—if that was who it was—had walked only a few steps, to the verge of the clearing, and then back to the carriage. Rhiannon surmised she had been allowed to relieve herself behind the tree. Rhiannon could see how she had stumbled and dragged her feet. Was she hurt, she wondered, or only overcome by grief and terror?

There were the footprints of another woman too, one

wearing sensible clogs. Rhiannon's eyes narrowed. That
would be Dedrie, the lord of Fettercairn's skeelie. The
skeelie had kindled a fire and sheltered it from the rain
with some kind of shelter hung from two sticks. Rhiannon
could see the holes that had been driven into the clay.
There was a mess of other footprints all made by males
wearing boots. They had sat on this fallen log, they had
moved about feeding and watering the horses, they had
gone down to the burn to fetch water. One had very small
feet for a man, but was evidently big and heavy, for his
boots pressed deeply into the clay. Then Rhiannon found a
great round indentation where he had sat. Or she. The
marks could have been made by a very large woman. In
which case Rhiannon thought she knew who it was.

Among all the mess of footprints, Rhiannon could see
none that clearly belonged to Owein MacCuinn, Olwynne's twin brother, or to the little boy Roden, son of
Rhiannon's friend and mentor, Nina the Nightingale. She
could only hope that they were here too.

Then, behind the fallen log, Rhiannon found a mark that
made her heart leap. There, quite distinct in the mud, was
the shape of a small bare foot. It could only belong to
Roden. Rhiannon smiled in relief and pressed her hand to
her chest. She had feared greatly for the little boy. It was
really for his sake that she had undertaken this perilous
hunt through the mountains. She had traveled many miles
with young Roden and had had many adventures with him.
She could not bear to think of him alone and afraid.

Rhiannon mounted and urged Blackthorn into a trot.
She was sure now that she was hot on the trail of her
enemy, the sinister Lord Malvern. Having found his trail
only brought her face-to-face with the dilemma of what to
do next. She had no desire to face Lord Malvern, or his
poisonous skeelie, or the band of loyal cutthroats who
served him. She had no idea how she was to rescue the prionnsa and his sister, or young Roden. She had formed a
vague notion of swooping down out of the night sky,

snatching up one or the other of them, and flying away to safety. That would do for one of them at least, preferably Roden, but it was a trick that could only be performed once, if at all.

Mentally she counted the arrows in the quiver that hung on her back. If she had to, could she shoot down the lord and his cronies? Rhiannon had killed a man once before, and the experience had been a disturbing one. It troubled her dreams sometimes, that moment when the arrow had sprung free of her bow and curved inexorably down, slicing apart the air with a singing hiss, and ended its journey deep in a man's fast-beating heart. She had not known how it could haunt you, the killing of a man. Could she do so again, knowing what she knew now?

Rhiannon hoped so. They had killed hundreds between them, these men she pursued, many of the deaths cruel ones. If she did not stop them, they would kill Olwynne and Owein and Roden too.

As she rode, Rhiannon listened intently to the rustle of the forest, her eyes moving constantly over the landscape. She paused often to examine the tracks before her, using every piece of woodcraft she had ever learned while running wild with her mother's herd of satyricorns. She saw that one of the horses had begun to lag behind the others. Perhaps it was the one who had slipped and fallen some miles back. It was favoring one leg, and then beginning to limp badly. Rhiannon forced herself to move even more cautiously.

It started to sleet again. Bluey came back and perched on the pommel, ruffling his damp feathers, then lifted the flap of Rhiannon's pocket and deftly hopped in. Rhiannon gritted her teeth and clenched and unclenched her numb hands, wriggling her toes in her damp boots. She tried not to think of roaring fires and hot mulled wine and roast venison. She tried to think only of Roden, crying out for his mother.

She came around a curve in the road and saw before her

a dead horse, lying still in the middle of the track. Rhiannon reined Blackthorn in sharply, her heart slamming. No one else seemed to be about. Rhiannon waited a long moment, listening, looking, then slowly rode up to the fallen horse. Its rider lay dead beside it. Rhiannon did not need to turn her over to see her face. She knew who it was at once. There could only be one woman so grossly fat her splayed arms looked like bolsters and her enormous rump like an overturned sofa. It was Octavia the Obese, the prison warder who had helped Lord Malvern escape. An arrow protruded from her shoulder. Another was embedded in the heart of the dead horse.

Looking about her at the pattern of hoofprints in the mud, Rhiannon could see clearly what had happened. The valiant horse, forced to carry the gargantuan weight of the prison warder, had begun to fail and grow lame. They fell behind. Another rider had wheeled back and come galloping up. He had shot the horse. It had fallen, trapping Octavia beneath it. The rider had come closer and coolly shot dead the obese woman as she struggled to rise. Then he had turned and gone galloping up the road again, leaving horse and woman to die in the mud behind him.

Rhiannon took a few deep breaths, shaken despite herself. She had hated and feared Octavia as she had never hated and feared anyone before. Rhiannon had spent one night in Octavia's charge and had seen the prison warder chain up a sweet-natured young woman called Bess for the rats to tear apart. She knew Octavia to be capable of acts of incredible cruelty. Rhiannon had dreaded having to face her again, and should have been pleased and relieved to find her here, dead on the road. Instead, she had to clench her hands together on the reins to stop them from shaking. It was such a ruthless, coldhearted act, to shoot down horse and rider simply because they were slowing the party down.

Dusk was falling. On they rode, going quietly. Rhiannon's heart was thumping. Blackthorn felt her unease and shied a little, ears laid back. Rhiannon soothed her and held her steady.

The drizzle that had tormented them all afternoon was turning into snow. Rhiannon did not dare pull up the hood of her cloak in case it muffled her ears. She tucked it closer about her throat and rode on. The bluebird was a soft, round mound in her pocket, and occasionally Rhiannon put down her hand to pat it.

There was a clink of metal ahead of her. Blackthorn froze midstep. Slowly Rhiannon backed her mare deeper into the gloom under the trees, then slid down from her back. Pressing against the mare's laboring side, she peered through the snow, listening for all she was worth. She heard another clink, and then a low curse.

Two large traveling carriages were pulled in at the side of the road, under the shelter of some big old trees. The eight exhausted horses that had dragged them up the steep muddy road all day were being untethered by a young man in rough homespuns and leather gaiters. There was still enough light for Rhiannon to recognize the surly, unshaven face of Jem, one of the grooms from Castle Fettercairn. He paused every now and again to gulp from a large, battered hipflask made of silver so tarnished it was almost completely black.

Jem tethered the horses under the trees and gave them a quick rub-down before scattering a few meager handfuls of hay before them. Rhiannon pressed her lips together. It angered her to see horses treated so badly.

Meanwhile, the outriders were stretching their backs and complaining about the cold and the mud and bony spines of their hacks. Jem grunted, and came and took their horses.

"Give us a wee dram," the bodyguard Ballard said. "Ye always have a drop o' something about ye to warm the bones."

"Get your own," Jem snarled.

"Go on! Be a sweetheart now," the coachman said.

"Else we'll tell the laird about your wee bottle, and then all o' us will go thirsty."

Jem grunted, and took the tarnished hipflask out of his pocket, tossing it to the others. They all took a swig, wiping their mouths with satisfaction and saying, "That's the stuff."

"No need to drink it all," Jem said, and held out his hand for the bottle. They all took another thirsty gulp, then passed it back to him. He carefully wiped the lip of the bottle with a handful of snow before tucking it away in his pocket again.

While Jem groomed and fed the hacks as desultorily as he had the carriage horses, the others lit smoky torches and stuck them all around the campsite. The wind shifted and the weary horses lifted their heads and looked towards the shadows where Rhiannon was crouched. She willed them to be quiet, and after a moment they lowered their heads again.

One of the men opened the door of the carriage, and a plump, middle-aged woman clambered down, a shawl huddled about her.

"Mercy me!" she cried. "Snowing again? What evil spell have those blaygird witches cast against us? If only I had kent, I would've packed my cloak, and some mittens, and a nice warm scarf, instead o' . . ."

"'Tis cold as a witch's tit out here," Jem said sourly. "Canna ye light us a fire and cook us up something hot instead o' clucking about like an auld hen?"

"Have ye gathered me any firewood?" she demanded. "I canna light a fire with naught but a snap o' my fingers, Jem, no' being a witch myself."

"Fine," he snarled and, huddling his hands under his armpits, went crashing into the undergrowth looking for fallen branches and twigs. "Come and help me, ye lazy bastards!" he called to the other men, who reluctantly followed him, muttering under their breath.

An elderly man put his head out the window of the

coach. "Irving!" he snapped. "Must I put the steps down for myself?"

Rhiannon stiffened and drew back farther into the gloom under the trees. Her heart raced. She had not seen Lord Malvern since he had stood over her in the dark with a knife gleaming in his hand, the night he had tried to take her from Sorrowgate Tower, the night before her trial for Connor's murder. If she had not screamed so loudly the guards had come running, she would be the one lying bound and trussed in the other carriage, not the Banprionnsa Olwynne. Or else she'd be dead. He was a dangerous man, the lord of Fettercairn Castle, and he had the uncanny ability of the witches to sense when he was being watched. He had once been an apprentice-witch, she had been told, until he had been disgraced and expelled. Then he had used his powers for the Ensorcellor, to seek out witches and bring them to the fires to be burned alive. Rhiannon wished she had not come so close, and tried to pretend she was snow and mist and rustling leaves.

The lord of Fettercairn was cold and stiff and hungry, however, and much too concerned with his own comfort to be casting out his senses into the darkness in search of any pursuers. Snarling at his servants, he clambered down from the carriage and sat in a cushioned chair while Dedrie kindled the fire, and Herbert, his valet, arranged a fur cloak over his knees and another over his shoulders.

"Damn this snow," he grumbled. "It's holding us back. I do no' ken how long the ship will wait for us. We should've pressed on."

"The horses were failing," Irving, his seneschal, said. "We do no' want to be bogged down here, so many miles from anywhere. Better to let the horses rest and push on again in the morning, when we can see what lies ahead."

"What about the sacrifices? Are ye sure ye should've drugged them again, Dedrie? I do no' want them to die afore we reach the graveyard."

"They've tried to escape once already," Dedrie said.

"We wasted close on an hour catching them this morning. It's kept them quiet all day, hasn't it?"

"Better feed them some o' your slop," the lord said contemptuously. "Let them walk up and down a bit, afore we lock them up for the night."

"Aye, my laird," Dedrie said, and went over to the second carriage, which had stood still and dark all this time. She called to two of the men to come and help her, and they unsheathed their swords and held them at the ready while Dedrie cautiously unlocked the carriage door and opened it.

Rhiannon quietly led Blackthorn some distance away down the road and remounted her. Facing away from the campsite, she urged the winged mare into a canter and then up into the air. The frosty wind stung her eyes, and she bent low over the mare's neck as she wheeled and flew back over the forest. She still had no real plan, but Rhiannon knew she had to seize opportunity when it came.

Horse and rider hovered above the firelit camp, the sound of Blackthorn's wings disguised by the constant ruffle of the wind in the trees. Below them, Dedrie was leaning inside the carriage and Rhiannon heard her make some exclamation of dismay. Then the two guards were sheathing their swords and clambering up into the carriage. Rhiannon watched as they carried out a small, limp body in a nightgown. At the sight of Roden's curly head hanging to one side, Rhiannon felt a lurch of horror in her stomach. *Dark walkers, no!* she thought.

As the guard laid the little boy down beside the fire, the other was lifting out another body. It was a tall redhead in a gorgeous silver satin gown. One arm dangled and her head lolled back. She was deposited by the fire also, Dedrie kneeling beside her in sudden alarm, fingers at the pulse in her neck.

"Ye better no' have killed her," the lord said menacingly. "Where will we find another sacrifice in time? If she's dead, Dedrie, I'll cut your throat instead!"

"She's no' dead," Dedrie said, and turned to rummage in her basket as the guards carried out another body from the carriage. "Happen I gave her too much o' the poppy and nightshade syrup. Though I only gave them a wee . . ."

Staggering under the weight of Prionnsa Owein, a tall muscular young man with the added weight of two great feathered wings as long as he was tall, the guards came up to the fire. At that moment Banprionnsa Olwynne rolled over and gave Dedrie a hefty kick in the backside that sent her sprawling onto her face.

"Run, Roden!" Olwynne screamed, and seized a stick from the pile of firewood, brandishing it in the face of the lord as he attempted to leap to his feet.

The little boy was up and running at once. The guards shouted and dropped the prionnsa, trying desperately to catch Roden as he bolted past. The prionnsa's wings and arms were bound tightly to his body, but his legs were free. He managed to kick the legs of one of the guards from under him, so that he fell back to the ground with a thud. The other caught the edge of Roden's nightgown and hauled him back, but Olwynne whacked him hard across the head with the stick and he let go with a cry of pain, both hands flying up to protect himself.

Irving slapped the banprionnsa hard across the face and she fell to her knees with a cry; just then the other men came surging back in from the forest, dropping their bundles of firewood. One ran to intercept the little boy, but Roden dodged him and ran on. For a minute there was a ridiculous game of hide-and-seek as he dodged and scrambled through the circle of men, then the seeking hands closed in upon him. Just as Roden was about to be caught, the black winged mare came swooping out of the sky and Rhiannon bent and seized him, dragging him up and into her arms. Blackthorn beat her great wings and soared away.

"Shoot them down!" the lord screamed, beside himself with rage. "Fools! Idiots! Shoot them down!"

The men scrambled for their bows and arrows. Irving drew his dagger and would have sent it spinning after Blackthorn had Olwynne not kicked out with her high-heeled silver shoe and gouged him so sharply in the shin that he cried out and jerked, and the knife spun away harmlessly into the snow. He turned and slapped her again, knocking her back down to the ground. She did not seem to care, she was laughing and crying at once, and Owein was cheering and calling Rhiannon's name. It was the last thing she heard as she and Roden flew up and away into the dark, storm-tossed sky.

The Stargazer

〜❦〜

Bronwen the Bonny, the new Banrìgh of Eileanan, came quietly into the bedchamber.

"How is she?" she whispered to the healer.

"The Stargazer is very weak still, Your Majesty, but there is naught wrong with her that time and rest willna fix," the healer replied in a low voice. Named Mirabelle, she was a gaunt, pock-faced woman of middle age, with greying hair coiled neatly at the back of her head and dark shadows under her eyes. Like her patient, Mirabelle was fighting the aftereffects of the drugged wine she had drunk on Midsummer's Eve. The wine had been laced with poppy syrup, nightshade, henbane, and powdered valerian root, a toxic mixture designed to induce almost instant unconsciousness.

"May I speak with her now?" Bronwen asked.

"Aye, Your Majesty. She is awake and coherent now, and very distressed about her daughter."

Bronwen nodded and picked up the somber folds of her black satin gown in one hand as she followed the healer around the screen to the Stargazer's bedside. She always felt rather awkward in Mirabelle's company, remembering how much she and her friends had teased the healer when she had been one of their teachers at the Theurgia. Bronwen remembered one particular day, when she had given in to the impulse to mock Mirabelle for her pox-ravaged face, just to make the class giggle. Mirabelle had not seemed to mind, using the jibe to issue a smiling warning about the importance of taking care when nursing highly infectious diseases, yet Bronwen felt rather ashamed of her cruelty and as a consequence was always very sweet and charming to Mirabelle when they met.

Cloudshadow was lying against a mound of pillows, her snow-white hair rippling down to stream across the green satin coverlet. She looked more frail and ethereal than ever. Her skin was so white it looked bloodless, and there were violet shadows under the strange, colorless eyes.

Bronwen bowed low. *Greetings, honorable one,* she hummed deep in her throat.

Greetings, the Stargazer hummed back.

Ye ken your daughter was dear to me, Bronwen thought. *I am as devastated by her loss as ye. My husband too is missing, and our land is plunged into chaos. Can ye help me find them?*

The Stargazer reached out her long, four-jointed finger and placed it between Bronwen's brows.

I cannot see my daughter, the Stargazer said. Her mind-voice was filled with anguish. *I cannot sense her.*

Is she . . . are they . . . dead?

I do not know. The Celestine's hand fell away.

Bronwen was puzzled. The mind ability of the Celestines was legendary. It was said they could see into every man and woman's heart and read what was written there, and that they could cast their senses far across the land.

We think they have traveled the Auld Way. We found Donncan's sash at the entrance o' the maze, and evidence that Johanna seeks to go back a thousand years in time, to the days o' the First Coven.

The Celestine closed her eyes. To Bronwen's dismay, tears began to slide down from under her closed lids. She had never seen a Celestine cry before. She had not imagined they could, let alone ordinary tears of water like a human.

Forgive me, honorable one, but is this indeed possible? Can one travel the Auld Way so far back in time?

So far, and farther, came the reply. *It is a perilous journey, and forbidden to us. Even when our kind was being hunted down and burned alive by your mother's soldiers, we did not take refuge in other times, as some among us argued we should. To do so would have been to break one of the most sacred taboos of our kind. To bend time is to remake history, and to remake history is to remake the world.*

There was a long silence.

Did Thunderlily know the secret o' traveling back in time? Bronwen asked.

The Celestine lifted one hand and wiped away her tears. *Thunderlily has learned the tree-language and the star-language, as any child of the Stargazers must,* she said very quietly. *These are the most sacred secrets of my kind, and never to be disclosed to one not of her blood. Even the man whom she shall sacrifice to the Summer Tree may not know all the songs.*

So she does know how to do it? Would she do so? Bronwen asked.

The Stargazer opened her eyes and stared straight into Bronwen's. It was like being stabbed with a bright pin. Bronwen found it impossible to maintain her gaze, despite all her majesty and authority as the banrìgh of all Eileanan and the Far Islands. She dropped her eyes, color staining her cheeks.

I would not have thought so, came the answer. *But if a knife was held to the winged one's throat . . . perhaps she would rather brave the dangers of the Old Ways and do as she was bid, than sully the perfection of the Heart of Stars with the blood of a murdered king. I cannot tell. I have been too long away from my daughter. I no longer know what is in her heart. She has folded secrets away inside her, and closed her eye to me so I cannot read them.*

The Celestine sounded unutterably weary and sad. Bronwen felt her own eyes sting in sudden sympathy, and a guilt she told herself was entirely irrational. *It is no' my fault Thunderlily grew so fascinated with us humans,* she told herself. *It was your decision to send your daughter to the Theurgia to study our ways. You canna blame her for taking advantage of her freedom, and learning to drink and dance and flirt. You canna blame me.*

Impaled upon the Celestine's crystal-clear gaze, she found this was a fiction she could not sustain. She shifted her weight, the silk of her heavy skirts rustling, and said with a frown, *We must go after them, we must get them back. Will ye show us the way?*

There was a long silence, during which the Stargazer did not move a muscle. She did not blink, she did not drop her gaze, she hardly seemed to breathe.

I know it is forbidden, Bronwen said desperately, *but if we do no' go after them, Johanna will kill Donncan and use his lifeblood to resurrect a cruel and evil sorcerer. Have ye no' heard the stories about Brann the Raven? How he lusted after Medwenna, his own son's young wife, and stole her for his own? How he drowned her when she tried to escape, and cut off her head and had it delivered to his son on a silver tray? Ye say it is forbidden to go back in time because it could re-make history. Just imagine a world where such a man has a second chance o' life! What would happen to all o' us? Would the world we ken now be here at all? Would ye and I exist at all? What would happen to us? Would we just turn into dust and blow away? Or would we be what our history had made us, a darker, crueller, bloodier history than the one we have had because Brann died? Or would Brann disdain the life and world he knew, and compel Thunderlily to bring him back here, to our time, to a time when the witches' power is still being mended and there are only a few sorcerers to withstand him. What would that mean to us? To me? Widowed afore I was even a wife, and banrìgh to a world gone mad?*

Bronwen found she was weeping. She stopped and took a deep, ragged breath, digging the heels of her hands into her eyes. Still the Celestine was silent and motionless.

Please, Bronwen said. *Ye are the only one.*

The only Stargazer left . . . Cloudshadow said, very low.

Aye . . . Bronwen said sadly. *Now Thunderlily is lost . . .*

What would be the greater wrong, to abide by the laws of my kind and respect the taboo against bending time, and thus allow great evil to be done, or to knowingly breach the most strict and revered of laws and attempt to avert the doing of evil?

To stand by and let Donncan be murdered so some horrible man can live again would be by far the greater wrong! Bronwen said fiercely. *How can ye even ask such a question?*

And my daughter . . .

Aye, Thunderlily! What would Brann do to her?

I must think on it . . .

No! There is no time! Already two days and two nights have passed since my husband was stolen from me. Aunty Beau says the best time to travel the Auld Ways is at dawn or sunset. It will be dawn in a few hours. Please. We may already be too late.

Once again tears unexpectedly started to Cloud-shadow's eyes. *Thunderlily, Thunderlily,* she murmured. *Oh, my beautiful daughter, where are ye?*

Will ye go and try to find her? Bronwen pleaded.

The Celestine nodded. *Yes. I must. Call together my people. We must make ready.*

Thank ye, thank ye, Bronwen gabbled. *We will do all we can to aid ye. Tell me what must be done.*

I have all I need here, the Stargazer said, lifting her hand to touch first her heart, then the pulse at her throat, and then her third eye, which opened under her finger, as dark and fathomless as a well.

The little boy was shivering. Rhiannon drew him close to her and wrapped her cloak about him.

"How are ye yourself?" she whispered.

"Rhiannon, Rhiannon," he wept, and clutched her wrist
with one icy-cold little hand.

"I've got ye now, ye're safe," she whispered. He shuddered and she pressed him closer, shocked at how cold he
was.

"What were ye thinking, running off into the snow with
naught on but a nightgown?" she admonished him.

"They were going to kill us," he whispered.

"Well, I've got ye now, ye're safe, no one's going to kill
ye."

"What about Owein . . . Olwynne?"

"I'll get ye to safety too, and then I'll go back and get
them," she promised. He sighed and laid back against her,
and soon his breathing steadied. She glanced down at him
and found he was asleep.

Rhiannon flew on into the icy darkness. She had nothing to guide her but her own internal compass. The Banrìgh
had sent soldiers to pursue the lord of Fettercairn, and Rhiannon guessed they were somewhere on the road behind.
She bent over Blackthorn's neck and strained her eyes to
see through the blackness, following the thin line of white
that she hoped was the snow-covered road.

After an hour or so, she saw the red eye of a campfire
gleaming through the ranks of dark trees. Rhiannon was
not taking any chances and so she brought the mare down
on an outcrop of stone some way above. It was too difficult
to dismount with the sleeping child in her arms, so she
merely sat there quietly and surveyed the scene, while
Blackthorn drooped her head down, her flanks heaving
with exhaustion.

The camp below her was a neat and orderly one. The
horses wore heavy blankets and each had a nosebag of
warm mash. They were tied to a single line that could be
released in a moment if need be. A fire pit had been dug
and surrounded by stones to protect the fire from the snow.
A small pot hung above it, and a man was stirring it with a
long ladle. More men sat on a fallen log that had been

drawn up close to the flames. Some were eating from small bowls; others were taking off their boots and setting them to dry near the fire, stuffing them with spare socks first to keep their shape.

Guards had been set. Rhiannon would not have seen them if she had not waited and watched for so long, for they sat very still, despite the bitter cold, and their cloaks were grey as the night. Still Rhiannon did not approach. She dared not take any chances.

It was not until one of the men sitting around the fire reached out and pulled a viola case out from a bundle of blankets, opening it and checking the instrument inside as tenderly as if it were a child, that Rhiannon was sure that she had found, if not exactly friends, at least allies. She knew Jay the Fiddler carried his viola with him everywhere he went. Rhiannon gave a little sigh and pulled Roden closer. Carefully she slipped down from the mare's back and, leaving Blackthorn in the safety of the darkness, began to make her way down the slope towards the camp.

"Halt! Who goes there?" came the cry.

"It is I, Rhiannon o' the Dubhslain, upon the Banrìgh's business," Rhiannon answered. To her surprise her voice was no more than a croak.

The guard came towards her with his sword drawn.

"Careful," she said. "I have the laddie here."

"The laddie?" the guard said incredulously, and seized her arm, drawing her roughly toward the fire so he could see more clearly. She shook him off.

"Sssh! He's asleep. Do no' wake him."

He could see the white shape of the boy in her arms. "No' the Viscount o' Laverock!" he cried.

"Aye," said Rhiannon irritably. She was very tired and cold, and her legs did not seem to be working properly.

At once the guard's manner changed. He put his arm about her and supported her towards the fire, calling for help. More men came running. Rhiannon was drawn in to the warmth of the flames, and then a tall woman with a long, untidy plait was kneeling before her in the snow, tenderly taking Roden from her. Rhiannon let him be taken.

"Look at him, the poor wee lad, he's blue with cold," the woman said, and seized a warm blanket to wrap him in. Another blanket was wrapped around Rhiannon, and then a cup of hot soup was thrust into her hands. Numbly she sipped, watching as the woman rubbed Roden's bare hands and feet, and called for hot bottles to be brought and laid against him.

For a while Rhiannon was content to sit and drink her soup, watching as the sleeping child was expertly cared for, but as soon as her cup was empty she remembered Blackthorn. It was in her mind to slip away and tend her mare in private, but the moment she pushed aside her blanket and stood up, three swords hissed out of their scabbards and were brought to bear upon her.

"I bid ye stay," the woman said, "and tell us what ye ken."

Her voice was calm, even conversational, but the look in her hazel-green eyes was whetted sharp as the blades at Rhiannon's breast. On her shoulder was perched a tiny black cat with long tufted ears and turquoise-colored eyes. It hissed, showing very sharp pointed teeth.

"I must tend my mare," Rhiannon said.

Jay the Fiddler and the woman—who could only be the sorceress they called Finn the Cat—exchanged a quick glance. "Ye are the girl who flies the winged mare, are ye no'?" Finn asked. As Rhiannon nodded, she continued, "The one who killed Connor?"

Rhiannon nodded again, warily.

"My men will tend the mare. Ye will stay here."

"My mare will no' allow these soldiers to approach her," Rhiannon said, raising her chin. "Besides, ye have no right to tell me to stay or go. I fly on the Banrìgh's business."

"Do ye just?" Jay said quietly, and again there was that quick flick of a glance between him and the sorceress. On his face there was only a gentle consideration, a sort of open watchfulness, as if he was waiting for some sign from her, some sudden movement. Finn's face was more guarded.

"Aye, I do," Rhiannon said angrily. "She sent me to rescue Roden, and that I have done."

"She sent *ye*? When she knew I was on the trail?" Finn sounded affronted.

"Aye, she did. Blackthorn and me, we are fast. We fly high above the world while ye must slog around down below. She kent I would save him, and I have." Rhiannon was aware that it may have been wise to moderate her tone, but she was cold and weary and she did not like having swords poked at her when she had just done a brave and clever thing.

Rhiannon knew that the sorceress had good cause to dislike her. After all, the man she had killed had been a dear childhood friend of Finn and Jay's. They had both sat through her trial for his murder with their hands clenched about the gold medals they wore, symbol of their membership of the League of the Healing Hand, a gang of beggar children who had banded together to help Lachlan the Winged gain his throne. There were only four members of that original gang left—Jay and Finn, now married and working in service of the Coven; Captain Dillon of the Rìgh's own guard; and Johanna, who had been head of the healers until betraying the Rìgh to his death and abducting his son and heir, Donncan. Johanna had wanted Rhiannon to hang for Connor's death. It was the news that Lachlan had planned to pardon Rhiannon that had driven her to help his murderers.

Finn and Jay must hate her too. They must have wanted her to hang. Rhiannon did not want to be near them. Every muscle in her body was rigid with nervous tension. If it had not been for the need to bring Roden to shelter as soon as possible, she would never have come near them. She wished she had not had to kill their friend. She was sorry Connor's death had caused so much grief. But that was the nature of life. People were born, people died. Sometimes they died out of time. He had been a soldier in the Rìgh's service and must have known the risks of riding into the wilds. She ran the same risk now, chasing after the lord of Fettercairn.

Finn was scowling, her hands on her hips. Rhiannon glared back at her. The tiny black cat on Finn's shoulder hissed furiously. Rhiannon hissed back.

Unexpectedly Finn's face relaxed, and she put up one hand to soothe the elven cat. "So Her Majesty has pressed ye into service, has she? Have ye papers to prove this?"

"In my saddlebag," Rhiannon answered. "Back with my mare."

"Handy."

"Where else would I keep them?" Rhiannon asked. "I had to carry Roden, I couldna be groping around in my bags in the pitch-black looking for a bit o' paper. If ye like, I will show ye when Blackthorn is here."

"How do I ken ye willna just fly off into the night again?" Finn demanded.

"Why would I do that?" Rhiannon asked. "Ye have fire here, and blankets, and hot soup. I'm cold and hungry and tired. Besides, what would it matter to ye if I did? I'm no' your prisoner. Ye have no right to tell me whether I can go or stay."

"I have no reason to trust ye," Finn said coldly.

Rhiannon gritted her teeth. "I'm the one who rescued Roden from the mad laird, remember?"

"So ye got him away from Laird Malvern?" The sorceress's voice was full of suspicion. "How?"

"I will tell ye all when I have seen to my horse." Rhiannon was inflexible.

There was a moment's pause, and Finn looked to her husband. Jay nodded. The soldiers lowered their swords.

"It's as black as pitch out there, and blowing a gale. Let me walk with ye, to make sure ye do no' get lost in the storm," Jay said.

"No need," Rhiannon said tersely. "Blackthorn will come to me. As long as your soldiers stand back and keep their weapons low. She doesna like soldiers." It was clear from her tone that she shared her horse's sentiments.

Jay nodded and made a swift gesture to the soldiers, who all drew back. Rhiannon called her mare's name, silently, with no more than a slight abstraction in her expression to show what she was doing. Within moments the black winged horse was hovering above them in the darkness, her powerful wings beating up a flurry of snow. Her ears were laid back, and her sharp horns were lowered. She pawed the air and neighed a challenge.

Rhiannon reassured her silently, and the mare dropped down to the ground, pressing close to Rhiannon's side and looking sideways at the soldiers with a white-rimmed eye and curled lip. Rhiannon stroked her damp neck. Blackthorn's back was frosty where her sweat had frozen, and she was trembling. Rhiannon was gripped with guilt. Blackthorn had flown far that day. She should never have left her to stand in that nasty wind, all sweaty and weary as she was. Rhiannon hurried to cover her with her own cloak and, teeth chattering and extremities numb, began to rub her down with a brush she snatched out of her bag. Jay brought her some heavy blankets that she threw over the mare's back, and one of the soldiers made up some warm mash for her.

Only when Blackthorn was as warm and comfortable as it was possible to be when camped on the side of a road in the middle of the snow did Rhiannon turn her attention back to the others at the campsite. She saw Roden had been put to bed in a little tent made from some kind of oilcloth slung over a stick. He was rolled in blankets and had a skin of hot wine at his feet, and another at his back. He was still fast asleep.

The soldiers had either gone back to guard duty or were preparing themselves to sleep. One was stoking up the fire for the night, and another was making some hot mulled

wine for Finn and Jay and Rhiannon. She accepted it gratefully, warming her numb hands on the tin mug and enjoying the aroma of spices. Then they brought her more soup,
and some hard black bread that she could only eat after
sopping it in her bowl. She broke off a piece and crumbled
it in her hand, and then coaxed a sleepy Bluey out of her
pocket to eat. At the sight of the bluebird, the elven cat
leaped down from Finn's lap and crept forward, low to the
ground, one paw raised. Alarmed, Rhiannon tucked the
bluebird away again, and kept a close eye on the elven cat
as it prowled towards her, its turquoise eyes slitted, its tail
lashing.

"No, Goblin," Finn said. "Leave it alone."

Goblin only hissed in response, then sat by the fire, its
eyes fixed on Rhiannon's pocket.

Finn and Jay were silent as Rhiannon ate and drank ravenously. When at last she had finished, and the soldier had
taken her bowl away to wash in a saucepan of melted snow,
Rhiannon sat back and returned the gaze of the two who
had been examining her with such curiosity while she ate.
She had spared them little more than a glance at the trial.
All her attention had been on the witnesses brought against
her, and the judges who had condemned her.

Now she looked them over with open curiosity. Finn
was tall and lithe, with messy brown hair that caught the
red of the firelight. The elven cat had stalked into her lap
and was now kneading its claws in and out of Finn's leg.
Finn stroked it absentmindedly, her head bent down to rest
on her other hand. She looked tired.

Jay was not much taller than Finn, and slender, with
dark hair and eyes and olive skin. Although, like most
witches, his hair was long, it was neatly bound back in a
queue and his beard was clipped. This may have been because it was rather sparse, or it may have been to prevent
attackers from seizing it and using it against him. Both
Finn and Jay were dressed in the clothes of a soldier—a
padded leather breastplate and gaiters and a thick grey

cloak. Rhiannon saw that their cloaks, like hers, were blue on the inside, and wondered that these witches wore the uniform of the Yeoman of the Guard, the personal body-guard of the monarch.

"So tell me, Rhiannon," Jay said. "Last time I heard your name ye were a prisoner o' Sorrowgate Tower. What do ye do here in the Whitelock Mountains?"

"The Banrìgh sent me to get back Roden, and the prionnsa and banprionnsa," Rhiannon said.

"Iseult sent ye?" Jay began, but Rhiannon interrupted.

"No' the auld one. The Banrìgh Bronwen. I have her paper."

When Jay spoke, she could hear the smile in his voice. "Poor Iseult! She is no' so auld. Only forty or so. But I suppose to a young one like ye . . . So it was Bronwen who sent ye?"

"Aye."

"I imagine the Banrìgh could see the advantages o' having a thigearn on the trail o' the laird o' Fettercairn. Certainly we've failed to lay them by the heels. Their plans were well laid."

"Aye," Rhiannon repeated. She still felt on guard with the fiddler, but his gentle voice and manner were doing much to calm her.

"We're on their trail," Finn said defensively. "We're getting closer all the time."

"So tell us how ye came to wrest Roden from them?" Jay asked.

Rhiannon gave him a brief explanation. By the time she had finished, she was having difficulty hiding her yawns, and she saw Finn was also yawning so wide her jaw cracked.

"It will no' be so easy next time," Jay said.

"No," Rhiannon agreed. "They will be watching the sky now."

"Did they say where they were going?" Finn said.

"Something about a ship," Rhiannon answered. "Naught more."

"That is no use," Finn said restlessly. "We've guessed already they head for the coast. What I want to ken is where on the coast they plan to embark. I hate trailing behind them like this, trying to guess their next move."

"Well, we ken they head to the Pirate Isles, to the grave o' Margrit o' Arran," Jay said. "Or at least we think we ken that is where they are going. Isabeau is convinced that is why they have abducted Olwynne, to sacrifice her to raise Margrit o' Arran from the dead."

Rhiannon nodded. "She wanted me. But they couldna take me. So they took the banprionnsa instead. Happen they realized she is the one who truly has the ruthless heart." She spoke with bitterness. Jay regarded her with a little frown, not understanding her final words but sensing the real hurt behind them.

"We will just keep following them and do our best to catch up," Finn said. "We need to get Roden home to safety first. Happen ye had best take him, Rhiannon."

Rhiannon regarded her suspiciously. On the one hand, she wanted nothing more than to take Roden back to his parents and see the smiles breaking across their faces. On the other hand, she wondered whether Finn was trying to shoulder her out of the main chase. Owein and Olwynne were still held captive. She wanted to save them and have done with it. She calculated swiftly how long it would take her to fly back to where Nina and Iven followed with more of the Banrìgh's soldiers.

Reluctantly she shook her head.

"Take too long," she said. "They reach the sea soon. Olwynne is the first sacrifice. I promised Lewen I'd save her."

There was a long pause.

Finn said slowly, almost reluctantly, "Ye ken Lewen and the banprionnsa have jumped the fire together? They are pledged one to the other, as man and wife, for a year and a day."

"I ken," Rhiannon said.

"These are no' vows to be taken lightly," Finn said. "Olwynne is a banprionnsa o' the royal MacCuinn clan."

"Ye think I do no' realize that?" Rhiannon said in exasperation.

Again Finn seemed to struggle with herself before speaking. "The tie between Lewen and Olwynne is strong, Rhiannon, no' easily overturned. Do ye ken what ye are doing?"

"Do ye mean, do I understand that Olwynne has ensorcelled my man?" Rhiannon demanded fiercely. "Aye, I ken. Why else do ye think I promised to save her? She has cast a spell on him that no one but she can break. So, I find her, bring her back, and if she doesna release my man, well, then I'll break her neck, aye, I will."

Finn stared at her for a moment longer, and then, unexpectedly, her face relaxed into laughter. "Well then, as long as ye ken."

"Och, aye, I ken," Rhiannon rejoined. "And there's another thing I ken—if she does no' undo her spell quick smart, she'll be wishing I never saved her!"

"So, how do ye plan to rescue her?" Finn said when she had composed her face again.

Rhiannon shrugged. "Now that I do no' ken," she answered. "Yet."

The Tomb

A t the heart of the witches' garden was a maze built of
ancient yew trees, planted more than eight hundred
years ago. Designed as a series of concentric circles that
spiraled in to the sacred Pool of Two Moons, it was a puzzle designed to lead the unwary in ever tighter turns of bafflement.

Once within the maze, its narrow gloomy corridors all
looked the same, leading to one dead end after another.
The ground was paved so that one could not draw a line
with one's foot to show where one had already been, and
there were no pebbles to mark one's progress. In some
dead ends lay the bones of those who had dared to try to
solve the puzzle and failed, new students at the Theurgia
were always told.

Certainly students were discouraged from wandering
the maze, except once a year at midsummer when the tall
iron gate was unlocked and the maze thrown open for the
amusement of the apprentices. Those who managed to find
their way through were rewarded with sparkling rose-
colored wine and honey cakes, and the privilege of looking
through the observatory and seeing the secret compartment
above the sacred pool where the Lodestar was hidden for
so many years. At dusk the witches went through with
torches and found the many hot, tired, and frustrated apprentices still wandering the pathways, and took them back

to the Theurgia for thin soup and weak ale. Making it through the maze was considered a rite of initiation for those who wished to join the Coven, and those who solved the puzzle never gave away its secret.

Isabeau, the Keybearer of the Coven, had learned its secret more than twenty years before and she walked its spiraling path at least twice a week, to watch the stars and moons through the far-seeing glass and to study the maps of the universe kept at the observatory. Even in the dark, and numb and stumbling with exhaustion after a week with very little sleep, she felt no hesitation when it came to choosing which direction to go at each intersection. She simply kept her hand on the left-hand wall as she walked. A big globe of blue witch-light hung above her head, casting an eerie light on the close-clipped walls of yew that towered over her head, and making those that followed after her look more unearthly than ever.

Directly behind Isabeau came Cloudshadow, the Stargazer of the Celestines, leaning on a tall gnarled staff. She was followed by one of her party, a young man named Stormstrider, who had insisted on his right to join the company, as he was, nominally at least, betrothed to Thunderlily.

He was a tall, lithe man, unusually broad in the shoulder and chest for a Celestine, with a proud, aloof face most remarkable for its high-bridged nose and angular cheekbones. Isabeau thought privately that he looked more like one of her kin, the Khan'cohbans of the Spine of the World, than one of the gentle forest faeries. Like Cloudshadow, he had taken off his usual long pale robe, and was dressed in sensible traveling clothes, like the rest of them—breeches, boots, a warm woolen jerkin over a soft shirt, and a waterproofed coat with a hood and deep pockets. It made him look a lot more approachable. Over his shoulder he carried a large sack that bulged with something large and round.

Behind him came Ghislaine Dream-Walker, a tall fair-haired sorceress with the ensign of the Summer Tree hanging about her neck. She was not yet thirty and considered a great beauty despite her general air of fragility, enhanced by the shadows under her eyes.

Cailean of the Shadowswathe followed her, his huge shadow-hound padding silently at his heels. He was a thin, serious-looking young sorcerer, with a quizzical expression and a habit of ruining his clothes by stuffing his pockets with books. All dogs loved him, and he was often to be found with a large pack trotting along behind him, composed of everything from mangy mongrels to high-bred hunting hounds and fluffy button-eyed pets that were normally carried in some noble lady's sleeve.

Bringing up the rear was Dide, two long daggers at his belt and a tiny one tucked in his boot. As well as the light pack of tools and supplies that everyone else carried, he wore a guitar slung on his back, its battered case painted with entwining tendrils of flowers and birds, much faded with time. Dide never traveled without his guitar and a pocketful of juggling balls.

Each of the three witches carried a sorcerer's staff, as usual, and Isabeau wore the familiar weight of the Key of the Coven about her neck. Her familiar, the little elf-owl Buba, flew silently ahead, white as a snowflake blown in the wind.

Isabeau was racked with impatience. She kept having to stop and wait for Cloudshadow, who walked as slowly and wearily as an old woman, her body still weak from the poison she had drunk. It was all Isabeau could do not to shriek, "Hurry! Hurry!"

She knew she was driven to the limits of endurance by the spell of compulsion that Brann the Raven had laid down in curlicues of his own blood, a thousand years earlier, in *The Book of Shadows*. The spell had been hidden behind another spell, the one that told the secret of resurrecting the dead, and so first Johanna and then Isabeau had unwittingly read the spell and were now subject to his implacable will. Johanna had kidnapped Donncan and Thunderlily, and forced them to travel back in time to the time of Brann's death, compelled to try to raise him from the grave. Isabeau could only reassure herself that, by chasing after Johanna, and her two royal hostages, she too was not compelled by Brann's hunger to live again.

They came at last to the circular garden at the very center of the maze, stepping out of the confined corridor with relief and taking a deep breath of frosty air. Mist drifted along the ground and wreathed about the cypress trees, but it was growing light enough for them to see the domed roof of the observatory.

In silence they climbed the steps till they reached the immense blocks of stones that surrounded the Pool of Two Moons. The stones were ancient, far older than the garden or the maze, and Isabeau knew that they were all carved with mysterious symbols, the stylized shape of stars and moons and planets and trees and rocks. These runes were called the tree-language by the Celestines, and despite a lifetime of study Isabeau still understood only the barest fraction. The symbols had all been carved so long ago they were barely visible even in brightest sunlight, yet one could feel them clearly with one's hand in the darkness. It was by touching these symbols, in certain formal sequences, that one was able to choose one's destination when traveling the Old Ways. Isabeau knew the symbol for the pool above her parents' home, at the Cursed Towers in Tírlethan. It was shaped like a crooked letter *M*, to represent the twin crags of the mountains above the lake there. Similarly, the sign for the Pool of Two Moons was like a *V*, representing the two rivers that came together to make the Shining Falls.

There were many thousands of runes in the Celestines' tree-language, however, and some were very similar. This was just one of the many reasons why it was so dangerous for someone who did not know the whole tree-alphabet to try to travel the Old Ways. It was all too easy to put the wrong rune in the wrong place and end up in a quite different place or time than one had intended.

The circle of stones had been built about the sacred tarn by the Celestines many thousands of years before humans had come to Eileanan. It had been discovered by the witches who had settled Rionnagan and built Lucescere, and they had at once sensed the latent power in the water and stones and sought to harness it for their own. The maze about the pool had been built by Martha the Wise, the great-granddaughter of Cuinn Lionheart, the sorcerer who had led the witches across time and space to this new world. It was her father, Lachlan the Astronomer, who first noticed that at dawn on the summer solstice light struck like an arrow of gold through a hole the size of a fist on one great menhir, illuminating a symbol shaped like a sun, or a face, on the stone opposite. Later he was to notice that certain lines drawn here and there marked the rise of key constellations, and that if one put one's eye to another great hole in a menhir at the time of the winter solstice, one could watch the red moon rise and fill its dimensions exactly. It was Lachlan the Astronomer who had built the observatory at the Pool of Two Moons, and he devoted his life to unraveling the mysteries of the great stones.

In time, the Tower of Two Moons was built nearby and this began a pattern that was repeated all over the country. Nearly all of the witches' towers were built on or around a stone-ringed pool of the Celestines, wittingly or unwittingly driving away the peaceful forest faeries and banishing them from their most sacred sites. Many of the circles of stones fell into disrepair or were damaged. The Pool of Two Moons was entirely encased in stones, and the great menhirs topped with arches to create a graceful colonnade that, pretty as it was, obscured many of the celestial events the circle of stones had been built to record.

What Lachlan the Astronomer and his fellow witches failed to understand was that the circles of stones were more than just some giant calendar that marked the cycles of suns and moons. They were Hearts of Stars, places charged with magnetic energy that radiated invisible lines of power that connected one to another across the entire planet. Reflecting the ellipses of moons, stars, and planets across the land, these lines were like magical roads that could be traveled, enabling the Celestines to move about the land invisibly and at great speed. They were seams in the matter of the universe, connecting space and time in a way that Isabeau could still only dimly grasp. All she knew was that the Hearts of Stars, the sacred pools in their circle of stones, focused power like a magnifying glass concentrated light until it could burn a hole in paper.

The secret of the Old Ways was one of the most closely guarded mysteries of the Celestines. Isabeau had been taught a little, because her guardian Meghan of the Beasts had been a great friend and champion of the forest faeries. She was not permitted to reveal what she had been taught, however, and so none of the others knew why it was Cloudshadow stood before the doors, tracing one shape after another with her long, four-jointed fingers.

"What does she do?" Dide whispered.

"She seeks to find the mark for the Tomb o' Ravens," Isabeau whispered back. "We must travel there first, in this time, afore we can attempt to go back in time. One canna do both at the same time."

Dide shifted his pack to the other shoulder. Somewhere a bird trilled. "It is almost dawn," he said and sighed.

"Aye, it is time," Isabeau agreed, and was glad that he too seemed to share her anxiety to be on their way. Three days had passed since Donncan and Thunderlily had been abducted. It was no consolation at all to know that they would all be traveling back to the exact same point in time, so it made no difference if it had been days or even weeks that had passed. Apart from the sick urgency the spell of compulsion had tattooed upon her brain, Isabeau was driven by anxiety about the young rìgh and what exactly Johanna intended to do with him.

Take hands, Cloudshadow said. *Remember, do not falter, do not look back, do not step off the path. Fix your eyes upon those that run before you, and do not listen to the ghosts. Run swiftly.*

They all nodded. Dobhailen, the shadow-hound, growled deep in his throat, and Cailean laid his hand upon his neck.

The sun rose above the horizon and struck at the great pillar of stone. It was three days past the summer solstice, and so they could see the great ball of fire through the hole punched in the menhir, although the miracle of the arrow of gold did not occur. Cloudshadow gently pressed one of the symbols on the pillar facing due south and then stepped through the archway. She disappeared, only the hand that held on to Stormstrider's still showing. He followed her, drawing Isabeau after him. She took a deep breath and ducked her head instinctively as she stepped into the glimmering, silvery haze that filled the archway. She knew to expect the shock that shot through every nerve, but it did not make the pain any easier to bear. Pulling Dide behind her, she broke into an awkward, stumbling run, keeping her eyes fixed on Stormstrider's flowing white hair. It seemed to shimmer in the strange greenish light, lifting and swirling in the lightning-charged wind that buffeted her face.

It was like trying to run through cold, rough surf. Her feet were almost swept away from under her, and she could hear the eerie wailing and sobbing of many, many ghosts, and could feel the icy clutch of their fingers. Some were bold enough to wreathe about her head, shrieking in her ear, pounding at her chest and throat, seeking to insinuate themselves into her nose and mouth. She choked, unable to breathe, and shook her head violently, throwing them aside. *Give us life,* one whispered in her ear. *Ye have the secret. Give us life again!*

"Begone, foul spirit!" she cried. "Your life is long gone!"

Behind her she could hear Dide shouting and cursing too, and Ghislaine was chanting an ancient prayer against harm. Isabeau took up the words as well, and heard Cailean and then Dide join in.

"In the name o' Eà, our mother, our father, our child, thee who is Spinner and Weaver and Cutter o' the Thread; thee who sows the seed, nurtures the crop, and reaps the harvest; by the virtue o' the four elements, wind, stone, flame and rain; by virtue o' clear skies and storm, rainbows and hailstones, protect us this day from all harm, O Eà, mother, father, child, spinner, weaver, cutter, maiden, mother, crone . . ."

Ahead of her the Celestines were humming deep in their throats, and behind Dobhailen growled and snarled, a strangely harmonic counterpoint. The words and the humming formed a rhythm that they could march by. Isabeau felt her stride lengthen and quicken, and her breath come more evenly. The ghosts seemed to shred away, until they were mere mist and shadows and a cold snaky wind about her ears.

All about them, above and below them, were sheets of silvery-green fire that leaped and roared and hissed. She could see vague shapes through the green fire, a forest of trees, a white rushing river, mountains behind. With each step the picture blurred and rushed past, however, and she never had the chance to recognize any landmark or realize where they were.

Then suddenly there was a great hiss of green sparks and Isabeau felt herself falling. She cried out and tried to wrench her hand free to save herself, but neither Dide nor Stormstrider would let her go. She fell painfully to her knees, with a great ringing in her ears, blind with vertigo. When her vision cleared, she looked about her and realized she was slumped on the ground in a cool, grey dawn many miles away from the Pool of Two Moons.

Crouched in the morning mist, on the crest of a small hill, was a great grey mausoleum, guarded by brooding stone ravens. A long avenue of yew trees led up to it, gaunt and dark in the dawn. In the forecourt before the mausoleum was a long, oblong pool surrounded by formal urns and statues. It reflected the dome of the tomb in its still, black waters.

We are here, Cloudshadow said wearily.

"I dinna realize this was a Heart o' Stars!" Isabeau exclaimed. "How extraordinary! When ye said we would travel to the Tomb o' Ravens, I thought ye meant we would walk the Auld Way as close as we could get, and then go cross-country. Is this truly a Heart o' Stars? Where is the circle o' stones, the summerbourne?"

All gone, the Celestine answered.

"But . . . why? When? Was it Brann the Raven who had the circle leveled? Did he no' ken?"

Of evil mind was the man who built this grave, and of evil intent. He knew this was a place of power and sought to use its magic for his own ends, Stormstrider said. His mind-voice was deep and grave, and had the same stern arrogance of his face.

"I never kent," Isabeau said slowly and looked about her with a troubled face. Now that she knew, she saw the three elements that always composed the sacred sites of the Celestines—the hill, the pool, and the erection of stones—but its shape and composition, its essence, were all wrong. The natural spring of water had been trapped and forced into this stiff, formal, stone-bound shape, and the pillars constructed did not celebrate life and the passing of seasons, but death and one man's vanity.

Buba came down to rest on Isabeau's shoulder, and she put up one hand and petted him, comforted.

The others were all stretching and moving about, murmuring the occasional comment to each other. Dobhailen did not like the look of the crypt, and he curled back his lip and growled, his green eyes glowing like marsh-candles. Cailean fondled his ears, and the shadow-hound, stiff-legged, crept forward and sniffed at the broad steps. Suddenly he raised his muzzle and bayed aloud, the call of a hunting dog that has caught a scent. It was a deep, loud, savage sound that echoed off the walls and made them all jump and cry out in alarm. Dobhailen lunged up the stairs and bayed again at the door. Cailean followed him, and so did the others, hurrying.

The dog led them in through the massive doors and into the shadowy chill of the crypt. Within was a long hall, lined on either side with small vaults protected by heavy iron grilles. Above were elegant arches, the ornate pillars topped with carvings of sharp-beaked ravens amid fronds of acanthus and oak. In every dark vault were sarcophagi, thick with dust and cobwebs, their stone faces crumbling in the damp. The air smelled old and musty, and Ghislaine cupped her hand over her mouth and nose. She was deathly pale.

As they made their slow way down the hall, their boots echoed on the flagstones. Unconsciously they all drew together, Cailean's hand gripping his dog's ruff and holding him back. Isabeau had conjured light to illuminate their way. Witch's light was a cold, eerie light to explore a crypt with, casting thick shadows behind every pillar and grave, and tricking the eye so it seemed the sarcophagi breathed.

At the far end of the hall was a large ornate tomb with another statue laid out upon it, arms crossed over its mailed chest, a sorcerer's staff clasped between the huge ringed hands. The tomb was carved with ravens, sleeping, eating, flying, nesting. One rested beneath the sorcerer's feet, beak curled into its chest.

"I have been here afore," Ghislaine said in a high, shrill voice, breaking the echoing silence. "When I walked the dream-road with Olwynne. We were led here, to this place, by a raven. We saw the dead sorcerer, trailing his shroud. He told us . . ." Her voice faltered.

"What did he tell ye?" Isabeau asked intently. Although Ghislaine had reported as much as she could remember of the dream-road she had walked with the missing banprionnsa, details of dreams were always vague afterwards and both Ghislaine and Olwynne had been struck down with sorcery sickness afterwards, making their account even more strange and wild than usual. Isabeau knew any details to be recalled could be of the utmost importance.

"He said . . . he said the dream world is o' no use to him, no more use than the world o' spirits. He said to come again in daylight, with a living soul and a knife, and then we should see him walk again." Ghislaine looked with dread at the statue lying on the tomb and repressed a shudder.

Isabeau nodded. "Indeed he is a greedy soul, and strong, to be reaching out to touch my niece in her dreams."

She bent her head and counted the rings upon the sorcerer's hands. There were ten. Isabeau felt a little giddy. A sorcerer of ten rings! She herself had only eight. For the first time she felt a miserable shrinking of her confidence. How was she meant to defeat a sorcerer of ten rings, one who had clung to life for a thousand years? Cailean and Ghislaine had been counting too, and she saw their faces blanch and their breath catch.

Dobhailen had been straining to break free of Cailean's grip and, at the involuntary relaxation of his master's hand, leaped forward and sniffed eagerly at the base of the tomb where the shadows were thickest. He raised his head and gave that great baying cry, and at once Cailean came forward and knelt, seeking to see what had excited the dog's interest. He cried aloud and picked something up.

"Look! It is His Highness's . . . His Majesty's . . ."

In his hand he held a long golden feather.

"He must have plucked it from his wing and hidden it there," Isabeau said, taking it from Cailean and turning it in her hand. "So we'd ken we are on the right track."

"How many days ago were they here, though, and then where did they go?" Dide asked.

Cloudshadow glanced at the feather, then continued walking slowly around the circumference of the tomb. Isabeau knew she was searching for some sign that her daughter too was alive and well.

Suddenly she hummed loudly and urgently and dropped to her knees. Isabeau came swiftly to join her. Laid down on the ground was a little collection of leaves, twigs, and a white pebble. Isabeau brought the globe of witch's light down to her hand so they could see the pattern clearly.

She was here, my daughter was here, Cloudshadow said. *They arrived at dawn the day after Midsummer's Day, and left again at dusk. They went back. Back to the beginning, she says.*

"Back to the beginning?" Isabeau asked. "Does she mean back to the beginning o' this building? To the time when the Tomb o' Ravens was built?"

The Celestine hummed a negative, a sound of bafflement and indecision.

Isabeau was trying to decipher the message written with twig and pebble. "What is this?" she asked, pointing to a little stick that had been broken and arranged in a jagged line like lightning. There was a long silence, and then Isabeau saw a drop of water darken the pale stone. She looked up in surprise and saw the Celestine was weeping.

It means good-bye, Stormstrider said.

A Night on the Road

No one slept well that night. It was too cold. Even with the fire roaring away in its circle of stones, and their thick cloaks and plaids wrapped well around them, the cold bit up from the ground and tortured them. It was not a night to spend on the road.

Rhiannon crawled out of her tent at dawn. The stick that formed the ridgepole of the tent was caked with ice, and snow rose in hillocks and hummocks all about, white and unblemished. The sky had a pale silvery radiance to it, which meant a fair day ahead. Rhiannon wondered whether the Dowager Banrìgh's grief had at last worn itself out. She hoped so. All had been turned summerset, and that alarmed Rhiannon. When the world was broken asunder, it left cracks through which dark walkers could crawl. Rhiannon had not left her satyricorn past so far behind that this was a notion that did not terrify her.

A raven called weirdly. Rhiannon spun on her heel, her heart pounding. A big black bird was perched on a branch nearby, observing her. It cried again, mockingly.

Rhiannon bent and scooped up a hunk of snow and flung it. Her aim was good. The snow broke against the bird and almost knocked it off its perch. It spread its wings and flew away, uttering its harsh, mournful call a third time.

"One for sorrow," a voice said behind her.

Rhiannon turned to face Jay, huddling her hands into the sleeves of her coat.

"It is a saying we have. One for sorrow; two for mirth; three for a death; four for a birth; five for silver; six for gold; seven for a secret, no' to be told; eight for heaven; nine for hell; and ten for the devil's own self."

The fiddler spoke beautifully. His words sent a shiver across Rhiannon's skin and reminded her of the sorceress Nina the Nightingale, whose magic was all contained in her voice. If the tales were true, then this slight, gentle man had magic in his fingers, in the sound he could coax from the strings of his viola. There was magic in his voice too, Rhiannon thought, though perhaps it was only the terror implicit in his words that struck such a chord with her.

"Any raven within twenty leagues o' Laird Malvern is trouble," she said sourly, sitting down on the log and warming her hands at the embers.

"Ye think that was his raven?" Jay asked, turning to stare after the bird.

"Could be," she replied, and thrust her numb feet into her boots. Bluey was perched on her tent rail, looking very cold and miserable, and she held out her hand to it. It flew across to her, and she lifted it to her shoulder, liking the feel of its slight weight there.

One of the soldiers, red-nosed and morose, threw some more logs on the fire and began to make some mess out of oats and water that these humans called breakfast. Rhiannon whickered a satirical comment to Blackthorn, who whickered back. *I'll have it, if you do not want it,* the mare said.

Rhiannon's eyes brightened when another of the soldiers came in with a brace of coneys, which he began to skin by the fire. Finn was still lying in her bedroll, but she suddenly rolled over, crawled out the end, and retched, noisily and publicly, under a bush. When she had finished, she looked positively green. Without a word or a look to anyone, she crept back into her little tent and dragged her cloak over her face. Her little cat, who had pranced away most indignantly, returned to pat her with one inquisitive paw. Finn did not look up.

Jay took her a cup of tea.

At the smell of roast rabbit, Roden at last woke up and poked his tousled head out of the tent, rubbing his eyes sleepily. He had been kidnapped from his bed, in the middle of summer, and so, dressed in a loose white nightgown, was woefully unprepared for this evil winter. They managed to find him a heavy woolen jerkin to wear over the top of his nightgown, and some socks that acted like knitted hosen. Wrapped in a blanket, with a scarf muffling him to his eyes, he was a comical figure, and evidently felt it. His lip stuck out sulkily, and his feet were turned inward, and every now and again he jerked at his clothes, as if trying to drag them to a different shape and style.

He wanted his mother and father.

"Brice will take ye back home," Finn said gently, indicating one of the soldiers who bent down to smile reassuringly at Roden. "It's a day or two on the road, I'm afraid, but—"

"I want to go home now," Roden said, his voice quavering despite himself. "Please, I want my mam."

"I ken, sweetie, and we'll get ye there just as soon as we can. Brice is very quick, he can ride like the wind, that's why he was sent with us. He'll get ye to your mam and dai just as quick as he can."

"I want my mam *now*!" Roden cried, and suddenly broke into sobs. "Please, please, I want Mam now!"

"I'll take ye back," Rhiannon said, putting her arms about the little boy. "Ye ken how fast Blackthorn can fly. If ye eat up your breakfast real fast, we'll be on our way and I shall have ye to your mam afore sunset."

"Really?" Roden asked, perking up at once.

"Really." Rhiannon felt Finn's curious gaze upon her, and said rather defensively, "He wants his mam. I'll be back afore ye ken it. It's better this way anyway. They'll be looking for me in the skies now, and I have no desire to be shot down by one o' their arrows. Once I have Roden safe and sound, I'll fly after them again, and see if I canna get ahead o' them and ambush them somehow."

Finn nodded. "Very well. Let me scry to Nina and tell her the glad news that Roden is safe, and I'll find out for ye where she is. Indeed, she'll be glad to have Roden back again so quickly."

As Roden happily chewed on a rabbit leg and inundated the soldiers with endless questions about battles they had fought, Rhiannon watched with intense curiosity as Finn drew out a small silver bowl from her pack and filled it with water. She set it on the ground before her and bent over it, as if gazing at her own reflection. There was a long silence. Rhiannon was puzzled. She had heard of scrying before, of course, and had watched the witch-apprentices attempt it a number of times. She had always thought the face of the person being spoken to appeared in the bowl, speaking as clear as if they were right next to you. But Finn's eyes were blank and the water in the bowl was still, reflecting only the pale wintry sky.

At length the sorceress's eyes lost their vacant, unfocused look and she shook herself and glanced at Jay.

"That was hard, harder than I'm used to," she said ruefully.

"Ye must no' try to do too much," Jay said admonishingly.

"Oh, fiddle! I'll be fine." Finn stretched her back and then poured the water into the kettle over the fire. She turned to Rhiannon and Roden, who was teasing the elven cat with a length of wool he had pulled out from his rumpled socks. "Your mam is absolutely overjoyed to hear that ye are safe, Roden, as ye can imagine. She and your *Daidein* are at a wee village called Alloway, on the Rhyllster. It is where this road begins, so ye should have no trouble finding it, Rhiannon. It is where Laird Malvern abandoned his boat and took to the forest."

"How do ye ken all this?" Rhiannon said suspiciously. "Ye saw it all in the bowl?"

"Aye. Witches can talk to one another through water or fire or gemstone, if they are well known to each other, and no' separated by a large body o' water or high mountains. It helps if one is waiting for the contact. Nina and I had agreed to scry each dawn and sunset."

"But ye did no' talk," Rhiannon said. "Ye were still and quiet."

"We talked mind to mind, as ye call your horse," Finn replied. "I have kent Nina since I was knee-high to a grasshopper. I couldna talk so to a stranger."

"Knee-high to a grasshopper?" Rhiannon asked in complete puzzlement, making a gesture with one hand as if trying to measure the knee height of a small hopping insect.

"Aye. Very, very small," Finn answered, giving a little wry smile. "No' as small as young Roden here, who's knee-high to an ant . . ."

"I am no'!" Roden protested, even as Rhiannon realized it was yet another of the endless meaningless phrases that humans were so prone to use. She smiled mechanically, and filed it away in her brain for future reference. It had not taken her long to realize that people were much more likely to accept you as one of them if you spoke the same cant as they did.

By the time the eastern rim of the valley was brightening and the birds were singing, Rhiannon was astride Blackthorn once more, feeling the mare's muscles bunch in her shoulders in anticipation of flight. Roden sat before her, wrapped up warmly in a blanket with a muffler up around his ears.

"We will see ye again soon," Finn said. "Give our love to Nina and Iven."

"Look after yourself, Roden," Jay said, and put his hand up to pat the boy's knee.

Roden nodded, looking very solemn.

Then Rhiannon wheeled Blackthorn about and urged her

into a canter. She went away down the road like a black streak, and then lifted her legs high up under her belly, spread out her magnificent wings, and soared up into the sky.

"Whoo-hoo!" Roden shouted.

Olwynne moaned. Her head thumped sickeningly and all her limbs felt weighted down. The mad phantasmagoria of her dreams still gibbered away behind her eyelids. She had dreamt she was on trial in a giant courtroom, the judges all leaning down and shouting at her, shaking their immense bony fingers, accusing her with their gimlet eyes. *I did it for love,* she had explained weakly, but they had shaken their heads in reprobation and, with great ceremony, turned their mantles inside out to red. Blood. Fire. Hissing red adders. Chains of her own hair binding her down. A rivulet of blood slashing across her throat like a crimson ribbon.

She had woken then, struggling up from the depths of her drugged sleep, but there was no sanctuary in wakefulness. The coach rocked and rattled and bounced and swayed and slid and skidded, and at times seemed to almost overturn. She and Owein were tumbled helplessly from one side to another, and tossed off the seat onto the floor till they were bruised and aching in every limb. The air was so cold their breath hung before their faces in little clouds of frost, and their limbs shuddered uncontrollably. They would have huddled together for warmth, but after Olwynne had half bitten her tongue off after cracking her head on Owein's jaw, and they had landed one on top of the other half a dozen times, they concentrated on trying to keep their seats, bearing the cold as best they might.

They could hear the shouting of the coachman and the crack of his whip, and the creaking and clatter of the carriage, the occasional high-pitched whinny of a horse and the shout of the men riding alongside. Owein braced his legs against the side of the carriage and did his best to protect Olwynne with his arm and wing. Despite the cold, his

curls were damp with sweat and his breath came in harsh
pants. Both had already been sick till there was nothing left
in their stomachs, but still nausea racked them.

All night they had driven through the forest, the men
lighting the road with pitch torches. Drugged with poppy
and valerian, both Olwynne and Owein had slept most of
the time, although uneasily. However, once it became light
enough to see, the horses had been whipped into this mad,
headlong rush as the road began to plunge downhill. They
could hear the screech of the brake being applied, and
someone shouting. Then the carriage swerved, swayed violently from side to side, skidded sideways, and then toppled over onto its side. Olwynne screamed as she was flung
head over heels, knocking her head violently on the ceiling. She landed in a heap with Owein on top of her, his
feathers smothering her.

She put her hand to her head and winced. Her fingers
came away bloody. Groaning, Owein managed to lever
himself off her. He supported one arm with his hand.

"How are ye yourself?" he whispered. "Olwynne? Are
ye hurt?"

She was so dazed with shock and the drugged potion
Dedrie kept force-feeding her that she could not frame an
answer. He helped her up, and she staggered and lost her
balance, falling again. The coach was lying at a peculiar
angle, so that the left-hand door was buried in an embank-
ment, and the right-hand door was above their heads, fram-
ing a patch of sky.

The carriage door was wrenched open, and the surly,
unshaven face of Jem the groom glared down at them.
"They're alive," he shouted to someone. "Blood everywhere, though."

"I told my laird we'd be over if we kept traveling at such
a pace," someone else said. "Here, get them out. Can ye
reach them?"

"Toss me a rope," Jem answered.

It was a bit of a struggle to get them out of the carriage,

both Owein and Olwynne being so shaken and bemused that they were incapable of helping much. It was a scene of chaos on the road. Lord Malvern's carriage was mired in the mud where a small burn crossed the road, at the bottom of a valley. No matter how hard they whipped the horses, the poor exhausted creatures could not manage to drag it free. Lord Malvern himself was standing knee-deep in the muck, hissing at his coachman in a low, vicious voice, two white dents driven deep from his nose to the sides of his mouth.

Owein and Olwynne's carriage had tried to stop before crashing into the first carriage, and had overturned. Half of the horses were lying in the mud, and two at least were clearly badly injured. One was screaming with pain, until Jem impatiently slashed its throat with his knife. He killed the other one too, without taking the time to examine the injury, and then unhitched the other horses and whipped them till they struggled to their feet.

Olwynne had entered a strange light-headed state that was almost euphoric. She could not keep her feet. Her legs just folded underneath her, as if made of old spinach stalks, and she found herself sitting in the mud again, her silver bridesmaid dress crumpled up all around her.

There was an angry exchange of shouts and accusations, which Lord Malvern's voice cut through like a sword. "We've already lost one o' the sacrifices due to your stupidity," he said icily. "And the Blue Guards are hot on our trail. We do no' have time for this. Take only what we can carry with us. Ballard, ye are the strongest, ye take the prionnsa. Bind him well. Piers, ye take the banprionnsa. Dedrie, ye will have to go up behind Irving. Jem, ride ahead and make sure there is no ambush waiting for us. Now, to horse, all o' ye!"

Olwynne found herself being passed up to a tall, thin man with grey eyes who murmured apologetically as he settled her in the saddle before him. Olwynne's wrists were bound tightly before her, and although the man who held her kept asking her pardon, he held her with a grip like iron. Olwynne could only be grateful she had not been put up before Jem, who had a hot lascivious stare, or Irving Steward, who looked like he hanged puppies for pleasure.

There were twelve in the lord's party, with Dedrie the only woman. Three of the men were old, bent, grey, and decrepit, and found it very hard to drive their horses on at the pace Lord Malvern demanded. Even when he whipped their horses himself with his long riding crop, and once, in frustration, whipped the old librarian Gerard, who would not stop moaning, still their pace flagged. So Lord Malvern ordered them tied to their horses, and the reins taken by the younger, more vigorous members of the company. The poor old men were jerked and jostled as badly as Owein and Olwynne, and their moans and cries of pain were a constant counterpoint to the uneven melody of the horses' hooves on the stony road.

Olwynne was a fine horsewoman and did her best to keep her seat, but with her hands bound, her movement hampered by her flowing skirts, and the pommel of the saddle jammed up hard against her pelvic bone, she was badly jolted. Many times she would have fallen if it had not been for the strong arms of the man behind her. At first she sat bolt upright, flinching every time her back brushed against his chest, but soon she was glad to lean her weight against him.

By dusk the horses were all foundering and Olwynne was weeping with exhaustion. She did her best to hide it from the others, but she could not conceal it from the man who held her. He felt every shudder and choke, and kept whispering to her, "I'm so sorry, Your Highness. No' much further now. Chin up now."

Olwynne could only mop her face on her arm and try to catch her breath.

The road had been going downhill for most of the day now, and gradually the landscape had changed from towering grey mountains with their roots in stands of dark fir and pine, to steep stony ravines and gorges that led down into rolling hills of green forest. As the light began to fail, Dedrie looked about for a campsite. The horses were so weary they could only plod along with hanging heads, despite the lash of whip and prick of spur. Olwynne kept feeling herself falling, and would jerk awake with a cry and a convulsive clutch at the arms about her waist.

"Easy now, Your Highness," the man whispered. "We'll stop any moment now, and ye can rest a wee."

"When?" she cried peevishly. "When can we stop?"

"When my laird gives the order," he said.

Olwynne choked back a sob.

Jem came trotting back along the road, his horse all in a lather, blood running down its flanks from where he had dug in his spurs.

"There are charcoal-burners ahead, my laird. With a dray and six horses."

"Excellent," Lord Malvern said. "Let us relieve them o' it."

He ordered the riders to draw up on the side of the road, and Olwynne was allowed to dismount, if sliding off the horse in a clumsy rush to collapse in the mud could be called dismounting. Owein was tossed down to the ground too, and Olwynne saw her twin had fared worse than she. He was unconscious, his freckles standing out orange against his white skin. Dried blood obscured half his face, and his bound wrists were a red, raw mess. She crawled to him with a miserable cry, and brought his head into her lap. She could do no more.

The old men were lifted down from their mounts and given water to sip. They were greyer and more decrepit than ever. Olwynne saw the man who had ridden with her lift one of the old men in his arms and lay him on the soft grass at the road's verge, wrapped in a cloak. The old man opened his eyes and smiled wanly, whispering, "Thank ye, Piers."

"Can ye manage any more, *Dai-dein*?" Piers said gently. "I wish ye had never come . . . I wish . . ."

"Far too late for wishing," the old man whispered, and closed his eyes with a sigh.

Piers gave his father something to drink out of a silver engraved flask. He swallowed gratefully, and some of the blueness around his mouth receded. Then Piers brought the flask to Olwynne and she wiped the lip fastidiously with the least filthy part of her skirt she could find, and sipped cautiously. It was whisky, and it burned a path like acid down to her gullet. Once she had finished coughing and choking, she felt an amazing return of strength and warmth and vigor. She lifted Owein's head and poured a few drops into his mouth. It roused him at once, and he took the flask from her with his bound, bloodied hands and swigged a good dram.

"Thank Eà for the water o' life," he gasped. *"Slàinte mhath!"*

"Slàinte mhath," she repeated ironically.

While Olwynne had been sitting with Owein's head in her lap, Jem and Irving and Kennard the coachman and Ballard the bodyguard had gone on down the road with grim expressions on their faces. No one seemed to worry much about the poor unsuspecting charcoal-burners ahead. Olwynne could only hope they would not fight to save their dray and carthorses.

Lord Malvern was sitting on a rock, his furred cloak slung about his shoulders, his valet on his knees before him, massaging his stockinged feet. Dedrie brought him whisky, and some bread and cold meat, apologizing for the roughness of the fare. She ignored Owein and Olwynne.

Olwynne had not eaten since midday, when they had been given some dry bread to gnaw on as they rode, and a mouthful of water. Her mouth was so dry her tongue felt like a lizard in her mouth.

"We need water and some food," she said loudly. "Do ye want us to die afore ye can sacrifice us?"

Lord Malvern made a bored gesture, and Dedrie brought them the water-skin and tossed them some bread. It was so dry and old there was no way Olwynne could eat it, even by dribbling water onto it. She satisfied herself with drinking deeply, and helping Owein to drink also. Piers offered them more whisky, with an unhappy twist of his mouth, and Olwynne accepted, even though she had never liked it. It was better than bread, bolder and hotter, and filled her with a courage she knew to be wholly spurious.

By the time Jem returned, it was twilight. Olwynne and Owein were forced to stumble down the road, the horses being too weary to carry their double load any more. Their humiliation was complete when Lord Malvern ordered ropes to be looped about their necks. Every time they staggered or tripped, they would be dragged up, the rope burning about their necks. *So this is what it would feel like to be hanged,* Olwynne thought, and was filled with a remorse so bitter it scalded her.

In darkness they came into a clearing. Olwynne could only be glad of the lack of light. Her captors had slaughtered the peaceable charcoal-burners who labored here, and tossed their bodies to one side. In the flickering light of the great bonfire Olwynne could see their slack bodies, like a pile of discarded clothes. It made her feel strange and cold and sick. She could not stop looking at them.

Jem and Irving and Kennard and Ballard were drinking out of Jem's tarnished hipflask with great gusto. A goat was turning on a spit over the fire, filling the air with the aroma of roast meat. It made Olwynne retch and weep.

Owein looked very grave. "These are evil men indeed," he whispered to Olwynne. "Keep close to me. I can only hope they wish to keep us unharmed until we get to wherever we are going. Try no' to attract any notice."

"What do they want with us?" Olwynne whispered in anguish. "Why do they call us 'the sacrifices'?"

"I do no' ken," Owein said after a moment. "I am afraid to even try and guess."

Olwynne shuddered. Piers noticed and brought them both some rough old blankets that, by the smell of sweat and wood smoke, had once belonged to the charcoal-burners. Olwynne huddled one about her gratefully. She was dressed for a midsummer wedding, not a trek through a wintry forest.

"Do ye think she will come again, for us?" Owein whispered some time later, when the men were busy about their meal and could not hear. He looked up at the night sky, studded with a thousand stars. The red moon was rising, gibbous as a moldy orange.

Olwynne felt tears sting her eyes. She could think of no reason why Rhiannon would risk her life or the life of her horse to come and rescue her, when Olwynne had stolen away the man she loved. Rhiannon would rejoice to know the humiliation and pain she was now suffering. Olwynne could not bear to quench the hope in her twin brother's voice, however.

"I'm sure she will come," she lied.

The Celestial Globe

Rhiannon was many miles away, sitting by the warmth of a fire in a small, rather rough village inn, with a mug of ale in her hands and a warm feeling about her heart as she observed Roden snuggled up in his mother's arms.

They had found Alloway without any trouble at all, simply following the thin line of the road back down through the forest to the river's edge. Nina had been waiting for them, leaning on a fence, her hand raised to shield her face from the sun. At the sight of Blackthorn, she had begun to wave and call, and Roden had almost fallen to his death as he leaned over Blackthorn's side, waving madly back. Rhiannon had to hold his wriggling, squirming little body in a firm grip until the winged mare could land in the meadow and she could drop Roden to the ground. He had run across the snow, shouting, and leaped into his mother's arms, while his father Iven had come running out from the inn to join them in one happy muddle of tears and hugs and kisses.

The sight of them had affected Rhiannon deeply. She had found her chest heaving with sobs that she was quite at a loss to explain, and quite fiercely ashamed about. She had taken her time removing her saddlebags from Blackthorn's back, and rubbing her down thoroughly, and leading her to drink at the trough. By the time Nina thought to turn and embrace her, Rhiannon's face had been scrubbed dry and she could be sure of her voice again.

Both Blackthorn and Rhiannon were very tired after the last few days, and so they had been easily persuaded to stay the night. Winged horses were not used to flying long distances. It was more natural to them to stay in their own territory, wandering along as they grazed. Their wings were usually only used to escape danger, or in the yearly migration from the summer breeding grounds high in the mountains to the winter meadows lower down the mountains, and back again. Rhiannon did not want to exhaust Blackthorn by keeping her in the air too much, particularly if they had a long flight over the sea ahead of them, as seemed likely. So she had stabled the winged mare for the night with some warm mash and a bale of hay, and a deep bed of straw, and taken the opportunity to enjoy her friends' happiness.

Iven Yellowbeard, a tall fair man with a long forked beard, was chatting companionably to the locals, hearing all their talk about the terrible weather and their distress over the murder of the Rìgh, and doing his best to allay their alarms. The hairy brown arak Lulu was sitting at Nina's feet, her arms wrapped about the sorceress's legs, her wizened old face pressed against Roden. The little boy lay with his head nestled on Nina's shoulder, his eyes shut, his cheeks rosy from the heat of the fire. Nina was rocking him gently, her hand patting his back.

"Poor wee laddie, he's worn out," she whispered. "What an adventure! Oh, Rhiannon, I canna thank ye enough for saving him. These last few days have been the most horrible nightmare. I am so glad to have him back again it hurts me, really hurts me, like I've been punched in the heart." She laid one hand on her breast, tears running down her face. "I shall never let him out of my sight again, not even for a moment." She took a deep, ragged breath and then took Rhiannon's hand. "If I can ever do aught for ye, Rhiannon, anything at all . . ."

"Thanks," Rhiannon said gruffly. "But there's naught."

Nina hesitated, then said softly, "Rhiannon, when this is

all over and ye are released from the Banrìgh's service . . . if ye find ye do no' wish to keep on serving her . . . and do no' wish to go to study at the Theurgia, as I ken Isabeau would like . . . will ye come to me? Wherever we are, ye would always be welcome."

"I ken Iven would very much like to add a flying horse to his show," Rhiannon said with a laugh. Nina and Iven were jongleurs, who traveled about the land singing and performing in the villages and towns, and secretly gathering information for the Coven and the Crown, respectively. From the moment he had seen Rhiannon and her winged mare, Iven had imagined the crowds they would pull if she was to join their small troupe. Both knew Rhiannon had neither the talent nor the inclination to be a jongleur, but it had become a running joke between them in the weeks they had traveled together through Ravenshaw.

Nina laughed. "Indeed he would, but ye ken that is no' why I ask ye."

"Aye, aye, I ken," Rhiannon replied. "Thanks, Nina. I'll keep it in mind."

"I will never be able to repay ye," Nina said. "Never."

"I'm just glad I could save him," Rhiannon said, remembering the sight of the little boy in his white nightgown, barefoot in the snow, dodging the big men with their outstretched hands and grim, brutish faces, all lit up from below with the red light of the fire. She shivered, and Bluey rubbed her cheek with its curved beak.

"So am I," Nina said, smiling through her tears. "Now, I'll just go and lay my lad in his bed, and then we'll have some supper. I must admit I'm hungry tonight for the first time since all this happened."

"I'm hungry too," Rhiannon said.

Nina smiled over Roden's curly head as she carried him towards the stairwell, Lulu at her heels. "Are ye ever no'?" she teased.

*   *   *

At the Tower of Two Moons, Lewen leaned on the stone balustrade and stared out across the witches' wood. It was cold. His nose and ears stung, and his feet in their heavy boots were numb. It made no sense that he would stand here, when inside the great hall of the Theurgia a fire was roaring on the hearth and the lackeys were doling out big bowls of hearty vegetable soup.

Yet he stood, watching the sun set like a giant red ball behind the tall dark columns of the yew trees, with his head and his heart in a tangle he had no hope of unraveling. Whom did he love? The wild girl Rhiannon, so quick to kiss or strike, so clear-sighted it frightened him? Or the Banprionnsa Olwynne, his dear friend who had seduced him and jumped the fire with him, and whom he had promised to love forever.

Lewen did not know. He loved them both, had betrayed them both, feared for them both, and wanted them both. Now he had lost them both. Somewhere out there, in the cold dark, his two loves faced the most terrible danger, and he could do nothing but watch and wait, and suffer the discomfort of cold feet.

"Lewen?"

At the sound of Fèlice's soft voice, Lewen turned his head and tried to smile.

A pretty, slender, dark-haired girl, Fèlice was one of the caravan of apprentice-witches who had traveled through Ravenshaw with Lewen, and had sought shelter from a terrible storm at Fettercairn Castle, thus finding themselves catapulted into an adventure of kidnappers and necromancers, ghosts and mad old ladies, that had ended with Rhiannon on trial for murder. Fèlice was not very tall. She barely reached Lewen's shoulder. But she had so much charm and animation that she was usually the focus of any room, particularly one filled with young men.

"How are ye yourself?" she asked, gripping the balustrade with her small, gloved hands.

He shook his head. "No' good."

"Me either."

They stared out at the smoldering horizon. A bright star showed over the mountains.

"Will she be able to save them?" Fèlice asked in a small voice.

"I dinna ken," Lewen said, too raw for false comfort. "I hope so. But . . ."

"But . . . ?"

"I think it's more likely she'll be killed trying, and Owein and Olwynne too."

Fèlice caught her breath in a sob, gamely suppressed.

"The world has turned topsy-turvy," Lewen said harshly. "Naught is in its right place. I do no' ken what is right or wrong, true or false, real or unreal."

Fèlice laid her hand over his. "Aye, ye do," she said softly. "Ye ken it as well as I do."

He shook his head, unable to speak.

"It's just because your heart is all in a tangle that ye feel that way," Fèlice said. "Once ye sort out the muddle ye're in, all will be well again, I promise."

"I do no' ken who I love!" he burst out. "I feel torn in half. One minute I am sure it is Rhiannon, that she's my one true love—but then I think o' Olwynne in danger and it makes me sick with fear. And I've promised to marry her! We jumped the fire together!" He stopped and pressed his lips together, then said with obvious difficulty, "I never thought love would be like this. I thought ye met the one ye are meant to be with, fell in love, and then everything was simple."

"It is simple," Fèlice said with the absolute certainty in the affairs of the heart that her sixteen years had given her. "It does no' matter who ye loved first, or who ye have promised to marry. What matters is who ye love the most."

He heaved a great sigh.

She patted his hand reassuringly. "Do no' worry so. It'll all come right in the end, I promise."

"And how can ye be so sure?" Lewen demanded, and

fixed his gaze on the far horizon, where darkness was rapidly swallowing the last of the sun.

At dusk, the witches and the Celestines were once again standing hand in hand by a pool of darkly glimmering water. The sun was setting in the west, and in the east the red moon was just lifting itself free of its cage of tree branches.

Isabeau glanced towards the far distant horizon, looking to see the bright star of the west, the planet they called the Fire-Eater. It usually appeared just as the sun was setting, particularly in summer. It was this bright red spark that was to be their guide on their mad, perilous rush back in time.

The day had passed slowly. Although all were weary, they were too cold, anxious, and uncomfortable to sleep. The crypt of an evil sorcerer was not a restful place to spend the day, particularly when one knew that the sorcerer had sworn to outwit Gearradh, the Cutter of Thread, and live again, no matter whose lifeblood was spilled to raise him.

"Hot blood, he wanted," Ghislaine muttered at one point. "And he a sorcerer o' ten rings."

"How are we to do it?" Dide asked as the shadows had begun to lengthen and the time of their stupidity grew nearer. "How are we meant to travel back to the time o' Brann the Raven?"

Isabeau hesitated for a long moment. Dide had his frowning dark eyes fixed on her face, and she saw how both Ghislaine and Cailean leaned forward to listen intently.

"The Celestines follow a lunar calendar," she said in a low voice. "They navigate by calculating the position and shape o' the two moons against that o' the stars."

Isabeau knew she was breaking a taboo by revealing the secrets of the Celestines, but could not think it mattered when in a few hours they could all be dead, or lost and wandering between worlds. She saw Cloudshadow raise her white, ravaged face and look at her, but the Stargazer did not protest and so Isabeau went on. "Apart from being gateways to the Auld Ways, the Hearts o' Stars help the Celestines to predict the positions o' stars and planets and comets in years to come, and also calculate where they were in years gone by."

You have listened well, Cloudshadow said.

Dide and the witches were leaning forward in interest. "But how can they possibly ken where the moons and the stars were a thousand years ago?" Cailean asked. "I mean, it's no' even exactly a thousand years. What is it? One thousand, one hundred and sixteen years, we worked out, since Brann died."

"The Celestines do no' judge time as we do," Isabeau said, trying her best to explain something she did not fully understand herself. "Their year is a lunar year; they mark the passage from new moon to new moon. To follow such a system one must, in some sense, release oneself from the idea of seasons—the sowing o' seeds in spring, the harvesting o' crops in autumn. The Celestines do no' sow and reap; they do no' celebrate the changing o' seasons as we do."

"But . . . surely such a system is flawed?" Cailean said. "The moons and the sun do no' move in perfect time together; they are out o' step. A year o' twelve lunar months is shorter than a year o' twelve solar months. One is but twenty-eight days long, the other thirty or thirty-one. Each month they lose a few days; over time they would lose a whole month in the cycle o' the seasons. How do they make their calendars work?"

"I am no' sure," Isabeau said. She glanced at Cloudshadow, who sat straight-backed, staring at the light striking in through the open tomb door. The Stargazer made no sign that she listened to the murmured conversation behind her. "I do ken they have seasonal points on the horizon to mark the arcs o' sunrise and sunset. When the sun rises behind a particular rock, for example, it is the shortest day o' the year, and when it has swung all the way over to that cleft in the mountains, it is the longest day. That sort o' thing."

Cailean taught alchemy, astronomy, and mathematics at the Theurgia. He was pained and puzzled by this.

"But . . ." he began, and Isabeau could tell by his voice that he was doubting the Celestines' ability to navigate through time. The Keybearer wanted no insecurity.

"It is no' just the moon they track, but the stars as well," she said. "Thunderlily has shown me. A star rises four minutes earlier every night. When it rises during the day, it canna be seen, o' course, but once it matches its rhythms to that o' the night, then it can be seen and tracked. The first day a certain star can be seen rising is most significant. The Celestines keep a record o' these. Moonrise, star-rise, landmark, it is very precise, over thousands o' years."

The others were baffled and skeptical.

"Space and time are linked for the Celestines," Isabeau tried to explain. "It is a calendar based on landmarks, a horizon calendar. I ken it seems strange to us, but ye must remember the Celestines are intimately linked to their landscape. They ken each rock, each tree, each pool o' water."

"Rocks can crumble, trees can fall, springs o' water can run dry," Ghislaine said heavily.

"Aye, that is true," Isabeau admitted. "And we have seen how even the circles o' stones the Celestines built have been destroyed." She made a vague gesture out the doorway, to the formal pool that lay in the forecourt. "Yet the memory o' the Celestines is very long; they teach the remembered lore to their children. Cloudshadow . . . the Stargazer says their calculations are very precise and we must believe her."

There was a short silence. Cailean had pressed his lips

together, and beside him Dobhailen lifted his head from his paws and growled softly.

"I often travel back to my childhood in my dreams," Ghislaine said dreamily. "Sometimes it is a glad journey. Sometimes I wake weeping. We have been experimenting with traveling back farther too, back past the moment o' one's birth, back to the lives that came afore."

Isabeau nodded. She was well aware of such experiments. Many sorceresses, herself included, had visions of previous lives while deep in a trance. It was always difficult to remember them upon waking, like any dream, but dream-walkers were trained to remember and record the images their deepest subconscious mind threw up, and to try to direct what they dreamt.

"To go back so far, though, and in my own body . . . indeed it seems impossible," Ghislaine said, and raised her eyes for a moment, to look directly at Isabeau. "I canna help being afraid."

"I have traveled every road in Eileanan, except this one," Dide said cheerily. "I think it may be the greatest adventure ever."

Isabeau smiled at him. "We would be fools no' to fear what lies ahead," she said. "There is no doubt about that. But I trust in the Stargazer. I am sure she will lead us true."

The frown between Cailean's brows deepened, and he pulled at Dobhailen's ears to soothe the low growl that again rose from the dog's throat.

The one who can whistle dogs is troubled, Cloudshadow said, rising to her feet and coming to stand before them. Hearing her voice in his mind, Cailean looked up, startled. *He is one that sees beauty in order and in knowledge. He loves to know that he can use the power and insight of his mind to make sense of what seems unknowable. In many ways, I have sympathy with him, for the desire to bring order out of chaos is something that my kin have in common with those of your kind. However, it is one of the fundamental laws of nature that disorder will always multiply.*

An apple is a shape and form of utmost perfection, yet it shall rot and fall apart and ultimately dissolve back into the earth, and from it shall, perhaps, in time, grow another apple tree, that shall in time fall also. This, too, is true. The stuff of this earth, this universe, cannot ever be destroyed. It simply changes from one form to another. An apple rots away and feeds the earth. An apple seed becomes a tree. A tree falls and becomes firewood, which is burned and becomes ash. Order breaks down and becomes chaos. It is best to remember this, dog-whistler.

They had all listened silently, entranced by her words.

We cannot undertake this journey beset by fears and doubts, she continued. *The malevolent spirits that haunt the Old Ways are drawn by such emotions. They feed off them, and become stronger. I do not wish to have you at my shoulder, dog-whistler, if you doubt my ability to navigate through time and space.*

Color rushed up Cailean's face. He would have protested, but she held up her hand and he fell silent, gripping his lip with his teeth.

We of the Celestines, as you of your kind like to call us, have learned over the centuries not to easily trust in you humans or, for that matter, in anyone. To keep our laws and lore secret is natural to us. These are high mysteries. They are sacred. However, this evening I shall in all willingness break one of our most holy taboos. Considering what we are about to embark upon together, I feel it is a small matter to reveal other secrets to you. Stormstrider, will you show these humans what you carry?

The young Celestine had been listening quietly, his arms folded over his chest. The knot of skin that concealed his third eye was clenched tightly shut, as if he was scowling. He did not respond to Cloudshadow's request for a long moment, long enough for Cloudshadow herself to frown and turn towards him commandingly.

Stormstrider, she said softly.

As you wish, my Stargazer, he replied then, and unfolded his arms and unknotted his brow. His third eye opened and raked them all with a dark, unfathomable look. Then he bent and retrieved from beside the door the large sack he had carried over one shoulder.

Very carefully he unknotted the cord and drew back the folds of the cloth to reveal a sphere of interlinked metal circles. He lifted it between his two hands and released a little lever that swung down and turned into a delicate stand set upon three feet. Stormstrider secured the sphere upon its stand, then gently spun it around. The witches all cried aloud in astonishment and wonder as the sphere sprang apart with a little whirr.

It was a celestial globe, illustrating the positions of the sun and planets and moons and stars. Unsprung, it had been no larger than a man's head, but once released it spanned twelve feet in all directions. In the center was the sun, a globe of burnished red metal inscribed with wavy lines. Around it, each on its own elliptical cycle, spun the planets. Their own planet was no bigger than a green crab-apple, and its two moons were as small as peppercorns. Around the whole were several metal circles inscribed with measurements and symbols. Isabeau recognized it at once as being very like the skeleton globe of the heavens that was kept in the observatory at the Pool of Two Moons. This was far larger and more intricate, however, and was driven by some sort of clockwork device so that all the little pieces swung and moved.

"It's like an astrolabe!" Cailean exclaimed. "A celestial astrolabe. See these disks, Beau? They must measure . . . what? The rising and setting o' stars?"

Stormstrider's face warmed at the eager interest in Cailean's voice. He nodded and began to explain the device to the sorcerer, showing how little bronze markers could be moved here and there on the outer dials to set the time and place, and how all the little globes swung in response, showing the exact celestial position of every cosmological marker.

"I dinna ken the Celestines had such things," Dide said softly to Isabeau. "I thought they lived simply in the forest, eating berries and fruit. I didn't think they kent how to work metal."

Just because we do not make weapons of war, or tools to rape the earth, or worthless follies to decorate our limbs does not mean we are entirely without the skill of forging metal with fire, Cloudshadow said coldly. *Stormstrider is of the Starforger family. Like all of his family, he has been taught the secrets of using metal to measure and record time and space. Other families are taught the secrets of stone, or water, or silk, or trees and flowers. We all share the common songs and stories, but the deep wisdom, that is the burden of the nine families.*

Both Isabeau and Dide were speechless. The more they learned about the Celestines, the more they realized they did not know, and the more shallow their assumptions seemed.

"Look, this is truly amazing!" Cailean turned to them with a glowing face. "It works just like an astrolabe really, but so much more precise! We are here . . ." With a touch of his finger he sent the delicate rings swinging about until they could see clearly where the earth was in relation to the sun and the other planets, and where the moons were in relation to the earth. Then he showed them where all the constellations were rising and setting in the night sky, his words coming in a tumble.

"Now, we ken where we want to go back in time, and so if we just move this little marker all the way round here, look, we can see exactly where everything was in relation to everything else a thousand, one hundred and sixteen years ago. The difficulty is, of course, calculating the difference between our solar years and their lunar years but because they mark everything in cycles, it is no' as hard as one would imagine. See, here? Two hundred and thirty-five o' their months exactly matches nineteen o' our solar years, each having six thousand, nine hundred and forty days in them. They call it a Great Cycle. If you quadruple that, you have seventy-six solar years or nine hundred and forty lunar months, each having twenty-seven thousand, seven hundred and sixty days in them, which is what they call a Sacred Cycle . . ."

"It's times like this that I regret no' having had a formal education," Dide said in a wry undertone to Isabeau.

"This outer circle is what they call the star dance, and it marks the times of star-rise and star-set, and this little one is what they call the mansions o' the moon, so you can see, just by adjusting this lever, what phases the moons were in at the time a certain star was either rising or setting, and by doing that, ye see, ye can figure out exactly what the sky looked like at dusk where and when we want to go. The Stargazer fixes these in her memory along with the landscape markers, that horizon calendar ye explained afore, and then sets her course as it were. It really is just like navigating, though across time as well as space."

"How amazing," Ghislaine said. "I wonder if I could use such a mechanism to aid me in dream-walking back in time? We tend to use memory markers. Ye ken, smells, shapes, the touch o' certain materials, music or other sound prompts. But they are very imprecise."

Cailean and Stormstrider spent the rest of the day studying the celestial astrolabe, and doing their best to explain its mysteries to those who did not have so much of a fascination with astronomy and mathematics. Ghislaine did not listen. She was off in a reverie, imagining her own navigational tool to aid dream-walking. Dide sat and strummed his guitar, and began composing a dirge in Lachlan's honor. Isabeau paced back and forth, biting her fingernails till her cuticles bled, and doing her best not to shriek with irritation at the dragging of the hours. Here, in Brann's tomb, it seemed his voice was louder and more compelling than ever.

Gradually the sun had dropped towards the horizon and the little party began to make its preparations. Dobhailen had gone hunting, and came back with a bloody muzzle and a few tufts of coney fur sticking to his mouth. The Celestines ate a frugal meal of seeds, nuts, dried fruit, and water; the witches had a slightly more substantial meal of bread and cheese and bellfruit jam, and dried apricots, and a bottle of goldensloe wine. This was a wine normally reserved for festivals and weddings, taking a great many goldensloes to make, and it gave their picnic a ritual feel, as if it was indeed to be their last supper.

When all had eaten and drunk their fill, and tidied up after themselves, they came to stand by the pool, linking hands in a chain. Cloudshadow had spent her time painting runic symbols into flat dark stones that she had gathered from the parkland about the mausoleum. She had arranged these around the pool in the same pattern that the menhirs would once have stood in. Now she held one of those stones in her hand. Painted upon it were four symbols, signs for setting sun, rising star, three-quarter moon, and rock. She stepped forward through two of her rune-painted rocks and disappeared, drawing Isabeau after her.

Isabeau fell into a whirlpool of roaring red light. It dragged at her arms and legs, sought to draw her head away from her body. Although she tried to run, as one must do when traveling the Old Ways, her body responded only very, very slowly. It was like one of those nightmares when one tries to scream but has no voice, tries to run but one's feet are stuck to the floor, tries to punch but finds the air has turned to treacle. Even drawing of breath was an immense effort and the air seemed to shrivel her lungs.

Normally, when one ran the Old Ways, one could see the landscape one traversed blurring on the other side, as if each step carried one a hundred leagues. What Isabeau saw through the red inferno of flames was quite different. The landscape in its essentials stood still. Everything, however, changed, and so rapidly Isabeau had no time to absorb any details before they were gone. Stars wheeled overhead, rising and setting in seconds, to be followed by the rapid blowing of clouds, the brightening and darkening of the sky, the swift passage of the moon from new to full, to new to full, over and over again. Grown trees shrank back to seeds, cleared land became forest again, storms raged and stilled, seasons flickered past. The courses of streams and rivers changed, and the thick, gnarled trunks of the ancient yew trees became young, slim saplings, newly planted. All this happened in the time it took her to take four painful, rasping breaths and to force her immensely heavy, unresponsive limbs four staggering steps forward. Her joints were screaming with pain, and her extremities were numb and tingling with pins and needles so that she could not feel Dide hanging on to her hand behind her.

Suddenly she was sucked down through the whirlpool. It happened so fast, so unexpectedly, that Isabeau could not scream. For a moment it felt as if she was being dragged apart by horses, the pressure on her limbs utterly unbearable. Then she was spat out at the other side, falling to her knees upon the flagstones, sobbing in pain and terror.

She was kneeling beside the pool in the forecourt of the Tomb of Ravens at dusk, in exactly the same place where she had been standing scant seconds before. Yet nothing was the same.

Winding and Watching

The bells tolled out, filling the air with their melancholy clamor.

The hearse moved slowly along the road, pulled by six black horses draped in heavy black caparisons. Their heads were hooded, and tall black plumes nodded from their forehead straps. Alongside them walked six black-clad lords, carrying banners that snapped in the cold breeze. The royal piper marched at the head of the procession, playing a mournful lament, with heralds carrying more banners behind him.

Iseult, clad in somber black from head to foot, walked behind the hearse. Not one strand of her red hair could be seen beneath her heavy headdress. Her dress was pinned at her throat with an ebon and glass brooch in which could be seen a lock of her dead husband's hair.

Behind her came Bronwen, dressed as soberly, her face bowed. The Lodestar clasped between her two hands shone like a pale star, the only brilliant thing in the whole solemn procession. The line of mourners stretched for two miles behind the hearse, making its stately way to the palace graveyard. All were dressed in solid black, and many among the crowd wept as Lachlan the Winged was taken at last to his rest.

For three days he had lain in state in the banquet hall, surrounded by tiers of candles, and watched over by his widow and friends and servants. Then the midwives had come to wash and wind him, swaddling him in white linen as tenderly and efficiently as they would a newborn babe. Flowers and herbs were placed between the bands—rosemary and sweet woodruff and lavender—to help combat the smell of putrefaction.

Normally the coffin would also be heaped with flowers, but the frost that had bitten after Lachlan's murder had laid the garden waste. The midwives had been hard put to find any living herbs at all to tuck inside the winding cloth. So Lachlan's coffin was topped with an arrangement of evergreen leaves—yew and ivy and holly—and those who walked behind the hearse carried sprigs of evergreen rosemary in their black-gloved hands.

Lachlan the Winged was buried beside the tiny grave of his daughter Lavinya, Donncan's twin sister, who had died at birth. Iseult did not weep. Her face was as expressionless as a plaster mask. The only sign of her bitter grief was the cold that clamped down upon the graveyard. Snow whirled down out of a leaden sky, and the breath of those that watched blew in white plumes before their faces. Everyone was glad to hurry back to the palace and warm their hands on goblets of mulled wine and draw as close to the roaring fires laid in the hearths as they could.

"Eà's blood!" Douglas MacSeinn, the Prionnsa of Carraig, growled to King Nila. "It's as cold as the Castle Forlorn in the dead o' winter. I wish I had brought my seal furs."

"Even I find it rather fresh," King Nila admitted. "May I offer ye some seasquill wine to warm your blood?"

The MacSeinn shook his head. "No' unless ye wish me to shame myself by falling down dead drunk," he replied with a wry twist of his lips. "I havena the head for it at all. I will have some whisky, though, to toast our dead Rìgh. To think Lachlan should be struck down in the very prime o' his life. It's a sad day indeed."

"Indeed it is," King Nila said soberly. "He was a great man."

"And now your niece sits the throne," the MacSeinn said. "I have no wish to cast aspersions on one o' your blood, Your Majesty, but I must admit it makes me uneasy, such a young slip o' a girl and one best known for dancing and partying."

"Aye, ye ken what they say," a grizzled old lord struck in. "A whistling maid and a crowing hen . . ."

"Her Majesty is descended from royal blood on both sides," King Nila said in a cold voice. "I think ye will find she is well aware o' the gravity o' her position."

The grizzled lord looked very doubtful, but no one wanted to insult the King of the Fairgean, a race known for their pride and temper, and so both he and the MacSeinn murmured something appropriate as they lifted their cups and drank.

The great hall was a sea of black. Every man, woman, and child from the most lowly to the grandest was dressed head to foot in the color of mourning. Many of them, having no time for anything else, had been forced to throw their entire wardrobe into giant vats of black dye made from oak galls, alder, meadowsweet, or even crushed blackberries, anything the city dyers could find to render material black, even if only for a few days.

Black swags of material hung above the mantel and down the grand staircase, and because the curtains were all drawn across the windows, the hall was dim and gloomy.

Bronwen stood by the foot of the staircase, greeting those who came in and accepting their commiserations. Beside her stood her mother, dressed in a low-necked gown of oyster grey. Her black hair was cut in a straight fringe above her eyebrows and then level with her ears so it swung forward onto her cheekbones in two smooth wings, emphasizing her exotic angular features and doing nothing to hide the gills that fluttered slightly just below her ears. Her eyes were icy blue, and one thin cheek was scarred with a fine fretwork of white lines, starring out from a central point, like glass that had been broken by a bullet.

Maya's grey dress gleamed amidst all the black with the sheen of mother-of-pearl. Bronwen would have much preferred it if her mother had bowed her head to the conventions and worn deepest, darkest black like everyone else, but if Maya had had her way, she would have been dressed in a gown of her favorite crimson red.

"But red is the Fairgean color o' mourning," Maya had said earlier that morning, smiling, when Bronwen had exclaimed in absolute horror at the sight of her in a dress the color of blood.

"But it is the color ye wore when ye were Banrìgh, more than any other color," Bronwen said, pressing her hands together in distress. "Your soldiers wore red cloaks in your honor, and the Seekers o' the Awl long red robes. It is the color most associated with the Burning, and the years o' terror."

"Was I no' in mourning then?" Maya said, anger sparking in her eyes. "Forced by my father to wed the king o' our bitterest enemy, and woo him into evil and madness? Forced to murder thousands and thousands o' people to serve my father's lust for revenge?"

"I thought ye wore it because it suited ye so well," Bronwen had said, trying for lightness.

Maya laughed, lifting her heavy red skirts and giving a small ironic curtsy. "Aye, and does it no'?" she asked. "Yet that is no' why I wore it, Bronwen. Red is the color o' Kani, goddess o' volcanoes and earthquakes, fire and destruction. I was upon Kani's work and so I chose to wear her color."

"Yet ye are no' upon Kani's work now," Bronwen said.

"Nay, but I shallna be a hypocrite and wear the black o' human mourning for a man whose death I do no' grieve for."

"Please, Mama," Bronwen asked. "Please. If black means naught to ye, it should no' matter if ye wear it."

"I have worn the black o' servants' garb for twenty long years as punishment for my sins," Maya replied fiercely. "I will never wear it again."

"Then grey. Dark grey is perfectly respectable."

"I have no desire to be respectable."

"But, Mama, red . . . it will cause such talk, such a scandal. Please . . ."

"And who are ye to worry about causing a scandal?" Maya scoffed. "I thought ye delighted in thumbing your nose at polite society."

"Aye, but that was afore. I am banrìgh now. I must tread very carefully."

"Then tread carefully, my dear. But do no' expect me to."

"I must," Bronwen said desperately. "Do ye no' understand, Mama? By allowing ye to remain unbound, by bringing ye here to the palace, I have already courted much disapproval. The crown is no' yet secure on my head! I may be a NicCuinn by blood and by marriage, but that does no' mean all will welcome my rule. Rìghrean have been deposed afore. My uncle Dughall MacBrann has MacCuinn blood through his mother; he could challenge my right to rule, being at least fully human. Then there are those that hate the MacCuinns' power and would welcome a chance to throw down the clan entirely. Please! I need ye to show the world a meek and humble face. Now is no' the time to flaunt your new-found freedom in the faces o' those who remember the Burning all too well."

Maya had gazed at her in silence for a moment, surprised, and then she had nodded, her pale eyes gleaming. "Ye are right, my love. I will change. I will no' wear black, I warn ye now, but I will find something suitable, I promise ye."

Bronwen could have wished for a darker, more sober

grey, but was so relieved her mother had changed at all she said nothing but squeezed her mother's arm in silent thanks. She could see that many among the court took umbrage at the half-mourning, but she could only hope no one would make a scene.

Just then she saw the old sorceress, Tully the Wise, tiptapping her way towards them. A tiny woman, with a face as wrinkled as a prune, the sorceress was dressed from head to toe in black. Bronwen braced herself. Tully could be shockingly outspoken at times, believing herself old enough to have won the right to speak her mind.

"It's an outrage," Tully muttered, pointing a shaking finger at Maya. "The Ensorcellor should be in prison, no' here at the palace flaunting herself for all to see." She looked around at the interested crowd and raised her voice. "How dare she show such a lack o' respect for our poor dead Rìgh? I say it was Maya the Ensorcellor who spat the poisoned barb at our Rìgh!"

Bronwen glanced hurriedly at Neil, who nodded at her in reassurance and went up to the old sorceress, bending his head over hers. He knew Tully well, having spent most of his childhood at the Theurgia with Donncan and Bronwen. He brought her a cup of hot mulled wine laced with a double shot of whisky, and when she had swallowed that down, smacking her whiskery lips in pleasure, gave her another. It was not long before he was arranging to have her escorted quietly back to the Tower of Two Moons. Bronwen could only smile at him gratefully.

It took a very long time to formally greet the guests, for the palace was still overflowing with those who had come to attend the wedding. Bronwen's feet were aching and her throat was hoarse by the time the last one had filed past her and into the great hall.

"Here, Bronny," Neil said quietly, and offered her a cup of steaming herbal tea.

"I'd rather have dancey," she said, making a face.

"Ye've been drinking too much dancey," Neil said reprovingly. "No wonder ye're having trouble sleeping. The healer Mirabelle has made this brew especially for ye. She says it's made with angelica and linden blossom, and bee pollen and honey. It's meant to make ye calm and happy and focused . . ."

Tears stung her eyes. *How can I be happy till Donncan comes home?* she thought.

"And I ken ye will no' wanting to be drinking the wine, no' today," Neil finished.

It touched her that he realized as well as she did that she could not afford to drink the potent mulled wine when she needed all her wits about her. Later, when all the guests were gone, she could relax and drink some wine. Now she was better off sticking to tea, much as she disliked it.

Bronwen sighed and took a cautious sip, then smiled in surprise. "Why, it's delicious!"

She swallowed another mouthful, and felt it spread through her, warming and relaxing her. Bronwen drank the cup to its dregs and passed it back to Neil with a grateful smile, before moving forward to speak to the Siantan ambassador.

Iseult, the Dowager Banrìgh, had not attended the wake. With eyes blind with the agony of her grief, she had gone straight up the stairs and to her own suite of rooms. Bronwen wished she could do the same. But she knew how important it was for her to move about the room, talking with the prionnsachan and banprionnsachan, who would all leave in the morning to go back to their own countries.

She knew they must all be reassured that the search to recover the lost children of the dead Rìgh was proceeding with all possible speed. There had been no time for the shock over Lachlan's murder and his heirs' abduction to wear off; the prionnsachan were all upset and frightened, and Bronwen took the opportunity to allay their concerns as much as possible. It was a tricky tightrope for her to walk. Most of the prionnsachan still thought of her as the flighty daughter of the Ensorcellor. She must treat them all with grave respect and esteem, while still impressing upon them her right to rule over them. She had to try to allay any suspicions that she and her mother had anything at all to do with the plot to murder Lachlan. The absence of the Keybearer did not help. It made everyone feel uneasy and vulnerable, and Bronwen was too young, too beautiful, and too controversial to assuage their fears.

In any other company she might have drawn upon just a little of her power to win some warmth and sympathy, and to impress her abilities upon them. The prionnsachan all had their own powers, however, and they were all accompanied by their court sorcerers. Any attempt to compel or manipulate with magic would have been noticed at once, and never forgiven. So Bronwen could only look fragile and yet brave, beautiful and yet sad, and reassure one prionnsa and banprionnsa after another that everything that could be done was being done.

The NicAislin of Aslinn was pale and frightened, tortured by nightmares; the NicThanach of Blèssem was sharp-eyed and sharp-tongued, and anxious for her family; the MacFaghan of Tírlethan was wearied and exasperated by the continued sleep of his wife, Isabeau and Iseult's mother Ishbel, and anxious to return to his land of snows and stony towers; his younger children, Alasdair and Heloise, were white and sick with anxiety for their lost cousins, and chafing at the restrictions of tradition and convention that prevented them from racing to their rescue.

The Prionnsa of Arran, Iain MacFóghnan, had not waited for the funeral to be over before leaving for his misty marshlands. Bronwen could only wish his wife, the white-faced, black-clad, glittery-eyed Elfrida, had gone with him. Much as Bronwen cared for Neil of Arran, she could not stand his mother.

The MacSeinn of Carraig was inclined to be sentimental, and wept openly at the dirge played by the court piper.

He reminisced loudly with anyone who would join in about the legendary Battle of Bonnyblair, where Lachlan had finally harnessed the power of the Lodestar and raised it against their enemies. Since that was a famous battle against the Fairgean, King Nila and Queen Fand were understandably stiff and polite, and very wary of any intimation that the death of Lachlan the Winged was part of a Fairgean plot to see their niece Bronwen rule. Bronwen, who longed to know more about her mother's aloof and mysterious people, was saddened to see how eager her aunt and uncle and their daughters were to leave.

The MacRuraich of Rurach had been content to let his sons and daughter attend the wedding on his behalf. The old wolf was grey now, and crippled with arthritis, Bronwen had heard, and it was thought it would not be many more winters before Aindrew MacRuraich inherited the throne. The young heir to the Rurach throne was often at Bronwen's elbow, helping her negotiate the perils and pitfalls of the room with his easy manner and winning ways. Bronwen could only be grateful to him, even though she was all too conscious of Elfrida NicHilde's disapproving frown, and the sly sideways glance of the Duchess of Rammermuir. She could only be grateful that Aindrew and his brother Barney were leaving the next day, to ride home for Rurach.

Brangaine NicSian of Siantan had traveled a very long way to attend the wedding, leaving her elderly gouty husband behind her, but bringing her son and two daughters with her for their first taste of the royal court. They were only children still, and too young to appreciate the sorrowful occasion. It made Bronwen smile to see them hiding under the table, gorging themselves on sugarplums and honey cakes, with the boy, Odell, reaching up a surreptitious hand every now and again to steal the last dregs of a cup of mulled wine. It was the only bright moment in this long, dragging morning of monochromes. It made Bronwen wish she was a child again, and running shrieking through elegant balls with Neil and Donncan racing after her, their hands full of plundered goodies.

The MacAhern of Tìreich accosted her by the long table of funeral meats. He was a tall man, brown-haired and brown-eyed, and dressed in a kilt and plaid in the old style, a long stretch of soft wool pleated about his waist and held in place with a thick belt. The plaid was pinned at his shoulder with a golden brooch in the shape of a rearing horse.

He did not waste time in the usual platitudes, addressing her with a heavy scowl and an abrupt question: "So, have ye laid the villains by the heels yet? Who would dare strike down the MacCuinn in his own banquet hall?"

"We believe it was a plot hatched by an old enemy o' his," Bronwen answered quietly. "Long ago, during the rebellion against the Burning, my uncle was the cause o' the death o' the laird o' Fettercairn and his young son." As usual, she found it difficult to speak of this period of history, for it was against her own mother that Lachlan had led the rebellion. Loving her mother as she did, and hating what her mother had done, Bronwen found it easiest to speak in the broadest of historical terms, as if Maya the Ensorcellor, and the terrible deeds done in her name by the Anti-Witchcraft League, was someone far distant to her in time and place, like the Red Queen of fairy tales who had executed her own cousin, after keeping her prisoner for decades, simply to make sure she did not dream of challenging her for the throne.

"The laird's brother had been a Seeker o' the Awl," she went on. "He blamed my uncle, and plotted his revenge for many years. It is he who kidnapped my cousins for his own nefarious purposes. We are certain we will catch up with him soon and drag him back here to face trial."

"I have heard, Your Majesty," the MacAhern said curtly, "that ye have a thigearna flying in your service? A satyricorn girl? I find it hard to believe. The satyricorns hunt the winged horses for food, I had always heard."

"She is only half a satyricorn, my laird, and indeed a true thigearn. I have seen her call her winged horse myself, without words or whistle, and seen her ride it. They are like one, my laird, just as I believe a thigearn should be."

He grunted, frowning. "Was the horse bridled and saddled? Did it wear a bit?"

Bronwen was amused. "Nay, sir. No bridle, no saddle, no bit. She had saddlebags, and a saddlecloth, but that was it."

She was aware that the MacAhern's daughter was listening avidly, and smiled at her, racking her brains to remember her name. The young woman flushed and moved away, pretending disinterest, and Bronwen returned her attention to the prionnsa, who was saying angrily, "I have heard many wild tales about her, including that she tamed her horse in just a day and a night. O'course I dinna believe such a tale. No winged horse could be tamed so easily, and no woman would have the strength to break it. She must have raised the horse from a foal."

"I believe no'," Bronwen said. "I am sorry ye did no' have a chance to meet her yourself. If things had been different . . . we had so little time, and I was, o' course, anxious to use her skills to help track down my cousins. It is no' often one can take a thigearn into service."

The MacAhern bowed his head. "No. A thigearn is no' for common hire," he answered softly. "Nor, for that matter, a thigearna, though I have never before heard o' a woman taming a flying horse." He glanced at his daughter, who was pretending not to listen.

"I am lucky she was willing to serve me," Bronwen said. "It will make all the difference having a winged horse in pursuit o' the villains. Otherwise, I fear, our chances of catching them are slim." She felt no need to tell the prionnsa that she had pressed Rhiannon into service as some kind of payment for saving her from the gallows. Let the arrogant old man feel his own lack of fortitude, she thought, rather unkindly.

The MacAhern hesitated. He had, of course, ridden his own flying horse to Lucescere, but both he and his beautiful rainbow-winged stallion were growing elderly now. There was no way that he could have volunteered his services, and he was the only thigearn left in Tìreich—at least he had been until this wild girl had popped up from nowhere. The flying horses had all been cruelly hunted by Maya's soldiers during the Burning, and were now more rare than ever. Bronwen was sure that the old prionnsa wished one of his sons had managed to tame a flying horse of his own, but it had not happened, and he was too proud to admit he feared the days of the thigearns were over.

"I would like to see this girl who can tame a flying horse," he said abruptly. "If she doesna wish to stay in your service, perhaps she will come to visit us, and tell us her tale? I must admit I am curious."

"Perhaps ye will see her at the Lammas Congress," Bronwen replied. "Will ye be there, my laird?"

"Happen so," he answered. "There will be much to talk about."

"Indeed there will be," Bronwen answered. "So much has happened in these last few dreadful days, there has scarcely been time to take it all in. But we must adjust. By Lammas, all o' us will ken better how to go on."

He nodded, his expression softening. "It has been hard on ye," he said, his voice much warmer. "To lose your husband on your wedding day, and your uncle too, and then to have so much thrust upon your shoulders."

"It has been very hard," Bronwen replied, swallowing a lump in her throat. " But I am a NicCuinn. 'Bravely and wisely' is our motto, and so brave and wise I must be. If, Eà forbid, we do no' succeed in rescuing Donncan, I must just do my best for the people o' Eileanan."

The MacAhern pressed her hand sympathetically and pledged her his support, before withdrawing back to his wife, shaking his head and murmuring about the poor, brave girl bearing her troubles so valiantly.

Bronwen, sipping another cup of Mirabelle's tea, hid a smile.

The MacBrann

"Come, Bronny, ye must eat," Neil said in a low voice, holding up a little tray of delicacies for her to try.

Bronwen gave him a quick frowning glance of reprimand, and he grinned. "I'm sorry, Your Majesty! After twenty-four years o' calling ye by name, it's hard to remember. Come on, try the fishcake, it's your favorite. I asked the cook to make it especially."

Bronwen smiled and took one, biting into it. As its delicate, salty flavor filled her mouth, she realized she could not remember the last time she had eaten a proper meal. She seemed to have been living on dancey alone.

"It's a hard row ye have to hoe," Neil said softly as she swallowed the morsel of food and reached for another. "Ye must keep your strength up, Bronny."

Tears stung her eyes. She glanced up at him and nodded in agreement. He was right. If she was faint and giddy from hunger, and jittery from too much dancey, she would make a mistake that could cost her the crown.

"Thank ye, Neil," she answered. "For everything."

"I am yours to command," he answered, his voice husky with deep emotion.

She wanted to tell him, once again, that he must not show his feelings for her so clearly when she became aware of being watched. At once she shifted her gaze, and saw she was being observed closely by her second cousin,

Dughall MacBrann, the Prionnsa of Ravenshaw. She felt herself stiffen. Dughall had been her father's cousin and best friend, and after Jaspar's death had joined forces with Lachlan to help overthrow Maya and return power to the witches. He had inherited the throne of Ravenshaw only recently on the death of his father Malcolm, usually called the Mad. Since his mother had been a NicCuinn, he was theoretically a contender for the throne, and there were no doubt many who looked on him more favorably than on Bronwen.

Dughall was a slim, suave figure, dressed all in black silk, with a neat, pointed beard. Although his hair and mustache were inky black, his face was lined and there were sagging pouches under his eyes. He leaned upon a slender walking stick of ebony, embossed with silver, and wore a diamond drop hanging from one ear. His fingers were laden with witch-rings, for the Prionnsa of Ravenshaw was an accomplished sorcerer, descended from Cuinn the Wise on his mother's side and Brann the Raven on his father's.

Bronwen took a deep breath and then crossed the room to his side, determined to try to ascertain for herself whether her father's cousin was to be a danger to her.

"This is an unhappy day indeed, Your Majesty," Dughall said to her, with what seemed like true feeling in his voice. "I kent Lachlan when he was but a lad, and feel this is a grievous end indeed for such a proud and noble man."

"Aye, true indeed, Your Grace," Bronwen replied. "Evil times are upon us indeed if the Rìgh o' Eileanan and the Far Islands can be poisoned in his own banquet hall."

"And on such a happy occasion. I feel for ye, Your Majesty, to have lost your husband on the very eve o' your wedding."

She examined his face for any sign of irony and, finding none, said, with a catch in her voice she could not disguise, "Aye, indeed, it was cruel. But we hope to have him back very soon. The Keybearer has gone herself to search for

him, with the help of the Celestines, and I am sure it will
no' be much longer afore he is home again."

"Let us hope so," Dughall replied. "And Olwynne and
Owein too. Indeed, it was a wicked plot that saw Lachlan
struck down and all three o' his children stolen."

Bronwen nodded. "He is a very wicked man, the laird o'
Fettercairn, if all the stories are true."

A shadow crossed Dughall's face. He frowned and
pulled at his beard. Bronwen remembered that the MacFerris clan, owners of Fettercairn Castle, were one of Ravenshaw's oldest and most respected families. She wondered
why they had been allowed to go on kidnapping and murdering for so long, and then remembered how vague and
senile Dughall's father, Malcolm, was said to be in the
years before his death. Ravenshaw had once been a prosperous and powerful country, but it had lost most of its
wealth in the Ensorcellor's Burning. Dughall's mother,
Bronwen's great-aunt, had died in the Burning, she remembered, and his father had never recovered. It must be
difficult for Dughall, inheriting a country that had been allowed to go to rack and ruin for forty-odd years.

"I feel . . . I feel in some ways responsible," Dughall
said in a low, passionate voice. "If only I . . . oh, if only I
had done so many things differently! If I had listened to my
father . . ." He pulled himself up short. "I'm sorry," he said.
"Would ye excuse me? I must go and pay my respects to
Iseult."

Bronwen inclined her head and watched him go, her
brows drawn together thoughtfully. Of all the things she
might have expected Dughall to regret, not listening to his
mad, doddering old father was not among them.

A tall, dark-haired man wearing the MacBrann plaid
and brooch had been standing silently at Dughall's elbow
all through the conversation. Now he bowed to her politely,
and turned to follow after the Prionnsa of Ravenshaw.

She restrained him with a quick gesture of her hand.
"I'm sorry, I'm afraid we were no' introduced. Am I right

in guessing that ye are Dughall's . . . adopted son . . . his heir?"

"Aye, Your Majesty," he replied gravely. "I am Owen MacBrann. His Grace adopted me when I was still but a lad."

"Why, then that means we are kin," Bronwen said warmly.

"I'm afraid no', Your Majesty. Dughall's mother was a NicCuinn, and your father's aunt. My grandmother was sister to Dughall's grandmother, on his father's side. There is no blood relationship between us."

Bronwen was disconcerted. She had only claimed kinship with him as a means to beginning a conversation. It was in her mind to perhaps charm or cajole him into casting some light on Dughall's rather cryptic last comment. His sober precision was rather like a dash of water in the face.

She recovered gamely. "Och, well, all o' the great clans have intermarried so many times it's a wonder we do no' all have two heads," she said. "I'm sure there's a kinship somewhere."

"I would be honored to think so," he responded with a polite bow.

She frowned, wondering on the difference between Dughall MacBrann, a man renowned for his suavity and wit, and this cold, polite young man. She glanced up at him and met his steady grey eyes, and thought again about the many whispers and innuendos that followed Dughall wherever he went. The MacBrann had never married, nor shown much interest in women at all. The court of Ravenshaw was said to be an idle place, much occupied with gambling, horseracing, dog-breeding, and the vagaries of fashion. Dughall, it was said, had lost so much money at the gaming tables that he had had to take out a loan from Lachlan, which Bronwen was sure was still outstanding. He was also, it was said, more likely to hire a servant for his comeliness than for his efficiency and had once, many years ago, caused a dreadful scandal with his intense friendship with another young man, the son of one of his father's courtiers.

Gossip like this had a way of never disappearing. It was like a harlequin-hydra, which grew another two heads every time you cut one off. It must have been hard for a handsome young man like Owen to be adopted by a dissolute old rake like Dughall. No doubt there had been a lot of talk.

"I am intrigued by Dughall's last words," she said, deciding on impulse that directness and honesty would work better with Owen than guile. "Why should he feel responsible for what happened? Did he mean he was sorry that such an evil plot was brewed in his homeland?"

"No doubt," Owen answered. "None o' us can feel proud that such men could thrive in Ravenshaw. By all accounts, they've been kidnapping, torturing, and murdering as they please for a quarter o' a century, without anyone the wiser. We kent, o' course, that no one liked to go near the Tower o' Ravens. We all thought it was because it was haunted. Certainly my laird . . . his mother died there, ye ken, and he has always had a horror o' the place."

"It does seem unbelievable," Bronwen said. "I have been told thirty-odd little boys were stolen and murdered, and countless graves desecrated, and others tortured and killed in the laird o' Fettercairn's experiments in trying to raise the dead. Was there no reeve, no sheriff, to report the dead and missing?"

Owen looked uncomfortable. "It does seem difficult to believe, especially, I imagine, for one no' familiar with the peculiar topography o' the highlands o' Ravenshaw. It is cut in two, ye see, by the Findhorn River, and there is only the one bridge now, Brann's Bridge having been destroyed on the Day o' Reckoning. The river itself is fierce and fast, and too dangerous to cross easily. So the valley o' Fetterness is very isolated, and Laird Malvern was like a prionnsa there, with Castle Fettercairn guarding the road down into the lowlands."

"Aye, I can see that," Bronwen said slowly. "But still . . . one wonders that the auld MacBrann could have no inkling o' what was going on."

"He was ill," Owen said stiffly. "The last few years he was completely bedridden."

"One wonders that Dughall did no' act as regent, if his father was so incapacitated," Bronwen said.

Owen flushed. "My laird has always had the utmost respect and affection for his father."

Bronwen nodded. "O'course. I did no' mean to imply otherwise. It just . . . concerns me that a plot to assassinate the Rìgh o' Eileanan and to abduct all his heirs could have gone unnoticed."

"I assure ye that now my laird is Prionnsa o' Ravenshaw, he is taking steps to make sure such a dreadful thing can never happen again," Owen replied stiffly.

"I am relieved," Bronwen said, and inclined her head as he bowed and excused himself, moving quickly to catch up with the MacBrann, who was climbing the stairs to the upper floor.

Owen had, she reflected, sidestepped her real question rather efficiently. Bronwen would still like to know why it was Dughall MacBrann wished he had listened to his mad old father.

Iseult sat in her wing chair by the fire, staring without seeing into the flickering flames. She had removed her headdress, but her red hair was scraped back from her face and secured so tightly at the back of her head that not one curl managed to escape. With her eyes so swollen and red from weeping, and her face so bony and white, she looked far older than her forty-two years.

She turned her head as Dughall came in, followed

closely by his adopted son, Owen, and his squire, a pretty young man with dark curls and a dreamy face.

"Dughall," she said in a flat, uninterested voice. "I'm sorry. I have no' seen much o' ye these last few days. I hope they have made ye comfortable."

Dughall came and bowed over her hand, and sat himself opposite, waving to his squire to go and sit by the wall with the other servants.

"I leave for Ravenshaw in the morn," Dughall said with the familiarity that comes from a long friendship. "I wanted to see ye . . . to tell ye how very sorry I am."

"Aye. Thank ye."

"It is my fault," Dughall burst out. "My father . . . he foresaw it, I think. In the weeks afore he died, he raved a lot. I paid no attention. He seized me by the hand and begged me, begged me, to take fire and raze the Tower o' Ravens to the ground. He said it was cursed, we were cursed. He said we must kill the ravens, that if we did no', the Rìgh would die at his own table. I thought it was all nonsense. He said ghosts were gathering all round his bed, that my mother was there, warning him, begging him . . ." He fell silent, unable to speak any further.

Iseult had roused from her cold abstraction. "Your father warned ye? That Lachlan was in danger?"

Dughall nodded unhappily. "But he was so incoherent . . . he said many things. We thought he had finally lost his wits. We soothed and swaddled him and gave him more poppy syrup to help him sleep. It just made him rave all the more."

"Did he tell Connor?" Iseult demanded.

"He must o'. Connor went to see him . . . and rode out that same evening. He must've realized it was no' just an old man's ramblings." Dughall's voice was bitter.

"Connor always had a knack o' seeing truth," Iseult said softly. She reached out her thin white hand and laid it on Dughall's arm. "Do no' distress yourself too much. We too had warnings o' what was to come. Olwynne . . . Olwynne dreamt it too. I thought we could keep him safe . . . I still canna understand how it happened . . . I was right there, beside him, and I saw naught! I, a Scarred Warrior! If anyone is to blame it is I."

"No, no," Dughall cried. "How were ye to guess?"

"I was sitting right beside him," Iseult said, her voice breaking. "We had just shared a toast. He rose to make his speech, to announce the pardons . . . and then this . . . this thing . . . just comes hissing out o' the shadows and strikes him down."

"It's a terrible thing," Dughall said, pressing her hand between his.

"The murderer was right there, right there! And I saw naught. And then I am so angry, so sure o' what I think happened, that I bungle everything, I just make it worse! I think it is this Rhiannon girl who has done the deed, because she had a blowpipe and poisoned darts, and because she chooses that very hour to escape from prison. And so I call the dragon's name and fly after her, to drag her back for the hangman's noose. Why did I no' fly after Owein and Olwynne instead? I could have saved them!"

"Maybe," Dughall said. "But maybe all ye would've done is endanger them. The dragon could no' have flamed the kidnappers without killing Owein and Olwynne too. They would've shot at Asrohc and perhaps injured her, or ye. And probably, if they had realized a dragon was on their trail, they would've just killed Owein and Olwynne out o' hand and fled . . ."

"Maybe," Iseult said unhappily. "I just wish I had thought more clearly. I could have asked Asrohc who the murderer was! Dragons can see both ways along the thread o' time, ye ken. Why did I no' ask her? It is too late now, I canna call her name again. One does no' call a dragon lightly, and she is raising her baby princess and was no' pleased to have to leave her."

"Who could think clearly at such a time?" Dughall asked. "I too was there. I too saw naught. I had been forewarned by my father's ramblings, I should've kent . . . if only I'd been watching! If only I'd seen whoever did it."

"We thought we were safe in our own banquet hall," Iseult said. "I had made sure Lachlan's food and drink were all tasted, I had made sure the palace was guarded. There was no one there but our friends and family. Who could have done such a thing? Who?"

Dughall had no answer for her.

"And now Lachlan is dead, and my bairns taken," Iseult said blankly. "My bairns . . . I am sick with anxiety for them, Dughall. Eà kens what they arc suffering in the hands o' that madman."

"Is there any news?"

Iseult shook her head. "Nay. No' really. I mean, I ken they are still alive, Owein and Olwynne at least. Bronwen recruited the lass, the one that tamed the black winged horse, the one I tried to hang. Her name is Rhiannon. She flew after them and managed to wrest back young Roden, Nina's lad. She said she saw both Owein and Olwynne then, alive and literally kicking." She paused and drew one hand across her eyes. "I canna help wishing . . ." she whispered. "Though I am glad, o' course, that Nina has Roden back. I just wish . . ."

"This lass, this thigearn, she flies still in pursuit?"

"Aye."

"I am sure she will manage to rescue Owein and Olwynne too," Dughall said comfortingly. "Finn and Jay arc in pursuit as well, remember, and the Yeomen o' the Guard."

"But will they be in time?" Iseult whispered. "He plans to kill them, to use their lifeblood to raise the dead from the grave." She shuddered and caught her lip between her teeth. "When? When will he do it? Can they possibly get to him in time?"

"She flies a winged horse," Dughall said. "They are swift, by all accounts. I saw her fly the other day, for the Banrìgh. She is a true thigearn."

At the mention of Bronwen, Iseult's gaze lifted and color rose in her cheeks. She pressed her lips together tightly and did not respond.

"And Donncan? What news o' the Rìgh?"

Tears spilled down Iseult's face. "No news."

"Isabeau will find him, I'm sure o' it. She is a powerful sorceress indeed, the most powerful we have had for many generations."

Iseult could not speak. She lifted her damp, crumpled handkerchief to her eyes and wiped them impatiently.

"Iseult, tell me, is it true . . . can it be true that it was a spell wrought by Brann the Raven that saw Donncan stolen away?"

Iseult stared at him. "Where did ye hear such news?" she demanded.

"Is it true?"

"I canna speak o' it," Iseult replied, and cast a quick glance at the squire, who was shyly chatting to her maid-of-waiting on the other side of the room, his legs swinging as he nibbled on a sugared plum. Owen was sitting quietly at a table some distance away, flicking through the daily broadsheets piled there. He did not look up at the touch of her eyes.

"Please, Iseult, by Eà's green blood, if it is true let me ken," Dughall said sharply. "Brann is my ancestor. I was raised with tales o' his doings. I ken he swore to outwit Gearradh and live again. I ken what a subtle and clever sorcerer he was. I must ken if there is any truth in these tales."

"Tell me first where you heard such talk," Iseult said softly. "For indeed, this is no' a tale we want told in every village square, Dughall. It is bad enough that Lachlan is dead and his heirs vanished away, with only an impudent slip o' a girl left to raise the Lodestar. If it was common knowledge what had happened to Donncan . . . if we take away the hope that we will soon have him back again . . ."

"There is a lad here who was squire at Ravenscraig last year," Dughall said. "A well set-up young man, really rather comely. He is a student at the Theurgia now and has plans to join the Yeomen. He was one o' the search party for Donncan on Midsummer's Eve. He kens he and the Celestine princess were taken into the maze by Johanna, and he kens Isabeau and the Stargazer have followed them onto the Auld Ways, to try and get him and Thunderlily back. He kens Johanna spent much time in the library researching the life and death o' Brann the Raven, and that Gwilym the Ugly has done so too. He kens the laird o' Fettercairn well, having been one o' the party that traveled through Fetterness with Nina, and so kens all about the necromancy, and the laird's search to learn the secret o' raising the dead. He and his friends are no' stupid, Iseult."

"Just loose-tongued," she flashed back.

"I do no' think so. He's a good lad. There is a lot o' gossip around, and as far as I can tell, none o' it anywhere near the truth. Indeed, the favored tale is that Donncan has run off with Thunderlily."

"What!"

"Aye. Most do no' realize that Johanna was in cahoots with the laird o' Fettercairn. That has been kept very quiet. I think they imagine she was assisting a tragic love story."

Iseult stared at him blankly, and then suddenly she began to laugh and could not stop. She pressed her hand over her mouth and rocked backward and forward, laughing and weeping at once, a condition Dughall's old nurse used to call "merry-go-sorry." He stared at her in some consternation, and she buried her face in her hands and fought to get herself back under control.

When at last she raised her face, her eyes were red-raw. "I wish . . ." she sobbed. "Oh, I wish that is all it was!"

"So is Cameron's guess right? Is it true that, by some ill chance, Brann is involved in this, strange and impossible as that may seem?"

Iseult nodded and scoured her eyes with the useless rag of a handkerchief. "He wrote a spell o' resurrection in *The Book o' Shadows* and somehow hid beneath it a spell o' compulsion. Whoever reads the spell is overcome by an irresistible need to raise Brann from the dead."

"But how is that possible? Brann has been dead over a thousand years."

Iseult nodded. "Och, I ken. That is why Thunderlily was taken too. Only the Celestines ken the secret o' using the Auld Ways to travel back in time. Johanna read the spell and fell under its compulsion, and that was why she kidnapped Donncan and Thunderlily, to do Brann's bidding."

"It must no' happen," Dughall whispered, his breath quickening, his eyes staring at nothing. "Iseult, ye canna ken . . . none but a MacBrann kens the truth o' Brann's evil. He must no' be allowed to live again, he must no'!"

"Ye think any o' us want him to?" she said wearily. "Quite apart from wanting to save Donncan and Thunderlily, Isabeau has gone to make sure it does no' happen."

"But did she no' read the spell herself?" Dughall whispered. "She acts under Brann's compulsion too! Believe me, Iseult, no one could shake off such a spell easily. If Isabeau has read the spell, she now does Brann's will, believe me. She willna stop his resurrection, she'll help it happen!"

THE DARK
BACKWARD

*"What seest thou else
in the dark backward and abysm of time?"*

—SHAKESPEARE
The Tempest, 1611

Time Past

How is one to measure time?

With each heartbeat, with each pulse of blood through an artery, with each breath taken and released, one counts the passing of time.

As the sun rolls over the sky, the shadow of the pointer moves around the sundial, and flowers turn their faces to its warmth. Sand falls through an hourglass. A melting candle devours the lines scored in its wax. The pendulum swings, and all the little wheels and gears of the clock click-clack through another tiny compartment of time. The moon rises and sets, waxes and wanes, and the tides mark out their hours on the strand. Seasons change and wheel about again, and the child grows into a man and then declines towards death.

All these things can be felt, seen, measured.

Yet they are merely shadow pictures of time's true being. Time is not the measure of the passing of seconds, seasons, centuries. It is not a river that flows smoothly and inexorably forward. It is the warp of the weave of the universe, and so hums at the very heart of all matter.

Spun like a thread through the eye of the needle, stretched like silk to breaking point, for a moment Isabeau had felt the cross-hatching of space and time in the very fibers of her being. It was only a moment, a pulse beat, a blink of the eye, yet it was unendurable. Then, with a great whoosh, she was spat out the far side, in another time, another world altogether. Or half of her was. The other half was still trailing behind her, somewhere else.

The only way Isabeau had to describe the sensation was the strange distortion of fever, when your head and your feet seem miles apart, and the membrane of the world shimmers before your eyes, pain whooshing in your ears like the coming and going of the sea in a cave. Every nerve in her body was shrilling, numb and yet tingling fiercely all at once, and her mouth was dry as a desert.

She stumbled to her knees, one hand gripped in Cloud-shadow's, the other still dragging through an infinite space, on the top of a hill in a world that seemed much greener, much wilder, much vaster, and infinitely more dangerous than her own.

Suddenly her hand was her own again, and Dide came with it, panting in fear and amazement. With him he dragged the others, one by one, all arriving in a rush and blur of red roaring light, like the fiercest of fires.

Shivering, sick and dizzy, none of them could move for an instant, even though all were desperately aware of danger. Then Isabeau became conscious of the pool of water right beside them, and managed to twist and half fall into it, drinking deeply, and splashing her face and breast and arms. The water was cold and delicious, and roused her from the strange trancelike inertia that had imprisoned her. As the others too drank and splashed themselves, Isabeau was able to look about her and take stock of where, or rather, when, they were.

It was sunset on a warm midsummer's evening. The Fire-Eater was a bright spark in the east, framed between a cleft in the hills. Before them was the Tomb of Ravens, new, white, and clean. The pool behind her was now a natural spring, roughly oval in shape, with a little stream that went burbling down the hill in a series of steps and starts. In the warm lambent light, the avenue of freshly planted yew saplings glowed vividly. As far as the eye could see was forest, rolling up to snow-tipped mountains on one hand and rolling down to a thin curve of water through the valley. Isabeau was startled and amazed. In her time, the Rhyllster was a mighty, broad river lined with rich green farmland, and with many crofts, villages, and small towns dotting its banks. It was the lifeblood of the land, busy with boats and barges, carrying trade and passengers from the highlands to the lowlands and back again.

It was a shock to see how much forest there had once been, and how very different in shape and size was the river. It was much rougher, with many patches of turbulent water, and a series of rapids foaming white over piles of fallen trees and storm wrack. There were many signs that the river was often in full flood. In places the mess of fallen trees and branches reached high on either side. Isabeau remembered that the locks and canals that protected the mouth of the Rhyllster would not be built for another few hundred years; it gave her a strange jolt, to realize how different the landscape was from the one she knew.

She did not have time to do much more than glance about her, though. She could smell tobacco smoke, and hear the low murmur of voices. To one side, in a patch of grass under a big hemlock, a grave had been freshly dug. The grave diggers rested there on the mound of earth, smoking their pipes and taking the occasional swig from a bottle they passed between them. If they turned their heads, they would see the six strangers who had materialized so suddenly out of thin air.

With a quick whisper, Isabeau hurried her companions away from the pool and into the shelter of some big old trees to one side. They crouched there, hearts hammering, palms tingling with perspiration. It was very warm, and they were still dressed for winter. They dared not remove their cloaks, though, which had been woven with potent spells of concealment and camouflage.

"Any sign o' Donncan?" Isabeau whispered, craning her head forward to look.

"Let me run out and see if I can find aught by the pool," Dide whispered. "Another feather, perhaps?"

"No, it is too dangerous. Buba will fly out and see what he can see." The little elf-owl had come down to rest on her shoulder, his feathers all ruffled up about his ear tufts, his eyes very round. At her words he hooted softly and took flight, making no sound.

"I wonder where they are," Ghislaine said.

"If we used the same constellations as they did, surely we should have landed on their heels, despite the few days' difference in the time o' our leaving?" Cailean asked with a frown. The huge shadow-hound was pressed close by the sorcerer's leg, his ears laid back, his muzzle lifted in a silent snarl. He had not enjoyed the journey back in time.

I cannot feel my daughter, Cloudshadow said. *Not here, not now. She has not been here.*

"No' been here!" Isabeau exclaimed. "Ye mean, no' at all? No' at any time recently?"

Cloudshadow shook her head.

"Where can they be?" Ghislaine said blankly. "Have we come to the wrong time?"

Everyone felt a sick, black anxiety. They looked about frantically. Although the sun had set, the light was still bright, for the gloaming lasted a very long time in midsummer. The grave diggers were still sitting, smoking and drinking on their mound of freshly turned earth. Buba flitted from tree to tree silently, unnoticed. The Tomb of Ravens glimmered whitely. Isabeau could see the scars in the earth near the pool where the sacred stones of the Celestines had stood till only recently. She turned and looked out towards the sea, hoping against hope to see Donncan and Thunderlily, sheltering in the forest perhaps, or foraging for food.

To her surprise she saw a small grey castle built on the high crag above the firth. In her time, the palace of Rhyssmadill was a palace of soaring pointed towers, built from dreamy blue stone. This was a much smaller building, built for formidability, not beauty. More than anything else she had yet seen, the grim stern castle made Isabeau realize that she had, indeed, gone back to the time of Brann the Raven. He had built Rhyssmadill, and lived there many years, unassailable and proud. After his death, his heirs had abandoned Rhyssmadill and moved their court to Ravenscraig, which had previously been their hunting castle. In time, Jaspar had built a palace on the site of the ruins, for his new wife, Maya, who longed to live within sight and smell of the sea.

Staring at the castle, she noticed that the green flags with their device of a raven upon it were all flying at half mast. Then she saw a heavily armed procession crossing the drawbridge across the ravine. Amidst all the jostling soldiers was a cart, and on the cart was a long wooden box that, she realized with a sharp juddering of her pulse, was a coffin.

Beside her, Ghislaine frowned. "I think we must've come to the wrong time," she said. "For though we are here for a death, it canna be Brann's."

Cailean turned to look where she pointed.

"That is a rude funeral procession for a prionnsa," he agreed. "Especially such a proud and rich man as Brann the Raven. If it was no' for all the soldiers, I would say it was a servant o' some sort they carried out there, feet first. Or a plague victim."

"Aye. It seems odd," Dide said. "Surely they would've had a piper? A procession? Mourning clothes? It canna be Brann."

"It is Brann," Isabeau said, her voice sounding strange. Dide turned to look at her, and saw how tense and hunched her shoulders were, and how sickly white her skin.

"Are ye all right?" he asked.

"Nay," she said. "It is Brann. His spirit is strong. I hear it in my ear."

It is time. Raise me!

Buba came back to rest on Isabeau's shoulder, and she

rubbed the owl's ear tufts compulsively, seeking comfort. He sank his head down into his wings, and she tried to soften the force of her touch.

Find-hooh they-hooh? she hooted.

No-hooh-hooh, he answered sadly.

Cailean sent Dobhailen slinking out to sniff around, to see if his keen nose could pick up a trace that Buba's keen eyes had missed. Although the shadow-hound was near as big as a child's pony, he was silent as smoke and seemed to float from shadow to shadow. Certainly the grave diggers packing away their pipes and tobacco did not see him, not even when one stood and stretched his back before shouldering his shovel. The dog came back to Cailean after a few minutes scouting around, and it was clear from his sunken tail and ears that he had caught no trace of the Rìgh either. Isabeau clenched her jaw and dug her fingernails into her palms.

"What are we to do?" Ghislaine whispered. "Where can Donncan have gone?"

"We must find them, and follow them," Isabeau said through her teeth. "We must go now!"

The compulsion to find Brann and resurrect him was like the lash of whip and spur, driving her mad with pain. It was like lust, or anguish, an emotion that could not be assuaged. She could feel him coming nearer and nearer. He was a black force of malice and rage, clinging to his corpse with hooks made of an implacable will. He was not long dead. No more than twelve hours, barely enough time for the meat of his body to begin to rot. Isabeau knew it took three days for a soul to relinquish its body. It was one reason for the long ritual of watching over the corpse, and praying for its soul's easy passage to the next dimension. Even in the heat of midsummer, it was unusual for someone to be buried so soon after death. The grave diggers must have worked hard all day to have such a deep pit ready and waiting.

All must have been done in haste and secrecy. There

would have been no time to do more than wash and wrap him, and order the coffin to be made and the grave to be dug. No bells were ringing, and no one was wearing the black of mourning. If Isabeau could not feel for herself, in every sick and shaky nerve and muscle, how dark a soul it was clinging to his empty sack of a body, she would have felt pity and regret, that he should be allowed to be hurried to his grave in this fashion.

As it was, she felt only overwhelming terror.

"Surely it would be dangerous, to attempt another trip through time so close on the heels o' the last?" Dide was saying. "We are all worn out. I feel like I've been chewed up and spat out by an ogre. We have no' eaten, or had a chance to rest. Surely we—"

"No," Isabeau said. "We must go now."

"But Isabeau . . ." Ghislaine protested. She looked sick and haggard. "Please!"

"Is it no' too late?" Cailean said. "Sunset has passed, and with it the shift in the tides o' power. Should we no' wait till dawn?"

"I do no' ken about ye," Dide said, "but I ache all over, and my legs feel all wobbly."

"I also," Ghislaine said. "I feel as if I have been dreamwalking all night. I would love a glass o' wine in a hot bath, and a big bed with freshly laundered sheets."

Cailean compressed a smile and looked away. He was absentmindedly rubbing his shoulder, as if it pained him. Stormstrider also looked weary, though he sat as straight-backed as ever, his hands resting protectively on the sack.

"No!" Isabeau shrieked. At their expressions of shock and hurt, she tried to control her voice. "This spell o' Brann's . . . is driving me mad. He speaks in my ear all the time, commanding me, compelling me. He is almost here. He's getting louder and louder. Please, please, we must . . . we must get away from here!" She tried to think rationally, to find an argument to sway them. "I fear . . . for Donncan and Thunderlily. If I . . . if I canna withstand

him . . . how will Johanna . . . she will be half crazed with
it . . . I fear what she will do . . ."

She could not go on. She stood up and seized her
satchel, throwing it over her shoulder. She could barely
hear the sound of the others' protests and questions. Her
ears were full of the voice of the spell. *I am Brann. It is
time. I will live again! I am Brann. It is time! Raise me!
Raise me from the dead, for I must live again.*

Thorns snagged in her cloak, and she dragged it free,
not caring as the material tore. Buba hooted at her anxiously from a nearby branch, and she did not hear, stalking
back towards the pool, her shoulders hunched, her fists
curled so tightly her nails cut into her palms. Dide caught
up with her and took her arm.

"Beau . . ." he said.

She tore her arm free and walked on. "Ye must help
me," she said hoarsely. "Please."

"Ye're frightening me, Beau. Is this wise? Should we
take such a risk? We'll be seen!"

She turned to face him. "Do ye no' understand? It is taking every bit o' my strength no' to seize my witch-dagger
and slash ye across the throat right now! He is almost here.
He demands blood! Someone must die if he is to live again.
I do no' want it to be ye."

Dide took an involuntary step back, his face shocked.

"He is close, Dide. He is very close. The spell is strong.
It is . . . it is like a madness . . . I can barely . . ." Again she
stopped, biting her lip, clenching her hands together. "I
must get away," she muttered. "Else . . . else I . . ."

"We'll go," Dide said.

She nodded, and strode out through the trees and towards the Tomb of Ravens glowing in the very last rays of
the sun.

She was too late. The cart with its roughly made
wooden coffin was drawn up near the graveyard, and the
soldiers were maneuvering it down and onto their shoulders. The voice in Isabeau's ears rose to a shriek.

Now! Now! Now is the time! Raise me!

Isabeau fell to her knees, her hands beating at the side of her head, her eyes screwed tight. "Stop, stop it, stop it," she was muttering under her breath. Cailean and Dide ran to her side and tried to help her up. She broke away from them violently, bending over as if about to retch, her hands clamped over her ears.

"Here, let us get her out o' sight, afore they see us," Dide whispered. He bent and put his hand under her armpit.

"Take . . . away . . . my . . . dagger," she panted. "Dide, please!"

He nodded and skillfully flipped her dagger out of its sheath and tossed it to Ghislaine, who caught it white-faced and backed away, holding it as if it was a viper. Then Dide and Cailean together lifted Isabeau and half carried her back into the shelter of the trees. Quick as they were, they were nearly spotted, for there were soldiers on guard about the cart, weapons drawn and eyes flicking about everywhere.

"We canna use the Auld Ways to escape while they are still here," Dide whispered. "We must wait. Beau, can ye stand it?"

He was bending to lower her gently to the grass. Her answer was to reach out one hand and seize the slim, black-handled dagger he wore always in his boot. Dide sprang away as she slashed the dagger towards him. "Brann *will* live again," she hissed.

"Beau!" Dide cried. "What do ye do?" His face showed his utter shock and horror.

Isabeau looked down at the dagger in her hand. Her eyes opened wide and she dropped it from suddenly nerveless fingers. Dide very slowly bent and retrieved it, then stood there staring at her with it hanging from his hand. She raised her eyes and looked back at him, tears suddenly burning her eyes. "I canna . . . I canna help it," she said. "It is . . . so strong . . . *He* is so strong . . . Dide, forgive me . . . help me, please . . ."

He could not speak.

"What should we do?" Ghislaine whispered. She looked fiercely at Cloudshadow and Stormstrider, who stood watching from the shadows of the trees, their third eye wide open and black as night. "Canna ye heal her?" she demanded.

Cloudshadow slowly shook her head. *She is suffering an injury of the soul, not an injury of the body,* she said silently. *This is a magic of your kind, not of ours. I can tell you, though, that the stain that has been laid upon her is spreading fast. It is black, like the scorch marks of fire upon wood. She is full of darkness.*

"What should we do, what should we do?" Ghislaine moaned, pressing her hands together.

"Bind her and gag her," Dide said harshly, "until we can escape from here."

He took a coil of rope from his pack and came towards Isabeau, who stared at him with widely dilated eyes. "It is for the best," he said, forcing himself to meet her eyes.

"No," she said. "Don't. I'll . . . it'll drive me mad. I . . . I canna be still. Let me . . ."

He came towards her inexorably, and with a quick flick she transformed herself into the shape of an elf-owl. One moment there was a redheaded woman standing in the gloaming, the next two small white birds were soaring away into the forest on soundless wings.

Dide stared after them, and let his hands fall by his sides.

Midnight in the Graveyard

❦

Once in the shape of an owl, Isabeau felt an immediate release from Brann the Raven's spell of compulsion. Dizzy with relief, she soared high into the sky, wheeling above the trees.

Soar-hooh, Buba hooted joyfully. *Soar-hooh high-hooh!*

Isabeau and Buba had flown the night skies together many times, snapping at insects midair, enjoying the ruffle of the night wind in their feathers, watching the scuttle of small creatures through the undergrowth with their superior owl-eyes. Isabeau had never felt such a keen edge to her enjoyment before, though. She felt as if she had broken out of a cage of red-hot iron that had pressed close about her limbs, branding her with pain.

After a while, she came swooping back down to the hillside, to hoot reassuringly at her friends and watch the work of the grave diggers as they buried Brann the Raven in an unmarked grave at the side of the hill, like a pauper, or a plague victim, or a suicide.

Although it was almost dark now, Isabeau could see easily. Her friends had taken refuge under the down-arching branches of one of the big hemlocks, for the soldiers were patrolling the hillside constantly, weapons at the ready.

The soldiers wore long green surcoats, with the black

raven of the MacBrann clan emblazoned upon them, and
the clan's motto, *Sans Peur*, embroidered in white on a
black scroll. They carried tall claymores or wicked-looking
pikes, and had daggers at their belts. There were archers
too, guarding the road towards the castle. They had arrows
cocked to the bow, and their eyes ranged over the landscape constantly, looking for movement.

Watching the grave diggers hurriedly fill in the hole was
a tall man with a very dark, frowning visage. His clothes
were heavy and archaic. He wore long tight hosen under a
massive striped doublet, with a strange little ruff of lace
forcing up his chin. His shoes had long, narrow points at
the toes and heavy jeweled buckles. His sleeves were huge
and elaborate, striped in green and black, and slashed to
show the white silk beneath. Many of his fingers were
weighted down with rings, showing he was a talented sorcerer, and he carried no weapon, but had a silver-embossed
wand of ebon tucked through his sash.

As the last clod of earth was shoveled into place, he
sighed and nodded. "Well done," he said in a low voice.
"Did ye cut the turf as I commanded? Roll it over the grave
and stamp it down well. We want no one to ken where he
is buried."

"Aye, Your Grace, we'll do our best," one of the grave
diggers said. "I brought a bucket so we can water it from
the pool. In this heat, it'll brown off fast otherwise."

"Good thinking," the lord said. "Are there some fallen
branches we can toss over the top, to help conceal it until
the grass begins to grow again?"

"Aye, Your Grace."

As Isabeau watched and wondered, the grave diggers
unrolled ribbons of green turf, and covered the grave site
over, and watered it in thoroughly. Soon it was difficult to
tell where Brann had been buried, though in broad daylight
and under the full glare of the sun, the disturbance to the
soil would be more obvious, she knew. When they were
finished, the lord thanked them and handed them heavy

bags that clinked and made the grave diggers smile in satisfaction.

"Remember, ye must no' speak o' what ye have done to anyone," the lord warned. "No' your wife, or your sweetheart, no' your sons or daughters. If ye tell a soul, I shall ken, and I shall wreak vengeance. Remember, I am Brann's son! I will ken, and I will make ye suffer!"

"Aye, Your Grace, o' course, Your Grace," they gabbled, and pocketed their coin bags and shouldered their shovels, then went away down the hill half running.

"Ye would have done better to have slit their throats, my laird," the captain of the guards observed in a low voice. "Ye think they'll no' talk o' this night's doing?"

"It is what my father would have done," the MacBrann agreed wearily. "But I refuse to be as my father was! O' course word will get out, it canna be helped. But their minds were well befuddled with whisky, and soon they will be forgetting exactly where he was buried. Once the grass grows back, there'll be no mark to show where his grave is, and I intend to keep this hill well guarded until all traces o' him have rotted away and there is naught left o' him to raise."

"But that could be years!" The captain of the guards was startled.

"Seven years or seventy, I'll do whatever I must to make sure he stays in his grave where he belongs!"

"But surely it was all just hot wind, all that talk o' his o' discovering the secrets o' immortality?"

"My father was close on eighty years auld, and looked no' a day over fifty," the MacBrann said in a low voice. "I have heard tell he learned to suck the life out o' his acolytes, who grew sick and pale as he grew ever more vigorous."

"He sucked their blood?"

"Their blood, their soul, their life-energy, who kens?" the MacBrann answered in the same low, weary voice. "I do no' ken the secret. I do ken he devoted much o' his life to researching the secrets o' life and death. He mocked me by promising to raise Medwenna from the dead. All I had to do was bring him a sweet young virgin to sacrifice, and hold her down while he cut her throat. I said I would rather die myself. He laughed and said that all men must die, except for him."

"He was mad!" the captain said.

"I have often thought so," the MacBrann said. "Mad, or evil, or both. A fine father to have. But do ye ken? I was tempted. For a moment, I hesitated. To have Medwenna back again, and the child still blooming in her womb! I had thought I would give anything to have such magic wrought. And my father knew I was tempted. He could see into my heart, and he knew all my disgust was half-sham, because for one moment, one second, I contemplated murdering some poor young girl just so I could have my wife alive again. So am I any less evil than my father?"

"Aye, ye are," the captain said passionately. "Ye are a good man! A good, kind, just man who—"

"Who today murdered his own father," the MacBrann said.

"Aye," the captain said, "and if that was no' a good deed, and a just one, I ken no better!"

"It is a sin and a crime I shall carry forever more," the MacBrann replied. "May Eà forgive me!"

"He was an evil, black-hearted snake o' a man, and ye've done us all a service ridding the world o' him," his captain said loyally.

The MacBrann did not answer.

"Have ye any orders for me, my laird?" the captain said after a moment. "All is quiet so far."

"They will come," the MacBrann said quietly. "They will wait until they think we are gone. Tell the men to withdraw. Most o' them may go back to the castle, but tell them to keep a close watch on the gate, and if anyone comes out, to follow them at a distance. Ask Darrell and Robin to take up positions by the road, and set a ring o' men about the hillside, well hidden. If anyone comes they are to hoot like an owl, three times."

"Aye, my laird. What o' me? Shall I ride with ye back to the castle, or do ye wish me to wait and watch here?"

"Ye and I shall wait in the tomb, Colin."

"In the tomb?" The captain swallowed and looked behind him at the ghostly white bulk of the crypt.

"Aye. They will think him buried there. That is where they will come."

"Ye are so sure someone will come?"

"He swore to outwit Gearradh. He swore he would live again. He had the power o' prophecy, my father. We must do all we can to make sure his words are no true foretelling."

"A pleasant task for a midsummer's eve," the captain said ironically.

Isabeau saw the MacBrann smile briefly.

"Just be glad it is no' the dead o' winter," he replied.

Isabeau flew overhead as the bulk of the soldiers marched back to the castle, carrying flaming torches to light their way. Then she flitted silently down to the tree in which Dide, Cailean, Ghislaine, Stormstrider, and Cloudshadow hid. Wrapped in their grey cloaks, they were invisible in the darkness. She told them what she had overheard in owl-language, having no desire to transform back into her spell-wracked human body.

At dawn-hooh, we flee-hooh, she said. *For now-hooh, snooze-hooh. Owl-hooh watch-hooh.*

Take care-hooh, Dide hooted back.

You-hooh too-hooh, she replied and rubbed her beak against his cheek, before swooping away into darkness again.

In the shape of an owl, human needs and passions dropped away and were subsumed by the needs and desires of Owl. Isabeau remembered her love for Dide, and her horror and guilt at drawing a dagger on him, and her terror at the power of the dead sorcerer to so overthrow her will.

But she did not feel these emotions. She was all Owl. When a moth blundered past, she snapped at it and swallowed it with pleasure. When Buba soared ahead of her, she stretched her wings and followed him, filled with a serene joy at the coming of the night and the moon-cool, the hours when Owl ruled.

She could see clearly in the darkness. She could see the men crouched in the shadows of the trees, watching the road from the castle. She could see the shape of the unmarked grave. When she and Buba flitted silently in through the doors of the mausoleum, she could see the two men sitting quietly in the darkness, their daggers drawn. They both jumped violently at the sudden rush of pale motion above their heads, and Isabeau hooted softly, to reassure them, before coming down to rest above their heads.

They did not speak. Slowly the hours crept past. The tomb was cold and they huddled their plaids about their shoulders. Isabeau amused herself by flitting about the tomb, catching a mouse or two, and reading the inscriptions above the few tombs already existent in the crypt. Brann had buried two wives, four daughters, two sons, and numerous servants, and there was a plaque commemorating his familiar, a raven named Nigrum. Most interesting was the centerpiece of the crypt, a great slab of stone on a raised platform, and with a sarcophagus carved from marble. It depicted Brann the Raven himself, lying with his hands crossed on a staff, and a crown on his head. Engraved on a tablet at his foot were the words "I will return," which was enough to make Isabeau shudder and huddle her feathers about her.

What man built himself a grand tomb before he had even died, and then wrote himself such an epitaph? A vain and arrogant man, certainly, but also one afraid of death, afraid of his own mortality. Or perhaps it was all just a trick. Isabeau knew, as very few did, that the tomb concealed a secret passage that led into the water-caves under Rhyssmadill. During the Bright Wars, Dughall MacBrann had led Lachlan and Dide and the rest of the Rìgh's body-guard down through the secret way and into Rhyssmadill, relieving a long and desperate siege that had seen many soldiers loyal to Lachlan die a slow and horrible death from starvation. Brann had built the secret way, and concealed its entrance with this spurious tomb that he certainly never expected to inhabit. It was said that he had buried all those who had helped build the hidden passageway within it, so that none but he and his kin should ever know the secret.

The hours passed. Finding herself weary and bored, Isabeau sank her head into her feathers and snoozed for a while, confident her owl-senses would alert her if anything happened.

A few minutes to midnight, the great bronze door to the crypt slowly eased open. Beau and Buba raised their heads and opened their eyes. In the dark grey of their night vision, they saw two dark-cloaked figures step cautiously within. They paused and looked about them, then stole silently to the tomb where the sepulchre of Brann the Raven lay.

After a long breathless moment of listening, a globe of witch's light sprang into being above the tomb. Isabeau blinked and swiveled her head away. When her owl-eyes had grown accustomed, she rotated her head back curiously.

A tall woman was standing on the flagstones, her hands folded before her, while a young man knelt by the tomb, leaning his weight on the ledger.

"It does no' shift," he whispered.

"Try harder," she replied. "Ye are young and strong, Irvin, ye should be able to move it easily enough."

He heaved harder, grunting with the effort. After a few moments, when all his bulging muscles had had no effect, she frowned and came to kneel beside him. She ran her hands over the crack that lay where the great slab of stone rested on the walls of the tomb, then she raised both hands high and clapped them together with a dramatic flourish, muttering a sequence of words that sounded like gibberish. Nothing happened.

"Ye always work so hard for effect, Aven," the MacBrann said from behind her. "Really, there is no need for all these histrionics. The will and the word, that is all ye need."

The sorceress jerked and cried aloud in surprise, then spun around, one hand at her throat. "Ye!" she hissed.

"Aye, I'm afraid so," he answered. "I am so glad that ye did not disappoint me and stay at home as ye were bid. Did ye really think I would leave the tomb unguarded?"

"I had great ease in passing by those blind fools ye had posted on the road," she said contemptuously. "They did no' hear a thing!"

"They are mere men, no' sorcerers," the MacBrann said softly. "I kent ye could walk right through them without them seeing a thing. Although ye are in many ways a fool, ye are a true witch with a true Talent. Ye canna deceive my eyes, though, Aven. I ken ye too well."

She nodded, and looked away. "Aye, we were bairns together, were we no'?" she said. "Practically brother and sister."

Suddenly her fingers flicked out sideways and lightning flashed across the tomb towards the MacBrann with the sizzling speed and ferocity of a viper. It hit an invisible wall before him and fizzled away, leaving only a faint drift of smoke and the dazzling imprint of its shape upon the retina.

"Aye, raised together as close as brother and sister," he said in his low, weary voice, waving one hand to disperse the smoke, "which surely makes your relationship with my father akin to incest, does it no'?"

Beside him, Colin had his sword drawn, his body crouched in the warrior's stance, ready to lunge. The young man Irvin was crouched behind the sorceress, his face white and frightened, listening with incredulity to the bitter exchange of words.

"Your father may have been the same age as my own father, but where my father grew bent and frail, and at last senile and drooling afore he died, your father was as strong and lusty as a much younger man. Lustier even," she snapped back, her lip curled in a sneer.

"Yet he is dead now, and in his grave where he belongs," the MacBrann answered quietly.

"Aye, murdered in his own bed, by his own son's hand!" she flashed. "Ye call him evil, but what are ye but a traitor and a murderer? A fine son ye turned out to be."

"Three times I struck him," the MacBrann said. "Once for my mother, once for my wife, and once for the wee babe that died in her womb."

"How did ye get in?" she demanded. "The gates were closed to ye, and all my laird's men warned to watch for ye!" Her breast was rising and falling sharply, and her eyes glittered in the pale witch's light.

"I see ye do no' ken all my father's secrets," he said contemptuously. "I suppose I should be grateful to ye. It is hard to catch my father unawares. He never seems to sleep. I was lucky to find him at the moment o' rapture, his senses closed to my approach. Else I do no' think my dagger would have found its mark."

"How dare ye!" she hissed. "Ye are contemptible!"

"I am contemptible? What then are ye, Aven?"

"I at least am loyal to my laird and master," she cried, clenching her hands into fists. "Ye are naught but a treacherous, murdering dog!"

"At least I do no' murder in cold blood, as ye have done in your master's service," he said, his voice trembling. "I do no' bathe in the blood o' my victims, and drink it like wine. I have right and justice on my side . . ."

She laughed out loud. "Oh, so very noble," she mocked. "Ye play your part well, Dugald. The poor wronged son, intent on revenge, and wrapping it up in the guise o' what is right and just. Oh, the bards will write songs o' this night's work!"

"I am glad it was ye in his bed and no' some poor innocent lass who may have been shocked at the sight o' so much blood," the MacBrann retorted angrily. "Though I must admit I was very surprised. I did not expect to find ye in his bed."

She flushed an ugly crimson. "And why no'?" she demanded.

"I thought my father had grown tired o' ye long ago," the MacBrann said. "After all, ye are no longer in the first flush o' your youth, Aven. I had heard ye had become his procuress, bringing him ever younger and choicer tidbits for his bed. Are there no young virgins left in Ravenshaw, that he was willing to spend his seed in ye?"

Her mouth worked, and the ugly flush deepened.

"Let me guess? Ye were determined to win your place in his bed again, and he acquiesced, having nothing better on offer, and no' wanting to offend his most faithful acolyte."

"I am no acolyte," she flashed, caught on the raw. "I am the Second Sorceress in Brann's circle, his most trusted and—"

"Brann is dead," his son said cruelly, "and his circle no more."

She smiled. "Do ye no' ken? Brann swore he would live again. If he says something shall be so, so it shall be. Ye may have stabbed your father a thousand times, for the thousand ills he has done ye, and it would be to no avail. He will live again!"

Her voice rang out rapturously, and even in the shape of an owl Isabeau felt the terrible power of the words and shrank down upon her rafter. Buba hooted softly in comfort and reassurance.

"He is dead, and dead he shall remain," the MacBrann said very quietly.

Aven gave a terrible cry, and again threw a whiplash of power at him. This time he staggered as he thrust it away, and she lashed him again and again. Each time he was able to block her, though the effort left him white and shaken.

"Ye canna defeat me this way," he said hoarsely. "I am still Brann's son, ye ken. There is naught ye can do, Aven."

She gave an eldritch scream of rage and frustration. Lightning bolts rained about him, white-hot and smoking. As he threw up his hand to protect himself, she darted at him, a dagger suddenly in her hand. It plunged down towards his unprotected armpit, but then Colin leaped forward, deflecting the dagger and taking off her head with a single sweep of his great sword. Blood spurted, and her head bounced and rolled to lie at the MacBrann's foot, the eyes wide and staring, the mouth still open in a scream.

Dugald MacBrann stared down at it for a long moment, panting and wild-eyed, then he gave the severed head a gentle kick with his foot so it rolled away to rest at the base of the steps, the dreadful staring eyes and mouth turned towards the stone. Then the MacBrann walked forward and dropped his hand on Irvin's shoulder.

"What do ye do here, lad?" he said gently. "Did I no' give orders none were to leave the castle?"

"She . . . my lady Aven said . . . she promised me a great reward."

"Do ye no' ken she meant to sacrifice ye to bring my father back to life?"

"Sacrifice?"

"Aye. It is the dark art, necromancy. Blood for blood, a life for a life."

"She meant to kill me?"

"Aye, lad. Come, ye are shaking. Colin, give the boy a wee dram and take him down to Robin, then come back to me. I shall need your help to . . . to clean away the blood."

He resolutely did not look at the headless body of the sorceress, crumpled in a pool of blood in the middle of the floor. Colin led away the shivering young man, wrapping him up well in his own cloak, and returned a few minutes later, his face grim. Isabeau and Buba watched as the

MacBrann and his captain hurriedly mopped up the blood with the sorceress's long dark cloak, and then wrapped her and her head up in it together.

"We shall bury Aven within the tomb," the MacBrann said, climbing swiftly up the steps and laying his hand on the head of the stone sorcerer's staff. "I do no' want any to ken o' this night's doings."

Colin carried the body up the steps, trying not to show his revulsion on his face. The MacBrann twisted the head of the staff; there was a slow grinding noise and the stone ledge swung sideways, revealing a dark gaping hole. Within was a very narrow and steep spiral staircase that wound down into the earth. With great difficulty, Colin managed to negotiate his way down the steps, the dead woman and her severed head in his arms. A few minutes later he climbed back again, looking very white, his jaw set hard.

The MacBrann raised an eyebrow, and he nodded. Together they swung the stone slab back over the secret staircase, and it clicked into place, the stone sorcerer resting supine as if he had never been disturbed. The only sign of Aven was the smears of blood left on the stone floor, and Colin polished these away with the hem of his own cloak.

"Can we go away from here now, my laird?" he said. "This place makes me nervous."

The MacBrann shook his head. "Others will come," he said with certainty. "Perhaps no' tonight. But they will come. Brann will no' rest quietly, I can assure ye o' that."

"Please tell me I do no' have to spend the rest o' my life guarding his grave," Colin said.

The MacBrann smiled briefly. "If no' ye, someone," he answered. "I will no' rest easy otherwise."

"Well, I'll no' rest easy spending another minute in this blaygird place. I swear I feel eyes upon me."

"I also," the MacBrann said. "Come, Colin, give me this one night, and tomorrow I shall set up a roster o' guard duty so the burden can be shared among us all. Indeed, I was no' jesting when I said I would guard the grave a hundred years if I had to."

"Well, I wouldna like the auld man to walk again," Colin said heavily. "Let us sit it out till dawn, just in case we get any more nasty surprises."

"Thank ye, Colin. I ken this is far more than anyone should demand o' their captain."

"All in a night's work," Colin answered, with a poor attempt at humor.

Back to the Beginning

❧❧❧

No other disturbances occurred that night. Dugald
MacBrann was able to sleep rolled in his cloak while
his faithful captain sat nearby, sword resting on his knees.
Isàbeau and Buba dozed, their heads sunk into their feath-
ery shoulders. They woke before dawn and flew out into
the silvery grey, coming down soundlessly onto a branch
above Dide's sleeping head.

The three witches and two Celestines had taken shelter
under an ancient hemlock tree. Curving down to the
ground, the heavy branches created a dim green tent that
hid them from the sight of any passersby. Ghislaine had
been given the dawn watch, the easiest of all, and she sat
quietly, her arms wrapped around her knees, deep shadows
under her eyes. In her rough traveling clothes, her long fair
hair plaited up under a brown tam-o'-shanter, she looked
very different from the cool, pale sorceress Isabeau knew
so well.

All well-hooh? Isabeau hooted.

Well-hooh, and with-hooh you-hooh too-hooh? Ghislaine hooted back in perfect owl-language.

Isabeau sat on her branch a while longer, her feathers
ruffled. She dreaded having to return to her own shape. She
knew Brann's ghost waited for her.

"Come down, Beau," Ghislaine said gently. "Ye must

have time to recover, else ye'll be sick as a cat. It is almost dawn. We do no' have much time left."

Isabeau shook herself all over, shifted from claw to claw, and then, reluctantly, flew down to the grass, transforming back into the shape of a woman. At once she heard the hammer of Brann's insistence in her brain.

I shall live again, and ye shall be the one to raise me. All ye need is a soul, willing or unwilling, and a very sharp knife . . .

Isabeau pressed her hands over her ears, but it was no use. The ghost did not speak with mouth and tongue but in the soundless voice of the mind, which could not be blocked out.

Ghislaine had her clothes ready and, dizzy and sick, Isabeau dragged them on. It was taking all her strength to resist the duress of Brann's spell, and so she had little energy left to recover from the shapeshifting, which was always a heavy drain on her powers. Her legs trembled so much she had to sit down and rest her head in her hands. Ghislaine was worried by her shivering and urged her to stretch out on a blanket, with another tucked around her. Isabeau obeyed. She always felt sick and shivery after too long out of her own shape, but this was different. It was like a giant hand had seized the strings of her nerves and was wrenching them this way and that, trying to force her to rise and find the dead man's grave, and dig through to his coffin with bare hands, if a shovel could not be found, and drag his limp, stinking corpse out into the fresh air, to lie staring sightlessly at the sky while she found a living soul, willing or unwilling, and a very sharp dagger . . .

I shall live again, and ye shall be the one to raise me.

Isabeau dug her fists into her ears and hummed loudly, trying to tune out the voice.

Biting her lip with worry, Ghislaine made her tea, heating the water with her finger, and warmed up some day-old griddle-cakes between her hands. She had to hold the cup to Isabeau's chattering teeth, for the Keybearer would not

stop rocking and humming, grinding her fists into her ears.
She could not eat, but she managed to swallow some of the
hot liquid and that seemed to help a little. Drawing Isabeau's head onto her lap and stroking a circular shape
round and round between Isabeau's brows, Ghislaine said
softly, "Rest while ye can. We have a long way to travel
today."

"Back to the beginning," Isabeau said under her breath.

"Ye ken where to go, to find them?"

Isabeau shook her head, her eyes shut. The soft stroking
of Ghislaine's fingers acted as a counterweight against
Brann's spell, making it easier to bear. Still she found her
muscles slowly tensing against the onslaught of his will,
the endless demand in her ears.

A soul, willing or unwilling, and a very sharp knife . . .

"We canna go wandering through times, willy-nilly,
hoping to find them," Ghislaine said. "Yet find them we
must."

I shall live again, and ye shall be the one to raise me.

Isabeau's breath shortened. Her limbs jerked every now
and again as her muscles went into spasm. She found it
hard to concentrate on Ghislaine's words.

*Come to the time o' my death, come and bring a living
soul, willing or unwilling . . .*

Isabeau shuddered.

"What is it?" Ghislaine's voice was very soft.

"I am afraid . . ." Isabeau answered, just as low. "Will I
ever be free o' this spell, this compulsion? I have no' had a
moment's peace since I read the blaygird thing. Except
while an owl, and I canna spend the rest o' my life in a different shape."

"We will find a way to break the spell," Ghislaine said
firmly. "Somehow."

"We must." Dide's voice came quietly out of the green
gloom. "I do no' want to spend the rest o' my life wondering if ye're going to pull a knife on me again."

"I . . . I'm sorry," Isabeau said inadequately. "It's like a madness. It's in my ear all the time, it's . . . it's very hard to resist."

"Then let us get as far away from Brann as we can," Cailean said, propping himself up on one elbow. "Ye must feel it so much more strongly here, 'cause we are so close to the time o' his death. Let us go and find Rìgh Donncan and Princess Thunderlily, and go home."

There was no surcease from his voice at home, Isabeau thought, but she nodded and sat up rather gingerly, clasping her hands together to try to stop their spasms.

"How are we going to find them?" Ghislaine said. "Cloudshadow, do ye know where they are?"

The Celestine shook her head. She looked very tired and sad. *Back to the beginning, my daughter wrote in the tree-language. Yet where is the beginning? There is no beginning, no end. Such words are only ways of ordering our experience, of making sense of what cannot be understood.*

Her words filled them all with a desperate melancholy and weariness.

Isabeau dropped her head into her hands, felt her fingers writhing through her curls, tugging at the roots of her hair. The sudden sharp pain drowned out the words beating at her skull, long enough for her to think. She tugged at her hair again and again, until Dide, in distress, tried to stop her.

"No! It's all right. Cloudshadow? The celestial globe Stormstrider carries? That was Thunderlily's, was it no'?" Isabeau said.

The Stargazer nodded. *It is one of the treasures of the Stargazer family. Thunderlily took it with her to the Theurgia so she could study the star-lore in her spare time, ensuring the traditions of our people were not forgotten. It was agreed between us, also, that she could come home at any time if she so desired, and she would need the star-map to help her navigate, not having ever traveled the Old Way by herself before.*

Isabeau remembered the first time she had traveled the

Old Way, carried on the back of the horse Lasair. She had had no idea of where they were going, or how. It made her feel very uncomfortable now, realizing how dangerous such a journey had been.

A living soul, willing or unwilling, and a very sharp knife . . .

"It will remember her touch," she said curtly. "There are six o' us here. We can make a circle o' power and use the star-map to show us where Donncan and Thunderlily are. It is a shame Finn is no' with us; none o' our Talents lie in searching and finding, and so we will have to rely on a spell." She looked about her. "We will have to be quick. It is almost dawn, and I canna stand much more."

All her years of training, of denying the body rest and food, of controlling her impulses and seeking tranquillity in meditation, these were the only things that stopped her from rising to pace from side to side, or gnaw her fingernails to the quick. Already she had torn the cuticles on her thumb, and bitten her lower lip till it was swollen and sore. She wished she could change back to Owl.

It was still dark and gloomy under the hemlock, though along the east the sky was flying banners of crimson and gold, and birds were singing. Isabeau conjured a tiny witch's light and hurriedly pushed the others into a rough circle, alternating male and female. She asked them to remove all their weapons and tools, and to lay their packs down beside the tree trunk. Dobhailen lay beside the packs to guard them, his massive head on his paws. Buba watched from above as Stormstrider set up the celestial globe in the center of the circle. His steady, deliberate care almost drove Isabeau mad with impatience, and she rocked on one foot and chewed at her thumbnail until at last the globe was ready.

Isabeau then cast the circle with her witch's dagger, having to take several deep breaths to stop herself from hurrying the ritual. "I consecrate and conjure thee, O circle of magic, ring o' power, symbol o' perfection and constant renewal, guardian and protector, eternal and infinite," she chanted, walking the circle three times, sprinkling first salt and then water from her water-skin. The familiar words helped calm and center her, and her anxiety eased a little.

She had a bundle of small white candles in her pack, and had removed six, anointing them with precious oils of angelica and hawthorn flowers for increased powers and protection from evil. Now she placed the anointed candles at the six points of the star she drew within the circle. Each of the six companions took up position before the candle, kneeling, and stretching out their arms so that they could hold hands. Isabeau glanced at Cloudshadow and Storm strider, wondering if they would protest or endanger them all by breaking the circle, but they both looked calm and focused. Isabeau realized with a little jerk of her heart that both of them had their third eye wide open. She took a few deep breaths to calm herself, feeling dangerously over-wrought. Her limbs were trembling and her heart pounded erratically. She waited until she was calmer before attempting to call on the One Power.

At last she felt able to begin the chant. Cailean, Ghislaine, and Dide chanted with her, their voices sure and firm, and then she heard a low sonorous hum rise from the throats of the Celestines as they caught the rhythm of the words and echoed it. Isabeau felt the hairs rise on her arms, felt the surge of the One Power within the circle.

She raised her arms and all around the circle the linked hands rose. "O blessed Eà, I call upon ye this day to show us those who have been lost, to point the way forward so that we may find them and save them and bring them home, in peace and in the blessed radiance o' your protection, so let it be, so let it be, so let it be."

The others murmured the refrain with her, their eyes shut.

The metal hoops of the celestial globe all began to slowly rotate, illuminated by the ghostly glow of the witch-light that hung overhead. Faster and faster they moved, under the fascinated eyes of the witches and the Celestines, until at last they came to a halt, in a different configuration to before.

Dide and Stormstrider would have surged forward to see, but Isabeau would not let them break the circle until she had blessed it and opened it with her dagger. Only then did she give in to her own urgent desire to see what the star-map would show them.

She said back to the beginning, Cloudshadow murmured when she had studied the new configuration of stars and moons and planets. *She meant before you humans came to Eileanan. She has gone back to the time when the Celestine ruled the forest and all were at peace, before the ship that sailed out of the sky.*

"She never meant to do as Johanna commanded!" Dide cried.

"Back to the beginning," Isabeau murmured and felt her heart bound. Surely she would be free of Brann's curse if she went farther back in time, to before he and the First Coven had even arrived in Eileanan?

"Come, let us go swiftly. We must run. If Brann's son sees us, he will try and stop us. We shall have only a few moments. Cloudshadow, are ye ready to lead us?"

Cloudshadow nodded. She had her head bent over a handful of small white stones, deftly drawing runes upon them with a nub of charcoal.

"When we are back in our own time, I shall have all the stones erected again," Isabeau said. "They should never have been thrown down."

Cloudshadow looked up and smiled faintly.

As if realizing she sought to escape him, the voice of the ghost was hammering at her again, getting louder and more insistent with every passing second. Isabeau's skull throbbed and her heart pounded.

Dide took her hand.

"Let's go," he said softly. "Run!"

Hand in hand, the six companions ran out from the shelter of the tree and sprinted towards the pool. Cloudshadow clutched one of the rocks in her free hand; at the end of the chain, Cailean ran, his hand on the neck of the huge black dog that loped behind him. Dobhailen was so very large the sorcerer did not need to stoop.

Cloudshadow was humming in her throat, and Stormstrider repeated her melody in a different key, so low it sounded like the earth rumbling.

The first light of the sun struck the surface of the pool, making it glint. Cloudshadow hurled herself towards it, and a deep red shimmer began to rise from the ground, marking the opening of the gateway.

"Stop!" a voice shouted. "Stop, I say, else I'll shoot!"

Isabeau glanced around. On the steps of the crypt stood Captain Colin, a crossbow in his hands. It was wound on, with a savage-looking bolt to the string.

"Let us be!" Isabeau cried back. "We mean ye no harm. Let us go!"

"Stop now, else I'll shoot!"

"Jump!" Isabeau cried.

Cloudshadow leaped forward, dragging Isabeau behind her. She felt the familiar red roar of the gateway suck her in, felt the strange spinning and stretching as if she were bound on an immense rack. For one long, unendurable second, she spun between times as stars bloomed and died around her, then there was a rush and a wrench, and once again Isabeau fell to her knees beside the Celestine's pool on the green hillside where Brann the Raven had built his tomb sixty-two years later.

Dide tumbled down beside her, then Ghislaine, then Stormstrider, then Cailean, his hand still on Dobhailen's thick ruff. And over their heads came whizzing a crossbow bolt, scraping Dide's cheek and burying itself deep in the tall stone menhir that stood, one of many, in a circle dance about the pool.

The first thing Isabeau realized was that she had brought the spell of compulsion with her. It was not so loud, not so insistent, but still it hissed in her inner ear and tormented her limbs with uncontrollable twitches and urges. *Blood, I must have blood,* it whispered. *I shall live again!*

The second thing she realized was that they were not alone beside that tranquil pool. Donncan and Thunderlily were backed up hard against the menhir of stone. The crossbow bolt had plunged home between their faces, missing them by less than an inch. Blood trickled down Donncan's cheekbone from a splinter of stone it had gouged up.

Standing before the young couple, menacing them with a dagger, was Johanna.

At the whizz of the crossbow she had spun on one heel. Her eyes dilated at the sight of Isabeau and her companions, all on their knees, sick, dry-mouthed, bent, and retching, trying to catch their breaths.

Johanna gave an exclamation, then sprang forward, wild-eyed, and seized Cloudshadow, holding the dagger to her throat.

"Ye do no' care enough for the life o' your friend Donncan to take me back? So tell me, do ye care enough for that o' your mother?" she spat at Thunderlily.

The young Celestine started forward, humming wildly in distress.

Johanna held up her free hand imperatively. "Stay back! I'll kill her, I swear I will! Stay back!"

Dragging Cloudshadow upright, she wheeled away from the group still on their hands and knees by the pool, putting the Celestine before her like a shield. Still dazed and trembling from their leap back in time, it took the others a few seconds to react. Then Isabeau was up and on her feet, calling to Johanna.

"Jo, don't! Please don't! I ken about the spell o' resurrection, about Brann. Ye mustn't . . ."

Johanna's lips curled back in a snarl. "Brann shall live again and I shall be the one to raise him!"

"Ye must fight the compulsion," Isabeau said. "Please, Jo! Ye are no' an evil woman, and yet this is an evil thing ye do. Please!"

"He must have blood, he needs blood. A living soul, willing or unwilling, and a very sharp knife."

"Jo, no!"

"A Celestine to heal his wounds, and a rìgh to offer up his blood. He will be pleased, very pleased with me," Johanna gabbled.

She was very white and strange-looking, with perspiration beading her face and hands that shook so much she could barely keep the knife steady. Her pupils had shrunk to pinpoints, giving her a strange look of blindness. Her lip was swollen where she had bitten it through, and her ragged nails were edged with red half-moons of blood where she had torn her cuticles to rags. She could not stop talking, repeating snatches of Brann's spell over and over, and every now and again her arm jerked, as if her knife was a living animal struggling to escape.

"He will live again, he swore it so, and I shall be the one. Blood, blood, blood, he must have blood. Blood. A living soul, willing or unwilling, and a very sharp knife. I have the knife, I have the soul, he will be pleased with me. I just . . . I just . . . I just need to get there. Back. Back. Back to the time o' his death. I must get back. Ye do no' care about *him*, well, I have your mother now. Do ye care about her? Blood. He needs blood. Does it matter whose? He wanted a young man, strong and handsome, and full o' power. Who better than the Rìgh himself? What a joke! What a hoot! Dedrie will be pleased with me. He will be pleased with me, everyone . . . everyone . . ."

Isabeau watched with horror as the knife jerked in her hand, cutting Cloudshadow's throat and drawing blood.

"Jo, please," she said, gripping her own hands together as she tried to ignore the eerie echo of her words whispering in her brain. *A soul, willing or unwilling, and a very sharp knife . . .*

"Blood, blood, blood, he needs blood. Her blood is red and hot, will it do, will it do? We must go back. Take me back or I will kill her, do ye understand?"

No! No! Thunderlily was humming in horror and distress. *My mother, what do you do here? I had thought to escape, to bring her back to a time before the passion and confusion of humankind, back to when all was sure and sweet and at peace . . .*

"I'll kill her, I tell ye! All o' ye, get up! We must go back. Back, back, back. Will ye lead me, or do ye watch your mother die?"

I will lead ye, Thunderlily said, and stepped forward, her hands held out in a gesture of peace and reassurance. *Please, leave my mother be.*

The knife hand jerked, and blood ran down and stained the Stargazer's collar.

Cloudshadow put up both hands and seized the knife, holding it firm and steady against her throat.

Do you think I value my own life above that of my daughter? What will happen to her if she takes you back to the time of the raven man? She will die. You think I do not know this? She will die, and many others, for the raven man takes pleasure in hurting and killing. Do you not think I would rather die myself and keep my daughter safe?

Then, with her third eye wide open and fixed upon the despairing face of her daughter, Cloudshadow dragged the sharp-edged dagger across her own throat. Blood spurted. The Stargazer choked, gave a strange burbling sound deep in her throat, and fell, dragging Johanna down with her.

The knife fell from Johanna's blood-slick hand as she fell backwards, knocking her head on the menhir behind her. At once Dide leaped forward and seized the knife. Thunderlily scrambled forward, weeping, and drew her mother's lifeless body into her arms. And Johanna, realizing she had gambled and lost, threw back her head and screamed.

Madwoman

The madwoman's scream echoed around the circle of stones, causing all within to flinch back.

Johanna's hands were soaked with blood. Her brown hair hung wet with it, and it was sprayed across half her face, looking like the painted mask of some bizarre ritual. Screaming still, she stared down at her hands, then she drew a deep breath and raised her hands to press against her mouth, drinking the blood.

Isabeau turned her face away. *Blood, blood. I must have blood.*

Thunderlily had laid her hands over the gaping wound in her mother's throat, tears streaming down her face. Dide wiped the dagger on his breeches so it would not slip in his hand, and held it threateningly, every muscle in his body ready for some quick movement from Johanna. She was licking her fingers with relish, though, laughing and muttering.

"Blood, blood. He must have blood."

Isabeau turned and began to retch helplessly. Ghislaine supported her with her arm, stroking back the wildly tangled red hair. Stormstrider had fallen to his knees beside Thunderlily, one arm about her back, the other hand holding Cloudshadow's. The terrible gurgling sounds from her throat were slowly fading.

Donncan stumbled forward and fell to his knees near Cloudshadow's body.

"Thunderlily, I'm so sorry, I'm so sorry," he gabbled.

Stormstrider raised his hard-planed face and stared at him angrily, lifting his hand in a gesture that clearly meant "Stop! Go away!"

Donncan sat back on his heels, distress etched into his handsome features.

Johanna finished licking her fingers, and lifted her eyes to stare at them. "Why do ye stare at me so? Do ye no' ken he shall live again? Naught left o' him now but grave-dust, and his will and his desire. It is all ye need. Will and desire. And blood. Blood, blood, blood." She laughed, a crazy laugh that made Ghislaine shudder and Isabeau shrink back down again in terror. "Ye think ye have stopped him. Ye think ye have won. But Brann the Raven never loses. Canna ye hear him? Canna ye hear him? He is calling, he is calling, and someone, somewhere, will heed his call."

She turned her blank eyes on Isabeau, who was whimpering and shivering with dread and the force of the spell of compulsion. "Ye hear him, Beau, don't ye?" she whispered. "He calls to ye like a lover. He calls to ye like a laird. He is your master now, as he is mine."

"No, no," Isabeau whispered.

"Yes. He shall live again, and who shall be the one to raise him? No' ye! No' ye! It should have been me! I'll kill ye myself first. He is mine, mine, mine, my laird and master, no' yours, no' yours." She flung herself towards Isabeau, and was caught by Dide and flung back roughly against the stone.

She raised her face to the brightening sky and howled like a dog. "I must go back," she wept. "I must go back. Take me back, please, take me back. I must raise him. I must, I must. Oh, blood, blood, blood. He must have blood. He must live again. He has sworn it. Oh, please, please, take me back."

"This is unbearable," Ghislaine whispered, and turned her face into Cailean's shoulder. He drew her closer, stroking the long fair hair that had tumbled down from under her tam-o'-shanter. Beside him, the dog Dobhailen stood quivering with tension, his keen nostrils scenting the blood, one paw raised as he thrust his pointed muzzle towards the madwoman rocking and sobbing beside the great block of stone.

"No, Dobhailen," Cailean said softly, and the dog snarled in frustration.

"What are we to do with her?" Dide said, his jaw clenched in distress. "She is quite, quite mad."

"That will be me soon," Isabeau sobbed. "I read the spell only a few hours after her. Already I can feel it happening. He's winning, Dide, he's winning! What a spell! He wrote it with his own blood, ye ken that?" She laughed wildly. "Blood-magic, the worst, the most powerful o' all."

"Blood, blood, blood," Johanna wept. "He must have blood!"

Suddenly she leaped up and hurled herself forward, her hands like claws, straight at Thunderlily, who was still crouched over her mother's body, hands cupping the Stargazer's throat.

"Ye must take me back!" Johanna screamed. "Now! Take me back, else I'll rip your throat open myself."

Dide lunged forward and caught her about the waist, dragging her back. Johanna screamed and writhed, fighting to reach Thunderlily. The nails of one hand scratched the young Celestine's cheek, raising red welts. Dide swung her away, and she struggled to reach the dagger he still held in one hand. He raised it high above her head, trying to hold her off with his other hand. She punched and kicked and slapped and bit and clawed, and he stepped back and kicked her full in the chest so she fell with a cry of pain. Breathing hard, Dide put one hand up to his cheek, where blood was flowing freely from the bite wound. She had torn away a hunk of flesh.

"Eà's eyes!" he cursed.

Johanna was up in an instant and hurling herself upon him. Instinctively Dide brought up both hands to protect himself, forgetting he held the dagger still. Johanna ran full upon it. It was well sharpened. It ran into her chest as smoothly as if she were made of butter, not flesh and gristle and bone.

Johanna's eyes opened wide in surprise. She looked down at herself and raised both hands to cup the knife, just as Dide, in horror, let go and stepped back. Johanna cradled the knife hilt and laughed. "Blood," she said, then dropped to her knees. For a moment longer she was alive and conscious. Her eyes sought Isabeau's, and for that one instant sanity seemed to return and Johanna's eyes begged for mercy, for forgiveness, for understanding. Then she crumpled and fell.

Dide knelt beside her. "She's dead," he said blankly. "Eà save me, she's dead!"

Isabeau would have liked to have said something to comfort and reassure him, and to mourn the passing of her friend, but Brann's ghost was suddenly seizing her and rattling her, shouting in her ear. *I must live again and ye are the one to raise me!*

"No, no, no!" Isabeau screamed.

"I'm sorry, I'm so sorry," Dide cried.

She reached out her hand to him and stumbled forward into his arms. With her head buried against his chest, the sound of his thundering heartbeat in her ears, she was able to drown out the worst of Brann's voice. Dide wrapped her close, rocking her, his words coming like sobs. She wrapped her own arms about his back, trying to press herself as close to him as she could. Too much blood, too much death, she felt as if she was being torn apart with pain. Isabeau had thought of Johanna as one of her dearest friends. Her death, Lachlan's murder, the horror of her niece and nephews being stolen away, Iseult's gut-ripping grief, which Isabeau shared as if it was her own, the dreadful ordeal of traveling through time, and the struggle with the spell of compulsion, the horror of Cloudshadow's self-sacrifice and Johanna's madness, all had wrought Isabeau to a high pitch of intensity. It was an utter relief to break down and sob in Dide's arms.

At last, though, her natural composure reasserted itself. Isabeau caught her breath and wiped her face with her sleeve, stepping a little away from Dide, who cleared his throat self-consciously and surreptitiously dabbed at his own eyes. Feeling weak and rather shaky, but somehow much better, Isabeau looked about her, eyes red-rimmed. Cailean was still comforting Ghislaine, Donncan was still kneeling before the limp body of Cloudshadow, his golden wings folded tight against his back, and Stormstrider still supported Thunderlily, who had bent her head over her mother so that her long mane of silvery-white hair fell across Cloudshadow's face like a curtain. A dark, sticky pool had slowly crept out across the dirt from beneath the Stargazer's body. Thunderlily's shoulders heaved.

Isabeau watched in pity and misery. Then Thunderlily raised her face. She was laughing.

For a moment, Isabeau feared that Thunderlily too had lost her mind in the horror of the moment. But then she saw Cloudshadow's blood-soaked breast rise and fall, and slowly rise and fall again.

"She lives!" Donncan cried. "Thunderlily, ye healed her! Thank Eà!"

Thunderlily laughed and cried together, and Stormstrider bowed his head formally, his two hands pressed together, humming low in his throat. It was a gesture of great honor and respect.

Isabeau went down on her knees beside the Stargazer, tears of gladness pouring down her face. She had known, of course, that those of Stargazer blood had magical powers of healing. It was the gift of the Summer Tree to them, and one for which they paid a high price. It had seemed impossible, though, that such a terrible wound could be

healed. Yet all that was left of the slash across Cloudshadow's throat was a thin pink line, and the dreadful
staining of blood on her dress and on Thunderlily's hands.

The act of healing had cost Thunderlily dearly. She was
white as moonlight, and her breathing was shallow and uneven. If it had not been for Stormstrider, she would have
crumpled. He held her gently, and she accepted his support, near fainting with exhaustion and emotion.

Isabeau took Cloudshadow's hand. The Stargazer
turned her face feebly towards her. "Is it over?" she whispered.

"Aye, thank Eà, it's over!" Ghislaine said, and freed herself from Cailean's arms, dropping on her knees beside Isabeau. "We must all rest and eat first, o' course, and give
Cloudshadow and Thunderlily time to recover, but then we
can go home!"

"Thank the Spinners!" Donncan said. "What a nightmare this has been. I canna believe all that has happened."

"I bet ye're keen to see your wife," Dide said, trying to
joke in his usual manner. "Cruel o' Johanna to kidnap ye
afore ye had a chance to consummate the wedding."

"Aye, indeed," Donncan said. "She could've waited a
couple o' hours, at least."

"Hours!" Dide said. "Lucky Bronwen."

Isabeau said nothing. She knew it was not all over.
Brann spoke to her still, and Isabeau knew her resistance
was wilting. It would not be long and she would be as mad
as Johanna.

They set up camp under the hemlock, which was now a
vigorous young tree, its branches not yet curving all the
way down to the ground. From here they had a view all the
way to the sea. There was no grey castle on the crag above
the firth. There was no town or village or croft or shep-
herd's hut, no roads, no bridges, no goat track, no apple
tree or vegetable plot. Nothing but thick, green, virgin for-

est rolling up to mountains on one side, and down to the strand to the east. The pale sand-dunes stretched for miles all along the coast, broken by the occasional shallow lagoon gleaming like an aquamarine, and by the narrow thread of the Rhyllster, which broke at the mouth into a great delta, a thousand tiny streams wriggling through the sand and into the sleepy blue ocean.

All were weary in body and spirit. Although Cloud-shadow lived, the dreadfulness of the moment in which she had drawn the knife across her own throat weighed on them still. For Isabeau and Dide, who had known and cared deeply for Johanna, the shock of her death would not pass easily. Sorrow is always made more bitter by guilt and recriminations, and both wished they had acted differently.

"If only I had seen something was wrong earlier. If only I had realized how bitterly angry she was that Lachlan planned to pardon Rhiannon, or realized that the lord of Fettercairn's skeelie had been poisoning her, body and mind, for so long. Perhaps she would no' then have gone looking for the spell o' resurrection in *The Book o' Shadows*," Isabeau said to Dide, who was doing his best to bury his grief and sense of self-recrimination in work. After helping make up soft beds of grass and leaves for Cloud-shadow and Thunderlily, he had gathered great piles of firewood and was now building a fire to cook up something hot for them all.

He paused and slowly put down the faggots of wood he was holding. "If only I had tossed the dagger away . . . If only I had realized how beside herself she was with this . . . this madness the spell brings."

"If only someone had listened to Rhiannon! She warned us about Lord Malvern, and Dedrie, and their search for the spell of resurrection."

"If only . . ."

They stopped and looked at each other. Isabeau's eyes were brimming over with tears.

"I canna stay here, in this body," she said. "It is too

much to bear. I will change into another shape and be free
o' the compulsion, for a few hours anyway. We must rest
here at least a day or two. Thunderlily and Cloudshadow
are both at the end o' their strength. I will no' be able to
maintain a shape that long, no' without risking sorcery
sickness. But if I stay at least part o' each day in another
shape, I should be able to escape the madness."

Dide nodded. "Have a care. This is no' the world we
ken. Stay close, so that I ken ye are safe."

Isabeau reached up and kissed him on the mouth. "Ye
too, *leannan*. Keep them all close. We must be ready to escape through the circle o' stones at any time."

"Yes."

"I will keep watch," she said, then, in a blink of an eye,
she transformed, flinging up great wings and taking flight,
choosing the shape of the golden eagle, the mightiest of all
the birds. Dide watched her fly higher and higher into the
sky, till she was nothing but a black speck in the blue, and
then he turned with a sigh, stoked up the fire, and wondered how he was to dig a grave without a spade.

Thunderlily lay quietly on her bed of bracken and leaves,
wrapped in a blanket, staring about her, soaking up the
sight of the wild green forest rolling away on either side.

Donncan hesitated, and then came and sat beside her.

"Ye saved me," he said very softly. "If ye had taken me
back to the time o' Brann's death, as she commanded, I
would be dead now."

No, she answered, humming very faintly in her throat.
*My mother and the Keybearer would have arrived on our
heels, using the same configuration of stars to travel by.
They would have stopped her. I just did not expect them to
know where we had gone. I still do not understand how
they came to find us.*

"Still . . ." Donncan said, and then paused, not knowing
how to express what he felt. They had traveled a thousand

years back in time together, and they had faced what they had thought was certain death. He felt in awe of Thunderlily, and yet closer to her than anyone, even Bronwen, his own wife, whom he had left behind in his own time. There were no words to express such emotion and so he did what Stormstrider had done—he pressed both his hands together and bowed his head in reverence.

Thunderlily smiled and put out one finger to touch his brow.

Look, is it not beautiful? she asked, sweeping out her other hand to indicate the landscape. *I have always wondered what it would be like.*

Donncan sat down beside her, braving the displeasure of Stormstrider, who was glaring at him from a distance.

It is beautiful, he thought in response. *So wild, so green.*

That was why I brought us here. I knew the configuration of the stars. I had often calculated them before, just wondering what our world was like, before humans came . . .

Do you dislike us so much? Donncan asked, hurt and surprised.

She smiled at him. *You know that is not true. I love you. All you humans. You fascinate me. You live so very lightly. Perhaps it is because your lives are so short. Perhaps you just do not fear as much as we do. You seem to have no taboo. This is my tragedy, that I am drawn to this lightness and joyfulness and recklessness like a moth to one of your flames. I am not human. I am not free to love so lightly. Yet love I do, and I do not have your courage. That is why I swing the celestial globe and dream of a time when life was simple for those of my kind, and my life would have been laid out before me in the unchanging pattern of my ancestors, and I did not ever need to fear the loss and grief that comes from loving too much.*

I too fear the hurt that can come from loving too much, Donncan thought with difficulty.

Thunderlily turned and regarded him with her three-eyed gaze. *Do you think I do not know?*

Do you think she realizes?

Thunderlily looked away from him. There was a long silence, and then she said, with a soft strum of sound in her throat, *Sometimes I fear so, sometimes I wish so. Of all the humans I know, she is the one that lives most lightly, most joyfully, most bravely. She is like a bright light that dazzles my eyes, like music that fills my ears. It is impossible not to love her. Does she know this? I think at times she does, and she revels in her power, and revels in her beauty, and cares not the harm her beauty can do . . .*

She has harmed ye then, Donncan said unhappily.

Yes. But do I wish I had never seen her? Do I wish she had never laughed at me, and drawn her arm through mine and bid me to dance? Of course not! I have been harmed, it is true. I will never be happy with my own kind now. All my life I will remember the brightness and the music, and all else will seem dull and clanging. But I do not grieve. At least, not often. I will go back to the forest, and I will lie with the mate my mother has chosen for me, and I will bear him a child, so that my line and my people will go on, undamaged. Sometimes, it is true, in the dusk when the first star can be seen and the light is fading, I will think of her, and I will sigh and smile, and press my eyelids together for a moment. And then I will pick up my child, and I will lay him on my shoulder, and think of her no more.

Thunderlily was weeping, in the dusk under the tree, and wordlessly Donncan put out his hand and took hers, long and bony, with its odd-looking four-jointed fingers, and she clung to his hand, and laughed.

I love her too, he said.

I know. You will go back and you will be happy, the two of you, and one day you both will have a child or two, or three, or four, and once or twice a year you will glance at each other and say, I wonder how Thunderlily is, away in her garden?

I will think o' ye often. I wish—

No, you do not. Happiness for me would be bitter unhappiness for you. This is so. You cannot change it, and I would not wish you to. You say that I saved you. Perhaps, in a way, there is some truth in that. If so, I am glad, for I saved you for her. You fear she does not love you. It is because of her beauty that you fear. And so you would harm her, your fear as cruel in its way as her fearlessness. If you are to be happy, you must not let fear blind you, but walk forward with courage and clear eyes . . .

Donncan was silent for a long moment. *I will try,* he said at last.

Then I will be happy too, she said, and turned her face to look at Stormstrider, who was regarding her with an intensity and darkness most unusual for one of his kind. Thunderlily smiled at him, her pale starry eyes shining and, taken by surprise, he smiled back, his whole face transfigured. The next moment he glanced away, hiding his expression.

Thunderlily's smile lingered. *I wonder if he too has lived among humans, to feel so much and show it?* Her mind-voice was so very soft Donncan barely heard it.

On the Wings of an Eagle

Isabeau soared high on the thermal winds, rejoicing as once again she left the white-hot cage of Brann's spell.

She had chosen the form of a golden eagle with good reason, even though she knew Buba would be disappointed to be left behind, his broad, short wings not built for flying as far and fast as an eagle. Isabeau wished to see as much of the land as she could, though, and the strong wings and keen eyes of the eagle would carry her much farther than those of an elf-owl.

She swooped around the whole basin of the river valley, seeing herds of satyricorns running wild in the woods, cluricauns playing through the trees, nisses diving and splashing in the rapids. She saw sand-lions basking on the dunes, and sea-stirks wrestling by the foamy water's edge. Both had been hunted almost to extinction in her day, one because of the danger they presented to a growing colony, the other for their delicious fatty meat.

She soared far out over the sea and saw the Fairgean in their summer migration to the south, the warrior-lords riding the sinuous sea-serpents, their bodyguards following behind on horse-eels, the women swimming alongside, some pushing narrow canoes piled high with supplies.

All day Isabeau soared above the land, raking the horizons with her fierce golden eyes. Only once did she drop to earth, to seize a donbeag in her talons and deftly disembowel it with her beak. She was hungry, and she had seen no coneys or rats or mice in her day's flight. There was just enough of the human left in her to note the irony.

As dusk approached, Isabeau winged her way across the strand to a tall rocky crag that rose like a gnarled finger out of the sand. In winter, this peak was an island, but now in summer, with the tides at their lowest, it was surrounded on all sides with rolling white sands, littered with barnacle-encrusted timber, rocks, bones, and dried seaweed. Writhing across one sand-dune was the long skeleton of a sea-serpent, its great fanged mouth wide open as if to bite the sky.

Isabeau had a reason for wanting to be perched on the tip of the rocky crag at dusk. She knew this was the day that Cuinn's Ship arrived, the first landing of humankind in Eileanan. Thunderlily had come to this time, this moment, on purpose, wanting to see the land before humans came and wrought such change upon it, wanting to see the magical act that had changed the whole destiny of the planet forever.

Isabeau wanted to see it too.

She had been raised on the story. Her guardian Meghan had often told her the tale, pinching the fabric of her grey dress between the fingers of either hand and bringing the folds together. "It was a great spell," she had said in her rather wheezy old voice. "In their own land, which they called Alba, witches were hunted down and tortured and burned to death on dreadful fires. The First Coven were determined to escape this horror and find a place where they could be safe and prosperous and worship their own gods. And so together they wrought this great, marvelous spell. They folded the very fabric o' the universe, as I now fold my dress between my fingers, and they crossed an unfathomable distance in no more than the blink o' an eye."

As we crossed a thousand years in time, Isabeau thought to herself, and wondered if there were perhaps Old Ways crossing space as there were crossing the earth.

There were many tapestries woven to tell the story of
the Great Crossing. They all showed a ship bursting
through a flaming rent in the fabric of the sky, and crashing down upon the sand. Behind them was this tall finger
of stone, pointing directly up at the first star of evening.
The passengers on board that ship had sought refuge on the
high rock, and Cuinn the Wise, leader of the First Coven,
had died there this very night. It was said you could still
see the very spot where he had died, for white heather grew
there, the only place on Eileanan where such a plant could
be found. He had carried it in his buttonhole from his
homeland, it was said, and it had fallen to the ground when
he was laid down, and taken root.

There were many more stories. Stories about how Sian's
Ship had been separated from Cuinn's Ship in the Crossing, and landed on the far side of Eileanan, not knowing
the fate of their companions. The descendants of each ship
had settled and fought the native faeries, and built castles
and walled towns to protect themselves, and in time had
flourished and spread. And it was not until Cuinn's great-
great-grandson, Hartley the Explorer, had built a fleet of
ships and gone exploring around the coastline of Eileanan
that they had met with the descendants of Sian the Storm-
Rider, Rùraich the Searcher, Seinneadair the Singer, and
Berhtilde the Bright Warrior-Maid, and their followers, all
of whom had settled the north coast of Eileanan, never suspecting there was another thriving human settlement on the
far side of the impassable mountains.

There had been thirteen witches in total in the First
Coven, and each had brought friends and family and servants, horses and dogs, goats and sheep, pigs, geese and
chickens, sacks of seeds and boxes of seedlings, and trunks
and trunks of books and tools and instruments and
weapons. With them had come the invisible marauders,
rats and mice and viruses, which had done more to wipe
out the native inhabitants than their swords and pistols and
arrows.

Isabeau knew all this history as well as she knew her own. She knew what incalculable damage the First Coven had done to the world they had pinpointed on a star-map because it was the world most like the one they had left behind. Yet Isabeau could not find it in her to be sorry. She knew no other world but Eileanan, and she loved it passionately. The First Coven had tried to build a world where they could be free. They had never meant to enslave others, or to destroy what had been there before them. The motto of the Coven of Witches had always been "Do as thy will, as long as thou harm none." It was a grand ambition, and a thousand years in the future, people still strived to live up to its spirit, sometimes succeeding, and sometimes failing, as people always seemed destined to do.

Dusk fell like a silver snuffer. Then, without any warning, it happened. The sky above the sand suddenly tore across with a gasp of fire, and out of this blazing tunnel sailed a great ship, billowing with white sails from its four masts, and flying flags that flapped in a storm from another world. With it came a great slap of wild grey water, a swirl of foam, a howl of wind. The ship rode this swirl of sea down, down, down, to crash into the sand-dunes, the ship keeling over under the weight of its suddenly limp and dragging sails. Isabeau's keen ears could hear screaming and the sound of cracking and splintering wood.

She took flight, soaring overhead. She watched as the thousand-odd people crammed on board were flung about violently, trapped under falling spars and sails, and crushed by rolling barrels and tumbling crates. Horses screamed in the hold. Sheep and goats bleated in terror, and a broken crate released a flock of pigeons into the sky.

The travelers from another world worked rapidly to return order to the ship, but fire had broken out in the stern, the consequence of a broken barrel of gunpowder. A young man and a tall dark-haired woman were shouting at each other. On the deck lay an elderly man wrapped in a cloak.

Isabeau swooped down, curious. She saw the strong aquiline nose and olive skin of her guardian, and knew the old man must be Cuinn the Wise. The young man must be his son Owein, and that tall supercilious woman Fóghnan the Thistle, who would leave this beleaguered ship and take her followers to the land she would name Arran. In time, Owein's son Balfour, the first human child born in Eileanan, would murder her and be murdered in turn by Fóghnan's daughter, Margrit. So would begin the feud that would not be healed for more than a thousand years, when Lachlan MacCuinn and Iain MacFóghnan became friends, and swore to put the age-old rivalry aside.

When Isabeau changed shape, she did not merely assume the look of a certain creature, she became that creature. As Isabeau, the Keybearer of the Coven, she abhorred the eating of meat. As Owl, she would eagerly snatch up a scurrying mouse, and think nothing of coughing up a little pellet of claw and fur later. As Snow-Lion, she would use her strong jaws to disembowel a little deer, and lick the blood off her whiskers with great satisfaction afterwards. As Eagle, she could watch a long chain of weeping, exhausted, and frightened people struggle across the sand, carrying what they could from the burning remains of their ship, with little more than a detached interest and a keen eye for the rats and mice scurrying away over the sand. She enjoyed a dainty feast and then circled once more over the settlers as they took refuge from the eerie fall of night on the rocky crag that would, in time, be called Cuinn's Isle.

Isabeau was fascinated by their archaic clothes, their strange incomprehensible speech, and their unexpected lack of magic. She was most surprised to see them lighting fires with tinder and flint, and not with their minds, and illuminating their way with smoky torches and a few simple glass lanterns, instead of conjuring witch's light as she would have done.

She had always been taught that the First Coven were sorcerers of incredible strength and power, but apart from

Ahearn Horse-Laird's obvious ability to calm terrified horses with a touch and a whisper, she could see no overt sign of their magical ability. She recognized Brann the Raven for his dark hair and mesmeric eyes, and even in the shape of an eagle felt a little thrill as she recognized the red hair and beard of her own ancestor, Faodhagan the Red. He was working side by side with his twin sister, Sorcha, to unload boxes of tools and weapons, and she was pleased when he turned and calmed the hunger of the flames with a broad gesture of his hand. She would have expected him and Sorcha together to have been able to quell the fire altogether, however, and thought to herself that perhaps, over time, the magical talents of humans had sharpened and focused, an interesting theory she would like to discuss with Gwilym and the other sorcerers some time.

At last it was too dark for even her keen eagle eyes to see, and she knew she had been too long out of her own shape. She turned and flew back towards the green hill with its crown of standing stones, finding it in the darkness by the bright eye of the fire Dide had lit by the pool. She landed lightly and let herself fall back into her own shape, feeling the usual bone-deep weariness fall upon her.

With the weariness came Brann's compulsion, crueler and sharper than ever. She was able to wonder if it was so intense because Brann was here now, in this world, and glanced out to the other small red eyes she could see in the distance, the bonfires by which the new arrivals huddled, frightened and homesick. Would he be able to sense something out there, some link between them, some inkling that out in the darkness was a woman whose soul was riven with longing to raise him from the dead? It was said Brann had the power of prophecy, and that he had foreseen he would live again in a vision. Could it be her presence here, burning with desire and madness, that gave him the presentiment? If she had not come to this time, chasing a stolen rìgh, would he perhaps never have conceived the idea of living twice? If so, he might not have spent his life studying the secrets of life and death, and he would not have written the spell in *The Book of Shadows*. Then she would not have read it, nor Johanna either, and none of the last few terrible days would have happened. She would not be here now, staring out towards Brann in the darkness. It made her brain reel, thinking of it. Meghan had always said events cast a shadow before them. Who had cast this shadow, Brann or herself?

Naked, weeping, Isabeau crept into the circle of stones and found the long shape of Dide, sleeping wrapped in his blanket. She crouched beside him and shook him gently until he at last awoke with a cry of surprise.

"Sssh," she whispered, and took him by the hand, tugging it.

"Beau! What is it?" he said sleepily.

"I need ye," she whispered.

"What? What's wrong?"

"Come with me," she said, and led him out through the menhirs and down the hill. Dide stumbled after her, blind and confused. She led him into the forest and then turned and flung herself against him, wrapping her arms about his neck. "Kiss me, Dide," she murmured. "Love me. Please."

Still half-asleep, Dide nonetheless did as she commanded, one hand sliding down her bare back, the other cupping the back of her head. Isabeau was near frantic with need. It was only in the pounding of her heart, the roar of climax in her ears, that she was able to drown out Brann's sibilant hiss in her brain.

Afterwards, as they lay entwined in each other's arms in the darkness of the forest, Dide said softly in her ear, "Is all well, *leannan*?"

"Better now," she answered.

"Is it this spell?"

She nodded.

"We'll find a way to break it, dinna ye fear, my love," he said, and kissed her ear.

Isabeau nodded again, although she knew she lied. Blood-magic could only be broken by death.

For the next two days Isabeau spent more time in the shape of a hollow-boned bird than in her own form.

It was dangerous, she knew. Too much time in another shape and she began to forget her humanity. She became more eagle than woman. It grew harder and harder to remember to return to the campfire and shift back into her own pain-wracked body. With each return she grew weaker, the fever of sorcery sickness gripping its sharp claws deep into her body. It was a swift downward spiral with nothing but madness or death at the end. Isabeau knew this, they all knew this, and yet there seemed nothing else to do. Both Cloudshadow and Thunderlily were weak and exhausted after their ordeal, and Isabeau would rather ravage her own body than risk the last of the Stargazers.

On the evening of the second day, she lay shivering and moaning under a blanket by the fire, her eyes shut, perspiration dampening her skin. Dide sat beside her, stroking back her hair, while Cailean stirred a thin broth in the saucepan hanging above the flames.

Their supplies had long since run out, but Cloudshadow would not permit any of them to step outside the circle of stones on the crown of the sacred hill to go exploring or foraging, or even just to stretch their legs. Beyond the sacred circle was a garden of the Celestines, faeries who had never before seen a human. Cloudshadow wanted to preserve their innocence as long as possible, knowing as she did that the faeries' doom had already arrived in a burning ship from another world.

The very first thing the Stargazer had done was leave a collection of twigs and stones in a formal pattern outside the ring of stones, explaining in tree-language that they were lost out of time and sought to heal and recover before attempting the journey home. It was one of the most sacred taboos of the Celestines, she explained wearily, that those who traveled the Old Ways back in time did nothing to change the world in which they found themselves. *Do not touch, do not make or break, do not speak,* she said. *For the smallest change can have enormous implications for the future, so much so that we may find we have no future to return to.*

The next morning they had found some food left on large leaves by one of the tall standing stones. There were berries of all kinds, bundles of herbs and bitter green leaves, mushrooms and some odd knobbly roots of a rather putrid yellow color, which when roasted in the coals proved to be utterly delicious. It was scanty fare for those used to palace feasts, but all were so hungry that they accepted it gratefully, filling up the gaps with long drafts of icy-cold spring water.

All except Isabeau, who showed no interest at all in food. So Cailean was cooking her up some soup with the latest offering of herbs and mushrooms in the hope of tempting her appetite or, at the very least, getting some nourishment into her sadly wasted body.

Isabeau's hands were both bandaged to stop her gnawing her fingernails to the quick. Ghislaine had combed back her hair and plaited it tightly, to try to stop her from tugging at it. It was no use. She clutched at her head compulsively, rocking back and forth, muttering, until her curly red hair was dragged free of the plait to snake wildly about her white face. It disturbed Dide to hear words among the garble. "Blood," she mumbled. "He must have blood. A living soul, willing or unwilling, and a very sharp knife. Must go back . . . blood, blood, blood. No! No! I won't! I won't! No blood. No more blood. No. No."

She sobbed out loud, and turned her head fretfully, grabbing at her skull with both hands. "Make him stop, make him stop," she begged. "I canna stand it. Dide, please!"

"Ssssh, dearling," he soothed. "Sssh. Sleep. All will be well."

"How?" she demanded. "Tell me how?"

"Try to rest, *leannan*. Ye must save your strength."

"Please, just kill me," she begged. "I canna stand it anymore. Please, kill me and have done with it!"

"We canna do that, dearling. Come, try to sleep. We'll find a way to break the spell, I promise."

Tears poured down her cheeks. "How? This is no' a ghost that has lost its way and needs help passing through to the next world. This is a ghost who is so determined to live again he is willing to drive me to madness to work his will. Ye do no' understand! This is blood-magic, o' the highest, most dangerous kind. Blood-magic. Blood. Only death will save me. Please, oh, please, Dide! I'm afraid o' what I will do. Please . . ."

She began to sob hysterically, and only calmed when Ghislaine the Dream-Walker touched her gently between the eyes and brought down the veils of sleep.

"She's getting worse," Dide said to Donncan.

The young Rìgh was very troubled about his aunt, and sat close by her makeshift bed, occasionally soothing her with gentle pats when she grew too fretful. At Dide's words he nodded, biting his lip and looking very anxious. "What are we to do?" he asked.

"Beau says the only escape is death," Dide said, dabbing at her hot forehead with a cool damp cloth. She opened her eyes and looked up at him, her pupils like pinpoints in the bright blank blue of her irises.

"Yes, death," she said in a low, husky voice. "Life, death, life, death. He swore he would live again. He shall live again. He shall! He must!"

"Ssshhh," Dide soothed, and she closed her eyes again, mumbling to herself.

"But we canna kill her!" Donncan cried.

"O'course no'," Dide replied.

"Then what?" Cailean asked, dropping a pinch of salt into the soup. "For we have to do something!"

"I can only think o' one thing," Dide said. He paused and took a deep breath. "We must raise Brann from the dead."

"What!" Cailean, Ghislaine, and Donncan all cried together. Thunderlily, who had been sitting staring out at the dusk-filled valley, turned her head and stared at them, eyes wide with horror.

"If we raise Brann from the dead, then the compulsion will have been fulfilled and Isabeau will be free," Dide explained.

"But then Brann will be alive," Donncan said hotly. "That is the very thing we fought so hard to avoid."

"We'll just have to kill him again," Dide said. "Surely if he is resurrected once, the terms o' the spell will be fulfilled? Then, once we have killed him and put him back in the grave, it will be done. It'll all be over."

"How are we to kill him?" Ghislaine asked. "Remember what Isabeau told us, about what his son said? The only way he was able to kill his father was to come across him at the moment o' rapture, when all his senses were closed to the world. He is a sorcerer o' ten rings, remember."

"He'll be newly raised from the dead," Dide said. "He'll be weak, disorientated."

"Ye hope," Ghislaine said.

Dide grimaced and nodded. "I must admit, it's a plan full o' holes. We will just have to make sure we are ready for him. A quick stab to the heart at the very moment he is resurrected, perhaps?"

"Do ye think it would really work?" Donncan asked, his dark eyes filled with hope. "Would Aunty Beau really be free o' the spell if we raise him and then kill him again?"

"I dinna ken," Dide said. "It is at least a plan, though, the only one we've got."

Cailean frowned, thinking this through. "I suppose so,"

he answered slowly. "There's one small problem I can see with your plan, though."

"What's that?" Dide asked.

"Someone has to be sacrificed in order to resurrect him."

"Och, I ken," Dide said. "O'course I thought o' that. It'd have to be me."

"Ye!" Donncan cried. "Ye want us to sacrifice *ye*?"

Dide nodded, and looked back down at Isabeau, who was turning her wild red head from side to side, saying at great speed, "Blood, blood, he must have blood, he must walk again. Aye, aye, blood for my master!"

"O'course," he answered. "Who else?"

Bright Things

It was a long and difficult night. Isabeau alternated long periods of fever where she recognized no one, with interludes of agitation where she struggled to get back to the time of Brann's death, cursing them, pleading with them, beseeching them to help her. Isabeau was convinced Brann's ghost was there in the circle of stones with them, watching her, commanding her.

"He says it is time!" she cried. "I must go to him, I must, I must! Let me go!"

Suddenly she disappeared where she stood. They searched desperately in the darkness, stumbling over each other, terrified they had lost her forever. Then Dide found a tiny mouse crouched trembling beside one of the great standing stones, obviously in great distress. He bent and picked it up very gently, and sat cradling it in his large, warm hands, crooning to it through the last hours of the night until at last the little creature stopped shivering and panting, and dozed a little, its tiny paw crooked over his thumb. Dide could not help but weep then, silently and shamefacedly, pressing his sleeve against his eyes so no one would see his tears.

When dawn began to finger-paint the sky with brilliant streaks of rose and gold and crimson, Cailean made tea with some of the herbs left for them outside the circle of standing stones, and said, "Well then, how are we to do this thing? For we canna go on this way."

Dide's face was haggard, his eyes red-rimmed. Cradling the sleeping mouse against his breast, he held the tin cup with his other hand, sipping at it gratefully.

"We go back to Brann's grave. It does no' have to be to the time o' his death again, for his son will have it guarded, and I have no desire to fight his men first. Maybe fifty, a hundred years after his death? We resurrect him, ye kill him, Thunderlily heals me and brings me back to life, we bury him and go home. Simple."

There was a long silence. No one wanted to begin to point out all the things that could go wrong with such a plan.

"Any other suggestions?" Dide asked, with an attempt at cheerfulness that rang extremely hollow.

No one spoke. Buba hooted softly from his perch above Isabeau's head, and the mouse cringed and shivered.

"But . . . but . . . Dide . . . who is to kill ye?" Donncan said at last. "I could no' do it, I could no'. The idea o' it fills me with horror. Now, Brann the Raven, I think I could kill, though no' with any ease o' heart. He was a wicked, wicked man and his resurrection would mean naught but evil for us all. If I had help . . . if I did it quickly enough . . . I think perhaps I could do it. But no' ye."

"Beau would have to do it," Dide said, stroking one thumb over the silky fur of the mouse, who looked up at him with beady black eyes, its whiskers quivering.

"Aunty Beau! But . . . but she canna kill a cockroach!" Donncan said.

"She's already drawn a dagger on me once." Dide tried, and failed, to keep the pain out of his voice. He cleared his throat. "She'll be acting under compulsion. This is no ordinary spell o' persuasion, Donncan, we can all see that. Isabeau is the strongest witch o' our time and she has failed to withstand this spell. Brann wrote it in his own blood, and with all the force o' his black heart."

"But . . ." Donncan protested again, and was so overwhelmed with emotion his voice failed him utterly. "How could ye stand it?" he whispered at last. "To let your lover cut your own throat, to let her kill ye . . ."

"Thunderlily will heal me," Dide said, trying to grin. "We saw how she healed Cloudshadow."

But what if I cannot heal your wound? Thunderlily said. She was sitting bolt upright, her ruined silver dress gleaming like water in the grey light of the dawn. Her third eye was open, staring at Dide in anguish. *What if I am too late? Or not strong enough? I have not yet eaten of the flower of the Summer Tree. My powers are not great.*

But mine are, Cloudshadow said. *I have killed my beloved and eaten of the Summer Tree's flower. I will heal the juggler, if I can.*

But you have lost so much blood, Thunderlily said. *You are frail still. It takes weeks to recover from such a blood loss, particularly since you are already much weakened by the poison in the wine Johanna gave us all. It takes much strength to heal a mortal wound. You could take yourself to the brink of death even trying.*

The juggler will be dead, Stormstrider said in deep concern. *Each second that the blood ebbs from his body, each second his heart does not beat and his lungs do not breathe, is a second farther away from life. I am not a Stargazer. I do not know your mysteries. But this I do know. The Stargazers do not have the power to bring the dead back to life. Once he is dead, dead he must stay. You can only heal while life remains.*

"Ye will just have to be quick," Dide said.

"Are ye no' afraid?" Donncan asked, regarding the jongleur with frowning eyes. "Of dying, o' no' being saved?"

"I have traveled many roads, had many adventures," Dide said, his eyes glowing strangely. "What is there left o' life to experience but death?"

"I do no' believe ye," Ghislaine said abruptly.

He turned to her, and this time his grin flashed with his

usual verve. "O'course I am afraid," he answered. "I'm afraid o' the pain and the blood, I'm afraid ye will fail and no' bring me back, I am afraid that there is naught after death but black emptiness. But I do no' lie. Death is the last great adventure. I have lived a good life, I have loved and been loved more deeply than I ever thought I deserved. My master, my friend is dead . . ." His voice faltered. ". . . and my dear wife Isabeau . . . do ye think I would no' rather face death than have her driven mad like this?"

Suddenly his arms were full of Isabeau, naked, weeping, her wild mass of red hair doing very little to preserve her modesty. "Ye called me wife," she wept. "Oh, Dide, no! What do ye plan? No, no. I canna . . . I canna let ye . . ."

He cradled her gently, bending his face to kiss her wet cheek. "Did ye hear it all?" he murmured. "Indeed, it's possible, dearling. We raise Brann, and then lay him to rest again, and with it his blaygird compulsion. Ye'll be free . . ."

"But ye'll be dead," she wept.

"Maybe no'," he answered. "In fact, definitely no'! Thunderlily and Cloudshadow between them have the power to revive me, dearling."

"But what if they do no'?" she cried. "What if they are too late?"

He shrugged. "It's worth the risk, don't ye think?"

"No, I don't!"

"Beau, listen to me. Ye are the Keybearer. Eileanan needs ye. These are evil times. Lachlan is dead. Iseult is beside herself with grief. There is only Donncan to rule, a mere lad whose mother's milk is still wet on his lips . . ."

He flashed a look at Donncan, who grinned.

"What am I but a good-for-naught jongleur, a singer o' pretty songs, a juggler o' pretty balls?" Dide said, reaching out one hand to grab his blanket and wrap it about her shoulders as he pressed her even closer to his chest.

"Ye're no'!" Isabeau was weeping in earnest now, and Dide mopped up her face with one corner of his blanket.

"If I should die, I'll be missed, that's true. No one sings a love song the way I do. But if ye were to die . . . if ye were to be sent mad by this evil spell . . . what would happen to the Coven? To Eileanan? Who would replace ye?"

Isabeau could not think, could not speak.

"I love ye," he said, very low, putting his mouth to her ear in the vain hope that no one else would hear his words. "I trust ye. I ken ye will bring me back."

"I canna . . . I must . . . I canna . . . I must . . ." She was fighting the compulsion now, shivering and weeping, gripping Dide's arm desperately.

"Aye, it is time," Dide said and lifted her free of his lap. "It is time to raise Brann the Raven from the dead, and ye are the one to do it."

Once they began to take steps to return to Brann's grave, some of the urgency of the compulsion left Isabeau and she was able to think and breathe more easily. She did not protest any more. Any attempt to avoid the compulsion only caused it to return in force. Acquiescence to Dide's plan made it much easier for her.

"Do ye think Brann's ghost is really here, watching us, forcing us to do his will?" Ghislaine asked Cailean nervously, looking about her with haunted green eyes.

Cailean shook his head. "No, I do no' think so. I think it's the spell. As long as the one ensorcelled is moving in the direction the spell wants, it relaxes. It's only when Isabeau tries to fight it or avoid it that it begins to pull again strongly. Spells o' compulsion are all about imposing one's will upon another. As long as she submits, all is well."

"When we get back to Lucescere, I'm going to go to *The Book o' Shadows* and rip that page out and burn it," Ghislaine declared.

"How will ye find it without reading it?" Cailean said

quietly. "We canna be sure that raising Brann from the dead will make the spell lose all its potency if he ends up back in the grave again. It'll release Isabeau from the spell, that I'm sure o'. But anyone else who reads it?"

"But we canna just leave it there!"

"We'll have to discuss later what is the best thing to do," Cailean said. "I must admit I hate the thought of it lurking inside the pages of *The Book o' Shadows* like a swarthyweb spider!"

As they packed up their belongings and tried to erase all signs of their presence in the circle of stones, they discussed every aspect of the plan. To all of them, the two murders involved in the plan were by far the most difficult. Isabeau was adamant that she would never be able to kill Dide, no matter how strong the compulsion, and he was as adamant that she would have to.

"It's the only way to be sure the compulsion is fulfilled," he argued.

I killed my beloved, Cloudshadow said, with deep sadness in her mind-voice. *It is the price we Stargazers must pay for the gifts of the Summer Tree. In time my daughter too must do the same.*

Donncan's eyes flashed to Stormstrider. The tall Celestine was, Donncan knew, Thunderlily's chosen husband. It was he who would die under her knife when the time came. How did he feel about that? It was impossible to tell from his face, which was as cool and composed as ever. Thunderlily did not have such control over her expressions. He saw her eyes drop and her lip quiver, and color rose under her pale skin. Living among humans had changed Thunderlily a great deal, Donncan thought. Surely she could not think of having to sacrifice her own husband with anything but deep abhorrence? Yet Thunderlily had said she would not seek to change her future, that she would submit to her duty. It must fill her with dread and horror, surely, the idea of lying with a man she did not love, bearing him children, then killing him for the blooming of their sacred tree.

She turned her head and looked at him. Her third eye was open, dark as night. *You do not understand,* she said silently in Donncan's mind, for only him to hear. *He is a good man, brave and true. His children will be born with honor. I may not love him with the desperate passion that you humans long for, and suffer for, but I will love him as Celestines love, with deep affection, trust, and tenderness. He will give me his seed and his blood, so that our kind may go on flourishing, and he will die among those who love him, honored and revered. Is there a better death?*

Donncan gazed back at her, feeling suddenly humbled. He thought of Bronwen, his wife in name only. He had longed for their wedding for years, longed to feel her skin next to his, to kiss her mouth and her silken hair, to lose himself in what Thunderlily so rightly called desperate passion. The very thought of Bronwen's strange beauty was enough to make his blood heat and his loins tingle. But Donncan had not thought much beyond those first days, weeks, months of their marriage. He had not imagined themselves growing stout with a brood of noisy children; or old, grey, and impotent. It had always been the now that had driven him. For the first time he began to imagine Bronwen as the mother of his children, as an old woman who looked up and smiled tenderly as he came into the room, despite his bald head and stooped shoulders. He was surprised to find that he wanted that desperately, wanted it, perhaps, even more than the passionate consummation of the now. He wanted to build a rich, happy life, he realized, and to grow old basking in the knowledge of having lived it well.

Donncan was brought out of his reverie by Ghislaine touching him gently on his arm. They were, he realized, ready to go. The sun was rising and Cloudshadow was running her hands over the great stone menhirs, setting their course. Stormstrider was shouldering his heavy sack. Isabeau was pressed close to Dide, her arm about his waist, her face pressed into his shoulder. The elf-owl Buba waited on top of one of the stones, and Cailean stood ready, his head on Dobhailen's big black head. Donncan nodded and tried to smile, taking Ghislaine's hand. She looked back somberly, her green eyes filled with fear. This was, he realized, no game of mere chance they played here. If they failed, Dide would be dead and Brann the Raven alive, and the future of the whole world changed. His hesitant smile faltered, and he took a deep breath and squared his shoulders. It was his job, and Cailean's, to make sure that did not happen.

The journey through time was not any easier for being their third time. If anything, it left them even more wrung out, sick, and exhausted. Isabeau fell to her knees, retching and gasping. They had to splash water in her face and sit her with her head between her knees before the swoon passed, and then she was very weak and faint, her hands trembling visibly. Buba perched on her shoulder, hooting in concern, and she rubbed his ear tufts, trying not to weep. Isabeau did not say so, but they could all tell that being so close to Brann's grave was putting her under unbearable pressure.

It was early morning at the Tomb of Ravens, seventy-five years after the death of Brann the Raven. Since they were navigating by the stars, it was once again midsummer at the full moon, at the first rising of the Kingfisher, the brightest star in the summer sky.

The Tomb of Ravens dominated the skyline, huge and grey, its stones now stained with moss. There were no guards. Brann's son Dugald would be dead by now, and some other MacBrann ruling. Donncan rather hoped it was Dugald's son, by another marriage. He had found the tale of Dugald and his murdered wife Medwenna very sad, and hoped that Brann's son had found some measure of happiness in his life. Donncan thought he would go and read the annals, when he was home again. There was so much he did not know about the history of Eileanan, the land he now ruled. Or, rather, the land he would rule if he made it back home alive.

They had a day to waste, since the spell of resurrection must be done at midnight on the night of the full moon. So they wasted it sleeping under the hemlock tree, taking it in turns to stand guard. Cloudshadow was particularly worn out by the journey through time, and she and Thunderlily both slept heavily, guarded over by Stormstrider, who sat very still, his hands folded before him.

Isabeau and Dide sought privacy in the forest, and wasted their time a little more energetically, if their flushed cheeks and languid limbs were any indication when at last they came back, arms about each other's waists. Donncan found himself longing for Bronwen very much.

Rather to his surprise, he found he was not the only one so affected. Ghislaine had watched them go and return with brooding eyes, then got to her feet, holding down her hand to Cailean and saying rather abruptly, "Fancy a walk?"

Eager desire flashed in Cailean's eyes. The young sorcerer let Ghislaine pull him to his feet and lead him down the hill into the forest, and they did not return for over an hour. When at last they did return, hand in hand in the dusk, Cailean was glowing with joy. Donncan realized with a start that Cailean had always been in love with Ghislaine, and never expected she would ever return his feelings. It was impossible to tell what Ghislaine felt. She was smiling and relaxed, it was true, but he saw none of the painful intensity of Cailean's emotions on her face.

Dobhailen was extremely put-out, and sat with his back to Cailean, his ears down and his tail tucked under his bottom. When Ghislaine went past to fill up her water-skin at the spring, he growled at her, lifting his lip to show his huge fangs. She only smiled, and went past unbothered.

Dide spent the rest of the day leaning up against a tree, with Isabeau asleep in his lap in the shape of a long-haired

red cat. He sat still, content to soak up the sunshine and gently stroke Isabeau's soft fur, while Buba slept in a hollow of the tree above, and Dobhailen watched hungrily from a distance.

Once Thunderlily woke, refreshed from her long nap, she and Stormstrider wandered together through the forest. When they came back, she wore a crooked wreath of clover and daisies on her long pale hair, and she too was smiling. Donncan was surprised to feel a pang of jealousy, though he could not have explained why. Perhaps because Thunderlily had been his friend for so long, and he was resentful of this new closeness with Stormstrider. Or perhaps it was just because he would so have loved to have made Bronwen a wreath of meadow flowers, and to have kissed her smiling mouth as he crowned her in the dappled dimness of the forest.

As the sun sank down in the west, Cailean and Ghislaine together contrived a feast of herb-stuffed mushrooms, grilled vegetables, honey-tossed greens, and fresh fruit. Dide took his guitar out from its battered case and played and sang for them. His voice was deep and sweet and true, and Isabeau was not the only one to weep.

> "O fare you well, I must be gone
> And leave you for a while:
> But wherever I go, I will return,
> If I go ten thousand mile, my dear,
> If I go ten thousand mile.
>
> The raven that's so black, my dear,
> Shall change his color white;
> And if ever I prove false to thee,
> The day shall turn to night, my dear,
> The day shall turn to night."

Donncan found himself blotting his eyes on his sleeve more than once, and at one point had to get up and get himself a drink of water from the spring. Thunderlily wept too, and Stormstrider moved closer to her, and after a while took her hand in his. Cloudshadow raised herself up on her elbow and watched and listened with her face softened with pity and regret. Ghislaine lay back in Cailean's arms, and he bent his head and touched her brow gently with his lips, and smoothed back her flaxen hair with his hand, and she looked up at him wonderingly, her eyes filled with sorrow. Dide was the only one who seemed genuinely cheerful and at peace, his only regret being, he said, the lack of whisky with which to drink his own health.

Death was near, Donncan knew, and so they all sought to feel alive. Love, laughter, music, comradeship, these were all bright things to set against the dark days behind them, and the darker night ahead.

All too soon the concealing veil of night had fallen, and it was time for Dide to put down his guitar, and for the men to start the hard work of disinterring Brann's bones.

"Damn it, I wish I'd brought a shovel!" Dide said, strapping closed his guitar case with a little affectionate caress to the battered leather. "Ye'd think they'd keep one lying around the tomb, for just this sort o' occasion."

Isabeau managed a smile. She was growing increasingly edgy and restless and now she could barely keep still, twisting and tugging at her hair, pacing up and down, wringing her hands, and biting her lip till it bled. With her hair all in a tangle, and her shaking hands and nervous mannerisms, she seemed a very different woman to the calm, serene sorceress Donncan had always known and revered.

"We need a spade," Cailean said. He glanced at Isabeau. "Why do ye no' transform into an owl and go find us a farmhouse or croft?" he suggested. "When ye have found it, come and tell us and we'll see if we canna borrow some tools. Else we'll be here all night."

Isabeau nodded, trying to hide her relief. She knew she could have sent Buba to do the searching for her, but it was utterly unbearable being so close to Brann's grave. So, with a quick glance of apology at Dide, she turned herself into an owl and, together with Buba, went flitting away over the forest.

It was not long before they returned, hooting through the darkness. Donncan spread his wings and soared into the air, following them across the shadowy trees. He had not been able to fly for days, confined within the ring of stones, and he found his own joy and celebration of life in that swift, silent flight through the moonlit sky, the dark trees below him and the wind in his face smelling of summer. Above him stars blazed in the wheel of the sky, and the two moons hung low, one golden-red and full, the other silvery-blue and waning, and both so beautiful it made his heart ache. They shone on the distant sea, turning it into cloth-of-silver, and illuminated the abandoned hulk of Rhyssmadill, falling into ruins on its crag above the firth.

The owls led him to a small croft where warm light spilled from the windows onto the cobbled barnyard. A dog lifted its head and barked a warning, but Donncan spoke to it in its own language and let it sniff his hand and feet and legs as he hovered a few inches above the ground. At last the dog decided he was no enemy and returned to its threadbare blanket on the porch, while Donncan crept into the barn and gathered together as many tools as he could carry—shovels and pitchforks and mattocks—all the while directed by the soft hoots of the owls who crouched on the rafters overhead.

It was not such a pleasurable journey back to the mausoleum, struggling as he was with armloads of heavy tools, and the knowledge of what they planned to do with them. But Donncan flew on as swiftly as he could, knowing they could waste no more time. As he landed lightly, dropping the tools to the ground, Isabeau landed beside him and changed back to her own form.

"It is time," she said, eyes shining.

"Aye," Donncan said, suddenly feeling very afraid.

Isabeau laughed out loud, even as the tears flooded down her face. "Eà, give me strength," she prayed. "Eà o' the dark face, let me do what has to be done. Let me no' fail ye now." She was shaking all over, though with terror or exultation, it was impossible to tell.

All had wondered how they were to find Brann's grave when there was no marker to guide them, but they need not have feared. Isabeau could not keep away. As if a rope had been hooked into her heart and snapped tight, she was dragged to the very spot and began to dig there with her bare hands, snarling at Ghislaine when she sought to draw her away.

Buba hooted plaintively, but Isabeau would not change back into Owl. Laughing and weeping together, she dug side by side with the men, her clothes and hands filthy, her hair wild as a tortured willow tree.

It took hours of back-breaking work, digging through the heavy clay of the hillside until a mound of earth rose high to one side and a dark mouth yawned before them. Then Isabeau's desperately wielded spade clunked on something wooden.

"He is here, he is here!" she cried.

Dide leaned on his shovel, panting, disheveled, and afraid. "So it is time," he said.

She glanced up at him, and nodded. In the darkness, it was impossible to read her expression. Her eyes were shadowed hollows, her hair streaming wildly in the rising wind. "Time to raise him!" she cried.

"Time for me to die?"

She turned away from him, staring down at the coffin. "Yes," she answered faintly. "For he must have blood, if he is to live again."

Dissolved to Dust

Brann's bones lay gleaming fragile and white in the moonlight.

They had laid him out on the grass. He was a pitiful thing, all delicate bones and dust, with a grinning skull that did not seem real, like something created to scare small children in a pantomime.

"Do ye remember the spell?" Dide asked Isabeau.

"Every word," she answered, tearing her gaze from the bones to look at Dide. She was trembling all over.

Dide drew his dagger and presented it to her, hilt first.

"Dide . . ." she said.

"See ye soon," he said, and tried to smile.

She uttered a gasp, laughed, and took the dagger. It protruded from her hand, sharp and cruel and bright.

"Ye need to lie down," she said. "On him. Hip to hip, breast to breast, eye to eye."

For the first time Dide looked truly discomposed. He glanced down at the bones. "Really?"

Isabeau nodded.

"All right," he said, and began to lower himself to the ground.

"Naked," Isabeau said.

Dide paused for three long heartbeats, then, grim-faced, he stripped himself naked. He was a fine figure of a man, with broad shoulders and lean flanks, and smooth brown skin marked with a plunging arrow of dark hair from his breast to the thicket of hair at his groin.

His long hair was tied back with a leather thong. Isabeau stepped forward and ran her hand up his arm and then to his shoulder. She took his ponytail in her hand and cut it off with a single slash of the knife. He jerked uncontrollably, and then set his jaw, willing himself to stand immobile.

Their eyes met. He stood naked and vulnerable. His hair fell forward over his face in a curve. Isabeau stood, his ponytail in one hand, the knife in the other.

"Lie down," she said.

He obeyed. He was trembling.

She knelt beside him, and used his own hair as a cord to tie his wrist to the two thin bones of the skeleton's wrist. He lay stretched out upon the hard white skeleton, trying to fit his body to it like a lover, eye to eye, breast to breast, hip to hip. He was too tall, and his long, pale feet stretched out beyond the skeleton's, soles turned upward to the starry sky.

He looked up at Isabeau. The moonlight bleached his face of all color. His eyes were sunk in shadows.

"I trust ye," he said, his voice very faint and filled with fear. "I do. I trust ye, Beau."

Isabeau's breath caught in a sob. She bent, cupped her hand around the back of Dide's head in a tender caress, then cut his throat.

He gasped. Blood bubbled in the second mouth that Isabeau had cut for him, stretched like a clown's smile from ear to ear. For several long, dreadful seconds he struggled to breathe, to get away, to drag himself free.

Isabeau held the knife low, so the black bloody stain dribbled down into the skull's unhinged grin and, with many hesitations and hiccups of tears, chanted the words of the spell of resurrection.

Standing in thrall about the two lovers and the bones of the sorcerer stood Donncan and the Celestines and the witches, watching in utter shocked fascination as Dide's body rapidly rotted and decayed away into dust and ashes. As he dissolved before their eyes, flesh began to grow on the bones of the skeleton—red, raw flesh, and blue throbbing veins, and white, hard-packed muscle and delicate traceries of nerve and capillary, all finally wrapped in translucent veils of skin.

"There's naught left to heal," Ghislaine whispered. "We canna bring him back, 'cause there's naught left o' him at all."

It was true. Dide's flesh had dissolved to dust, and in his place lay Brann the Raven, tethered to a frame of bare bones with a cord of black hair.

Brann shook the bones off him impatiently, and they fell to the ground in a muddle. Dide's skull rocked on its hook and rolled free, to stare away into the darkness. The sorcerer stretched languorously, then stripped off the handcuff of hair, rolled and stood up. He was, like Dide, dark-eyed and dark-haired, but there all similarity ended. Brann the Raven was far older and heavier, with grey streaks at his temples, and heavy lines of dissoluteness weighing down his mouth.

Isabeau stood still close by, the knife now hanging limply in her hand, her eyes wide and shocked, unable to believe that there was nothing left of Dide but tumbled bones.

Brann smiled at her. "And ye're a beauty too," he said, "though a little auld for my taste. Never mind. Well done." Reaching forward his large, living hand, he drew Isabeau to him and kissed her on the mouth.

Isabeau stood, unresisting, for a second, then suddenly her knife flashed up. Brann laughed and sidestepped. "Naughty, naughty," he said and divested her of the knife. "Ye need prettier tricks than that to kill me," he said, and lifted the knife so he could lick its shining blade. "Mmmm, tasty."

They were all so numb with shock and horror they could

not move. Brann looked them all over with a sardonic eye.
In the brilliant moonlight he could see almost as well as by
day, though everything was sucked dry of color.

"Celestines. Excellent. Indeed, ye are a worthy acolyte,
my dear. Come, heal me, *uile-bheistean*!" Brann took three
strides towards Cloudshadow and Thunderlily, the dagger
raised threateningly. Donncan managed to lower his eyes,
and saw three slits in Brann's skin that oozed blood. He
could move no more than that. He realized suddenly that
this inertia was more than shock and horror and dread. He
was frozen in place, and by the looks on the faces of his
companions, they too were unable to lift a finger.

"Heal me, *uile-bheistean*! I have only a few minutes
afore the blood-magic fails. Come, lay your stinking hands
upon me and heal these slits in my side, else I'll gouge out
the little one's eyes, all three o' them."

Suddenly he had his arm about Thunderlily and his
knife point at her crystalline eye. Cloudshadow cried out
loud in pain and terror, the first time Donncan had ever
heard her mutter more than a faint hum in her throat. Thunderlily tried to shrink back, but she too was held immobile,
the sharp tip of the dagger only a hairbreadth away from
piercing her eye.

"Ye, Celestine, lay your hands upon me and heal me, or
by the dark fiends o' hell, your daughter will be blind!"

Cloudshadow lifted shaking hands and laid them upon
Brann's bare skin. At once the bleeding dagger cuts in his
breast and belly began to close over. Within seconds he
was healed.

Brann laughed aloud. "So I am alive again! Alive and
kicking! And it was a man in his prime whose blood raised
me, a man o' power. I feel young again, young and lusty."

He gazed down at Thunderlily shrinking back into the
embrace of his arm, the dagger still poised above her eye.
Brann laughed and pretended to shift his grasp, ready for
striking. Thunderlily sobbed and flinched back, Cloud-

shadow shrieked aloud and Stormstrider gave a low, guttural groan in his throat.

Brann considered them, smiling. "It may also be worth suffering *uile-bheistean* flesh to see the anguish on all your faces," he mused. "But no! Sweet human flesh for me tonight. Ye!" He looked at Ghislaine. "Ye're a pretty piece. Come kneel before me, sweetling, and pleasure me. I'd enjoy that."

Ghislaine did not move, and he crooked a finger. Step by awkward, jerking step, she moved forward and fell to her knees before him. Her eyes were huge and terrified, but she was unable to resist.

Inwardly Donncan writhed and shouted. He had Dide's daggers hanging on his belt. He had been supposed to leap forward and plunge them into Brann's black heart before it had had time to beat more than a few times. He longed to be able to reach down and seize them, and stab them into Brann's chest again and again. But he could not even twitch his finger.

How could they have been so stupid? Donncan thought. They knew Brann was a powerful sorcerer who had always taken pleasure in forcing others to his will. He was practiced in the arts of compulsion, while the witches of the modern-day Coven had no defenses against such an attack, having never been forced to face such a thing before. The only one powerful enough to have withstood him was Isabeau, and her will had been utterly enslaved by his before he had even been resurrected.

Ghislaine was fighting Brann's will desperately, turning her face away, digging her fingers into the ground in an attempt to stop them from rising and cupping the engorged penis of the man standing naked and smiling above her. He only laughed, and her hands jerked up, and her head jerked around, and her mouth jerked open in a silent scream. Brann forced himself into her mouth.

Cailean took a deep, gasping breath and then uttered

one single word, his voice hoarse with the effort. "Dob!"
he said.

The shadow-hound leaped forward like a streak of black
lightning. He leaped straight over Ghislaine's bowed head
and closed massive jaws about the sorcerer's throat. Brann
fell backwards, his scream cut short. Ghislaine flung herself backwards, coughing and retching, and Cailean
crawled to her, drawing her into his arms. She turned her
face into his shoulder, shaking with angry sobs.

The only sound was that of tearing flesh.

"Enough, Dob," Cailean said gently.

Dobhailen lifted jaws dripping with blood and gore, and
turned his head to Cailean, seeming to grin. Beneath him,
Brann lay still, his eyes staring in astonishment up at the
moons, his throat a bloody mess. The fingers of one hand
twitched.

Able to move again, Donncan gasped a deep breath,
moaned aloud, and covered his face with his hands.

All around him his companions did likewise. Thunderlily turned her face into Stormstrider's chest, sobbing.
Cloudshadow found herself caught up in Stormstrider's
strong arms too. Cailean lifted Ghislaine's face and kissed
her, and she brought her arms about his neck and kissed
him back, sobbing, "Thank ye, thank ye, thank ye." Isabeau lifted both bloodstained hands up, and stared at
them, mute, shivering, unable to catch her breath.

"Dide," she whispered. "Dide."

"We must bring him back," Donncan cried, scrambling
to his feet.

"How? How?"

"The spell o' resurrection. Quick, quick. Gather up his
bones. Is there anything else left o' him? Any blood? Any
dust? Gather it all together. We must be able to do it."

Isabeau fell to her knees in the moonlight, gathering up
the flimsy articulation of her lover's bones, reaching out
for his skull and scooping it up into her arms. "Is it too
late? Is it too late?" she wept.

Donncan found the knife, the blood upon its blade smeared and beginning to congeal. Then he found, with his heart bounding with excitement, the rope of black hair. He laid Dide's skeleton down upon Brann's body, and tied their wrists together. Brann's lifeblood had been pumping fiercely, but now it merely bubbled as the sorcerer fought to take one last breath. Donncan thrust the knife, still red with Dide's blood, into the pulsing wound at Brann's throat and slashed from side to side, chanting, low and fast and fierce, the words of the spell of resurrection. He remembered it well. He thought he would never forget it.

Brann's body began to rot away, and then rise and swirl about, like a little whirlwind of red dust caught up by the wind. It found Dide's bones and began to wrap itself about them, building his body again in frail layers of flesh and sinew and skin. Strangely, miraculously, Brann dissolved away and Dide materialized upon the bed of his bones.

He took a deep, shuddering breath. His eyes opened. He lifted one hand desperately, and they saw his throat still gaped wide. Thunderlily and Cloudshadow stumbled forward, ululating in their throats. They fell to their knees together, one on either side of his head, and laid their hands about his throat, fingers meshed tight about the dreadful wound, humming and weeping. The air throbbed with magic. Donncan's hair rose on his arms and a shiver ran down his spine.

Then the Celestines sat back, smiling through their tears, and lifted away their bloody hands. Dide sat up, pushing Brann's bones away violently.

Isabeau fell on her knees beside him, embracing him passionately, weeping. "Ye're alive, ye're alive. Thank Eà, thank Eà!"

Dide put her aside. He was frowning, his eyes wide and very black. He put up one hand to feel the scar on his throat. It was thin and white and swooped from the base of one ear to another.

"Dark," he said. His voice was hoarse and faint. "So dark. Where . . ."

"All is well," Isabeau said. "Ye are here with us again, ye're alive."

"Alive . . . Was I dead?"

"Aye. Do ye no' remember?"

"I was here, I remember that, and then . . ." He looked at Isabeau. "That's right. Ye killed me."

"I'm sorry, I'm sorry," she wept. "But all is well now. Ye're back, ye're alive."

"What do ye remember?" Ghislaine asked gently.

"It was dark . . . and the bones, I was tied to the bones. And then . . . Beau cut me . . . there was blood . . ." Dide put his hand up to his throat again. "I felt . . . a rushing. Like I was flying. I tried to look back, I wanted to see . . . But behind all was dark. All I could see was light . . . ahead o' me . . . like stars spinning. It was so bright . . ."

"What did ye see?" Ghislaine prompted him after several long moments.

He shook his head, fingering his scar again. "It hurt my eyes . . . I could hear music, I think . . . a song my mam used to sing . . . but I canna remember the words . . . and then they spoke to me. They said . . ."

"They?"

"Who?"

"What did they say?"

Everyone was leaning forward, listening intently. Dide shrank back from their vehemence. "I dinna ken . . . I dinna remember . . ."

"What happened then?" Cailean prompted.

"I came back. I was jerked. It hurt. Then I was here." As Dide spoke, his voice strengthened. He looked from one face to another, all bone-white in the moonlight.

"I'm so glad," Isabeau said, seizing his hand in hers and lifting it to her mouth. "We were so afraid we could no' bring ye back."

"Back . . ." he said, very quietly. "So that was it? I was dead?"

"Aye," Isabeau said, wiping her face with her free hand. "Ye were dead, but now ye are alive again. We saved ye." She laid down her head on Dide's hand. She could speak no more.

"Can we go home now?" Ghislaine asked with a quaver in her voice.

"We'll go at dawn," Cailean said. "I've no doubt it would be best if we all spent a week in bed first, but I'm sure I'm no' the only one that canna wait to shake the dust o' this graveyard off my feet."

"Och, aye!" Donncan agreed. "We'll go to Rhyssmadill. It's only a short walk to the castle from the Tomb o' Ravens, and there's staff there who'll be able to feed us and look after us. I'll be able to send a message to Lucescere right away."

To Bronwen, he thought. *My wife* . . . "We must time it very carefully," Cailean said, glancing at Stormstrider, who nodded gravely. "I guess it would be easiest to return on the night o' the full moon, which is two weeks from the time we left. That way we can be sure we do no' run into ourselves."

Ghislaine shuddered. "That would be horrible," she said in a low, intense voice.

It is an impossibility, Stormstrider said. *The universe could not endure such wrongness.*

"What would happen?" Cailean asked, his eyes alive with interest.

Stormstrider shook his head and shrugged expressively.

The center could not hold, Cloudshadow said. *The universe would splinter. We would find ourselves in another world, another universe, like unto ours but not ours.*

"Another universe?"

She nodded her head. *So our songs say, and they are wise.*

"Would we ken?" Cailean thought aloud. "Or would we wander around in another Eileanan, never realizing we've caused the world to split? I wonder how many times it has happened already? Are we the original world or only the facsimile? And if so, how many worlds have me in them, living another life? I wonder how many o' me there are? And how many Ghislaines?"

"Dinna!" Ghislaine cried.

"Only one," Cailean said, his eyes softening. "There could only ever be one Ghislaine."

They were much of a height, the young sorcerer and sorceress. Their eyes met, and color rose in Ghislaine's cheeks. In all the years Donncan had known her, he had never before seen the dream-walker blush.

"All this time-traveling has worn us out," he said. "Stormstrider is right. It is a wrongness. I am glad we can go home now."

"All I want is a long hot bath, and a fire, and a big bed with clean sheets," Ghislaine said.

"Sounds good to me," Cailean said, and she glanced at him and smiled in such a way that it was his turn to flush.

"We need to hide any sign that we've been here," Donncan said with a sigh, looking down at the clutter of bones and dirt and tools. "We'd best get to work right away, then I'll take the tools back to the farm, and we'll do our best to hide the grave again. Aunty Beau, do ye think ye are strong enough to encourage the grass and weeds to grow all over the dirt again?"

"I think so," Isabeau answered with a tremulous smile.

"Excellent. Let's get to work then."

They simply kicked Brann's bones back into the hole and threw his coffin down on top of him, then all set to with a will, to bury him deep under the earth again. Dobhailen once again proved immensely useful, digging the earth back into the hole joyfully.

Isabeau had got to her feet with a weary sigh, but Ghislaine stopped her with one hand on her arm. "Ye're exhausted," she said gently. "These past few weeks have been utter hell. Go with Dide, lie down and rest. There are enough hands here to get the job done."

Isabeau looked at her gratefully. "Thanks," she said, and taking Dide's hand, they went together to lie for the last time in the shelter of the hemlock tree, where moonlight struck down through the leaves and branches and made for them a canopy of mottled silver.

"I thought I had lost ye," Isabeau murmured. "I thought ye were dead and gone. Oh, Dide! I am so sorry, so very sorry!"

He did not speak, looking up through the formalized shape of leaf and twig.

"Will ye ever be able to forgive me?" she said.

"I dinna ken," he said at last.

There was silence between them.

"I ken I am no' being fair," he said. "I ken it was my idea to stand sacrifice for ye. But . . . but . . ."

"I am so sorry," she whispered. "I did my best, Dide. I fought and fought, but the spell . . . it was so strong. It almost broke me."

"I think it broke me," Dide said quietly.

She took his hand and kissed it passionately. "No," she whispered. "Ye are the strongest o' us all. Ye must no' say so. Ye must no' let Brann have any victory over us. We stood together, and we beat him, and he is dead again and in his grave, and ye are alive. Alive, Dide!"

"Alive," he repeated, and looked up at the vast and implacable beauty of the night sky. "Aye, I'm alive," he said, and stretched out his arms and legs, and suddenly smiled up at the sky. "What an adventure!" he cried. "Eà's eyes! I have died and I live again. How many other men can say that?"

"None I ken," Isabeau said, and curled her body against his, suddenly so desperately weary she thought she might swoon. Lying there, his shoulder under her cheek, his arm about her waist, both of them staring into eternity, Isabeau thought she felt the earth spin beneath her, and she was suddenly deliriously happy.

"Alive," Dide whispered.

CLOCK HANDS CREEPING

*"And even as wheels of clockwork so
turn that the first, to whoso noteth it,
seemeth still, and the last to fly . . ."*

—DANTE ALIGHIERI
Divina Commedia, 1314–1320

Chasing the Lord
of Fettercairn

⟨⟨⟨⟩⟩⟩

Rhiannon was flying through a cold, rough, rainy wind, her numb hands clenched in Blackthorn's mane, when she saw something ahead that made her raise her face in wonder and a little fear.

It was a blazing line of silver light, drawn across the horizon with a sure hand. It was like a slash in the under- belly of the gloomy sky spilling out quicksilver, or like a chink under a heavy grey curtain, allowing a glimpse of a realm made purely of light. Rhiannon had never seen such a thing before. It made her heart quicken and lift, and her eyes dilate. Sensing her sudden accelerated pulse, Black- thorn raised her head and neighed loudly. Rhiannon soothed her with one hand on her neck, even while she leaned forward, willing the horse to fly faster, to take her closer to that miraculous shining line of light.

They had already flown far that day. The past week had been one of constant motion, where they seemed to fly and fly, yet never gain any ground. The forest over which they flew all looked the same, and no matter how hard Rhian- non drove herself and her horse, they were never able to catch up with the lord of Fettercairn.

He seemed to have an uncanny instinct for knowing when she was near, and Rhiannon had been taken by sur-

prise more than once by a sudden flight of arrows out of
the dense forest below her. To have so caught her unawares, the archers must have been hidden in the treetops
waiting for her, and Rhiannon was forced to be more careful, terrified her beloved winged mare could be injured.

Finn and Jay had also found it hard to come anywhere
near the lord of Fettercairn. Their progress had been hampered by the persistently foul weather. So concentrated
was the rain and fog and hail upon their stretch of road that
they were all convinced the weather was being manipu-
lated by Lord Malvern to slow their pursuit.

"He can whistle the wind, that's for sure," Finn had said
gloomily, "we saw that at Lucescere Loch. Why no' mist
and rain too?"

Rhiannon had told them about the unnatural storms that
had plagued them in the Fetterness Valley, and how Lord
Malvern had once been an apprentice-witch at the Tower of
Ravens, where he would have learned the rudiments of
controlling the One Power.

"Our only chance is to get ahead o' him and stop him on
the road," Jay had said. "Do ye think ye can outfly him,
Rhiannon?"

"O'course," she had answered. "Blackthorn's as fleet as
the wind!"

So Rhiannon and Blackthorn had flown as fast as they
could through the storm and out the far side, to find much
fairer weather ahead, and signs of Lord Malvern's lead
stretching. So, armed with the Banrìgh's letter and precise
instructions from Finn and Jay, Rhiannon had roused the
men of a small mountain village called Sligsachen. They
had set up a stout barrier across the road, and guarded it
well with men armed with bows and arrows, pitchforks and
heavy staves.

Despite all their commands to stop, Lord Malvern's
men had simply whipped up their team of six huge
carthorses and plowed straight through the barrier, knocking over one of the local men and injuring him badly. Ge-

rard, the lord's librarian, was shot and fell from the dray, its iron-bound wheels rolling over him and crushing him into the ground. The archers swore at least another three arrows had found a mark, though evidently not accurately enough to kill. It made no difference. The lord galloped on, and Rhiannon found the dray abandoned some miles on, with signs that the lord's party had followed a goat track into the hills. The six carthorses had been abandoned too, without feed or water, their great shoulders and backs cruelly lacerated from the repeated lash of a whip.

Rhiannon did what she could for them, finding a stream where they could drink and she could wash their cuts and smear on some of the heal-all balm she carried in her pack. She used up the last of her oats to make a warm porridge that they all shared, and then she showed them the way back to Sligsachen. She was sure there was someone in the village who would have use for them, and feed them and care for them.

The carthorses went slowly and wearily, and she sighed, feeling the same heavy fatigue weighing down her bones. Blackthorn did not wish to fly any more, and Rhiannon was anxious not to miss any tracks that might show which way the lord of Fettercairn and his party were headed. So she led her exhausted horse up the steep path at an easy pace, her bluebird darting on ahead of her through the overarching trees, catching bugs in its beak.

As the light faded away into an early dusk, Rhiannon found a dead man lying on the side of the goat track, and recognized the lord's valet, Herbert. They had not even taken the time to lay him out neatly, or cover his face. He lay tumbled on the side of the track, an arrow still protruding from his back. Rhiannon did not like dead people. She left him as he lay, telling herself the imploring voice she heard in her ears was just her imagination.

She had found plenty of evidence of Owein and Olwynne along the way—a discarded silver shoe, some long red feathers from the prionnsa's wings caught in the

bushes, scraps of their fine satin clothes, a bloody footprint
on a stepping stone across a stream. She was relieved to
know they still lived, having feared the lord of Fettercairn
would grow weary of their dogged pursuit and kill them
out of hand.

Two days later, the track led her out onto another road,
a wider thoroughfare with waystones engraved with a large
R marking out the miles. Here she found further proof of
the lord's utter ruthlessness. Evidently the villains had
come across a peddler, for Rhiannon found his body
thrown down by the side of the road amidst a clutter of pots
and pans, spades, bolts of cloth, unraveling coils of ribbon,
and the poor, pathetic corpse of a little black-and-white
dog.

Her stomach twisting with revulsion, Rhiannon straightened the peddler's limbs and covered him with a length of
fine red twill, tucking the little dog up beside him. It was all
she had time to do. She was now even more determined to
catch up with her enemy and bring him to some kind of justice. The death of the little dog had angered her the most. It
was so unnecessary.

On she flew, catching up with the lord by that afternoon.
The peddler's stolen caravan was being pulled by a fat,
spotted pony who had never felt the lash of the whip in her
life. Now she was galloping for dear life, Kennard laying
about her ears with the whip, the caravan bouncing madly
behind them. Dedrie and Piers both sat up on the seat beside Kennard, clutching on as tightly as they could, while
Jem and Ballard hung off the back. Of the others, there was
no sign. Rhiannon could only guess they were all inside the
caravan.

Careful not to be seen, Rhiannon wheeled away and
urged Blackthorn on to greater speed. Weary as she was,
the mare responded magnificently and Rhiannon came that
evening into a fairly large town, called Mullrannoch, an
hour or two ahead of Lord Malvern. She sent her bluebird
with a note to Finn and Jay, telling them where she was,

then went to find the town reeve. He agreed to barricade the road and find men willing to arm it. It took much of the afternoon, Rhiannon determined that this time it would be stout enough to withstand any assault, and then they all waited in the rainy darkness, straining their ears for any sound of hooves. The night plodded past with no sign of any peddler's caravan, or any other traveler. The men were all understandably angry and sarcastic, having spent the night shivering in a nasty wet wind, but Rhiannon begged them to continue standing guard. In the thin, grey dawn, they at last heard hooves approaching fast. The reeve raised his pistol, calling out fiercely, "Halt! Halt, I say, in the name o' the Banrìgh!"

The hooves clattered to a halt and then, to her dismay, Rhiannon heard her name being called. It was Finn and Jay and their soldiers they had bailed up, all wet through, exhausted and in as foul a temper as the reeve. Somehow the lord had escaped in the night.

Everyone was so frustrated and weary, they retired to the village inn for hot porridge laced with whisky, and mugs of steaming tea by the fire. Finn the Cat was clearly unwell; she spent ten minutes or more loudly throwing up in the privy, then sat morosely nursing her cup, and snarling at her husband every time he opened his mouth. Wet through, the black elven cat sat on the hearth, its tufted ears laid flat on its skull, licking itself dry and glaring with slitted eyes at anyone foolhardy enough to try to warm themselves by the hastily stoked-up fire. Rhiannon was careful to keep her bluebird on her shoulder. The evil-tempered elven cat had already stalked the little bird as it fluttered about the common room, and had managed to snatch a mouthful of blue tail feathers.

Rhiannon had hardly slept in three days, and the floor was rolling strangely under her feet. Jay quietly paid for a room each for her and his wife, who swore at him when he insisted on taking her up to bed, but nonetheless went willingly enough in the end. Rhiannon did not blame her. The idea of cuddling up in a warm bed and listening to the rain streaming down the windows sounded like bliss to her too. Blackthorn was snug enough in the stable, with two young grooms overwhelmed with the privilege of caring for her, and Rhiannon was simply too tired and dispirited to even think of trying to find out how Lord Malvern had got past them.

The reeve came in the miserable dusk of that evening to tell them. Rhiannon and Finn had both slept most of the day and were breaking their fast by the warmth of a fire in the common room. It continued nasty outside, with hail battering the old inn and clouds hanging close about the village. The reeve was flushed with self-importance, standing dripping on the hearth with his legs apart and his hand on his sword. The miscreants had apparently abandoned the horse and caravan at the first sight of the town lights, he said portentously, and circled around the village on foot. They were long gone now.

Finn wept to think how worn out the poor prionnsa and banprionnsa must be, soaked to the skin, squelching through the mud of the fields after the punishing pace the lord of Fettercairn had set those past few days.

"Oh, Eà grant them strength," she cried, "and forgive me for failing them!"

"Finn," Jay said placatingly.

Finn crossed her arms over her stomach, her hazel eyes bright with angry tears. "O' all the bad timing!" she cried.

"Dinna say that, dearling. No time is bad timing for us, and it is no fault o' the babe's that the weather has been so bad, and Lord Malvern's plans so well laid."

Rhiannon looked from one to the other.

Finn looked cross. "Still they elude us though! I should've caught them by now. It's ridiculous! More than a week in the chase and still they keep giving me the slip. It's no' good enough."

"We will catch up with them, never ye fear, my darling," Jay said. "It is better that we stop and rest and think about our next move than we keep running around the countryside in circles. Ye were exhausted and so was Rhiannon. Let's take another night to rest up, and in the morning, when we are all fresh, we'll think about what to do next."

Finn gave a harsh, ironic laugh. "Fresh? In the morning? Me?"

Jay smiled at her. "Go to bed, Finn. Ye'll feel better after a good night's rest, I promise ye. They canna have gone far in this blaygird weather. In the morning we'll have fresh horses and locals to advise us on the roads, and Rhiannon to fly ahead and scout. We'll catch up with them tomorrow, I promise."

Yet when they rose in the morning, refreshed and eager to set off, it was only to find that someone had spent the night stealing or slaughtering every horse in the village, including Finn and Jay's own weary mounts. Only Blackthorn had escaped the massacre, by knocking down her midnight assailant and escaping on wing. Lord Malvern's coachman, Kennard, was found unconscious in the straw of her stall, the two young grooms lying nearby in spreading pools of blood, their throats slit.

Rhiannon was distraught. She had been so weary that she had slept heavily, waking in the late morn in exactly the same position she had fallen asleep. She remembered nothing of the night, not a dream, not a sound, not a feeling of disquiet. All the soldiers had slept as heavily, and Finn and Jay, and the innkeeper and his wife too, and no one could help suspecting their food or drink had been doctored. They had all eaten from the same pot of vegetable stew, but who would have had the audacity to slip into the inn's kitchen and drug the stew with so many people bustling about?

"Dedrie," Rhiannon said darkly.

"So bold," Finn said, half-admiringly. "What a risk to run! What if ye had seen her?"

"She would probably have slit my throat like those poor lads," Rhiannon answered.

"Aye, why did they have to kill them?" Finn asked, her mouth twisting. "A quick knock on the head . . ."

"They seem to like killing," Rhiannon said.

Jay was white with anger. "This laird o' Fettercairn has much to answer for," he said quietly. "We must stop him! There is no point us trying to catch up with him now, I think. He has horses and we do no'. We come close to the sea now. He will have a ship waiting for him, probably in one o' the hundreds o' little coves on the Ravenshaw coast. Finn, ye and I will backtrack to the river and get ourselves to Dùn Gorm. The Banrìgh will have made sure *The Royal Stag* is armed and provisioned and ready to go. We'll see if we canna catch him on the open sea."

"Wonderful," Finn said with a groan. "A good dose o' seasickness is just what I need."

"Ye can stay in Dùn Gorm," Jay said, looking troubled.

"Stay behind? No, thank ye! I'll be just fine. The sea air will do me good."

"Well, then, if ye're sure . . ."

"Sure I'm sure. I'll scry to Nina right now and let her ken our plans," Finn said. "She will get a message to the palace for us."

"What o' me?" Rhiannon asked. "Should I no' fly after them, see where they go?"

"Aye, that would be best," Jay said. "Do no' put yourself in danger, though, Rhiannon. These are cruel, ruthless men, they'd have no hesitation in shooting ye out o' the sky."

"They could never catch me," Rhiannon said scornfully, and was rewarded by Finn's quick nod.

"That's the spirit, lass," the sorceress said. "I wish I had the time to teach ye to scry, though. It'd be good if ye could send us word o' where the blaygird laird is heading."

"I can send my wee birdie again," Rhiannon said.

"Goblin almost caught it last time," Finn said. "It thinks it looks like a tasty mouthful indeed."

"There are homing pigeons at Rhyssmadill," Jay said.

"Send a message to the garrison there, and they'll make sure Captain Dillon hears any news. And ye can leave a message for us at the Black Sheep Inn in Dùn Gorm."

"Ah, the Black Sheep Inn," Finn said, her eyes brightening. "Best ale in Dùn Gorm."

"No' that ye'll be drinking any o' it," Jay said.

Finn sighed.

Rhiannon had found herself rather reluctant to leave the couple in Mullrannoch and fly off by herself into the dismal weather. She had had enough of being always wet and cold and tired, and so many hours spent on horseback had chafed her inner thighs badly. Blackthorn was not happy to leave the warm, comfortable stable either. She had spent most of the night flying about in the rain, trying to avoid the arrows of the lord of Fettercairn's men, and doing her best to rouse Rhiannon by neighing shrilly outside the inn. She was most disgruntled at being led outside into the rain and having the familiar weight of Rhiannon's saddlebags thrown over her withers. Rhiannon had to talk to her quite severely before she stopped sidling about, tossing her head and hurrumphing her displeasure.

All day they flew and galloped, flew and galloped, stopping only to rest and eat in short stretches, and to make sure they were still following the lord of Fettercairn's trail. He was driving his party hard, and Rhiannon was not surprised to find another old man lying beside the roadside six hours past Mullrannoch. It was the old harper, Borden, and he still lived, though he looked grey and ill. He looked up as Blackthorn landed near his head, and said wheezily, "Ah, the thigearn. Ye will have to fly fast to catch them, lass. They are riding to the very devil."

"Are ye hurt?" she asked, kneeling beside him warily.

He tried to laugh. "Hurt? Nay. Sick and auld and weary, aye. I'm too auld for all this nonsense."

"I do no' call dead men and boys nonsense," Rhiannon said coldly, thinking of the two young, lighthearted grooms who had died so unnecessarily, and the old peddler with his little dog.

"Nay," he said. "None o' it was nonsense. If only I had kent . . ."

"Kent what?"

His rheumy eyes swam with tears. "If only I had kent where my laird's experiments with death would take us. I never meant to end up like this, a murderer and kidnapper, and a traitor to my rìgh. I wish . . ." He fell silent.

"Why did ye do it?" Rhiannon asked. "Ye do no' seem an evil man."

"He promised we would raise my wife," the old man said sorrowfully. "I dinna ken it would take more than a quarter o' a century afore we learned how. By then it was too late. We had done so many dreadful things, killed so many people, desecrated so many graves, all in our hunger to bring back the dead. We could no' stop then. What was it all for, if we were to stop then?"

"Making sure no one else died?"

"But by then my boy was caught up in it too. If I had betrayed my laird, if I had tried to get away, my boy would've suffered. They hang people for necromancy, do ye ken?"

"Aye, I ken," Rhiannon said coldly. "And hang, draw and quarter them for treason."

"Aye, ye would ken, wouldna ye? How did ye get away? My laird was sure they'd hang ye."

Rhiannon thought of Lewen, who had wrapped his body about the clapper of the bell so it would not ring. She smiled, and did not answer.

The old man rested his head on the iron-cold ground again. "Give it up," he said wearily. "My laird will no' be thwarted. What are these MacCuinns to ye? Let my laird have his way and raise his brother again, and his wee nephew too, and then it will all be over."

"The dead are dead, and should stay so," Rhiannon said tersely. She bent and heaved the old man into her arms. Frail as he was, he was still heavy and awkward.

"What do ye do?" he asked in surprise.

"Ye think I can leave ye to die by the side o' the road?" she said angrily.

"But . . . but why?"

"Ye may be a very stupid auld man, but I still canna just fly on and leave ye to die," she answered. "Do no' squirm so, else I'll drop ye!"

She managed to fling him over Blackthorn's back, and then, cursing her own stupidity, led her mare along the rutted road until they reached a crofter's cottage. Depleting the royal purse even further, she paid the crofter and his wife to feed and shelter him, and asked them to send a message to the local reeve to come and take him into custody.

By then it was dark again, and she gladly accepted a bowl of hot bean and potato stew from the crofter, and a bed in the dry straw of the barn, curled up against Blackthorn with the mare's wing tucked over her. She rose in the dawn, shared a bowl of porridge with the crofter and his wife, checked on Borden the Harper and was glad to see him with a better color, then once again grimly wrapped herself up in her cloak and went out into the cold, damp, misty morning.

"If only it would stop raining!" she said to Blackthorn, who shook her mane and whickered in agreement.

That day passed much the same as the one before, though the wind was fresher and more boisterous, and the road was swallowed up in forest once more. It was easy enough to follow the trail left by Lord Malvern and his party, for their horses were weary now and having to plod through deep mud. Rhiannon was able to soar high above the forest and follow the road's thin line through the trees.

Which was where she was when she first saw the gleaming line of light on the horizon, far brighter than anything she had ever seen before. It dazzled her eyes, so she could hardly bear to look at it, yet she could not wrench her gaze away.

As Rhiannon came closer, she saw it was water that gleamed so brightly, a great swath of water like a robe of grey satin edged richly with silver thread, where somewhere far distant, the storm clouds ended and sunlight was reflected at the sky's edge. The water stretched as far as Rhiannon could see. This was, she realized, the sea. Rhiannon had not realized it was as vast as the sky. It smelled as though it was alive, like a fish, or a woman, and moved sinuously, like the silky scaled skin of an immense snake. Or so she thought, until she came closer yet, and realized it moved in a rush and a fume, heaving, seething, sighing and foaming, splashing and spraying and swirling. It was grey, darker than the sky, and stormier. It made her want to run, or dance, or laugh out loud, yet the very immensity of it, the surge and grab of it, frightened her. She brought Blackthorn down onto a curve of rocks and pebbles under a dark overhang of cliff, amazed at how big the waves were, and the thunder and roar they made on the stones.

The sea, she thought. *At least I have seen the sea.*

She was anxious to try to rescue Owein and Olwynne before the lord set sail, for the idea of leaving solid land behind her and flying out across that deep immensity was terrifying. Once they took to the wing over the ocean, there was nowhere to rest, nowhere to sleep, nowhere to land if body or heart grew too weary.

So Rhiannon dragged herself up onto Blackthorn's back once more, and the mare sighed and snorted and pawed the ground discontentedly, but at last stretched out her wings and took to the air. They flew along the coast, looking in every bay and cove, but there was no sign of the lord of Fettercairn, nor of Olwynne and Owein.

It was growing dark. The waves grew greener and gloomier, and still Rhiannon flew along the wild, rocky seascape, looking, looking, but the coast was as wild as if no one had ever lived here.

Then the setting sun slipped down from under the heavy-bellied clouds and suddenly the sea was transformed. It gleamed and shone all around, golden as coins, and the curve of the wave on the shore was pale green and translucent as glass. Rhiannon came down onto a headland, sitting and watching until the gold was all gone and the sea was violet as dusk and the air was filled with the white wings of screaming seabirds. She sat and watched until the sea was swallowed by darkness and there was only the smell and the sound of it. She sat and watched until the red moon rose and built a ladder into the heavens. Only then did she stir and sigh, and realize she would have to make camp in the darkness. She did not care. Rhiannon had finally seen the sea.

Islay-on-the-Cliff

❧❧❧

Olwynne moaned in her sleep.

In her dreams, she was walking down an overgrown path. Thorns snagged in her dress and tore it. Mist swirled up around her legs. It smelled dank and old. All around her old gnarled yew trees loomed out of the gloom. She came out onto a hillside. Before her yawned an open grave. Olwynne's steps faltered and dragged, but she forced herself to walk on. Dread weighed on her limbs and froze her heart.

In the grave was a skeleton. It was dressed in the tattered remains of a satin bridesmaid's dress. As Olwynne stared down at it, transfixed, it turned its hollow eyes and looked up at her, raising one bony hand beseechingly.

Olwynne screamed. Screaming, she woke herself. She sat bolt upright, her hands pressed hard against her chest, where her heart was pounding like a blacksmith's hammer. Despite the cold, she was drenched in perspiration.

"Olwynne?" Owein whispered. "What's wrong? Are ye all right?"

"I dreamt . . . I dreamt . . ." Olwynne said, and could not go on. Too often, the worst of her dreams had come true. It was terrifying to think she was dreaming her own death. Not all dreams tell of the future, she told herself. Some are only phantoms thrown up from the deep, a vision of our most dreadful fears.

"Don't worry," Owein reassured her, shifting closer to her so he could drape an arm and a wing over her. "They'll be close behind us. Any time now, we'll hear them come bursting in, a whole regiment o' Blue Guards, blasting away with their fusils."

"It's been nine days," Olwynne said in despair. "Nine whole days. Surely . . ."

"They'll have Finn the Cat on our trail," Owein said. "Ye ken Finn always finds what she seeks. This blaygird laird is a slippery bugger, that's all. They'll be drawing the net tight about him, never ye fear."

Olwynne swallowed a sob and pressed closer to her twin. They were both lying on hard boards in a dark hold that smelled unpleasantly of bilge water. The captors had cut their bonds, giving their badly chafed wrists some relief, but there was no chance of escape. Owein and Olwynne had already crawled over every inch of the hold, which was piled high with sacks and barrels and coils of rope, but contained nothing they could use as a weapon. Not even an old lantern or a box of nails. It was difficult to keep track of time in the darkness, but Olwynne did not think she had slept for long. It had been late when they had been thrown in here, and by now the night must be almost over. They would sail at dawn, she knew.

The last week had been one long horror. Bound and often gagged, they had been hustled from one stolen conveyance to another, or pushed out and forced to walk miles and miles over rough tracks that bruised and cut her bare feet. Sometimes they were thrown over a horse's back and bounced until they were retching as the horses were whipped along at a cruel pace. Other times they were forced to hide in thorny thickets as soldiers searched for them, knives at their throats and knees in the smalls of their backs, pushing them into the ground. Once she had seen the black winged horse soaring away over the forest, and Olwynne had not been able to help making a small sound and gesture, whether of hope or hopelessness, she hardly

knew. One of the men had seen, and they had got off the
path and hidden until Rhiannon and her horse were long
gone.

Somehow the lord of Fettercairn had managed to keep a
step ahead of their pursuers. Olwynne remembered that he
had once been a witch-sniffer, a Seeker who had hunted
down witches and faeries for Maya. That finely honed
extrasensory perception was now being used to avoid capture, and Olwynne was filled with a sense of utter despair.
She did not share Owein's confidence that they would be
rescued in time.

Snuggled under the warmth of Owein's wing, Olwynne
was just dozing off again when a faint thrumming in the
boards beneath her roused her. She sat up, both hands flat
to the floor, feeling the ship come to life. Owein sat up too,
and she heard his sharp indrawn breath.

Timbers creaked. Sails flapped. Men called to each
other, and the ship began to sway, gently at first, then more
strongly as the wind filled the sails. Tears welled up in Olwynne's crusted eyes. She had been to sea often enough in
her father's great ship, *The Royal Stag*, to know what the
sounds meant. They had raised anchor, and were setting
sail.

They'll never catch us now, she thought, and the tears
seeped from under her eyelids and ran down her face.

Rhiannon had suffered a cold, uncomfortable night on the
beach, too afraid to light a fire in case it drew unwanted attention. She had gnawed on a hard heel of stale bread and
drunk the last of her water, cursing herself for wasting so
much time staring at the sea instead of finding a better
campsite, with a spring of fresh water.

She had been woken in the middle of the night by the
inrush of the tide, and would have drowned if it was not for
Blackthorn. Cold and wet and utterly furious with herself,
she had managed to grab her gear and leap onto Black-

thorn's back, the black water swirling around her knees.
The winged mare had soared up into the night sky, and they
had found a safe landing place on the cliff-top, more from
luck than anything else. Rhiannon had spent the rest of the
night huddled under Blackthorn's wing, shivering in her
damp clothes and wishing she was snuggled up in a warm
bed, firelight flickering on the walls, Lewen's knee flung
across her leg.

At first light they were aloft, Rhiannon determined to
find Lord Malvern and stop him somehow. She unslung her
crossbow and hung it from the pommel of her soft saddle,
even though the idea of shooting a man dead made her feel
strange and shivery inside. Rhiannon had killed once before, and it haunted her still, as did the ghosts of all the
people she had seen die since—Bess Balfour with her
crooked face and imploring eyes, a mad girl who had murdered her tiny baby and been hanged for it, Shannley the
groom who she had knocked out with a chamber pot and so
helped him on the way to the gallows, the massive shape of
Octavia casting its hideous shadow on her dreams. Those
ghosts had been with her a while now, and to their gallery
were added new ones—an old valet dressed all in black, a
peddler and his faithful little dog, and two eager-faced
grooms. It was no use Rhiannon telling herself it was not
her fault. She felt she was to blame, for not shooting Lord
Malvern dead when she had had the chance. She had tried,
during that mad chase the first time Lord Malvern had kidnapped Roden, but his seneschal Irving—the father of his
present seneschal—had flung himself in front of his master and taken the arrow meant for Lord Malvern. If she had
not hesitated for just a scant few seconds, the whole dreadful affair would have ended there, at the gates of Fettercairn Castle. She would not hesitate next time if the
opportunity presented itself. She was a soldier now, in service to the Banrìgh, she told herself, and Lord Malvern
was an enemy of the Crown.

The coast of Ravenshaw was riddled with countless tiny

bays and coves, each hidden by steep cliffs. Rhiannon flew along the edge of the cliffs, the rain in her eyes, the bluebird darting ahead of her. Then she felt a rush of wind at her back, strong enough to almost knock her from the saddle. Rhiannon felt the chill and tingle of it, and knew it was an enchanted wind. She urged Blackthorn on, bending close over the mare's neck, gripping her knees tight. The wind rushed past, blowing her hair forward, cutting through her clothes. Blackthorn fought to keep her wings steady.

There was a high singing sound that Rhiannon had never heard before, and the slap of canvas and rope. Then, from a deep hidden cove directly before them, a ship suddenly sailed out into the open. It was a big, ocean-going craft, with three tall masts and another lying almost flat at the front of the boat. Rhiannon had never seen such a big ship before. It was laden with sails, both square and triangular, and they bellied out, filled with the enchanted wind that streamed sure and strong past Rhiannon.

She cried aloud in dismay and seized her crossbow, firing arrow after arrow into the ship. A few tore the sails and made them flap wildly. One caught a man in the rigging, and he tumbled down and fell into the sea. No one made any attempt to rescue him, and Rhiannon was relieved to see him bob up and begin to swim strongly for shore. Rhiannon wheeled Blackthorn about and swooped down low over the ship. She saw Dedrie turn her face up to her and point, and the big bodyguard Ballard fired an arrow at her, which Blackthorn deftly dodged. Then she saw Lord Malvern standing up on the high poop deck, a cloak wrapped about him, his raven perched on the rail behind him. He stared up at her and then shouted an order to one of the ship's crewmen. Rhiannon put her last arrow to her bow and bent forward, taking careful aim.

There was a gigantic bang and a huge puff of black smoke. Rhiannon flinched, and instinctively Blackthorn flung out her wings and wheeled away. It was sheer luck that saw her turn to the left and not to the right. An iron cannonball came whizzing up from the ship, barreling through the air at incredible speed. It missed Blackthorn by only a few scant feet, enveloping them all in foul-smelling smoke. Rhiannon was shocked and astonished. She had never seen cannons before, or even heard of them, and had no idea what had just occurred. There was another bang, and then another, and Rhiannon took Blackthorn soaring up into the sky. Below them, the ship turned and gathered speed, and Rhiannon watched it go, clenching her jaw in bitter self-recrimination.

It was her urgent desire to speed after them, but her quiver was empty of arrows, her water-bag was dry, and her supplies almost all gone. Common sense prevailed, and Rhiannon brought Blackthorn's head about and headed back to land.

She found a small fishing village a few miles down the coast, called Islay-on-the-Cliff. It was a rough collection of huts, built halfway up the cliffs, with a narrow path down to the cove, guarded by a stone wall and a sturdy gate. It had an inn with one big common room opening onto the steep cobbled street, and one shop where anything and everything could be bought. Prudently keeping Blackthorn well out of sight, Rhiannon went into the shop and replenished her supplies.

The shopkeeper was amazed to see her. "I havena seen a strange face hereabouts in close on a year and then so many in the last few days! What brings ye here, lass?"

"I travel on the Banrìgh's service," Rhiannon said, "and I'd be most interested to hear all ye can tell me about any other strangers in the area."

"On the Banrìgh's service! Ye mean the young lass, the Ensorcellor's daughter? Och, that's a sorry tale! To have her wedding day ruined like that, her father-in-law murdered and her husband stolen. Is there any word o' the young Rìgh? Is it true the whole family was taken? We could scarce believe our ears when we heard the news!"

The shopkeeper was all agog, and Rhiannon was sorry
to have declared herself. She wanted the news, though, and
so she did her best to answer the shopkeeper's questions
and to impress upon him the importance of telling her anything out of the way.

The ship had been hired elsewhere, she learned, and
brought to this part of the coast a full two weeks ago. The
crew had grown bored with waiting about and had visited
the Islay Inn a few times. They had had plenty of money to
throw about, but had been a rough nasty lot with quick
tempers and a few too many weapons for the villagers' liking. The innkeeper had been careful to keep his pretty
daughter out of their way, and once had had to break up a
knife fight between two of the men over a dice game.

"Did they give any clue as to where they were heading?" Rhiannon asked as she hesitated between a string of
smoked herring and a hank of bacon. Anything she took
with her had to be carried, and Rhiannon was so hungry
everything looked good.

The shopkeeper shrugged. "Ye'd have to ask Martin up
the inn. They dinna come in here at all, Eà curse them. I
could've done with some new customers, but their ship was
well provisioned, I believe, and they wanted naught."

So once Rhiannon's saddlebags were again bulging, and
her quiver filled with what she considered very poor quality arrows, being used to Lewen's finely balanced and
beautifully fletched creations, she trudged up the street to
the inn.

Martin-up-the-inn was a big, burly man with a red face
and a shrewd eye. He had kept a close eye on his unruly
guests, "no' liking," he said, "the jib o' them." When Rhiannon asked him if they had given any clue to where they
were sailing, he nodded and said, "Aye. They made much
o' the fact they'd be leaving this cold, benighted coast and
sailing to warmer waters. They were off to the Fair Isles,
they said, and indeed I thought it the place for them, it
being the haunt o' pirates and cutthroats still."

"The Fair Isles," Rhiannon repeated, and he nodded and jerked his thumb at a map that had been rather crudely painted on the wall behind him. It showed all the crooks and hooks of the Ravenshaw coast, and every rock, reef and island all about.

"Painted by my great-grand-dai," Martin said proudly, "and what any foreigner wouldna give to have a copy."

Rhiannon examined it closely. She could see the six islands named the Fair Isles, far off to the south, separated from the coast of Eileanan by a very large stretch of sea, painted bright blue and populated by an improbably large sea-serpent. Her heart sank. She did not think Blackthorn could fly so far without coming down to land at some point.

"How far to sail there?" she asked, wondering if the map was to scale and guessing it was not, considering the size of the sea-serpent.

"Three days with a fair wind," Martin said with a shrug. "It's rare for the wind hereabout to be fair, though."

Rhiannon tried to calculate in her head how long it would take for Blackthorn to fly the same distance, but it was impossible for her to know. She had never learned to count any higher than twenty, the number of her fingers and toes, and the books she had been brought to read in Sorrowgate Prison had all been storybooks and histories, not mathematical textbooks. Lewen would have been able to estimate the distance and time in a flash, she thought to herself unhappily, and wished once again that he was here, to lend her his strength and wit and common sense.

She saw another village marked on the map, about the length of her first knuckle away from Islay-on-the-Cliff. When asked, Martin told her it took about half a day's walking to get there, which Rhiannon thought she could probably fly in a few hours. So, using her forefinger to measure, she plotted out a rough course for herself on the map, jumping from rock to island to reef. Martin was in-

valuable. He knew every mark on the map and was able to
tell her their names and properties.

"Och, aye," he said, "we call those the Demon's Teeth.
They're only uncovered at low tide, and even then they're
dangerous indeed, the waves break over them pretty
steadily. It's high summer, though, and the tides are at their
lowest. Ye couldna take a boat into them, though."

"What about this one?" Rhiannon asked.

"Aye, that's a fair rock, we go there in summer to gather
the kelp and hunt sea otters. It's a fair stretch from here, a
day in one o' our wee boats. We stay there overnight,
there's a spring o' fresh water, and plenty o' redfruit and
other things to eat."

"What's this over here?"

"They call that Sailors' Ruin," Martin answered. "The
number o' ships that run aground on that auld rock! It's
low, ye see, especially in autumn when the tides run high,
and if ye are no' looking out for it, it's easy to miss. But
why do ye need to ken all this, lassie . . . I mean . . . ma'am?
If ye're wishing to chase after those pirates, surely ye'll be
taking the quickest sea route, no' exploring all these auld
rocks?"

"I like to ken what lies ahead," Rhiannon said.

"Aye," he said, nodding his head wisely. "Well, then,
this wee island here may interest ye. It's small but it's high,
and it's got fresh water on it, which is rare enough. We call
it Muckle Roe, Eà ken why."

Rhiannon measured the distance with her eye, tried to
fix its position in her mind, and thanked Martin for his
help. She had been tormented during their conversation by
the rich smell of fish stew wafting from the kitchens. So
she ordered a bowl of it, and a mug of weak ale, and asked
Martin for some pen and paper. Very laboriously she
wrote: "Ship gone Fair Iyell. Magic wind. I fly after. Rhiannon." She always liked writing her name. It looked like
a horse in full gallop, mane and tail flying. It was the only

word she could write with full confidence, and she liked to give it a little flourish at the end.

She folded the slip of paper over, sealed it with wax and the seal-ring she had been given by the Banrìgh, and gave it to Martin with a coin, asking him to make sure it got to the garrison at Rhyssmadill. Then she ate up her stew with great enjoyment, swallowed down her ale, shouldered her saddlebags, and left Islay-on-the-Cliff behind her, having done all she could to make her task easier.

Blackthorn was grazing in the forest, the bluebird swooping about her, catching the insects she stirred up from the grass. The winged mare raised her head at the sight of Rhiannon and whickered in greeting. Rhiannon had bought a small sack of oats for her, and gave her half of them, having no desire to carry any extra weight on their journey over the sea. She then repacked her saddlebags so the weight was equally distributed, and led Blackthorn to the stream to drink her fill. After that, she could think of no other reason to linger, and so mounted up and rode Blackthorn to the top of the cliff. It had stopped raining, but the sea was rough and wild. The wind dragged at her hair and at Blackthorn's mane. The little bluebird, finding it too strong, came down to rest on Rhiannon's shoulder. She tucked the little bird inside her pocket, with a cob of corn to peck at, and fastened the flap securely. She did not want to risk Bluey.

Then Rhiannon took a deep breath. Far off, she could see the tiny white sails of the lord of Fettercairn's ship. Otherwise, the ocean stretched as far as she could see, limitless, fathomless, wild.

"Let's fly," she muttered, and urged Blackthorn into a gallop, straight at the cliff's edge.

Iseult lay in her bed, her eyes shut, tears oozing under her red, swollen lids. Although it was morning, her room was dim, for the curtains were pulled tight across the windows. The air smelled of rotting flowers.

Iseult's grief was like a giant boulder that lay on her chest, pinning her down. All her energy was taken in just breathing. She did not want to thrust the boulder away, because to do so would be to lose all that she had left of Lachlan. Instead she hugged the boulder to her, allowing it to press her down, crushing her ribs, her lungs and heart, her stomach. It hurt even to roll over, to find a dry spot on her pillow in which to press her aching eyes. So she lay as still as she could, and let the hours and the days slip past in a daze that was not quite sleeping, not quite swooning, not quite living.

She heard someone rap on the door to her sitting room, and then heard the low murmur of voices as her lady-in-waiting answered. Iseult did not open her eyes. She had given strict instructions that she was not to be disturbed, not by anyone.

"Resting?" a familiar voice roared. "What do ye mean she's resting? Wake her up."

Iseult pressed her hands over her eyes. *Go away, Father,* she thought.

There was the soft murmur of her lady-in-waiting's protest, and then the door slammed open. Light flooded into the bedchamber. Iseult moaned and covered her eyes with her hands.

With a few quick strides, her father was standing by her bed. He was a tall, strong man, with red-grey hair tied back with a leather thong, and two thick curling horns that marked him as a Khan'cohban, one of the Children of the Gods of White. His dark, aquiline face was slashed on both cheeks and forehead with seven white lines that matched the two thin scars on Iseult's cheeks.

"Iseult, get up!" he commanded.

"Leave me be," she moaned, and turned her face away.

"I will no'! Iseult, ye must get up."

"Why?" she wept. "Why must I?"

He sat down beside her and took her hands in his. "Iseult, do ye want to lie sleeping for sixteen years, like your mother did? Lie sleeping, and leave your children to suffer and struggle and shift for themselves, as ye and Beau had to?"

"My children are gone!" she spat. "Have ye no' heard. Gone!"

"Then why are ye no' out searching for them?" he demanded.

She turned to glance at him. "What's the use?" she whispered. "Lachlan is dead, my babies have all been stolen away, they mean to kill them too. What's the use in anything?"

"Ye may be able to stop them," Khan'gharad said.

She raised one hand and let it drop. "How? I have no power, no authority. I'm no' the Banrìgh anymore. Maya's daughter has seized that title with the throne. I am no' a witch, or a warrior, or anything anymore."

"Ye're still a Scarred Warrior," he said, tracing the scar on either cheek. "No one can take that away from ye."

"I'm forty-two years auld," Iseult said. "If I lived on the Spine o' the World, I'd be thought an old woman. Too auld for hunting, too auld for fighting."

He nodded and sat down beside her. "Aye, but this is no' the Spine o' the World. They revere their auld here. They think them wise. So it may be time for ye to start being wise, Iseult. And locking yourself away in your room is no' wise."

She turned her face away.

"Your mother lies in her bed, sleeping too," Khan'gharad said, frustration strong in his voice. "I canna wake her. Whenever something terrible happens, whenever she canna deal with what is happening, Ishbel falls asleep. I love your mother, ye ken that, Iseult, but I could strangle her with her own hair! How much o' her life has she wasted sleeping? Decades! Most o' your childhood. Do no' end up like her, Iseult, sleeping your life away!"

"I'm no'!" Iseult cried.

"Aye, ye are," he said. "I ken how much ye are grieving! I ken how terrible these last weeks have been. But lying here in bed with the curtains drawn, refusing to eat, is no' helping your bairns! Get up! Do something! Try and save them."

"How?" she asked again. "I have done everything wrong! It is my fault that all this has happened."

"Well, start doing something right," he answered. "Get up, wash your face, get dressed, and eat something, for the White Gods' sake. And then think what can be done! I do no' want to lose my grandchildren, as well as my son-in-law and my wife."

Iseult heaved a big sigh, and then tremulously sat up. "All right," she said, and tried to smile.

"That's my girl," he said, and bent and kissed her brow.

Banrìgh in Black

❧

Black did not suit her, Bronwen decided, staring at herself in the mirror. It made her look pale and weary and old. It made her *feel* pale and weary and old. She sighed and turned away from the mirror, smoothing down her somber gown with both hands.

It was time for her morning briefing with the Privy Council. Bronwen would very much like to have started her morning more pleasantly—curling up in bed with a cup of dancey and the broadsheets, for example. She knew how important these meetings were, however. Their perceived failure to catch Lachlan's murderer or to rescue his kidnapped children was causing a great deal of talk and speculation. There were many who did not trust the Ensorcellor's daughter and who privately believed she and her mother had plotted together to overthrow Lachlan and his family and win back power for themselves. No one dared say so to Bronwen's face, of course, but everywhere she went she heard whispers hurriedly shushed.

Bronwen actually preferred that brand of gossip to the rumors that Donncan had not been kidnapped at all but had fled his cold, arranged marriage to be with his true love, the Celestine princess Thunderlily. Whenever Bronwen heard even the faintest whisper of such talk, she felt herself turn rigid, blood draining from her face. "It's absolute hogwash," she had snapped at Neil when he had first brought her the tale. "I've never heard such a ridiculous story. Donncan would never . . . and besides, Thunderlily does no' . . ."

To her horror, words had failed her. Tears bit at the back of her throat. She turned away from Neil, breathing in deeply through her nose. He came up beside her, touching her shyly on the shoulder. "I ken that, and ye ken that, but these tattle-mongers, they'll say and believe anything," he said gently.

"It's absolute rubbish!" she cried.

"I ken," he replied, "but I thought ye ought to ken what they were saying."

She took another deep breath and said, "Aye. Thank ye."

"I'll do what I can to scotch the rumor," Neil said. "Everyone kens how honor-bound the Celestines are. Thunderlily kens she must marry as her family decrees."

"Aye," Bronwen said blankly, and bit her lip.

The rumors had persisted, though, as the days had stretched out past a week and still there was no news, nor any sign of the missing couple. Everyone knew that Isabeau and her companions traveled the Old Ways in their search for Donncan and Thunderlily; everyone also knew that only the Celestines knew the secret of the magical roads. What kidnapper could possibly know the secret?

It seemed obvious that it was Thunderlily who had chosen the escape route, and guided Donncan and Johanna along it, and no one truly believed the Celestine princess was party to any kidnapping attempt. It was a love story, then, many among the court and city decided, and their sympathies were definitely with the persecuted couple, not with Bronwen, who had wasted no time in seizing control. Johanna had known the prionnsa since he was a baby, and with her talents in healing magic, Thunderlily had spent much time studying with the head of the Healers' Guild. Obviously Johanna had been aware of Donncan and Thunderlily's secret love and had sympathized with it to the extent that she was prepared to assist an elopement.

Knowing the truth, these stories made Bronwen grind her teeth and clench her hands into fists. She could not blurt out the truth, however. Firstly, it was such a fantastic tale that surely no one would believe her; and secondly, Isabeau wanted no one to know about the spell of resurrection and the possible raising of Brann the Raven from the grave. The lord of Fettercairn was not the only madman in the world who dreamt of bringing back a loved one to life. And knowing Johanna sought to raise Brann could only cause fear and consternation, and possibly even panic. There was enough anxiety in the land already, without releasing the true story of Donncan and Thunderlily's disappearance.

Bronwen stopped outside the door of the Privy Chamber and took a few long, slow breaths, smoothing down her dress and making sure the little coronet she wore was straight. Then she nodded to her new page, Joey, who had been a gift of sorts from Neil, who thought she needed someone to fetch and carry for her, and run messages, and carry her mantle and gloves. A dark-haired, eager-faced boy who had grown up at the Tower of Mists in Arran, Joey had been Neil's page, like his brother before him. His brother Brant was Neil's squire, and Bronwen knew him quite well, as he always rode behind Neil and served him at meals. Joey was thrilled to be serving the new Banrìgh and was very quick and willing to serve.

At Bronwen's nod, he sprang forward to open the door for her, bowing low as she passed. Bronwen walked into a babble of noise, as the privy councillors argued angrily among themselves. The noise died away at her appearance, and everyone rose and bowed.

Bronwen nodded and allowed Joey to pull out her chair for her. As she seated herself, spreading out the dull black silk of her skirts, she looked around the room, carefully noting every expression and posture.

The Banrìgh had only chosen her privy councillors after a great deal of nail-biting and floor-pacing. She had to

have councillors about her that she could trust, yet she
knew how important it was to pacify the more powerful nobles. Most important, Bronwen realized she needed wise
and canny heads about her. There was much she did not understand about the management of the government, despite
all her lessons in economics, politics, history, and law. She
was ashamed to think how she had wasted her years at the
Theurgia, yawning through her classes and scribbling friv-
olous notes to her friends.

It had been important to her to reward those that she
perceived as supporting her, while punishing those that
muttered about her and her mother behind her back. Yet
Bronwen was clear-sighted enough to realize that many of
the courtiers who clustered about her whispering honeyed
words were mere sycophants, while some of those that
questioned and challenged her the most publicly were in
fact the cleverest and wisest men in the land.

In the end, she had kept many of her uncle's advisers,
replacing only those she truly disliked or distrusted. Neil
had already been appointed as her new master of horse, a
role that made him the third most powerful officer in her
household. On Neil's advice, she appointed herself a new
secretary, a young but vigilant minor lord named Maddock
MacNair, who had studied at the Theurgia with her, and ex-
celled in all the subjects she found most boring. It did not
bother her that Maddock had always disapproved of her. It
showed, she thought, great sense, and she at least could
trust him not to toady to her, which so many of her old
school friends were prone to do.

She had not forgotten that the Lord Steward had spoken
against her, the night of Lachlan's murder, when she had
seized control of the Privy Council. Bronwen took pleasure
in dismissing him and promoting a man who had always
been kind and respectful to her, a lord named Hargreaves,
whom Neil knew well, since he had served his father for
years. His elevation caused a lot of discussion, but in his

first week of office he had served well and efficiently, and Bronwen was pleased.

She would have liked to dismiss the Lord Chancellor too, for he was an elderly man and completely overcome by dismay and grief. He had spent much of the week wringing his hands and asking, over and over again, "What should we do? What should we do?" The Lord Chancellor had served her father before he had served Lachlan, however, and she could not bring herself to humiliate him. So she appointed a keen-eyed, firm-mouthed lord to act as his secretary, and replaced the Keeper of the Privy Seal, who had also spoken against her, with a younger, more vigorous man, one also highly recommended to her by Neil.

None of these were easy decisions to make, and Bronwen received so much conflicting advice from those around her that she found herself unable to please one without offending another. Many warned her against showing too much favor to the Fairgean, while Alta, the Fairgean ambassador, had at once begun pressing her for further trade concessions. There were lords who had lost all their lands in the rebellion and wanted some restitution now that Maya had been publicly pardoned and released from her subjugation; while the lords who had risen to wealth and power by fighting on Lachlan's side had no intention of relinquishing any of what they had won. There were those who were jealous of the Coven's power and believed Bronwen should take the opportunity of the Keybearer's absence to pass laws to curb their influence. Others feared her intentions, and made veiled threats that any attempt to undermine the witches would result in arms being taken up.

Some wanted taxes to be lowered; others wanted old debts to be paid immediately. The Prionnsa of Carraig wanted the controls on the production of saltpeter to be lifted, hinting that Bronwen may find a need for gunpowder in the near future. The Guild of Ancient Firework Magicians agreed; others argued against it vociferously.

The Banprionnsa of Blèssem was eager for Bronwen to use her friendship with Neil to encourage more roads to be opened up through the marshes of Arran, facilitating trade with the northwest; while those who distrusted Arran and Tirsoilleir muttered about Neil's quick advancement.

Much talk had been caused by Iain of Arran's decision to ride home to the marshes while his wife stayed behind at the royal court, her pastor and spiritual adviser her constant companion. If they had not both been so stern and virtuous, most would have assumed Iain a cuckold and the pale-haired pastor Elfrida's lover. But it was impossible to imagine, and so they assumed the Banprionnsa of Tirsoilleir saw her son's friendship with the new Banrìgh as a means to advancing the cause of her country and religion.

So many people warned Bronwen against the two that she lost her temper one afternoon and snapped, "Ye need have no fear for me, my lairds! Their sour faces make me want to rip off my blacks and dance about the hall half-naked!"

She regretted her comment immediately, but to her surprise it caused a little stir of amusement, and she found a new warmth towards her from some of the courtiers who had, she realized, begun to fear her new-found gravity and sobriety were an indication of sympathy with the stern religion of Tirsoilleir.

Not everyone was amused, however. The nobles of Eileanan feared another war with the Bright Soldiers almost as much as they feared war against the Fairgean, she knew, and so Bronwen found herself walking a tightrope between offending one race or religion, or another.

All seemed to hope to gain what they wanted in these first few days of uncertainty, as if expecting Bronwen to succumb to their flattery and their threats as if she was nothing but a wool-headed lass with more interest in the cut of her sleeve than the state of the nation. Bronwen had to remind herself grimly she had no one but herself to blame.

In all this rush and turmoil, the only peace she found was in her daily ride with Neil. He had found her a very dainty white mare and had insisted on her riding every day so that the mare would grow used to her. Bronwen knew he realized how tiring she found all the business of the government, and was grateful. Often they rode on alone, the other lords and ladies falling behind, so she could talk over problems with him and ease herself with frank and often humorous portrayals of all the different supplicants wearing out a path on the carpet that led to her rooms. It was a relief not having to watch what she said with him, and he surprised her sometimes with his knowledge of the political intricacies of the land.

Neil was, she reminded herself, heir to two of the great countries, and had been raised with full knowledge of what his role would one day be. She found his advice invaluable, and knew she could trust him in a way she could trust no other at the court.

She began asking him to attend her in the evening so he could go over the day's events with her, explain anything she did not understand and give her his advice. She made sure his mother was always present, as well as a number of other sober, respectable ladies and gentlemen, so no breath of scandal would be attached to these meetings. It was all so very grim and boring Bronwen could hardly bear it, and she longed to call for musicians and jugglers and singers, and lose herself in pleasure for a few hours. She resisted the temptation, however, and knew those who thought her too giddy and flighty to rule the land were surprised and some even pleased.

This morning, Neil was waiting for her in the Privy Chamber with all the other lords and councillors, his squire standing behind his chair as usual. He smiled at her, and suggested quietly that Joey pour her out a cup of her special angelica tea, which the squire did at once with a blush and an apology.

Bronwen smiled and thanked him, and drank a mouth-

ful of the invigorating brew before drawing her papers towards her.

"What news, my lairds?" she asked.

"No news yet from the Keybearer, I'm sorry, Your
Majesty," Gwilym said. "I have been keeping watch in the
Scrying Pool, just in case I should be able to see where
they are, and what is happening, but I have seen nothing,
nothing at all."

There was a stir of unease. Bronwen tried to hide her
disappointment, but she felt the Lodestar warm under her
hands and heard its crooning melody lift, as if it sought to
comfort her.

"Eà grant them success in their mission," she said softly,
and the lords all murmured in response.

"What o' my other cousins?" she asked. "Surely we
must have some more news by now?"

Captain Dillon of the Yeomen gave her a succinct re-
view of the difficulties Finn and Jay and their accompany-
ing soldiers had suffered. Bronwen's brows drew together
as she heard of the broken-down barricade, the injured
men, the slaughtered horses and grooms, the foul weather,
and the continued evasion of authorities by Lord Malvern
and his men.

"We have some good news, though, Your Majesty,"
Captain Dillon said. "Two o' Laird Malvern's men have
been laid by the heels and are being brought back to
Lucescere as we speak. One, at least, we should have no
trouble condemning to hang. He was found with a bloody
knife in his hand, right by the bodies o' the two lads he
slaughtered. He is sullen and recalcitrant, and has tried
several times to escape, but we have him well under control."

Bronwen sighed in relief. "That is good news," she said
warmly. She knew there must be some kind of public trial
and punishment for those who had dared commit such a
grievous offense against the Crown. As long as there was

no one to punish for Lachlan's murder and his children's abduction, Bronwen would continue to be suspect.

"And the other?" she asked.

"He is an elderly man, and weak and sick," Captain Dillon said, frowning. "He refuses to speak unless we promise him a full pardon for his son, who is still one o' Laird Malvern's party."

"No pardons!" Bronwen cried. "Make sure ye gather enough evidence to condemn them both and we will no' need his confession."

"My thoughts exactly," Captain Dillon said with a grim smile. "We also have two corpses to add to those of the traitorous prison warder, Octavia. We will be able to display them to the public, as more miscreants brought to justice."

"Their heads should be hung upon Sorrowgate," the Lord Constable said. "We need to make an example o' them."

Bronwen nodded, though she winced inside. She had never liked riding out of the city by the southern road, with those dreadful rotting heads hanging from the gate's lintel.

The news created a great deal of discussion, and Bronwen was pleased to discover it was her own thigearna, Rhiannon of the Banrìgh's Guard, who had been instrumental in the capture of the criminals.

She was less pleased to hear that Rhiannon had failed to rescue Owein and Olwynne before Lord Malvern's ship sailed. They had always known that this was a possibility, however, and so the royal navy had been on stand-by, fully provisioned and manned, and ready to sail in pursuit. Bronwen gave the Admiral the order to mobilize, and he scrawled a quick message and sealed it with his signet ring, before sending a page scurrying with it to the pigeon loft.

There was a great deal of business to attend to after that, the minutiae of government that Bronwen found tedious at the best of times. Now, with anxiety and grief her constant companions, she found it almost intolerable. She was determined to show that she could rule well, however, and so she sat and listened with a most unnatural patience, doing her best to listen and understand the arguments and counterarguments, and signing sheet after sheet, passing them over to the Keeper of the Privy Seal to stamp.

Bronwen was ashamed of her longing for Donncan. Again and again she told herself that she had no need of him, either as a woman or as the Banrìgh. "It is no' as though I love him," she said to herself. "I mean, there is no doubt that he was . . . is . . . the handsomest man at court, but such a stuffed shirt! So proud and disagreeable he could be at times. Look at the fuss he made over the lock o' hair I cut."

Bronwen did not like to think of that dreadful argument she and Donncan had had at the May Day feast when he had discovered she had chopped off a lock of her hair from the back of her head. Donncan had at once leaped to the conclusion that she had given the lock as a love token to one of her many admirers. She had been unable to tell him that she had used the lock of hair to bind about her mother's neck, so that all would believe Maya was still constrained by the magical ribbon of nyx-hair.

Woven by the oldest of the nyx from her own wild mane of hair, the ribbon had struck Maya mute, unable to speak or sing or even hum. Since all of Maya's power to charm and ensorcel was expressed through her voice, this had rendered her powerless, and she had spent the last twenty years a dumb servant to the witches. The death of the nyx had seen the black ribbon crumble to dust, releasing Maya from the spell and giving her back her voice.

Bronwen had known that Isabeau would simply have ordered another nyx hair ribbon woven, and so, on impulse, she had hacked out a lock of her own hair, and quickly plaited it into a ribbon with a few simple spells so that Isabeau would not suspect her mother was now returned to her powers. She could not confess this to Donncan, else the ruse would have been revealed, and so he had gone on thinking her unfaithful to him, in thought if not in deed, and a coldness had grown between them that had not had time to thaw. If only she could have told him the truth before he had been kidnapped! Everyone knew it now, for Maya had spoken after Lachlan's murder, and no longer tried to conceal she had her voice back, and with it all her powers.

Bronwen utterly refused to admit, even to herself, that she would have found the business of governing much easier with Donncan beside her. He had always been the serious one, who had studied hard at school and done well in his exams. She had no doubt he would have little trouble in grasping the ramifications of the sudden devaluing of coin as a consequence of Lachlan's murder, and deciding what action was best taken to solve the ensuing economic crisis. She had sat up half the night reading through the reports and trying to make her tired brain make sense of the unfamiliar terms and phrasing. Now she had to make sure no one in the Privy Council realized how little she knew, for any sign of weakness or folly in her could be disastrous. So Bronwen asked advice, listened with great care to all the responses, and tried to sound authoritative as she gave her orders, glad to see Neil's little nod that showed she had made the right decision.

The hands of the clock stood well after three o' clock when Bronwen was at last released from the Privy Chamber. Wearily she went down the hall to her room and rang her bell for some more angelica tea. Sitting down at her paper-laden desk, she drew a quill and the ink pot to her and began to make notes of the things she needed to do. Luckily she had prepared for the eventuality of Lord Malvern reaching the coast; now she just needed to make sure there was a fleet of ships on his tail as soon as possible, preferably with some weather-witches aboard to try to counteract the storm the lord of Fettercairn had raised.

She was just scattering sand over a note to Stormy Bri-

ant and reaching for her bell to summon her page to carry
the message for her when the door suddenly crashed open.

Bronwen jerked violently and knocked over her ink pot.
Ink flooded everywhere, all over the papers she was meant
to sign and return to the Keeper of the Privy Seal that afternoon. Bronwen gasped in dismay, but scrambled to her
feet and looked to the door, too afraid of a possible assassin to worry about spilled ink for the moment.

It was her mother-in-law, Iseult.

Relief was followed an instant later by anger, but Bronwen forced herself to take a few deep breaths before speaking. "Ye startled me, my lady," she said. "Is something
wrong, that ye come barging in without knocking?"

The Dowager Banrìgh had always been slender, but now
she was slim to the point of gauntness. Her blue eyes
seemed huge in her pale face, and her skin was blotched
red from days of weeping. She was dressed entirely in
black, with her red hair hidden under a heavy black coif.
For days she had been huddled up in her rooms, refusing
visitors, locked in her grieving. Bronwen had made the effort to go up and see her twice, and had been refused ad-
mittance each time. The Dowager Banrìgh was resting, she
was told. So Bronwen had not gone up again, even though
if truth be told, she would probably have welcomed Iseult's
experience and knowledge in many matters.

"Aye, something's wrong," Iseult snapped. "I've just
heard that you've failed to stop that madman that's stolen
my bairns and he's taken to the sea! Did it no' occur to ye
that I would have liked to have been told?"

Bronwen gaped at her for a moment, then busied herself
mopping up the spilled ink while she tried to think of the
best way to answer.

"I'm sorry," she said. "I've only just had the news myself."

"Three hours ago," Iseult said. "Long enough to send a
pigeon to Rhyssmadill, mobilizing the navy."

"Well, aye," Bronwen admitted, "but we have only just adjourned the Council . . ."

"I should've been told at once," Iseult said icily. "These are my children whose lives are at stake. Ye think I would no' wish to ken?"

"Nay, nay, o' course no'," Bronwen said. "I truly am sorry, my lady. It was just . . . the Council went on for so long, there were so many things to discuss and decide, and I . . . I . . ." To her utter dismay, Bronwen felt her voice shake. She stopped, and took a deep breath. When she looked up again, her voice was cool and steady. "I am sure ye must realize how very many affairs o' state there are to deal with, my lady. I am sorry if ye feel we were amiss in focusing our attention on those rather than in sending you a message at a time when I believed ye would be . . . resting."

She saw color rise in Iseult's cheeks. The Dowager Banrìgh pressed her hands together, her lip gripped between her teeth.

"I will no' sit in my rooms waiting and fearing any longer," Iseult said in a low, passionate voice. "I have allowed ye full rein, Bronwen, and what have ye achieved? Naught! Naught! Donncan is still missing, and Owein and Olwynne are still in the hands o' that madman. I will go myself and I will bring them back!"

She swung about with a loud rustle of her heavy skirts, and Bronwen gaped at her back in surprise. Then, as Iseult began to sweep from the room, she jumped to her feet.

"Wait!" she called.

Iseult turned.

"Ye canna mean to set sail after them yourself, my lady?" Bronwen asked. "It is too dangerous!"

"I am a Scarred Warrior!" Iseult replied coldly. "Ye think I fear these . . . necromancers! They are auld men, almost in the grave themselves."

"The laird o' Fettercairn can conjure wind and storms," Bronwen said. "He has Finn and Jay stalled on the road,

lashed with rain and hail. His ship runs afore an enchanted
wind."

Iseult smiled. "Ye think I do no' have powers o' my own
to command?" She snapped her fingers and the water in
Bronwen's glass turned at once to ice. The fire died, and a
bitter cold wind tore around the room, making the curtains
rise and twirl and Bronwen's hair whip across her face. In
the center of it all stood Iseult, her black skirts swirling.

"I have sat and grieved too long," she said. "My children are in danger, dreadful danger, and I have allowed ye
and everyone else to bungle their rescue. I will go, and I
will bring them back."

Bronwen smoothed back the hair blowing wildly about
her face, catching it in one hand. "Aye, my lady," she answered, hearing a new respect in her voice. "What will ye
need? Can I do aught to help?"

Iseult regarded her thoughtfully, and the wind slowly
died down until the room was quiet and peaceful again,
though bitterly cold without the fire.

"A fleet o' ships," the Dowager Banrìgh said then. "And
Dillon o' the Joyous Sword."

"Ye shall have them both," Bronwen answered. "Speed
well!"

Iseult regarded her for a long moment, and then she
nodded curtly, turned, and was gone.

Bronwen could only envy her.

Squires and Stowaways

❦

Lewen delicately transplanted the seedling into a small tub of soil and watered it gently, before putting the pot on the shelf to his left.

To his right were thousands of similar tiny plants, all of them magically grown from seed in an attempt to replace the frost-blighted plants that had died in the terrible snowstorm Iseult had conjured up on the night of her husband's murder. A whole season's crop had been lost, and many people would go hungry that winter if the Coven were not able to replace some at least of the ruined harvest. Lewen had always had a talent with growing things, and so he, along with the other earth-witches, were using their powers to speed along the growth of many key crops such as oats, corn, barley, beans, and potatoes.

The greenhouse was one of the few places where he felt any surcease from the terrible anxiety that racked his every moment. With his fingers buried in earth, his attention focused on unfurling leaf and flower, Lewen was able to put aside, for a moment, the aching loss and fear he felt for both his dear friends, Owein and Olwynne, and his lover, Rhiannon, who had put herself in danger purely for his sake.

Lewen could not believe he had let Rhiannon go. He knew he had been dazed and weak after the beating he had taken from the bell, but he felt that was no excuse. No ex-

cuse for lying with Rhiannon when he was hand-fasted to
Olwynne, no excuse for allowing her to fly off into the
night, one young woman against a gang of ruthless ruffi-
ans. He was so sick with fear for all of them that he could
not eat or sleep or settle to any task, apart from monoto-
nous, mindless jobs, like grooming a hundred horses, one
after the other, or carving and fletching a thousand arrows.
As soon as his hands were still, his mind began to gnaw
again at what he had done—or rather, what he had failed to
do—and he would find himself pacing restlessly, his hands
clenched into fists.

There was little else for him to do. The Tower of Two
Moons was deathly quiet, having closed for the rest of the
term in honor of their dead Rìgh. Most of the students had
gone. Only those who lived too far away to travel home
easily, like Lewen, had stayed. Most had been put to work
in the glasshouses, or out in the huge kitchen garden, wrapping up the fruit trees in sacking to save them from the
frost, and laying straw down over the rows of blighted vegetables. There were no classes, no homework, and the meal
they ate together every night in the Theurgia's great hall
was glum and miserable.

The palace was as quiet. Nearly all the wedding guests
had gone home, and many of the usual court too, affronted
at Bronwen's seizing of power, or simply desiring time to
see which way the wind blew before showing their hand.
Like Lewen, Bronwen had nothing to do but wait for news.

Lewen washed his hands at the pump, and dried them on
the towel hanging nearby, then shrugged himself back into
his coat, hat, scarf, and mittens before going out into the
snow.

Lucescere Palace was still gripped in a cold, white
gauntlet. By all accounts, the farther one traveled from the
palace, the warmer the weather grew. It was only here, in
Lucescere, where the widow of the murdered Rìgh
brooded alone in her rooms, that the bitter black frost still
bit, and showed no signs of relenting.

Lewen walked slowly back towards the witches' tower, his shoulders bowed. Then he heard the sound of running footsteps and looked up. A young woman was hurrying towards him, her cheeks pink from the cold, her satiny brown hair flying about her face. She wore a very pretty coat of raspberry red with a fur-lined hood and matching muff, and fur-lined brown boots.

"Lewen!" she cried.

"Hey, Fèlice," he said, unable to muster more than a faint smile.

She caught his arm between hers. "Lewen, there's news!"

He straightened at once, grabbing her hand. "What!"

"Laird Malvern's made it to the coast, and has set sail," she gabbled. "The Banrìgh is calling up the navy to chase after them. Finn and Jay are heading for Dùn Gorm now, to meet up with the Admiral. But Lewen! The Dowager Banrìgh has decided to go too. She has had enough, she says, o' sitting and waiting for news."

"What o' Rhiannon?" Lewen demanded.

She bit her lip. "She has flown after them."

"Across the sea?" Lewen was aghast.

"Aye. She sent the message from Ravenshaw, and then went after them. She says they are heading for the Pirate Isles."

"Is she mad? Blackthorn canna fly so far without coming down to land! Doesna she realize? She'll kill them both."

"Is it so far?" Fèlice said in a small voice.

"It's three or four days' sail, at least," Lewen said. "Maybe less, I suppose, with a spell-wrought wind behind their sails. But that's six hundred miles or more, she canna expect Blackthorn to stay in the air so long."

"Are there no' other islands where she can land and rest?" Fèlice asked.

"Aye, I suppose so, but no' many, and how is she meant to ken where they are? She's never seen the sea afore, she

has no idea how big it is, how dangerous! Oh, Rhiannon!"
He pressed both hands against his face, coming close to
breaking down.

"Why does the laird take them to the Pirate Isles? What
does he plan to do there?" Fèlice asked.

He looked down at her. She was a dainty girl, and barely
reached his shoulder. After a moment he shook his head. "I
do no' ken."

"He means to sacrifice them, doesn't he? I am no' a
fool, Lewen, I ken what is going on. Oh, Lewen, I am sick
with fear for them all!"

"Me too," he answered. He could barely frame the
words.

"We must go as well," Fèlice cried. "Ye ken the Dowager Banrìgh, ye have been her squire for years. If we went
to her and begged her, would she no' take us too?"

Lewen stared at her, and felt a sudden quickening of his
blood.

"Canna we go and ask her? She must be taking men,
servants, why no' us too? Come on, Lewen, let's go and
ask her now. She's preparing to leave this very moment.
Come on!"

She took his hand and dragged at it, and Lewen went
with her, his heart beginning to pound. It was the waiting
that was so hard. The hours went past so slowly. All along
he had been thinking, *If only I could have flown with her!
If only I could have gone too!*

As they hurried over the lawn towards the palace, two
tall, brown-haired boys raced towards them, their faces
alive with excitement. One was nineteen, the other eighteen, and they had, with Fèlice and her friend Landon and
two other girls, traveled with Nina and Finn's caravan
through Ravenshaw.

"Have ye heard the news? The laird o' Fettercairn has
got away," Cameron cried.

"He's out to sea, headed for the Pirate Isles," said
Rafferty.

"The Dowager Banrìgh sails after him today . . . she and that weather-witch, Stormy Briant."

"And the captain o' the guards!"

"She has no squires left but ye," Cameron said. "Fymbar o' Blèssem is heading home with his mother tomorrow, and Alasdair MacFaghan and his sister are both attending their mother, who sleeps still, is it no' peculiar? And Aindrew and Barnabas MacRuraich have left court too."

"That only leaves the MacAhern's son, and they ride home for Tìreich this afternoon," Rafferty interpolated. "So ye see . . ."

"She has no squires left but ye," Cameron said in a rush.

"Surely she'll be wanting someone to wait on her, and run messages, and . . . and pour her wine," Rafferty said. "If ye ask her . . ."

"Maybe . . ."

"Maybe she'll take us too!"

"Will ye ask her, Lewen? Ye'll be going, won't ye?"

Fèlice had been dancing up and down in her excitement and now she butted in impatiently, "That's where we're going now, to ask her!"

"What, ye too?" Cameron jeered. "Lassies canna be squires!"

"Nay, but I could be her lady-in-waiting," Fèlice replied. "Come on! Let's go!"

They all hurried towards the palace. Lewen felt an almost painful anxiety, in case they were too late, or in case Iseult did not wish for him to attend on her. He had not seen the Dowager Banrìgh since the night of Lachlan's murder. He had been confined to bed, with concussion and a few cracked ribs from tying himself to the clapper of the big bell, and she had been locked away in her room, grieving. He did not even know if she realized he was the one who had saved Rhiannon from hanging. It was Iseult that had given the order for Rhiannon to be hanged, and he feared she might resent his intervention. His friends seemed to have no doubt that Iseult would want him back, but Lewen felt no such confidence. She was very proud and stern, the Dowager Banrìgh, and Lewen had never felt anything but an awestruck respect for her. She was not one to forgive easily, he felt, and he could only hope she did not know, or mind, that Lewen was the one who had stopped her orders from being carried out.

Their friend Landon was waiting for them outside the ornate palace gate. He wore his black apprentice robe as usual, having few other clothes, and it hung off his bony shoulders. "I just heard the news?" he gasped, breathless. "Is it true?"

"That the Banrìgh . . . the Dowager Banrìgh, I mean . . . that she sails after the laird o' Fettercairn? I dinna ken," Lewen replied. "I think it may be. She is a Khan'cohban, remember, and a warrior. She has always ridden to war."

"I would so love to be there, at the end," Landon said, his face glowing. "Think o' the ballad I could write! Do ye think . . . ?"

"We go to ask," Fèlice cried. "Surely she will let us go! We are the ones who first discovered what Laird Malvern was up to! If it was no' for us . . ."

"And Rhiannon," Landon said.

". . . no one would ken aught about him at all. Come on, Landon, can ye run? I'm so afraid we'll be too late and she'll have gone already."

They raced up the back stairs, avoiding servants who were scurrying everywhere with armfuls of armor, or piles of thick grey cloaks, or scrolls of maps, or trays of food and drink. The guards outside the Banrìgh's suite of rooms knew Lewen well, and although they frowned at the sight of his mob of excited friends, they agreed to take word to Iseult that Lewen was here, begging for audience. One went in, and the other stood on guard, staring straight ahead and trying to ignore the excited students, who milled about, waiting expectantly, and chattering nineteen-to-the-dozen.

At last the other guard came back and opened the door for them, saying tersely, "She will see ye, but be quick! She leaves for the riverboat in less than ten minutes."

Lewen led the way into Iseult's suite, his hands suddenly clammy and his throat thick. The Dowager Banrìgh was standing in the middle of the room, dressed in old leather gaiters and boots, and a scarred leather cuirass worn over a mail shirt of supple, gleaming silver. Under one arm was her steel-enforced leather helmet. In her other hand she held her crossbow, with her quiver of arrows set on a chair nearby. Lewen was pleased to see it was heavy with arrows he had fletched himself. This gave him hope that the Dowager Banrìgh had forgiven him for what she must see as a betrayal, at worst, and insubordination at best.

Her expression was not encouraging. She glanced up as Lewen came in and made his bow, and her eyebrows rose at the sight of Fèlice, Cameron, Rafferty, and Landon clustering close behind him.

"What is it, Lewen?" she demanded. "Make it quick, for I have a boat waiting for me on the loch, and I wish to make Dùn Gorm afore dawn."

Lewen was startled, for it was a journey of several days along the river from Lucescere to Dùn Gorm. She must be very confident of the wind she could whistle up to fill their sails.

"Please, Your Highness . . . I mean, my lady . . . I beg o' ye, may we come too, to serve ye and help ye?" Lewen said in a rush. "We are all part o' the story, from the very beginning. This is Lady Fèlice, the daughter o' the Earl o' Stratheden, and Cameron MacHamish, who was squire at Ravenscraig afore he came to the Theurgia, and Landon MacPhillip, from Magpie Wood in Ravenshaw, and Rafferty MacDonovan from Tullimuir. We all traveled with Nina and Iven, if ye remember, and took refuge at Fettercairn Castle in the storm. We all ken Laird Malvern . . . we've fought him once afore and we . . . we

want to help lay him by the heels." He had been going to
say something about Rhiannon, but at the last moment did
not dare, and so ended rather lamely, wishing he had Iven
Yellowbeard's way with words.

Iseult frowned, looking at them each in turn, then returned her attention to her weapons belt, which she was
strapping about her waist.

"Please, Your Highness," Lewen said again. "We'll do
anything we can to help."

"Having a mob o' bairns on board is no' going to help
me," she replied coolly. "I'm sorry, but we must travel fast.
This is no' a pleasure trip."

"Please, Your Highness," Cameron cried. "We can be
your squires! We can carry your bow and arrows . . ."

"Thank ye, but I'll carry them myself," she answered.

"We can run messages for ye."

"On board a ship? What messages would I want run?"

"We ken Laird Malvern," Fèlice cried. "We can point
him out to ye. We can tell ye how he thinks."

Iseult looked at her long and hard. "So ye are Lady
Fèlice o' Stratheden, are ye?" she said. "The one that sang
the ballad o' Rhiannon's Ride and stirred up so much trouble with the faeries?"

Fèlice colored and dropped her gaze. "Aye, my lady."

Iseult regarded her with a long, frowning gaze, Fèlice
growing pinker by the moment, then switched her gaze to
Landon. "And ye are the poet?"

"Aye, my lady." Landon pressed his thin, bony hands together imploringly.

Iseult's frown deepened. One of her ladies came with a
thick grey cloak and fastened it about her shoulders, then
Iseult bent and picked up her quiver, slinging it over her
back.

"I will need a squire," she said. "Lewen, I can see from
the bruise on your temple that ye are no' yet in the best o'
shape. Stay here at Lucescere and recover your strength.
Lady Fèlice, the fact that ye are here does no' give me a

very high view o' your intelligence. Do ye seriously think your father would thank me for allowing ye to join such a dangerous venture?"

"But, my lady!" Fèlice cried, tears starting to her eyes.

Iseult narrowed her eyes. "Stay home and sew your sampler," she advised. "Ye, the poet. I'm sorry, but ye do no' look strong enough for the job. Ye are a scholar, no' a squire. We will be sailing fast, and the seas will be high. This blaygird laird has conjured up a tempest to try and stop us. I need someone who can stay the course, and can fight if needed."

As Landon drooped with disappointment, she turned to the last two, who stared at her pleadingly. She looked them over critically.

"Cameron. I've heard o' ye. The MacBrann said ye were a good lad, but I have doubts about your discretion. Flapping ears and a flapping tongue are no' qualities I want in a squire."

Cameron went red to the tips of his ears. There was no doubt he knew what Iseult was talking about. He wished he dared explain to the Dowager Banrìgh that the MacBrann had known him since he was a mere lad, and had quizzed him thoroughly about everything that had happened on his journey from Ravenscraig to Lucescere, keeping him answering questions for over an hour. The MacBrann was his lord and prionnsa; it had not even occurred to Cameron that he should not make as full a report as he could. Given the same circumstances, he would again.

Iseult had turned her attention to Rafferty. "Ye are the lad that ran messages for Lewen on Midsummer's Eve, are ye no'?"

"Aye, my lady," he answered eagerly.

"I would've done it too, if Lewen had no' asked me to help him search for the prionnsa . . . I mean, the Rìgh!" Cameron said indignantly. "Oh, please, my lady, canna we both come? Ye'll want someone on hand all day and all night!"

She looked them over critically. "Can ye ice-skate?" she asked abruptly.

"Och, aye, my lady, o' course we can," Cameron said. "We come from the highlands o' Ravenshaw! There's naught else to do there in winter."

Iseult sighed. "Very well. Both o' ye can come. Ye'll no' have much time to prepare, though. Report to the mistress of the wardrobe, and she'll give ye a surcoat and badge, and a sword. I'm presuming ye ken how to use one?"

"Aye, my lady!" the boys cried in great delight.

"Ask her to fit ye for ice skates. Auld ones o' Owein and Donncan's would probably do. Ye may need a change o' clothes too. There's no time for ye to go back to your own rooms, so ask the wardrobe to give ye aught ye need. Meet us down at the wharf in half an hour. Ye'll have to run! We're taking a river barge called the *Jessamine*. If ye are no' there when I am, ye will be left behind. Is that clear?"

"Aye, my lady!"

"Get going then. I'll see ye at the *Jessamine*."

Joyously the two boys hurried out of the room, punching and jostling each other in their usual fashion. Scoured with bitter disappointment and hurt, Lewen bowed and then turned to go, Fèlice and Landon leading the way disconsolately.

"Lewen," the Dowager Banrìgh said gently.

He turned back, barely able to see for the shameful tears that rose up in a mist before his eyes. Fèlice glanced back at him, her face pinched with misery, then went on with Landon, gently shutting the door behind them.

"I'm sorry, I ken ye are disappointed," Iseult said. "Ye are o' little use to me, though, with a broken head and ribs. Ye're far better resting here, and recovering."

Lewen put one hand up to the nasty bruise at his temple. "It's just a bruise," he said defensively. "Owein's given me worse bashing me over the head with a practice sword."

"They tell me ye were badly jarred and shaken up," Iseult said. "Ye lay unconscious for close on a day. The seas will be rough and nasty indeed. I do no' want to risk hurting ye again."

"Please, my lady. Please."

She shook her head. "I'm sorry. Indeed, I think it for the best."

Unable to speak, or even bow his head again, Lewen turned to go.

"I am glad your thigearn lass managed to save Roden," Iseult said, with obvious difficulty. "And she almost had the laird by the heels, I heard. They've lost four or five men, did ye ken? She did well."

"She's flown after them," Lewen said miserably, not turning around. "Over the sea. Blackthorn canna fly so far. They'll never make it."

"She seems a canny lass," Iseult said after a moment. "I'm sure she will no' risk her horse unnecessarily. And remember, Isabeau flew to the Pirate Isles in the shape o' a swan. It can be done."

Lewen turned back to her, hope lighting his features. "Isabeau did?"

"Aye. When Margrit o' Arran kidnapped Donncan and Neil, when they were but bairns. Isabeau flew after them and rescued them. That was when Margrit died. That is how her body comes to lie in the Pirate Isles. Ye have no' heard that story?"

Lewen shook his head dumbly.

"One day, when I have time, I will bid Dide to tell ye the tale. For now, do no' worry so for your wild girl. If Isabeau can fly to the Fair Isles in the shape o' a swan, so too can that winged horse."

"Except a swan is built for long-distance flying," Lewen said glumly. "A winged horse is no'."

"I'm sure she'll be fine," Iseult said, trying not to sound impatient. "Let us hope she catches up with them quickly, and saves my bairns for me! Then I'll be grateful for your damned interference, Lewen."

He managed a faint smile, bowed, and left her, conscious only that once again he was being left behind.

As soon as the door shut behind them, Fèlice turned and seized Landon by the arm.

"Come on!" she cried.

"Where are we going?" Landon asked, bewildered, as she towed him hastily down the corridor.

"Ye do no' think I'm really going to just sit at home and sew my sampler, do ye?" Fèlice was seething with indignation. "No, we have to get on that boat somehow. It'll be tricky, no doubt o' that. We'll have to have one o' those badges she was talking about."

"Ye want us to stow away?" Landon was aghast.

Fèlice smiled at him. "If we can. If no', we'll have to pretend to be cabin boys or something. Come on! We havena time to go back to the Theurgia if the boat sails in half an hour. Have ye got your dagger, on ye?"

Landon nodded dumbly, his hand going to his witch's dagger, which hung at his side as always.

"Excellent," Fèlice said, and opened a door at random, dragging Landon behind her and banging the door shut behind them. "Give it to me."

"What are ye going to do?" Landon asked, even as he unsheathed his knife and gave it to her.

"Cut my hair, o' course," she answered impatiently. She seized a hank of her silky brown hair in one hand and sliced it off just below her ear with the sharp edge of the knife. Landon gasped in horror as she dropped it and sliced off another hank.

"Fèlice, no!" he cried, even though it was too late.

"I canna pretend to be a cabin boy with hair down to my knees," she answered impatiently. "Is there a mirror in here anywhere? I have to make sure it is even."

She looked about the dim, quiet room. All the furniture was covered with dustsheets, and the hearth was clean and bare. Fèlice uncovered a tall mirror in the corner by the empty washstand.

"I look perfectly horrid," she said in delight. "Look at me! If it wasna for the dress, ye'd think I was a snotty-nosed cabin boy for sure! Now, what are ye wearing beneath your robe, Landon?"

He crimsoned, and said in a rather stifled voice, "Just my shirt and breeches. It's cold, ye ken, and I havena anything else to wear, so I . . ."

"Excellent," Fèlice cried, not bothering to listen to the end of his sentence. "Strip them off, there's a good lad."

"But why?" He made no move to obey, shrinking away from her in mortification.

"Unless ye want to be the one to go to the mistress o' the wardrobe and get us a badge, like Rafferty and Cameron? No? I dinna think so! Much better if ye wait here and I go. Once I'm dressed in your clothes, no one will guess I'm really a lass."

"Ye really mean to go ahead with this? It's madness! We'll be caught for sure."

She shrugged. "Well, at least we would've tried. What can they do to us? Rake us over the coals, no doubt, but so what? Better than going home like good little bairns, while Cameron and Rafferty get to have all the fun. Come on, Landon! Stop arguing with me, and give me your clothes, else we'll miss the boat and I'll have cut my hair for naught."

Shivering in the cold, Landon did as he was told, hiding himself under the voluminous folds of his apprentice robe. Fèlice grabbed his clothes and retreated behind a screen to change. When she emerged, she looked entirely different. With her cropped hair and her slim body clad in the shabby, threadbare clothes of the young poet, she looked just like a rough country boy. She gave Landon a jerky bow and said, with the broad accent of the highlands, "'Scuse me, sir, but I was wondering if ye could be telling me the way to the docks?"

"Amazing," Landon said.

"I need to be a bit grubbier," Fèlice said critically and ran her finger over the mantelpiece, looking for dust. She frowned when her finger came up clean, and got down on her hands and knees to swipe under the dressing-table. Landon averted his eyes, blushing. Fèlice's hand came up grey with dust, and she smeared it on her forehead and cheek, and then rubbed in a bit of spit to make it streaky. Eyes dancing, she curtsied to herself in the mirror, saying, "Oh la, Lady Fèlice, what a figure ye cut! I would never have recognized ye!"

"Fèlice, dinna ye think . . .?"

"Oh, shhh, Landon, stop worrying. I'll be back in a jiffy. Huddle up under the dustsheets to keep warm, and I'll be back afore ye ken it."

Fèlice opened the door cautiously, looked up and down the corridor, then ducked back inside as a pair of serving girls passed, their arms full of clean linen. They did not notice her, and Fèlice was able to sidle out and hurry along the corridor once they had passed.

Fèlice had never been inside Lucescere Palace before, but she had grown up at Ravenscraig, the royal court of the MacBrann clan, and so she knew the ways of a large castle well. She had no trouble finding her way to the wardrobe, which was always located near the solar, since the ladies of the court were expected to help the seamstresses with the enormous amount of sewing such a large establishment required.

As she had expected, the room was frantically busy, with clothes heaped everywhere, draped over the backs of chairs, hanging from rods or piled upon the floor. Women bustled around, sorting and packing away, or discussing the state of a pile of clothes to be mended. Others sat near the big windows, squinting as they threaded a needle, or chattering quietly among themselves as they expertly sewed together the seams of a new outfit. Several worked away at huge looms pushed against the walls, and several more were operating spinning wheels, the clatter and whirr of their machines almost drowning out the soft murmur of the women's voices.

"'Scuse me, ma'am, I'm looking for the mistress o' the wardrobe," Fèlice said in a deep, gruff voice that she hoped sounded just like Rafferty.

"What can I do for ye?" one of the women asked, dropping the hem of the gown she was examining and coming forward with a frown. Fèlice was conscious of being raked with shrewd grey eyes. She gave a little bow, and said, "I was told to report to ye, ma'am. I'm to go to sea with the Dowager Banrìgh. She said to get a cloak, and a badge, and a sword, and anything else I'd need."

"Well, ye willna get a sword here, ye need to go to the armorer for that," the woman said. She measured Fèlice expertly. "Ye're a bit small, aren't ye, to be squiring? And I've already had two lads through here, asking for the same. Big, strapping lads, they were. I'm surprised at Her Highness. She doesna usually pick scrawny wee lads like ye to take into such danger."

"I'm to be a cabin boy," Fèlice said desperately, her voice coming out in a squeak. Dismayed, she cleared her throat, and said again, in a much lower register, "Ken about boats, I do."

The women all laughed, and the mistress of the wardrobe said, rather acerbically, "Well, ye willna be needing a sword then, lad. Last I heard, cabin boys were no' armed like cavaliers!"

Fèlice bit her lip but, as the woman was rummaging about in a cupboard, said nothing, folding her arms, swinging one foot and trying to look as much like a boy as she could. The woman turned about with her arms full of clothes. "Here's some good stout breeches for ye, lad," she said. "Those ones look a trifle threadbare. And some shirts. They're no' new, but better than what ye have. And a warm woolen jerkin, 'cause it's cold about the Dowager Banrìgh, there's no denying that."

"I need two o' everything," Fèlice said, trying out a winning smile. "There's two o' us going."

The woman's smile faded, and she fixed Fèlice with a frowning stare. "Where's this other lad then?" she demanded.

"Running messages," Fèlice answered. "For the Dowager Banrìgh. The boat leaves in less than half an hour, ye ken. There's an awful lot to do."

The woman's suspicious look faded. "Too true," she replied with a sigh. "I do wish we'd been given some warning. My lady's armor has been packed away for years, and I had a hard time laying my hands on it at such short notice. And ice skates! Where was I meant to lay my hands on twelve dozen ice skates! What on earth does the Dowager Banrìgh want with ice skates on the high seas?"

"I have no idea," Fèlice answered truthfully.

The wardrobe mistress sighed. "Well, happen she needs her squires to wear ice skates since she turns everything about her to ice and snow," she said. "Snowstorms in midsummer! And me with all the winter clothes packed away for the season! Topsy-turvy, my storeroom now. I'll be lucky to be able to lay my hands on a thing."

Fèlice waited politely.

"So do ye need ice skates too?" the woman asked in a long-suffering tone.

"I guess so," Fèlice answered, determined to have everything Cameron and Rafferty got, bizarre as it seemed. Indeed, she could not help wondering if the Dowager Banrìgh had run completely mad. None of her actions since her husband had died seemed entirely rational—the snowstorm, the calling of the dragon's name to hunt down Rhiannon and drag her back to be hanged without a trial, the fortnight of seclusion in her curtain-shrouded room, and then this sudden mad impulse to motion, with people scurrying everywhere looking for ice skates and old-fashioned armor and maps to the Pirate Isles. Fèlice did not care. If it was taking her closer to Owein, the winged prionnsa whose smile Fèlice thought about every night before she drifted off to sleep, then that was all that mattered.

"Two o' everything, ye say?" the wardrobe mistress was grumbling on. "Very well—though fitting out four boys in as many minutes is going to strip the cupboard bare. At least I dinna have to give ye court dress! And since ye're no' to be a squire but merely a cabin boy, I needn't give ye a surcoat with the MacCuinn arms."

Fèlice gazed regretfully at the long blue silk surcoats the wardrobe mistress folded away, wishing she had not said she was not really a squire. The next moment her arms were filled with a great pile of clothes, though, with two long grey cloaks laid on top.

"And here are your badges," the woman said, unlocking a small chest and taking out two badges that bore upon them the ensign of a golden stag upon a dark green background. "Take good care o' these. They show ye are in the MacCuinn's service. If ye lose them, ye'll be sacked for sure!"

"Thank ye!" Fèlice cried, forgetting to lower her voice. The woman only smiled, obviously thinking Fèlice's voice was just breaking. Fèlice ducked her head and turned to go, only to be called back by the woman who had drawn a thick ledger towards her and was dipping her quill into her ink pot.

"No' so fast, laddie!" she said. "I need your name and the name o' your friend afore ye go, and your authority."

Fèlice gaped back at her, her brain for once refusing to respond. "Sorry?" she said at last, trying to buy time.

"Your name, lad! And who ye'll be reporting to."

"Oh! O'course. Well, my name is Phillip," Fèlice said. "Phillip, son o' Landon, from Magpie Wood in Ravenshaw. And my friend, my friend is Max . . . Maxwell, son o' . . . Rafferty the cobbler, from Tullimuir."

She could feel her cheeks getting hot, and cursed herself for her slow wit.

"Interesting, we've just had another Rafferty from Tul-

limuir," the wardrobe mistress replied, writing laboriously.
"No' a name ye hear every day."

"Really?" Fèlice said. "It's a common name in Ravenshaw."

The woman raised her eyes. "Ye all from Ravenshaw?
Now that is interesting."

Fèlice squirmed under her suspicious gaze, and did her
best to look innocent and soulful. "Really? Why? There's
lots o' us lads from Ravenshaw about, us no' having our
own Tower, ye ken, and it being too far for any o' us to
travel home now the Theurgia's closed down. The school is
full o' us, lounging around and doing naught. I guess the
Banrìgh is just trying to keep us out o' trouble."

"Good luck to her," the woman responded sourly, and
sprinkled sand onto the wet ink. "Well, then, lad, off ye go,
else ye'll be missing that boat."

"Och, aye, I dinna want that," Fèlice answered, and hurried out of the room, conscious of sweaty palms, hot
cheeks, and a thumping heart. She could not help a big
smile breaking out on her face, though, as soon as the door
of the wardrobe shut behind her. She'd done it! With a little more luck, and hopefully a lot more wit, she and Landon would be on that boat!

The Thistle Ring

⟨⟨⟨⟩⟩⟩

Bronwen sighed, shuffled her papers, got up, and went to the window, looking down on the fountain in the courtyard below. People were bustling everywhere, preparing for Iseult's departure. Bronwen was stabbed with envy. What she would not give to be going to the sea! She clenched her teeth together, crushed her skirt between her hands, and paced back and forth. She hated Lucescere! No wonder her mother had made her father rebuild Rhyssmadill for her. Oh, to live within sight and sound of the sea!

A stifled groan escaped her.

Maura, the old bogfaery who had been her nursemaid ever since she was a little girl, looked up from her sewing.

"Bron fidget-fadget all the time," she complained. "What wrong with my girl?"

"I'm bored!" Bronwen said. "And I'm sick o' being Banrìgh. I'm sick o' being in mourning. I'm sick o' everything."

"Ye need some fresh air," Maura said. "Why ye no' go out for a ride? Pretty girl like ye shouldna be stuck indoors all day with her head in books and papers. Go out, gallop, have some fun. Then ye feel better."

"Maura, ye're a treasure!" Bronwen smiled at her. "Will ye send that page o' mine to ask Neil to bring the horses round?"

"Anything to save my poor auld legs," Maura said, and got stiffly to her feet, sighing as she limped over to the door and spoke to the page, who was sitting just outside. Joey went running off to do her bidding and the old bog-faery came stumping back to help Bronwen change.

Standing, she only came up to Bronwen's waist and the Banrìgh had to bend low to embrace her. Maura patted her back affectionately. Her leathery hand was black and covered all over with ripples of fur, and her round black eyes were very bright.

"Do I work ye too hard?" Bronwen asked anxiously. "Neil was only saying yesterday that I should have a proper lady's maid. Would ye like that? If I got some lass to do the hard work, I mean, and give ye a bit o' a rest."

"That Cuckoo, he thinks he kens all, but he kens naught," Maura said grumpily. "He says this, he says that, and ye jump, jump, jump. He no' your husband, lassie, and he no' your lover. Ye be careful how much say ye give him over ye."

"Och, Maura! Do no' be silly. It's Neil jumping about all over the place for me. I have to be careful no' to let him work himself to the bone." Bronwen turned around so Maura could unlace her black silk dress. "I do no' think he's slept more than a wink this past week. Why, it was past midnight when we finished up last night, and he was at the Council table at breakfast. That's more than I can say for half the Privy Council!"

"Ye tell that Cuckoo ye need a new lady's maid like ye need a hole in the head," Maura said. "The nerve o' that boy!"

Bronwen smiled to hear Neil called by his childish nickname, and stepped into the riding dress that Maura held out for her, standing still as the bogfaery buttoned her up.

"How come ye stayed here in Lucescere instead o' going back to Arran?" she asked curiously, never having thought to wonder about this before. Bogfaeries were native to Arran, and Maura had been born there, her mother, Aya, nursemaid to Neil's father, Iain, when he was a boy.

Maura snorted. "That Tower o' Mists, it too filled with ghosts and bad dreams for me," she answered. "Besides, ye were my girl. Ye think me just say bye-bye and go, and leave ye all alone? Hmmphf!"

She would have been all alone too, Bronwen realized, with her mother a mute servant of the witches, and her uncle never quite learning to trust her, let alone love her. There had been Donncan and Neil, of course, vying for her affections all through their childhood and adolescence, and Isabeau, who had been more of a mother than an aunt to her, practically raising her from a babe, and looking out for her all of her life. But Isabeau had been the Keybearer, with a whole Coven to take care of, and certainly unable to give her the concentrated love and attention Bronwen had longed for. Without Maura to fuss about her all her life, and bring her hot chocolate in bed, and brush down her dresses for her, Bronwen's life would have been much lonelier.

"Aye, aye, I miss the marshes at times," Maura mumbled as she combed out Bronwen's hair and pinned it up for her again. "But no' that tower, oh no! Ye stay at that tower too long, ye get sick, ghosts start walking in your skin. Aye, aye, we ken, we bogfaeries do. We see. Ye should listen to your auld nursie, Bronny-lass, and watch out for those ghosties."

Bronwen was amused. "Donncan said he had nightmares the whole time he was there too," she said. "The air must be bad."

"Bad air, bad dreams, bad people," Maura said.

"No' any more, surely," Bronwen said. "Why, Iain o' Arran is an auld dear, really, and Cuckoo's an absolute sweetheart. I must say his mother's no' my favorite person on earth, but apart from having an odd taste in religion, there's no harm in her. That pastor o' hers, well, he gives

me the creeps, no doubt o' that, but he's no' from the Tower
o' Mists, strictly speaking."

"Ye just watch out for them ghosties, missy," Maura
said, and stood back to survey her charge, who was looking very dashing in a dark blue riding dress that, although
it covered her from chin to wrist to boot-toe, was fitted so
closely to her body it was almost scandalous. Bronwen had
not had time to have a new, more demure riding dress
made, nor, if she was to be truthful, the inclination. It was
a very beautiful costume.

By the time Bronwen was dressed and ready to go, Joey
was waiting excitedly for her outside her bedchamber, with
her riding crop and tall hat in his hands. One of Bronwen's
bodyguards, Dolan the Black, fell in behind her as she
made her way down the stairs, the tail of her skirt looped
up over her arm. Joey bounded just behind her, carrying
her gloves, hat, and whip reverently.

Neil was waiting for her out in the forecourt, holding
the reins of Bronwen's white palfrey and his own handsome bay, while a few other lords and ladies waited nearby
for Bronwen to appear before mounting. It was a fine, crisp
day, and the breath of the horses puffed out white. Since
most riding costumes were soberly made anyway, none
had been dyed black and so it was a relief to the eye to see
rich russet reds, forest greens, pearl greys, and autumn
browns instead of the unrelenting black that had met Bronwen's gaze day after day. The only black to be seen was the
two pillars of Elfrida and her pastor, who were taking a
promenade together around the forecourt and frowning
with disapproval at the high spirits of the courtiers, all of
whom were glad to be escaping the monotony of a court in
mourning, if only for an hour.

Just as Bronwen was preparing to be thrown up into her
saddle, a large party of people came out of the palace and
at once came over to speak to her. It was the MacAhern and
his family, who were riding for Tìreich that afternoon.
Each was followed by only one servant carrying a few

small packs, which made Bronwen open her eyes wide in amazement.

"My heavens! Is that all ye've got!" she exclaimed. "I swear, if I was coming to visit ye in Tìreich I'd have ten times as many chests as that, just for me."

"We like to travel light," the MacAhern said.

"We do no' have need of much," his wife said with just the faintest trace of scorn in her voice.

"A horse, a swag, and away we go," Hearne MacAhern said cheerfully, grinning at Bronwen. She could not help smiling back. She knew Hearne well, of course, since he had been one of her uncle's squires and so around the royal court a lot.

"Is this your new filly?" the MacAhern said, eyeing Bronwen's palfrey with an experienced eye. "She's a pretty piece. How does she run?"

"Smooth as silk," Bronwen said proudly. "Neil got her for me."

She smiled with pleasure as the MacAhern, the acknowledged lord of horses, ran his hand down her mare's flank and nodded approvingly as the palfrey danced away, curving her neck and tossing her mane.

"She's got spirit," the MacAhern said.

"I told the man I was wanting a horse for the Banrìgh and he tried to sell me an absolute slug," Neil said with a laugh. "He could no' believe I'd risk Bronny's neck on a spirited mare like Snowfall. I was adamant, though. I said, if I buy her that flat-footed, sway-backed beast, she'd make me ride her! I daren't risk it."

As everyone laughed, Bronwen saw that a sulky-faced young man with a shock of fair hair was watching disconsolately from the steps. It was Fymbar MacThanach of Blèssem, another of the Rìgh's former squires. Like Hearne MacAhern and Barney MacRuraich, his court duties had ended with Lachlan's murder and his family were eager to take him back home with them, at least until the assassin had been found and punished, and life at court seemed safe once again.

She waved at him and smiled, and he beckoned her over.

Bronwen sighed, being impatient to get away for her ride, but she excused herself politely and moved over to where he stood, his arms crossed over his chest.

"Hey, Fymbar, how are ye yourself?" she asked. "I have no' seen ye in days." She spoke warmly, sympathetic to the young man, who must be fed up at being tied to his mother's skirts all the time. The NicThanach of Blèssem had not let her precious son and heir out of her sight for a moment.

"Nay, ye've been too busy with your Cuckoo," he said sarcastically.

Bronwen frowned. "I beg your pardon?" she said icily.

Fymbar was nursing a strong sense of injured pride. The only son in a family of five, he had been petted and pandered to all his life by his powerful mother and four loving sisters, and he was not used to not getting what he wanted. Well, he had wanted Bronwen ever since he had first come to the palace, and yet she had never done more than laugh at him and send him to get her drinks while she flirted with someone else. He had been prepared to stand nobly aside for Donncan, knowing how important their marriage was strategically, but he had no intention of being tossed aside for Neil of Arran, who was a blackguard for endeavoring to seduce his best friend's wife in the first place. So, even though Bronwen's face and voice should have warned him to be quiet, he plunged on nonetheless.

"For shame, my lady," he said. "Your uncle no' a fortnight dead and your husband missing, Eà kens where, and ye amuse yourself with his best friend. It's no' worthy o' ye . . ."

Bronwen had lost all the color and animation that the prospect of an hour's freedom from the palace had given her.

"How dare ye!" she cried, then remembered to lower

her voice. "How dare ye insinuate that I have been unfaithful to my husband, and to the Crown," she hissed. "I have done naught but my best to govern this country since the role was thrust upon me so forcibly at Midsummer. Ye think I have time or energy for dalliance? Ye are a fool, and a dilettante. Ye think a country this size runs itself? Ye think I am but a puppet, that signs the papers put afore me without even glancing at them? Ye wrong me, sir! I have spent every waking hour since my husband disappeared trying to find him and bring him back, and doing my best for him while he is gone. And Neil has been my prop, my support, all this time, the best and dearest friend that either I or my husband could have. Ye owe me an apology, Fymbar, and him one too!"

She was close to tears, her breast heaving, while he was scarlet with anger and shame.

"Me, apologize to a MacFóghnan!" he cried. "Never! Do ye no' ken they canna be trusted? Ye've been duped, Bronwen. He plays ye for his own ends, and ye dance to his tune. Do ye no' ken all that clan are like snakes in the grass? Our lands have marched side by side for centuries, and we have learned to our cost that—"

"One does no' touch a Thistle without pain," a very soft, sneering voice said at Bronwen's elbow. She jumped as if stuck by a pin, and spun around, only to see Elfrida and her pastor standing right behind her. They must have heard every word.

Elfrida was standing very straight, with one hand pressed to her chest. She wore a very large black ring, Bronwen noticed, carved with the thistle crest of the Arran clan. She was smiling at Fymbar, who shrank back, his words dying in his throat.

"Ye would be best to remember that, young Fymbar," Elfrida said. "Touch no' the Thistle."

No one said anything.

Elfrida laughed.

"Shall we walk on, Your Grace?" the pastor said, offer-

ing her his arm. He was tall and thin and angular, with fine
blond hair cropped close to his skull, a pointed chin, and a
bony nose that he carried very high, all the better for looking down it.

Elfrida put up her hand and caressed the thistle seal
ring. "Aye, it's so pleasant to feel the sun after so many
days o' snow," she said. "I'm sure ye must agree, Your
Majesty."

"Aye," Bronwen said stupidly.

Elfrida laughed again and walked on, her full skirts
swaying beside the narrow robe of the pastor, like a black
poppy drooping from a black stem.

Bronwen turned back to Fymbar. "If ye ever speak to
me like that again, I will have ye charged with treason and
thrown in the tower," she said, very low. "If ye were no'
such a young fool, and if we had no' been friends for years,
I would do so now."

All his bravado had shriveled away. "I . . . I'm sorry," he
gasped. "It's just . . ."

"Neil has done naught to dishonor himself or me,"
Bronwen said. "He is the Rìgh's true friend. I bid ye remember that, and try to be as good a friend to me as he is."

She thought Fymbar might cry at that. Certainly there
was a choke in his voice as he tried again to apologize.
Bronwen did not wait to hear him out. She turned and
walked back to the group still talking and laughing by the
fountain, most of them thankfully unaware of the odd little
scene by the steps. Neil, however, had noticed something.
His eyes questioned her as he threw her up onto her mare,
and she smiled at him reassuringly. She saw the way he
turned to look anxiously at his mother, who had resumed
her promenade as if nothing had happened.

Bronwen, too, pretended nothing had happened. In a
way, nothing had. It had just been so disquieting, the way
Elfrida had laughed. And certainly it was odd to hear her
speak as if she was the Banprionnsa of Arran, and not its
neighbor, Tirsoilleir. Her family motto was "From Strength

to Strength," and her badge was a hand wearing a sword. Bronwen found it most peculiar to see her wearing the MacFóghnan thistle, and quoting Arran's family motto instead of her own. Puzzling over it occupied her thoughts all through the ride and back again, until Neil brought his horse up beside hers and asked her, with a troubled expression, if all was well.

"Och, aye," Bronwen said, with a brilliant smile. "I mean as well as it can be, given the circumstances."

His face cleared a little. "Aye, it's been a terrible time for ye. I do no' ken another woman who would no' have fallen to pieces, given the same situation. I do think ye're marvelous, Bronny!"

"And me ye!" she returned, flashing him a smile over her shoulder.

His eyes lit. "Really?"

"Aye. I couldna have done it without ye, Neil. Thank ye."

"It's my pleasure to serve ye, my lady," he responded with a mock courtly bow, and she laughed.

"Race ye to the old oak tree!" she cried, and dug her heels in Snowfall's sides. At once the white mare leaped forward, and Neil's gelding a second later. Neck to neck, the two horses galloped through the falling bars of sunlight, and Bronwen felt all her disquiet fall away behind her.

Golden Horses

Lewen was rather surprised not to find Fèlice and Landon waiting for him outside. He wondered whether they were upset with him for failing to convince Iseult to take them all with her. Or perhaps they were just as sick with misery and disappointment as he was himself, and had rushed back to their own rooms at the Theurgia to grieve in private.

Lewen had no desire to go back to his own room. Its coldness and emptiness tormented him. What he needed, he decided, was to get right away from the palace. He needed a good gallop in the fresh, cold air, the wind blowing in his face. He would go to the stables, he decided, and take his stallion Argent out for a good gallop.

Lewen had always spent a fair amount of his spare time at the stables, earning extra money as a groom, and paying for Argent's upkeep with his labor. He had always had a way with animals, and had a calm, gentle manner about him that horses liked. Usually the stables were as busy as an ants' nest stirred with a stick, and his help was always greatly appreciated, but lately things had been quiet, with half the court gone back to their own residencies. So Lewen was surprised to walk into the big, cobbled yard and find the place seething with activity. Grooms were busy saddling a great many horses, and servants wearing the warm brown livery of the MacAhern clan were loading up packhorses. Huge red-gold dogs lay around everywhere, their breath steaming in the icy air, and a large group of men and women dressed in brown plaids, crisscrossed with yellow and red, were standing about waiting.

Lewen remembered someone had mentioned the MacAhern clan was riding out that afternoon, and at once looked for his friend and fellow squire Hearne MacAhern, whom he had hardly seen since the night of the murder. Lewen saw him at once, talking with his sister, Madeline, and his brother, Aiken, both tall and brown with dark hair tied back with leather thongs. Lewen had met them once or twice before, when they had been studying at the Theurgia, but both had graduated some years before and had not returned to court since. The MacAherns disliked cities and palaces, he knew, much preferring the freedom of the wide brown plains they called home.

"Hearne!" he cried, and waved his hand.

Hearne turned and smiled brilliantly at the sight of him, lifting his hand and beckoning him over. "Lewen!" he cried. "Well met! I was hoping to run into ye afore I went. I've hardly seen ye all week. Do ye ken my sister, Maddie, and my brother, Aiken?"

"I remember ye from when ye first came to the Theurgia," Madeline said, offering him her hand. She shook it like a man, firmly and swiftly. "Ye had a beautiful grey, a big lad, looked like one o' Vervain's line."

"Aye, that's my stallion, Argent. He's in here somewhere, eating his head off and getting fat from too many oats. I've come down to take him for a gallop."

"Be careful, the roads are icy still," she said. "Ye do no' want to slip and fall."

"I will, thank ye," Lewen answered. She nodded and turned away, moving with a swift, long-legged stride to join her mother and father nearby. Aiken nodded too, abruptly, and turned to follow her. Although he was as tall and handsome as his sister, his face was dark and brooding, and did not have the same pleasant openness as Hearne's.

"Do no' mind Aiken," Hearne said rather apologetically. "He's no' much o' a talker."

"Well, neither am I," Lewen said.

"Except to horses," Hearne said, and they grinned at each other.

"So ye're heading home?" Lewen said.

"Aye, and glad I am o' it too. I mean, the Theurgia's closed for the rest o' the term anyway, and my parents are worried about what could happen next. They want to get home and keep us all close until it's clear there'll no' be war, or any other kind o' trouble."

"Aye, black days," Lewen said.

"Aye. Is it no' awful? I can hardly believe all that has happened! The Rìgh murdered, Prionnsa Donncan and Prionnsa Owein stolen away, and Banprionnsa Olwynne too. Ye must be absolutely gutted. Is there any news yet?"

Lewen shook his head and said tersely, "They've taken to the seas. The Dowager Banrìgh is setting off after them, hoping to catch them afore they reach the Pirate Isles."

"Is it a pirate who has kidnapped them?" Hearne asked in lively curiosity. "What on earth for? Do they want ransom?"

"I dinna ken," Lewen said. "Happen so."

Hearne sensed a black cloud descending over Lewen and so asked no more, even though it was clear he would have loved to. Instead he said, "Do ye want to see my father's horse?"

"Aye!" Lewen responded eagerly. "O'course I would. May I?"

"They'll bring Brimstone out last," Hearne said. "Else he'll just take off, and then we'll be in trouble."

"He's not the docile sort then?" Lewen said, following his friend into the stable.

"Nay, he's well named. He's quiet enough when *Daidein* is on his back, but willna let anyone else near him. He hates being kept in a stable, so he'll be in a foul mood.

They had to bring him in because o' the snowstorm, but he was no' at all pleased."

They heard the stallion as they entered the stable, whinnying and trumpeting in rage. His hooves thundered on the cobblestones as he danced about his stall, rearing back and fighting to free his head of the halter and rope that kept him tightly tethered.

Kenneth MacAhern, Hearne's father, was the last of the thigearns, so Brimstone was a huge old winged beast, with a warm honey coat shading to silver around the muzzle and eyes. He could not spread his rainbow-colored wings properly in the stall, adding to his anger and frustration, and so he held them high, half-furled, the tips sweeping the wooden walls on either side. On his head were spreading velvet-coated antlers like a stag, and he tossed them in his wrath, and repeatedly butted them against the door, which had stoved in under the pressure.

"He's magnificent!" Lewen said, gazing at him in awe. The golden winged horses of Tìreich were far larger and fiercer than their black cousins in Ravenshaw, and were now almost as rare, having been hunted almost to extinction during the Ensorcellor's reign. Since winged horses rarely bred in captivity, they had to be caught and tamed in the wild, and few had the strength or the determination to manage it. It was said the only way to tame a winged horse was to stay on its back for a year and a day without dismounting, a task few managed.

"Aye. He's getting auld now. My father has tried to breed him, to see if we can preserve his line, but none of the foals born have been winged, unfortunately."

"And no one has succeeded in taming another?"

"Nay. Aiken tried again last spring, but couldna even get close to one. I think that's why he's so surly."

"Och, well, it's up to ye then."

Hearne flashed a smile. "Aye! I'm no' allowed until I reach my majority, and that's another four years away, but

I mean to find one and tame it then, even if I must stay on its back for three years and three days!"

The winged stallion in the stall reared and neighed, as if in challenge. Hearne grinned again, shoved his hand in his pocket, and stepped forward quietly, holding out his hand and whickering softly. The stallion quietened and rolled one wary golden eye his way. Hearne moved forward another step, and the silvered muzzle dropped towards his hand and delicately took the lump of sugar that Hearne held there. He crunched it with relish, and then danced away, tossing his antlered head. Hearne stepped back, smiling widely. "What a beauty!" he cried.

Lewen's eye was caught by something gold at Hearne's shoulder, and he leaned forward for another look as his friend returned to his side.

"Is that your family brooch?" he asked.

"Aye, it is. Have ye no' seen it afore?" Hearne unpinned it and passed it to Lewen. It was a beautifully wrought badge of gold, depicting a rearing horse with tossing mane and tail.

"Nay, I havena. I guess ye were always either in court gear or your apprentice robe. It's bonny."

"Thank ye." Hearne took it back and fastened his brown and red plaid together again.

"Hearne, what would it mean to have a brooch very like that, but with a running horse, no' a rearing one?"

"The horse rampant is the royal family's badge, the horse passant is the badge o' our guard," Hearne answered. "Much like the badge o' the Blue Guards, and us squires. We wear the charging stag, while the MacCuinns themselves wear the crowned stag rampant."

Being a country boy from the highlands of Ravenshaw, Lewen did not know much about heraldry but he was able to follow this fairly well, guessing that "rampant" meant in the rearing position, and "passant" the running position.

"So someone who had a badge like that, a golden badge

with a running horse, that would mean they were one o' your people?"

"Aye, one o' the Royal Horse Guard, which is the special cavalry unit that guards the royal clan and rides to the forefront o' any attack. Only the very best are accepted. Most o' them used to be thigearns, but o' course there's none left now. Why do ye wish to ken?"

"Rhiannon . . ." Lewen started to stay, but his voice snagged in his throat. He tried again. "Rhiannon carries a badge like that. She said it was her father's."

"Rhiannon? The girl with the black flying horse?" Hearne was at once alert and interested.

"Aye."

"How strange. I wonder . . . Come, let's go tell my *Daidein*. He will want to ken."

Lewen followed Hearne back out into the sunshine, unable to help feeling a sharp spurt of eagerness. Even though Rhiannon rarely mentioned her father, who had died when she was five, he was sure she would wish to know more of him.

Kenneth MacAhern was overlooking the strapping of his family's luggage on the backs of the packhorses. He turned at the sound of his name, and smiled to see Hearne and Lewen approach. Hearne hurried through the introductions, and then launched into a description of Rhiannon's brooch, which caused the MacAhern and everyone around him to look at Lewen with great interest.

"Laird Farnell, will ye come here, please?" the MacAhern called.

A tall, elderly man with grizzled black hair came at once to his lord's call, a look of inquiry on his weathered face. He had the bowlegged swagger of a man who has spent most of his life on horseback and, despite his age, moved with swift grace. Lewen noticed the lord's eyes were a most unusual luminous blue grey, and felt his heart begin to accelerate.

"Will ye show Lewen here your badge?"

Puzzled but obliging, the elderly cavalier showed Lewen the badge that pinned his plaid at his shoulder.

"It's the same," Lewen said. "Exactly the same."

"We do no' forge many o' these badges," the MacAhern said. "Most o' them are very auld, passed down from father to son, or retrieved from the bodies o' the dead to give to those newly inducted into the Horse Guard. Gold is very rare and very precious in Tìreich. We do no' waste it."

"Rhiannon said the badge belonged to her father."

"How auld is this girl . . . this thigearna?"

"She is no' sure. She was never taught to count, or to remember anniversaries like birthdays. She could be seventeen or eighteen, at a guess."

The blue-eyed cavalier was standing very still and stiff, listening intently.

"It is eighteen years since Conall was lost, is it no'?" the MacAhern said to him in a very gentle, kind voice.

The cavalier nodded, struggling to conceal his shock and dawning hope. "Do ye think . . . is it possible?"

"Maybe," the MacAhern said. "We would need to see the brooch, and hear this lass's story." He turned back to Lewen. "This is Laird Farnell MacAhern, once the captain o' the guards, and my father's cousin and dear friend. His son, Conall, disappeared near the end o' the Fairgean Wars. He was taking a message to Ravenscraig, warning the MacBrann that Fairgean had been seen in the bays and coves along the coast. He was a thigearn. Last we heard he was flying over Bald Ben, taking the shortcut over the mountains. He never arrived, and we never found what happened to him, although we sent search parties into the hills."

"Rhiannon's herd live at Dubhglais, a loch that lies between Bald Ben and Ben Eyrie," Lewen said.

"Are ye suggesting that this . . . satyricorn herd somehow captured my son?" Lord Farnell was obviously struggling between horror that his son had been a captive of the satyricorns, and hope that he may have fathered a daughter, one who had managed to tame a winged horse herself.

"It's a possibility," the MacAhern said with a shrug.

"Rhiannon has eyes the same color as yours," Lewen said to Lord Farnell, and watched them widen and kindle in sudden excitement. "And she carries a bow like yours too." He nodded at the longbow the cavalier carried slung over one shoulder.

"The thigearn's weapon," Hearne said in excitement. "Roasted rats, it sounds like she really might be related!"

"My laird, may I be excused from service?" Lord Farnell asked. "I must meet this girl and see if it is at all possible that she is my granddaughter."

"O'course," the MacAhern replied with an understanding smile.

"She is no' here," Lewen said, misery weighing down his words. "She flies in the Banrìgh's service, trying to stop the kidnappers."

"Dangerous work," Lord Farnell said proudly.

"Aye," Lewen responded.

"I will wait for her nonetheless," Lord Farnell said. "Surely it will no' be long afore she returns, and I can see her badge for myself, and ask her about her father."

"She does no' remember much," Lewen said. "She was only five when he died."

"Poor lass," Lord Farnell said, his eyes growing misty. "What a terrible life she must have had, brought up among the satyricorns, without any idea o' who she really was."

"Well, then, if ye must stay, my laird, I will leave ye a regiment o' cavaliers to help ye and guard ye," the MacAhern said. "Bring this thigearna back to Tìreich. I am most curious to meet her, as are we all, I think."

There were nods and murmurs of agreement from the onlookers, except for Hearne's brother, Aiken, who scowled and looked most displeased. Lewen felt his heart sink. The last thing he wanted was Rhiannon riding off to Tìreich and discovering a whole new family. But he casti-gated himself for his selfishness and said nothing, manag-

ing to summon a smile of farewell for Hearne as he
mounted a tall chestnut stallion.

"Ye come too, Lewen!" Hearne shouted, as if guessing
his friend's thoughts. "Horse whisperers are always welcome in Tìreich!"

Lewen smiled and waved, then stood back to watch as
Brimstone was brought out by four of the prionnsa's cavaliers, rearing and bucking and fighting the rein. His wings
were fully spread now, and Lewen was able to appreciate
their full beauty. The MacAhern stepped forward, leaped
up and onto his back, and cast off the reins with an expression of utter disdain. Brimstone should have bucked and
reared even more at the freedom from restraint, but instead
he calmed instantly, folding his wings down by his sides
and turning his head to nuzzle affectionately at the Mac-
Ahern's boot.

"Come, let's ride!" the MacAhern shouted, and wheeled
his arm up and down. At once the whole cavalcade of
horses leaped forward as one, pouring out of the stable
gates and along the road in a living river of black, bay,
chestnut, and grey.

Lewen watched them go, then turned away, his heart
heavy.

Then he realized the old cavalier with the blue grey eyes
was watching him closely. "Ye ken this lass, this thigearna
well?" Lord Farnell asked.

Lewen nodded.

The old man dropped his callused hand on Lewen's
shoulder. "Come, share a dram with me and tell me all ye
ken," he said. "Is it true she tamed her winged horse in
only a day and a night?"

"Aye, it's true," Lewen answered, pride swelling his heart.

"Marvelous! Come, tell me all about it."

It was late when Lewen finally got back to the Theurgia, and
his head was swimming from all the whisky he had drunk.

Lord Farnell had been most interested in hearing everything about Rhiannon, and Lewen had found himself getting rather choked up with love and pride as he had recounted all their adventures, and Rhiannon's bravery and quick thinking. He found himself longing for her more than ever, and had to remind himself that he was betrothed to Olwynne, not Rhiannon. Once again, his dilemma plunged him into utter misery, and as a result he drank more than he should, and rather thought he had revealed more of his feelings to the old cavalier than was wise.

As he came into the great hall at the Theurgia, hoping to grab some bread and stew to help soak up the whisky, he saw Edithe and Maisie, both looking rather cross, sitting together at one of the long tables. All in all, there were only about a dozen people eating in the hall, when usually there would be several hundred. Lewen blanched and tried to duck away without being noticed, for he was not comfortable in the company of either of the two other girls he had met while traveling through Ravenshaw. Edithe was a stuck-up, toffee-nosed, supercilious snob, while Lewen was very much afraid that Maisie had conceived a warmer emotion than mere friendship for him. She had been badly mauled by wild dogs during their journey, and Lewen had saved her from being even more seriously injured and then had helped care for her afterwards. They were an unlikely couple, these two, Edithe being the daughter of one of Ravenshaw's oldest and most respected families, while Maisie was the daughter of a village cunning man, and very unsophisticated. She wore her mousy brown hair in plaits wound over her ears, and tended to clomp around the halls of the Theurgia in hand-hewn wooden clogs, unable to afford a cobbler's fees.

Lewen almost made it out the door, but unfortunately Edithe, screwing up her nose at the simple fare being offered for supper, saw him and beckoned him over imperiously.

"Lewen! Where is everyone? Have ye seen Cameron and Rafferty? I havena seen them all day."

"They've gone to be squires to the Dowager Banrìgh," Lewen said, too weary and drunk to be tactful.

"What! Those sly boys. I kent they were angling for advancement. How on earth did they win my lady's notice? Did ye introduce them?"

"Aye, I did," Lewen answered, and sat down with a sigh, grabbing a hunk of bread and dunking it in the bowl of rather watery stew. The cooks at the palace were much better than the cooks at the Theurgia.

"I do think ye could've introduced me to the Dowager Banrìgh," Edithe whined. "I am a NicAven o' Avebury, after all! Rafferty is naught but a clockmaker's son! Why, what does he ken about serving a banrìgh? I would have been a far more suitable choice . . ."

"My lady dinna want a lady-in-waiting, she wanted a squire." Lewen drank down some water, and rested his throbbing head on his hand.

Maisie looked at him closely. "Are ye all right, Lewen? Ye look a bit green. Is your head aching?" Maisie wanted to be a healer more than anything else in the world, and had come to the Theurgia to study at the Royal College of Healers.

Lewen nodded, and then wished that he had not.

"Here, let me rub it for ye," Maisie said, blushing rosily. She got up and stood behind Lewen, gently massaging his neck and shoulders. "Would ye like me to get ye some willowbark?"

"Nay, I'm fine," Lewen said and jerked his shoulders free of her touch. Usually he was more gentle with her, feeling sorry for her and not wishing to hurt her feelings. Tonight, though, he was simply too heartsick to care.

Maisie flushed crimson, and moved away from him, tears in her eyes.

"What about Landon, though, and Fèlice? Where have they got to? Oh, please, do no' tell me the Dowager Banrìgh has taken on that shameless hussy as her lady-in-waiting! Really, I am shocked! For a gently born girl, Fèlice is most forward in her ways. O'course, she wants to get her claws into Prionnsa Owein, and that is why she wishes to smarm up to his mother. I do believe—"

"I told ye, Her Highness has no need for a lady-in-waiting!" Lewen said impatiently, and then he dropped his hands from his eyes. "Ye mean, ye have no' seen Fèlice or Landon all afternoon either?"

"Nay, we have no'," Edithe said crossly. "And very boring it's been too, with no one but Maisie to talk to. We've looked for her everywhere, but canna find her. She's probably sneaked off into the city, the hussy!"

"I wonder," Lewen said slowly, and felt his heart sink. *What was Fèlice up to this time?*

Fèlice and Landon were finding out just why Iseult had been so confident of reaching the port by dawn.

Although she had three weather-witches on board with her, and was acknowledged as having strong if rather improperly controlled powers of her own, Iseult had no intention of adding to the turmoil of the weather by whistling up a wind.

Instead, Iseult had called up a loch-serpent from the depths of Lucescere Loch.

A great, sinuous beast with slimy, green grey scales, the loch-serpent had risen slowly from the very depths of the great expanse of water, responding to the strange language Iseult had wailed.

Lifting up the lid of the barrel she was hiding in, Fèlice could see the cold green boiling of the water, and then a thick loop of scaly skin that slowly rolled and unrolled. She shivered and crouched lower, holding her breath against the strong smell of the ale the barrel had originally contained. She wondered how Iseult knew the language of the loch-serpent, and wondered if it was akin to that of the dragons. She remembered that Iseult had, like Isabeau, been apprentice to the great sorceress Meghan of the Beasts, who, she had been taught, could speak the language of every living thing. It had been a long, wild ululation, the cry that had sounded from Iseult's throat, and which was now being echoed by the beast rearing its crested head from the loch.

Iseult ululated again, and the loch-serpent replied. Fèlice gave herself a crick in the neck trying to see what was happening, but dared not lift her barrel lid any higher. Soldiers were crowded everywhere on the boat, some in the blue cloaks of the Yeomen, some wearing the heavy furs of the Khan'cohbans, still more in the grey of the general army. There were dogs too, a whole pack of them, yelping and snarling and leaping about on the end of their leashes. The sight of them made Fèlice very afraid of discovery, and she could only hope that the overwhelming stench of the ale would hide her own.

Suddenly there was a massive jerk that saw Fèlice bang her head hard against the wooden barrel, and then the boat took off at an incredible speed. Fèlice heard shouting and cheering and, putting her eye to the crack once more, saw foam flying high over the side of the barge.

"Has the word gone ahead for all riverboats to heave-ho?" someone shouted.

"Aye, sir!" someone else shouted back.

"Hold fast then, laddie, 'cause we're going hell for leather now!" the first man yelled, obviously enjoying himself hugely.

Fèlice wished she felt the same. The smell of the ale, the dank closeness of her hiding place, and the wild rocking of the boat were all together making her feel very sick. She gritted her teeth, thought of Owein, and endured.

Long Past Midnight

B ronwen heaved a great sigh and sat up. It was no use. She could not sleep. Even though exhaustion hung on all her limbs like lead weights, she could not stop her brain from grinding around in the same old circles.

Her unhappy relationship with her husband was one well-worn track. Wondering where he could be was another. Worry over the consequences of the impulse that had caused her to pick up the Lodestar, and with it the crown, was a third. Fourth was wondering who could possibly have murdered her uncle, and worrying about whether that hidden assassin had murderous plans for her too. The last, and not least, subject occupying her mind was Neil and his love for her. She did not know how to manage him; how to keep him at arm's distance and convince him he had no chance of winning her heart, when it must be obvious to everyone that she was coming to rely on him more and more.

Thinking and worrying made no difference, yet she could not help herself. So night after night Bronwen lay awake for hours, only to fall into an uneasy doze sometime before dawn. She only knew she slept because of her dreams, which were all horrible, and so near to true life that she had to reassure herself they were only nightmares.

She swung her feet out of bed and thrust them into her fur-lined slippers, then wrapped her luxurious blue silk

dressing-gown about her shoulders. Although the weather
had improved remarkably since Iseult had left earlier that
day, it was still unseasonably cold. Bronwen walked over
to her fireplace and stirred the coals with a poker, then
threw on some small lengths of wood. Yellow flames began
to lick along their sides.

Bronwen felt a sudden longing for the sweet, fragrant
tea she had taken to drinking, and glanced at her bell.
There was no reason why she did not ring it and rouse
some poor servant to get it for her. It would probably be
her little page, though, she thought, and he was so young,
he needed his sleep.

She lit her lamp with a long piece of kindling, not having much skill with the element of fire, and sat down to
read over the reports from the Privy Chamber. There was
so much to do, so many demands on her time and energy,
that she felt like she was scaling a mountain of paper, all
covered with incomprehensible words. After a while, her
head was aching fiercely and her longing for tea was so
acute she kept glancing at the bell, even though she knew
it was long past midnight, and cruel to ring it.

So she stood up, stretched, and went through the flickering darkness to her door, opening it gently. To her surprise Joey was fast asleep outside, wrapped up in his cloak.
She frowned. Surely her page had a bed of his own? She
bent to wake him, but he was sleeping so peacefully she let
her hand fall, and stepped over him.

Two of her bodyguards stood in the hallway outside her
room, the corridor lit by bright lanterns in either direction.
She knew them well; they had guarded her since she was a
child.

"Canna ye sleep, my lady?" Dolan the Black asked,
raising one thick eyebrow.

She shook her head ruefully. "I thought I would go
down and get myself some tea," she said.

"Send that lad o' yours, that's what he's for," Dolan said
with amiable contempt.

"He's asleep," Bronwen replied. "Outside my door! Why is he there? Does he no' have quarters o' his own?"

"Has some notion he's guarding ye," Dolan said tolerantly. "Seems he fears for ye, my lady, and thinks he's better equipped to guard ye than us, Eà bless his foolish heart."

"I can go for ye, Your Majesty," said the younger guard, a fair, red-faced man called Barlow.

"Thank ye, Barlow, but I want to stretch my legs. I'm all . . . twitchety."

They laughed. "Ken that feeling," Dolan said. "I'll accompany ye, my lady."

She knew better than to argue. Dolan had first been appointed to her when she was little more than eight years old. He brooked no argument.

She went on down the corridor, Dolan following quietly a few paces behind. Once she reached the end of the corridor, the palace was all dim and quiet, lit only by the occasional lantern. It was cold, and she huddled her hands into her sleeves and wished summer would return.

The tea Mirabelle made up for her would be kept in the butler's special pantry, she knew, along with her own sack of dancey, a tin of her favorite biscuits and sweetmeats, and anything else she might take a fancy for at any time. The pantry was not in the kitchen wing, a completely different building to her own, but just on the floor below, so that she need not wait when she rang asking for something. She went silently down the stairs, moving from one dim point of radiance to another through oceans of darkness, her guard moving as quietly behind her.

Someone came sighing along the corridor. All Bronwen could see was a white floating face and two white disembodied hands, cupping the soft flickering light of a candle. Bronwen stopped where she was, suddenly seized with terror. If it was not for the tip-tap of shoes, she could have imagined it a ghost, or some phantom from one of her nightmares. The face was so white, the eyes so cavernous, and the night itself seemed to drag behind her in a vague rustle and crackle.

Then Bronwen saw the heavy black ring on one of the hands, and recognized it as the thistle seal-ring Elfrida of Tirsoilleir had been wearing earlier that day. Only then could she sort out the pattern of white and black, and see Elfrida's face, blank and wretchedly unhappy, lit demonically from below by the candle. Bronwen took a deep breath of relief, and would have made some move to declare herself, upon the stairs in the darkness, had she not heard a low mutter of words rising from Elfrida's mouth.

"Go away, go away," she was saying. "Why do ye torment me so? I have done all that can be done. I have done it all, what more can I do? No, no, no, no. Too much. Too much. Oh, why canna ye let me rest? I am so tired, so tired. I'm too tired to do any more. All is going well. All is fine. What more do ye want?"

She stopped. She seemed to cringe. Bronwen hardly dared to breathe.

"Ye canna do that," Elfrida breathed, so softly Bronwen could hardly make out the words. "Ye wouldna. Ye couldna. No."

There was a long pause. Every hair on Bronwen's body rose. She shivered and wrapped her arms close about her.

"Aye," Elfrida said, and sighed, her candle shaking. "Very well. What harm in it? None. Hardly any at all."

She seemed to be staring at a point beside her, as if someone walked with her in the cold darkness, but there was no one there. Bronwen wondered if she was sleep-walking. She was fully dressed. If she had slept, it was in her clothes. Bronwen could not have explained why the sight of Elfrida wandering the hallways at three o' clock in the morning, fully dressed and muttering to herself, was so disturbing. Perhaps because Elfrida always seemed so in control, as if she had never given in to a mad impulse in her life. Perhaps it was just the hour of the night, when everything seemed strange and spooky.

Bronwen was trying to gather the courage to go down the last ten steps and take Elfrida by the arm, waking her, or at least challenging her, when Dolan laid his hand on her arm, shaking his head and endeavoring to draw her away. Bronwen hesitated.

Just then another pool of light began to advance towards them down the corridor. Warmer, gladder, more golden, it filled the hallway. Instinctively Bronwen retreated a few steps, back into the darkness. Elfrida seemed to hear her movement. She turned her head, glancing up the stairs, and would have stepped a little closer, except that the light from the lantern reached her, and she cringed back, shielding her eyes.

It was Mirabelle the healer.

"Your Grace," she said in a soft voice. "Ye should no' be wandering the hallways at this time o' night. What is wrong? Can ye no' sleep again?"

Elfrida heaved a sigh. "Sleep, sleep, when did I last sleep?"

"The poppy tincture I gave ye is no' working?"

"I have bad dreams," Elfrida replied. She shuddered so visibly the candle flame undulated like a snake, and hot wax dripped down over her hands. She did not seem to notice.

"Come, ye need to sleep. Let me mix ye up a stronger potion. Ye need your strength, Your Grace. Now is no' the time to be giving in to doubts and weaknesses. Let me take ye back to bed . . ."

Elfrida turned her head and looked up the stairs. "She says to beware the silent watchers."

Now Bronwen wished she had taken Dolan's advice and gone back to her room earlier. Yet what was there to fear? A weary old woman who could not sleep, and a healer tending to her needs. Yet what was Mirabelle doing here, in the palace, at three o'clock in the morning? Why were both women fully dressed, and why were all the hairs on Bronwen's arms standing upright? Even while she was castigating herself for being a suspicious, superstitious fool, Bronwen was inching back step by slow step.

Mirabelle moved closer to the foot of the stairs and raised high her lantern. It illuminated the edge of Bronwen's embroidered blue dressing-gown. Bronwen managed a deep breath and then walked down into the light.

"Mirabelle!" she said gaily. "Well met! I was just wanting ye."

"Cannna ye sleep either, Your Majesty?"

Bronwen shook her head. "Nay, I'm afraid no'. Guilty consciences for us both, I guess, Your Grace," she said laughingly to Elfrida. Neither she nor Mirabelle saw the joke, staring up at Bronwen with blank faces. Bronwen smiled winningly to show she had only been teasing.

"Let me give ye a sleeping potion, Your Majesty," Mirabelle said. "Ye need your beauty sleep."

It was said deadpan, unsmiling, but Bronwen smiled in response anyway, and said, "Thank ye, Mirabelle, but I thought perhaps some o' your delicious tea . . ."

"The tea is a stimulant," Mirabelle said, "and ye need something to calm and soothe ye. Here. I have some mixed up already. Drink only two fingers o' it, no more, and try no' to drink any dancey or tea in the evening, Your Majesty."

Bronwen sighed, thinking of the cups and cups she drank every night as she tried to force her tired brain to understand the pyramid of papers delivered every evening to her private suite. She took the little brown bottle Mirabelle held out to her, however, and thanked her with a smile.

"Go back to bed now, Your Majesty," Mirabelle said. "I will see Her Grace back to her room."

Bronwen glanced at Elfrida, who was staring blankly at the wall.

"Is all well with her?" Bronwen said in a low tone. "I mean, she seems . . ."

"Her Grace suffered greatly as a child, in the hands o' the Fealde and her henchmen," Mirabelle answered gently.

"She has nightmares, and suffers insomnia. In times o' stress, her dreams and flashbacks are worse than ever. There is no' much any o' us can do, except try and help her to dreamless sleep."

"I see," Bronwen said, remembering her aunt mentioning Elfrida's dreadful childhood. "I'm so sorry. I did no' realize."

Mirabelle raised an eyebrow, a response that somehow made Bronwen feel terribly thoughtless and guilty, and said in a colorless voice, "I will come and see ye in the morning, Your Majesty. For now, go back to bed, drink some o' the medicine I have given ye, and try to get your sleep. Ye need your strength."

"Aye, indeed I do," Bronwen answered, trying to smile, and she turned and went back up the stairs, Dolan following close behind.

They reached her door, and she turned to Dolan, feeling uncomfortable about the little scene she had just witnessed. Dolan was frowning, but at her troubled look he said kindly, "Now get back to bed, my lady, and no more fussing. The healer is right, ye need your beauty sleep. Do ye want some warm milk or something?"

"Nay, nay, I'm fine," Bronwen answered hurriedly, hating to be treated like a child. She went back into her suite. Joey still slept before her bedroom door. She stepped over him, closed her door, drank down two fingers of the heady, sickly sweet medicine, and got into her cold bed. Huddled up into a little ball, inching her feet down the bed, Bronwen tried to think over what she had just seen and heard. A few things niggled at her, seeming odd, but even as she tried to tease them out of her subconscious, sleep swooped down upon her and took her falling into the abyss. She did not dream at all.

Bronwen woke late the next morning, feeling heavy-headed and lethargic. Remembering all she had to do that day, she groaned and dug herself deeper into her eiderdown, wishing she could stay in bed.

There was a very slight noise over by her door, but at once Bronwen was wide awake and preternaturally alert. Listening intently she cracked open one eye, and saw Mirabelle bending over a tray upon the table.

"What do ye do?" Bronwen asked sharply.

Mirabelle straightened and turned. "Och, I'm sorry, Your Majesty, did I wake ye? I came to see how ye were this morning, and found your little maid preparing your tea, and thought I'd bring it up myself. Here it is. It's hot. I told the bogfaery she should let ye sleep longer today, as ye had a disturbed night, but she said ye have a breakfast meeting with your councillors."

"I do, unfortunately," Bronwen said, accepting the steaming cup with a little nod of thanks, and fluffing up her pillows so she could sit up. She took a sip of tea and sighed in pleasure. It was the most delicious tea, and sent warmth and strength radiating through her at every mouthful.

"I have brought ye a little gift," Mirabelle said, placing a glass jar with a golden lid upon Bronwen's bedside table. "We would no' want our Banrìgh losing her looks because o' a lack o' beauty sleep, now, would we? It's made of elderflowers and celandine, which may sting a little when ye first put it on, but greatly brightens one's complexion."

"Why, thank ye," Bronwen answered, feeling a little pang of guilt. She had once, she remembered, laughed at Mirabelle when she was teaching them a recipe for making just such a skin lotion, asking her if she thought her own complexion was a great inducement for her students to trust her formula. It had been a long time ago, when Bronwen was only sixteen and first discovering the power of her own beauty. She hoped Mirabelle did not remember.

"Put it on just after washing your face," Mirabelle said. "I think ye will find it has a most pleasant aroma."

Bronwen wondered if she should mention that her aunt, Queen Fand, had given her a big pot of the skin lotion the

Fairgean women used, which was made with seaweed, after Bronwen had commented on how fine and soft the Fairgean women's skin was. She decided it would be more tactful to simply thank Mirabelle, and put the pot away for when the lotion she was using now had run out. So she smiled and said, "Thank ye, I will."

Mirabelle smiled in response, the expression lightening her heavy, pockmarked features, and then went away, leaving Bronwen to finish her tea and drag herself out of bed in peace.

It was a long, long day. The clock hands crept around very slowly. Bronwen found it hard to concentrate. Several times she had to jerk herself out of a reverie in which she daydreamed she had gone in search of Donncan, saved him from dreadful danger, and won his heart forever. The mental image of him clasping her against his chest and whispering, "Bronwen, my love!" in her ear was so enticing it brought a lingering smile to her lips, which she had to banish very firmly before someone noticed, it being entirely inappropriate to a discussion on revaluing the currency. She had to remind herself sternly that her days of freedom were over. She could not even afford to daydream of escaping the court to go in search of Donncan, let alone doing it. She had to concentrate on being the best banrìgh she could.

By the end of a very long session of the Privy Council, Bronwen had a headache and felt perilously close to tears. She withdrew to her bedchamber and, after about sixteen unwelcome interruptions and interludes, took the coronet off her head with a sigh of relief and begged her maid Maura to bring her some more of Mirabelle's special brew.

The bogfaery frowned. "Me no like that tea. Makes Bronny all twitchety. Me make Bronny some nice chamomile tea."

"I'd fall asleep if ye did that," Bronny said. "Please, Maura, just bring me the tea. It really does have a marvelous way o' clearing my head."

Grumbling, the bogfaery did as she was told. Bronwen

sat down and rested her face in her hands, whispering to herself, "Donncan, where are ye?"

Tears slipped out through her fingers.

The door opened but Bronwen did not look up, expecting it to be Maura returning with her tea.

She heard a quick step, then saw a grey silk gown blossom out as her mother sank into the chair beside her, the dark wings of her hair falling forward onto her cheekbones as she leaned forward in concern.

"Bronny, my dear, what's wrong?"

Bronwen hurriedly wiped her face and sat up. "Naught! I'm just tired. And sick o' waiting for news. When will Aunty Beau be back? It's been days and days. What is taking so long? I thought it was simply a matter o' following Donncan and Thunderlily along the Auld Ways, overcoming Johanna, and bringing him back. What can have gone wrong?"

Maya laid her work-roughened hand on Bronwen's silk sleeve.

"Ye may need to prepare yourself, sweetling," she said. "Isabeau may no' have been in time. Donncan may . . ."

"Donncan is no' dead!"

"I fear he may be, my dear. Ye must prepare yourself."

Bronwen was silent. She sat with her back stiff, her jaw clenched, her hands crushing the stuff of her gown.

Maya frowned. "I ken ye have always been close to your cousin," she began delicately, "but I had no' thought ye cared for him in that way. Ye did no' seem to miss him at all while he was away, visiting Neil in Arran over the winter. In fact, ye seemed relieved to have him gone."

Her daughter looked away, pressing her lips together.

"Then, at the wedding, ye seemed positively cold. I wanted to tell ye to at least try and keep up a semblance o' marital bliss, for appearance's sake, but could no', since I was meant to still be rendered mute." There were little ironic flourishes to Maya's voice that gave a piquancy to the beauty of her golden voice. "I was no' the only one who thought the marriage purely one o' convenience. Was I wrong? Do ye have deeper feelings for Donncan?"

There was a short silence, then Bronwen suddenly burst out, "I am banrìgh now. I should be happy . . . I should be gloating that fate has delivered everything I ever wanted into my hands . . . the throne, the crown, the Lodestar . . . yet it is no' how I dreamt it would be . . ."

"Naught ever is," Maya murmured.

Bronwen seized her mother's arm. "Was it no', Mama? Really? For ye never loved my father, did ye? Ye ensorcelled him into marrying ye, and ensorcelled him into giving all his power into your hands. Ye ensorcelled *me* into life! I thought ye loved it, the power, the control. I thought ye loved being banrìgh, and having everyone rush to do your bidding. Ye hated being thrown down."

This time it was Maya's turn to flush and bite her lip and look away. She was silent a long time, long enough for Bronwen's shoulders to droop and her breath to sigh out.

Then Maya said, very quietly, "No, it was no' enough. I told myself it was, but . . ."

"But what?"

"I wished . . ."

"Wished what?"

"Sometimes . . . many times . . . I wished your father had lived . . . and loved me for myself . . . and we had naught to do but love each other and rule the land together . . . But . . ."

"But?"

"It was no' to be. They . . . My father . . . they would never have let me be . . ."

"I ken."

Another long silence.

"It would never have worked. Besides, by the time I realized, it was too late . . . and he . . . Jaspar . . ."

Bronwen realized that her mother was struggling to hold back tears. She had never seen her mother cry. She stared at Maya, surprised and uncomfortable, and then reached out a hesitant hand to comfort her. Maya suffered it for a moment, then shook Bronwen away, straightening with a sigh.

"It is no use thinking o' what might have been," Maya said. "All we can do is play with the hand we've been dealt. And ye have a royal flush, Bronwen. Use it."

"It is just that I . . ." Bronwen sighed, then shut her mouth. She did not wish to tell her mother that she feared this new-found power, and longed to have Donncan relieve her of some, at least, of the load. She did not want to say she missed his steady presence at her side, his quick wit and insight, his intelligence and strength. Most of all, she did not want to admit she longed to melt into his arms, and raise her face to his, and have him kiss her again, like he had the night of the May Day feast. This was something she had trouble admitting to herself, let alone her mother.

"All I am saying, Bronny, is that ye must prepare yourself to rule alone," Maya continued, taking no notice of her daughter's agitation. "Donncan may well be dead, and if that is so, ye will have to fight to keep your throne. If your thigearn lass succeeds in rescuing Owein and Olwynne, ye may find yourself facing a challenge ye canna withstand. Indeed, perhaps it would be best to make sure she does no' succeed, and Owein and Olwynne never make it back alive."

Bronwen stared at her mother with wide eyes.

"One should always look ahead," Maya said serenely, and then smiled at Maura as the bogfaery came in, grumbling at the weight of the tray she carried. "Ah, good! Tea. Shall I pour, Bronny?"

SHIP IN A
BLACK STORM

*"My soul, like to a ship in a black storm,
Is driven, I know not whither."*

—JOHN WEBSTER
The White Devil, 1612

The Pirate Isles

Olwynne lay on the bare wooden boards, groaning.

She stank of vomit and sweat and urine and excrement. No matter how hard she tried, it was not possible in the heaving, rocking, swaying hold of the ship to always make the bucket on time. And Olwynne had never been so vilely ill in all her life.

Racked with cramps so severe they made her gasp out loud, her stomach in constant rebellion against the ceaseless motion and the dreadful diet, Olwynne could do nothing but weep and moan.

If it had not been for her twin brother's company, his staunch courage and valiant optimism, Olwynne thought she might have given in and died. In the darkness she could not see his face, but his strong hand and shoulder, his warm wing, his gentle voice rarely failed her, even though he was quite as sick as she was. Olwynne had always thought she was the strong one, the one with the quiet inner core of certainty and fortitude, but Owein had proved her wrong these past two weeks.

It was impossible to know how long they had been imprisoned in the stinking belly of the ship. Yet, counting the number of times Jem had come to bring them some dreadful slop of maggot-infested gruel, and to empty the bucket with many curses and jeers, Owein thought it was at least three days, maybe as many as six. It depended on whether he came only once a day, or twice. Olwynne found the young man filled her with the utmost terror. He never failed to stand over them, mocking them, threatening them both with rape and torture, death and abandonment.

"No one here to see or care," he would say with a leer. "Always wanted to shove my prick up the arse o' a banprionnsa. Guess I'll never get the chance again; may as well enjoy myself on this Truth-begotten journey." He would loom over her, his lantern held high so its cruel radiance would fall harshly upon her, and jerk his crotch with one hand. Olwynne would shrink back against Owein, who would steady her with his bound hands, trying to reassure her and keep her strong. Then Jem would snort with laughter. "Though I think I'll wait for a nice clean lass. Dinna want my prick to fall off!"

Another time he would focus his attentions on Owein. "Always thought ye were so fine, dinna ye? No' so high and mighty now, are ye? How does it feel to lie in your own shit and piss, and ken ye're no better than any other man? Shit and piss, that's what it's all about, and having a Rìgh for a father doesna make a fart's worth o' difference."

Owein just stared back at him, not saying a word. They had both learned that any defiance only earned them a kick in the ribs. Once, after Owein had lost his temper and given back as good as he had got, Jem had even unbuttoned his trousers and urinated on them, much to their disgust. He had not done any worse, though, despite all his foul words and threats, and with time they had found him easier to ignore.

The ship had been running fast before the wind, that they could tell from the creaking of the timbers and the pitching of the floor on which they lay. Now the ship was coming into gentler waters, and the wild rolling had calmed, allowing Olwynne to slip into an uneasy sleep.

She dreamt she walked down a dark corridor, groping her way forward, unable to see. Ahead a door stood ajar.

Light fell through the crack like a rent in a curtain. Olwynne crept towards it, and put her eye to the crack.

Inside Lewen sat, peel after peel of white bark falling away from his knife. He was carving a knob of wood away into nothing. Gladly Olwynne put her hand to the door and pushed it open. Lewen looked up at her, his face twisted in misery and hate.

"My blade must have blood," he said. He rose to his feet and stepped forward swiftly, slashing his knife across her throat. As Olwynne fell, gasping, blood fountaining up between her hands, he repeated the words unhappily, gazing down at her on the floor. "My blade must have blood."

Olwynne woke with a jerk. She shivered and crept a little closer towards Owein, who bent his tattered wing over her.

"Bad dreams again?"

She nodded her head.

Owein felt the movement in the darkness and said, with forced cheerfulness, "Never mind, it's only a dream."

"It seems so real," Olwynne said, her voice trembling.

"It's only a dream." Owein did not sound convinced. He knew as well as she did that dreams were rarely without meaning, particularly for Olwynne, who had seemed to be developing a talent for dream-walking. She had dreamt of her father's death before it happened; that at least was one dream proved prophetic. He dreaded thinking of the meaning of some of her other nightmares.

A silence fell between them.

"The ship has stopped rolling," Olwynne said.

"Aye. I'd say we're wherever we're meant to be."

"Where? Where?" she cried.

Owein shrugged. "Nowhere good, I'd say."

"What do they mean to do to us?"

"Nothing good, is my bet."

She heard the bitter humor in his voice, and had to swallow down a rush of tears.

"What do they want with us? Why did they take us?"

"To kill us," he answered. "Why, I do no' ken, but it is clear they hate us, our clan, our blood. Olwynne, ye must be brave. I do no' ken if we can save ourselves or not, but we must try. If only I could get my hands free! But I canna. I've chafed my wrists raw trying, but that brute Jem has tied me too tight. Olwynne! We must take our chance, if it comes. Be ready. If I give the signal, run. Can ye do that?"

Olwynne thought of her legs, trembling with weakness and seeping with sores where the ropes had rubbed again and again. She nodded and tried to smile, even though Owein would have no chance of seeing her expression in the darkness. He knew her well, though. His hand patted her feebly, and he said, his voice hoarse, "Good girl."

A few minutes later, the ship docked. They recognized the familiar sounds, having often traveled on their father's ship, *The Royal Stag*. Then Jem came down to jerk them to their feet, and force them up on deck.

It was dusk. The air over the shimmering water was warm and smelled of strange spices. Olwynne looked about her; this was no land she recognized. Rising in high peaks all about, the island curved like an ammonite about the lagoon. The peaks were black against the curve of the twilight sky. To the west, where the sea broke in little waves over a reef, the first moon was rising. It was huge, red, misshapen. It made Olwynne shudder.

Owein and Olwynne were so weak and disorientated they could barely walk. Their eyes were so used to darkness, the light of the lanterns hurt and they shrank away, shielding their faces.

Lord Malvern stood on the bulwark, his eyebrows drawn down close to his nose. "Ye fool!" he said to Jem. "I thought ye were taking care o' them! Look at them. They're filthy and sick. We need them to be strong and healthy when we sacrifice them, no' with poisoned blood and fever. How could you be so stupid?"

"They've been comfortable enough." Jem spat over the side.

"If they are sick, I will sacrifice ye in their place," the lord answered icily. Jem went pale, and cast a quick glance at the royal twins, who were doing their best to hold each other up.

"Dedrie!" Lord Malvern called. Slowly the skeelie climbed up from below deck. She was pale and trembling, and by the way she hunched over her stomach it was clear she too had suffered from seasickness.

"Aye, my laird," she answered in a weak voice.

"Look at the sacrifices! Is this what ye call looking after them? The banprionnsa will no' be pleased! She doesna want blood poisoned with pus and filth, she wants pure, clean, youthful blood, like we promised her. I want them washed, fed, tended, and given something to make them well again, and I want it done now! It is full moon tomorrow. Ye have until then to have the girl in particular strong enough to kill. Else it'll be ye I bind to the altar stone! Do I make myself clear?"

"Aye, my laird, o' course, my laird," Dedrie gabbled in very real terror, and then Owein and Olwynne were hurried back downstairs to a cabin that was obviously Dedrie's own, given the sour smell of vomit and the bottles and jars of potions and medicines on every available surface.

Hurling imprecations at Jem, the skeelie had jugs of hot water brought up from the galley and poured into a tin basin. Jem stood by, scowling, his dagger at the ready, while Dedrie carefully cut away the blood-stiff ropes and cleaned their sores, anointing them with some kind of ointment that stung badly, then bandaging them neatly. They were forced to drink bitter green nettle tea, to purify the blood, and a foul mixture in which Olwynne recognized the taste of burdock root, St. John's wort, and borage.

More water was brought, and Owein and Olwynne did their best to clean themselves up, washing their faces and

hands, their necks and armpits, their arms and legs. Olwynne would have loved to have washed her hair, which
was matted and filthy, but there was not enough water and
no shampoo or comb. She had long ago lost her pretty
high-heeled sandals, and her feet were filthy and covered
in nasty cuts and bruises. All she could do was sit wearily
on the bunk and soak them in another basin of warm water,
in which Dedrie poured some cloudy liquid that smelled
awful. Owein was in slightly better shape, still having his
boots, and having spent much of his youth out hunting,
camping, fishing, and riding, years that Olwynne had spent
in the library with her nose in a book. Still, there was no
need for Jem and his dagger. Neither of the twins could
muster up the strength to do more than sip at the hot soup
Dedrie brought them, and to lie down together to sleep,
their matted red heads sharing the same pillow, Owein's
wing folded over them both.

"Sleep tight, little babes," Jem cooed mockingly, going
out the door. "Enjoy your last night together."

As he shut the door they heard Dedrie saying crossly,
"Now make sure ye do no' drink too much o' the water o'
life and fall asleep on watch again, Jem, for I'll no' be taking the blame! My laird wants us to get to the auld fort
afore sunrise, so just make sure . . ."

The door nicked closed, and they heard the sound of a
key in the lock. Olwynne sighed and turned her cheek into
the sour-smelling pillow. She was asleep in moments.

Once again Olwynne's sleep was disturbed by images of
knives and mist and gravestones, blood dripping down her
neck, and the sound of a woman laughing in utter glee.
When she awoke, it was to find black misery crouching on
her chest like a malicious imp, choking her.

She turned and gave her brother a little shake, too afraid
to lie there in the darkness by herself. He came awake at
once, tense and alert. "What's wrong?" he whispered.

"What's wrong? What's wrong? Did ye no' hear what
the laird said? They mean to kill me tonight," she whis-

pered back. "They mean to sacrifice me. Sacrifice! I canna believe it's true!"

He nodded. "This is no' just some plot to destroy the MacCuinn clan," he murmured. "There's more going on. I wish I had paid more attention to . . . to Lewen . . . when he told us about the laird o' Fettercairn. They are necromancers, I ken, trying to rise the spirits o' the dead. *Daidein . . .*" His voice broke, and tears began to run down Olwynne's cheeks. Their grief over the death of their father was still raw and incredulous. There had been no time, no peace, for acceptance and healing.

Owein raised his hand and drew it across his nose. "*Dai-dein* killed the laird's brother and his nephew, I ken, years ago," he went on, his voice low and hoarse, "and Laird Malvern seeks revenge for that, and seeks to raise them from the dead again. So I can understand why I was taken and Roden, but no' ye. Who is this banprionnsa they seek to raise?"

"Tonight," Olwynne whispered. "This very night! Owein, what are we to do?"

"I canna believe the Yeomen are no' hot on our trail," Owein said. "They will have guessed the laird's plans, surely? They'll be here in time."

"But what if they are no'?" Olwynne's voice was paralyzed with terror. She could hardly force the words out.

Owein gripped her shoulder with his hand. "Bravely and wisely, Olwynne, remember that! Bravely and wisely."

She was trembling violently, but at her brother's words she did her best to calm herself.

"We'll try to escape," Owein said, shifting his weight in the narrow bunk, seeking to find a more comfortable position. One red-feathered wing was pinned behind him; the other was still folded over Olwynne, comforting her with its soft warmth. "They have cut our bonds, thank the Spinners! Let us pretend to extreme weakness and faintness; they will no' suspect we mean to escape. If they try to bind us again, scream in pain."

"That I can do with true sincerity," Olwynne said grimly. Her wrists and ankles were throbbing hotly.

"Let's look for a weapon o' some sorts. That skeelie must have a knife or a pair o' scissors somewhere. Let us look now while we are alone."

He got up and prowled quietly around the room, but Dedrie had taken all her belongings with her the night before, leaving the room bare.

Olwynne took advantage of him being gone to stretch out in the cramped little bunk. She was amazed they had been able to sleep at all, for both were tall and Owein was broad-shouldered and had his wings to add to his bulk as well.

The bunk was fitted in against the curved hull of the ship. Above were heavy beams, with a round porthole. Moonlight spilled in through the thick glass, filling the room with cold light. Lying back, Olwynne saw a small bottle silhouetted against the glass. She reached up her hand and took it down from the deep recess where the porthole was fitted. Obviously Dedrie had put the bottle there so it could be within easy reach when lying in the bunk. It had a glass stopper that was easily removed. Olwynne sniffed at the liquid inside, and felt a faint warming of hope. It was a tincture of poppy and valerian, to aid in sleep. A drop or two under the tongue was enough to relax and ease into sleep; the full bottle emptied into a strong-tasting drink like dancey or whisky would be enough to knock a man unconscious.

She had time only to whisper to Owein what she had found, before they heard someone at the door. As Owein slipped in beside her again, pretending to be still asleep, Olwynne hid the bottle under the blanket.

It was Dedrie, bringing them some hot porridge and more nettle tea, which they drank and ate obediently, by the light of a lantern. The night before, the skeelie had given Olwynne a clean chemise in which to sleep. Now she brought them some clean clothes—a rough brown dress and a pair of wooden clogs for Olwynne that obviously belonged to the skeelie, and some leather breeches for Owein. His shirt, which was especially made to fit around his wings, had been washed and dried, and Dedrie had brought him a big cloak to wrap over his wings, concealing them from view. There was a cloak for Olwynne too, with a hood. She surreptitiously slipped the bottle of sleeping potion into its pocket when the skeelie's back was turned.

Both Owein and Olwynne were feigning much greater weakness than they felt. Dedrie was worried about them, and clucked around them, mixing up another of her foul-tasting medicines and insisting they drink it.

Olwynne pretended to have so little energy she could not even lift the cup to her lips, and Dedrie bent over her solicitously, saying, "It's skullcap and rue, my lady, to stop ye feeling dizzy. My laird must no' see ye so sick and faint."

Owein exchanged a quick glance with Olwynne, and crept a little closer, preparing himself to knock the skeelie unconscious while her back was turned. Just then Dedrie straightened and turned around, however, and Owein pretended to stagger and fall. Dedrie caught him and called to Jem, who at once came rushing in through the door, making the twins glad they had not attacked the skeelie after all.

"Why could ye no' have looked after them properly?" Dedrie raged as they maneuvered the slumping Owein back onto the bed. "Ye said ye had it all under control!"

"Ye're the skeelie," Jem sneered, "it's your job to keep them healthy, no' mine."

"I was sick as a cat," Dedrie retorted. "Ye said ye'd look after them."

"I did," Jem said. "I changed their filthy bucket, dinna I? And made sure they had food. What else was I meant to do?"

"Keep them alive!" Dedrie snapped back. "Come on,

help me. We've got to get them up on deck. My laird wants
to leave the ship well afore dawn, so we're up at the auld
fort afore anyone's up and about."

Auld fort? Olwynne thought and glanced at her brother.

"No one ever sleeps in this pirate-infested hole anyway,
so what's the point?" Jem grumbled. "The streets will be
filled with drunken sailors and filthy whores, all drinking
and carousing till dawn."

Pirate-infested hole? Olwynne felt as much as saw the
sudden spark of comprehension that lit Owein's eyes. *The
Pirate Isles!* she thought. *But why? What is here apart from
pirates and cutthroats?*

The Fair Isles had been under the control of pirates for
so long that few called them that anymore. Periodically,
Lachlan had sent in his navy to wipe the nest of buccaneers
out, but they simply took to ship the moment they saw sails
on the horizon and escaped to the high seas, coming back
again later to rebuild their inns and brothels, their jetties
and warehouses. Lachlan had stationed a company of soldiers here for a long while, but they had gradually died of
fever or treachery, or had been seduced into piracy themselves. So then he had sent out an incorruptible com-
mander called Iron John, who had kept the islands fairly
free of thievery and corruption for seven years, but after
Iron John was poisoned by his own valet, there had been a
gradual return to the bad old days.

The Pirate Isles were a constant thorn in the Rìgh's side
and every Lammas Congress the lairds and the merchants
called for stronger measures, and Lachlan made promises
he had done his best to keep.

The problem was that Eileanan was one of an archipelago
of islands scattered across a seemingly boundless ocean.
Many, many ships had set off to explore the distant seas, and
most had never returned. The exceedingly wide swing of the
tides, dragged by the pull of two moons, made sea travel
treacherous indeed, and so most ships hugged the coast of
Eileanan, doing their best to avoid the natural hazards of

sandbank and sea-serpent, harlequin-hydra and whirlpool.
Only the pirates had succeeded in exploring the outer islands, and an illegal trade flourished in the produce of those
most distant islands, particularly in tobacco, cinnamon, and
rhinfrew, which would only grow in the Fair Isles, and in
moonbane, that most addictive—and expensive—of drugs.

Limp and heavy-footed, Owein and Olwynne were
pushed, dragged, and wrestled up the ladder and onto the
deck by Dedrie and Jem. It was still dark, though the two
moons, both at the full, were sinking behind the island's
peaks to the east. The water glimmered an eerie blue in the
moonlight, and the stars overhead were very large and
bright.

Olwynne clung to the rail for support, staring at the pirate town. Even though it was very late, lights were still
strung all along the shore, and she could hear faint sounds
of music and drunken laughter.

Hundreds of other ships were moored along the jetty, or
bobbed at anchor in the wide circle of the bay. Most of the
buildings were rough wooden structures, but Olwynne
could see a large square stone building high up on the cliff
that must be the old fort. It was a grim-looking place, half
in ruins, with arrow slits and battlements.

Jem dragged his hipflask out of his pocket and took a
generous swig, grunting with satisfaction and wiping his
mouth. A thought flashed between the twins. At once
Owein straightened up and made a bid for freedom. With a
cry of surprise, Jem shoved the stopper in his flask,
dropped it, and raced after him. Dedrie turned and began to
holler down the hatch, "Ballard, ahoy!"

Quick as a flash, Olwynne dropped on her knees,
grabbed the hipflask, and emptied the little vial she carried
in her pocket into it. It only took a moment, though her
hands were shaking so much she could barely put the stopper back in. By the time the bodyguard Ballard had
bounded up the stairs and helped Jem seize Owein and
drag him back, Olwynne was where she had been, leaning

weakly on the rail, and the hipflask lay where Jem had dropped it.

Owein was limp and senseless, much to Olwynne's horror. She fell on her knees beside him, weeping, but to her relief he gave her a secret wink when the others were not looking. She saw Jem bend and pick up his flask, and take a deep mouthful, and then at Ballard's jerked thumb, passed the flask to him so he too could drink. Olwynne dropped her eyes so they would not see the excitement and hope in them.

Lord Malvern came hurrying along the deck, wrapped up well against the cool of the night, with Irving and Piers a few paces behind him. The lord's raven flew ahead of them, coming down to perch on one of the yardarms.

"What was all that commotion?" the lord snapped. "Did I no' order ye to keep it quiet?"

"The prionnsa tried to escape," Dedrie explained, clutching her hands together in dismay. "Jem and Ballard caught him, though."

"Obviously the sacrifices are well recovered then," the lord said. "Hoist him up, Ballard. We'll pretend he's dead drunk. Now, remember, I want no attention drawn to us in the town, if at all possible. Let us get through quickly and quietly, and go on up to the fort. In the morning, these disreputable sailors I hired will unload their cargo and sail away, and no one will ever ken we have been here."

"Aye, my laird," they replied in unison.

"Keep the sacrifices quiet as we go through the town. I do no' wish to have to pay a ransom to get them back again should they alert anyone to who they really are."

Jem lifted his dagger and grinned.

"Very well. Try no' to kill them unless entirely necessary. I am looking forward to using MacCuinn blood to resurrect MacFerris blood. It will no' be anywhere near as satisfying if I must use one o' ye."

His followers exchanged uneasy glances. "Aye, my laird," they said.

Lord Malvern led the way across the gangplank and onto the jetty. Dedrie followed along behind, then Jem grunted at Olwynne and gestured her forward. Trying to avoid his touch, Olwynne stumbled and almost fell, and Piers came and took her arm and assisted her. He did not speak, but she was glad to get away from Jem and his constant staring, and so allowed herself to accept his support. Ballard had Owein hoisted up over his shoulder, and Owein lay quiescent, waiting for another opportunity.

No one paid them any attention as they went through the town, being too busy among their own concerns. Ballard made a show of pretending to be assisting a drunk friend, and Jem showed a mouth full of bad teeth in what he thought was a smile. Olwynne kept her head down, and her hood over her distinctive red hair. Owein was well muffled up in a cloak too, so that not one red curl or red feather could be seen.

Beyond the town was a steep cobbled road that climbed up the hill to the fort on the top of the cliff. It was dark away from the light of the town, and Ballard had to stop often, to shift Owein's dead weight on his shoulder, and to share another drink of whisky with Jem. Irving drank once or twice too, but Piers did not, and his hand under Olwynne's elbow did not slacken.

By the time they reached the top of the road, both Jem and Ballard were swaying and stumbling. Piers was remonstrating with them under his breath, and then let go of Olwynne to go to Ballard's assistance as the big man suddenly dropped to his knees. Owein slid over his shoulder to the ground, and lay quietly as Piers and Jem together tried to rouse Ballard, who dropped onto his face and began to snore very loudly.

Jem was giggling helplessly, much to Piers's anger, then suddenly keeled over onto his face as well. Olwynne slowly backed away, until she was beside Owein and was able to surreptitiously help him up. Step by slow step they edged away into the blackness, being careful to keep close to the inside edge of the hill so they did not slip over the cliff in their blindness.

Suddenly they heard shouts and the harsh cry of a raven. Seizing each other's hands they began to run, forcing their stiff, trembling legs forward, their breath already catching in their sides.

Then a great bluish sphere of light illuminated the whole road. Owein and Olwynne glanced back over their shoulders and saw Piers and Irving both bounding down the road after them. Irving had a dagger in his hand. At the top of the hill Lord Malvern stood, one hand raised high, a huge witch's light illuminating the hill all around. His raven was swooping towards them, calling raucously.

Owein and Olwynne could only stumble forward as fast as they could. They heard the pound of running feet behind them and expected, every moment, to feel heavy hands on their shoulders.

Then, out of the darkness, came a new sound. The beat of great wings. Olwynne glanced up, terrified, and saw Blackthorn dropping down from the sky, Rhiannon on her back. Desperate hope leaped in her heart. Rhiannon reached down a hand to her. Their eyes met. There was a moment of complete knowledge between them, smoldering with anger and shame and bitter hatred. Then Olwynne reached up her hand, and Rhiannon caught it and swung her up. Desperately, her legs hampered by her heavy skirts, Olwynne managed to lie across Blackthorn's withers, the bulge of the saddle-pad digging painfully into her stomach.

"Why?" she managed to gasp.

"Lewen wanted me to," Rhiannon answered, then she was leaning forward, shouting at Owein, "Fly! I canna carry ye both! Can ye fly!"

Owein at once spread his wings and leaped up into the air. Olwynne realized with a start of tears to her eyes that her brother could probably have escaped any time during the last hour, since they had not bothered to bind his wings to his body as they had done for so many days.

Rhiannon dug her knees into Blackthorn's side, and the winged mare wheeled about, making for the cliff's edge. Just then, something sharp and icy-cold pierced Rhiannon deep in her left shoulder. She jerked and cried aloud. A roar of pain filled her ears and eyes. The ice became a fire, a conflagration. Her head whirled. She realized she was falling. A scream tore at her vocal cords. She flailed out her arm, grasping for something to steady her. Her hand met something soft. Her fingers closed. The next moment, between the horror of falling that was every thigearn's greatest fear, and the pain and shock of the dagger driven deep into her shoulder, Rhiannon realized she was dragging Olwynne down with her. There was no time to think. Rhiannon let go, and fell.

Strong arms seized her. Rhiannon was pressed close to a linen-clad chest, and heard all about her the beating of strong wings. Intense pain stabbed through her, and for a moment she blacked out.

Then another jolt of agony dragged her halfway back to consciousness. Vaguely she heard screaming and shouting, and bluish light flashed in her eyes. Something hard knocked into her, and then she felt again the dreadful, heart-stopping sensation of falling.

All went dark.

The Old Fort

※

Rhiannon slowly swam back into consciousness. Her first sensations were the feel of a hard cold floor beneath her and the smell of dank stone and sour, unwashed hair. The smell was so familiar it brought a wave of panic crashing through her. Her heart accelerated, her breath hitched, and she thought, incoherently, *Oh no, no' again! No' Sorrowgate Tower . . .*

Trying to catch her breath, she opened her eyes and struggled to sit up. Pain lanced through her shoulder. She gasped out loud, and froze, one hand going up tentatively to touch the source of the pain. She felt as if a red-hot rod had been drilled through her shoulder and she was hanging upon it, pinned like a still-fluttering butterfly.

"Rhiannon, are ye all right? Owein, she's awoken!"

At the sound of the banprionnsa's voice, Rhiannon lifted her bleary gaze. She saw Olwynne sitting opposite her, leaning forward in concern. Her red hair was a bird's nest, rising up around her face in a wild frizz stuck with old leaves and burrs. They were in a dark cell or dungeon, with nothing but moldy old straw on the floor to soften the damp stones. Above them in the wall was a narrow slit of a window, through which light filtered. Beside the banprionnsa sat her twin brother. Although Rhiannon had never met him before, there was no mistaking his identity. Like Olwynne, his hair was red and curly, his eyes were brown, and he had the magnificent long wings of his father, though colored as flame-red as his hair, not night-black like Lachlan's had been. He was watching her with the same intent concern as Olwynne.

"What happened?" Rhiannon said faintly.

"Irving threw his dagger and got ye through the shoulder. Ye fainted and fell. I tried to catch ye, but Olwynne fell too. I couldna hold ye both, though I tried. We all fell, all three o' us. Luckily we hit the road, else we'd all be dead, I think. Your horse tried to save us, but there were too many o' them."

"They got her?" Rhiannon gasped in horror.

"Nay. She escaped, but only just. There was no hope for us. They dragged us up the road and threw us in this place. That was about three or four hours ago."

Rhiannon's eyes stung with tears. She dropped her face into her arms, refusing to let them see her weep.

"Ye tried," Olwynne said, her voice trembling. "Ye did your best."

"How did ye get here?" Owein asked eagerly. "Did ye come with the Yeomen? Are they here somewhere too? Maybe they'll—"

"No Yeomen," Rhiannon answered curtly. "I flew after your ship on Blackthorn. It was very hard. We almost dinna make it. The storm . . . I have never seen aught like it. The waves were tall as mountains."

"No wonder we were so sick," Olwynne said to Owein.

"And Dedrie and all the others too."

"Ahead was always fair skies," Rhiannon said, "but behind ye, blackness and storm like I've never seen afore. The lightning and the thunder, the wind . . . it was like frost-giants making war. So I . . . we flew ahead. It was too hard to just follow. We would never have made it. But once we got ahead o' ye, we had an easier time o' it. We came to this island last night, and made camp up in the auld ruin. Then we waited for ye."

She had to concentrate hard to form the words and make

sure they came out right. She felt sick and dizzy and utterly shocked and miserable. The pain in her shoulder was intense. Gingerly she reached over her shoulder and felt the point at which the dagger had pierced her. Someone had bound it with some kind of cloth, but it fell away when she moved, dropping to the floor like a mangled crimson flower. Beneath her fingers the wound was wet and pulpy and hurt like hell. Her fingers came away bloody.

"I could no' do any better," Olwynne said apologetically. "We managed to tear up Owein's shirt, but ye were bleeding so much. Most o' it got ruined." She made a gesture with one hand and Rhiannon saw a pile of bloodstained rags tossed in one corner. "Ye've lost a lot of blood," she went on unhappily. "But I do no' think anything important got nicked. No' your heart or your lungs, or anything."

"That's good," Rhiannon responded, feeling rather blank and strange. She wanted to get up, and rip the room apart searching for a way out, or a weapon, or tool. But she simply did not have the strength. She could not imagine even trying to stand.

"So ye do no' ken if the Yeomen are on our trail or no'?" Owein asked. She could hear from his voice that he was trying to hide his bitter disappointment. She looked at him with an effort, and managed to shrug one shoulder.

"I sent them a message. I told them where the ship was going. But I do no' ken if they even got it. And if they did, they are days behind. Maybe more, for they were sailing into that storm."

Despite herself her voice dragged with a sense of utter hopelessness. Rhiannon could not see how anyone could possibly survive the black storm Lord Malvern had conjured up. They were on their own.

Iseult clung to the railing.

"I will no' turn back!" she screamed.

"My lady, if we do no' heave-to we'll all drown!" Captain Tobias yelled back. As well as being the captain of *The Royal Stag,* the great war galleon whose wheel he was now clinging to in an effort to keep the ship from foundering, he was the Lord High Admiral of the royal fleet. Twenty ships spread out behind *The Royal Stag,* endeavoring to make their way through the heavy seas to the Pirate Isles.

They had to shout at one another, for there was no other way to be heard above the howling of the wind, the crash of the waves over the stern, the crack and whistle of the tormented sails, and the thunder that rattled about the heavens like a river of cannonballs tumbling down a grand staircase. Rain lashed their faces. *The Royal Stag* climbed a great black swell of water, looking as frail as a stormy petrel. Seawater streamed away down the deck, knocking sailors off their feet and dragging anything not tied down away in a wild welter of foam and spray. Higher and higher the ship climbed. It seemed the crest of the wave must break over them and smash them all to pieces. But then the ship broke through, and teetered for an instant. The sails filled. The ship tipped over and began the descent down into the black abyss, high walls of ocean swelling on either side. The sailors fought to keep their footing as water sloshed back down the other way.

"We canna sail through this storm," Captain Tobias shouted.

"We have to!" Iscult shouted back. "My children are out there somewhere. We have to find them, we have to catch up with that ship!"

"It's madness!"

"Maybe so, but we're doing it anyway! All I ask o' ye is ye hold the ship on course until we can get this wind back under control."

He barked a harsh laugh. "Control this wind? Ye're fools as well as madmen!"

"Do no' forget who ye speak to," Iseult said, her eyes narrowing. The captain shivered in the breath of arctic air that suddenly swirled at him from the folds of her cloak.

Icicles hung from her hood, and the deck about her feet turned white and slick.

"I have no' forgotten, my lady," the captain cried, "but ye canna expect me to take my fleet and all my men to the bottom o' the ocean without at least trying to make ye see reason."

She laughed. It was a wild, almost exultant sound. "Trust me, Captain! We're no' beaten yet."

He glanced out at the huge rolling seas and shuddered. "If ye could just keep the wind at our backs . . ." he said rather hopelessly.

"We can do that, at least," Iseult answered. "It's just a matter o' holding it steady."

Lightning ripped open the underbelly of the vast black cloud. Thunder roared. Captain Tobias made the sign of Eà's blessing, then shouted himself hoarse as sailors slipped and slithered about, doing his bidding.

The upper sails all came tumbling down, and were swiftly wrapped and stowed.

One little storm sail was hoisted aloft at the stern to help the captain retain control of the steering, while another was hoisted on the mizzenmast. The ship bucked and danced as the wind and the seas together wrenched it awry. The captain called for help to hold the tiller steady, and everyone grabbed at the rail as another grey beast of water came snarling and foaming over the rail and down the decks.

Iseult scanned the turbulent seas anxiously, then, as the ship labored up out of the trough again, took a deep breath and hurried back to her companions on the forecastle.

Stormy Briant was standing before the foremast with his hands gripping the rail, his dark hair blowing about his face and his eyes exultant. He loved a good storm. On either side of him were the two weather-witches who had trained as his apprentices. The elder, named Cristina, had been accepted into the Coven some four years earlier and was working towards her first sorceress ring. A tall attractive woman with grey eyes and brown hair, she was, it was rumored, more to Briant than just his assistant. The younger witch had only recently sat his Third Test of Power, and looked rather frightened to be facing such a wild storm so soon after being accepted as a witch. Named Fredric, he was in general called Freddy by his mentors, much to his disgust.

Finn the Cat was crouched in the shelter of a canvas lean-to, looking very ill. She was not, Iseult thought, a good sailor. Jay sat beside her, one arm about her back, the other holding a bucket, which he passed to her as needed. Nina the Nightingale sat on her other side, helping brace her against the pitching of the ship. Roden was with his father up on the poop deck, begging the captain to let him spin the wheel. The captain merely shook his head, and bade him go below deck and stop getting in everyone's way. Rafferty and Cameron were both doing what they could to make themselves useful, although neither had ever been on a ship before and had absolutely no idea what to do.

Captain Dillon was ordering his men to lash the cannons in place, and to make sure the barrels of gunpowder were well secured and not being ruined by water. He glanced at Iseult as she went by, and she nodded her head briefly to indicate that their course was to remain steady. He nodded, and ordered all the soldiers to make sure they wore a rope about their waists, tying them to the ship. He did not want to lose a man overboard if the seas were to grow any rougher, which he imagined they would.

"Finn, are ye well enough to try and raise the circle o' power again?" Iseult asked, bending over the prostrate sorceress. "We must try and calm this storm!"

Finn nodded and tried to get up, her hand pressed hard over her mouth. Her legs were wobbly, though, and Nina and Jay together needed to help her. The other witches turned from the rail, coming to join hands in a circle, with Stormy Briant in the center.

"What a magnificent storm!" he cried. "This laird has power, no doubt o' that!"

"Have we enough power to leash what he has unleashed?" Iseult asked.

Briant grinned and shrugged. "It is far easier to raise a storm than it is to control one. He conjured the wind to drive his ship, however, and we merely follow in his wake. If we had a full circle o' sorcerers, I'd say, easy! If we had even a half-circle o' weather-witches, I'd say not too difficult. A half-circle o' witches, half o' whom have no Talent with weather whatsoever, well, let's say it'll be a challenge." His eyes shone with excitement.

"Well, let us try again," Iseult said. "Nina, will ye sing the chant for us?"

Nina nodded. Her power all lay in her voice, and so, with her eyes closed and her energy focused, she began to sing, drawing upon the One Power until the air all about grew so chill it was hard for the sailors and soldiers working nearby to breathe. Icicles began to form on the halyards. The rain turned to sleet.

The other witches chanted with her then, as the song reached its ultimate crescendo, flung their hands high in the air, directing all their power to Briant. He took it, and wove it into a noose to seize the wind and bring it back under control.

It was like trying to lasso and ride a herd of wild flying horses. The wind was so strong and so turbulent, it would not be tamed so easily. Briant staggered and almost fell, almost as green as Finn, who was doing her best to control the urge to vomit until Nina had opened the circle again. Cristina ran to support Briant, who leaned his hands on his knees, his head hanging, dragging in deep lungfuls of the sleety, salty air.

The ship keeled and almost capsized, and everyone seized the closest mast or rail as water poured all over the decks. Briant was knocked off his feet and dragged sideways. If it had not been for Cristina clinging to him desperately, he may well have gone overboard. For a moment it seemed as if the ship could not possibly right itself.

Screams and cries of horror could be heard all over the ship. Then the galleon somehow steadied and plowed on, and everyone struggled to their feet again, coughing and spluttering, and wiping the salt water from their eyes. The wind bit through their wet clothes and dragged at their wet hair, and the witches were not the only ones to hurriedly make the sign of Eà's blessing with their fingers.

"May the Spinners spare us," one young sailor groaned.

"It's madness to go on," another cried.

Iseult looked at Briant, who clutched the rail, Cristina hugging her arm about his waist. He shrugged. "I almost had it," he said. "Och, but it's a wild one, this storm. If Cailean was here, to lend me his strength, I'd be riding it now, I swear. But we just havena the power."

"If only I dinna feel so sick," Finn murmured. Jay pressed her closer, smoothing back her wet, bedraggled hair. She was fighting tears.

"Sir!" a voice cried.

Captain Dillon turned at once. His eyebrows snapped together over his nose as he saw two soldiers come clambering up from below deck, each holding firmly onto a small, struggling figure.

"What's this?" he demanded.

"Stowaways, sir!"

"Stowaways!"

"Aye, sir. We found them in the store hold. If ye had no' sent us to check on the gunpowder, I doubt we would've found them till we reached shore. They've made a camp down there, sir, with beds o' sails and blankets, and water and food too. No' that they were feeling very hungry, sir. Both have been as sick as cats."

"Stowaways on the royal ship!" Captain Dillon cried thunderously. "How is this possible?"

"They have passes, sir. I dinna ken how. They must've used them to get on board ship when we were getting the stores aboard. There were men everywhere, sir, and boys too, loading up the provisions and the weapons, and helping make the ship seaworthy. They must have snuck into the store hold then, sir."

Captain Dillon looked utterly furious. "Find out for me who was responsible for securing the ship's safety while the Dowager Banrìgh was on board, and bring him here," he cried, over the roar of the storm. "Drop those ship-rats here first!"

"Aye, sir!" the soldiers said and let go of the two stowaways, who fell to their knees before him.

"Who are ye, and what is your business on board this ship?" Captain Dillon commanded.

One of the stowaways lifted a pale, grimy face. "Please, sir, it's no' Landon's fault. It was all my idea. Ye see, I wanted . . . we wanted . . ." The stowaway's voice failed, and one hand came up to scrub furiously at wet eyes.

"Fèlice?" Nina said incredulously.

Just then another great wave broke over the prow and came rushing down the deck, knocking sailors off their feet and swirling about the masts. Captain Dillon gripped tight to the rail with both hands until the water had subsided again. Then he looked down very sternly at the two scruffy figures at his feet. They had only managed to avoid being swept away by seizing his legs with both hands.

"Thank ye, ye can let go o' my boots now," he said coldly.

"Aye, sir, sorry, sir," they said and released his ankles.

"Fèlice, Landon, is that ye?" Nina asked, and came forward with a rush. So dirty and shabby were the two figures that she could barely recognize them, especially Fèlice, whose cropped hair stuck up all over her head like a hearth brush.

"Aye, Nina, it's us," Landon said unhappily.

"Landon?" Rafferty cried. "What are ye doing here? Eà's eyes, is that ye, Fèlice? What have ye done to your hair?"

"Cut it," Fèlice answered defiantly.

"Did ye stow away?" Cameron demanded. "Gracious alive, what a lark!"

"Such bad luck they had to come and check on the gunpowder," Fèlice said. "We'd been there for days and days and no one was the wiser."

The other witches had all gathered around, exclaiming in surprise and some amusement as Nina explained tersely who the miscreants were. Iseult, however, was not amused.

"Lady Fèlice, what are ye doing here? Ye are too auld for such a silly, childish prank. This is no' some pleasure cruise!"

As she spoke, another huge wave crashed over the prow of the ship, as if to prove the truth of her words.

"I ken that," Fèlice cried, struggling to hold her feet. "Ye think we do no' understand how desperate a mission this is? We ken Laird Malvern! We have seen what he is capable o'. Do ye no' realize . . . do ye no' see . . . we couldna just stay behind and wait! Owein is in terrible, terrible danger! Do ye think I could just sit around and do naught to try and help save him?"

"And Olwynne," Iscult said softly.

Fèlice blushed so hotly the color could be seen through all the grime. "Aye, o' course. And Olwynne."

There was a short silence, in which the tortured groaning of the ship's timbers and the howl of the wind seemed louder than ever.

"Would ye have just sat around and watched the clock, waiting for news?" Fèlice demanded, tears spilling down her face.

"Nay, I do no' think I would," Iseult answered. "But then, I am a Scarred Warrior. Ye are a gently reared court lady. What do ye possibly think ye could do to help?"

Fèlice clenched her hands into fists and stared up at Iseult rebelliously. "We could lend our strength to the magic circle," she said. "We are apprentice-witches, ye ken, and quite well trained, thanks to the court sorceress at Ravenscraig. And Landon's very strong, he'll be a sorcerer one day. If ye pull in Rafferty and Cameron too, ye'll have almost a full circle, that's got to be better than only half a circle, even though they've got more bone between their ears than brains."

As she spoke, she made a face at the two squires, who grimaced back at her.

Iseult looked down at Fèlice with something like respect dawning in her eyes. "Captain Dillon, we called upon ye once afore to make up a full circle, may we do so again?" she asked, not taking her eyes off the scruffy, crop-haired girl standing so defiantly before her.

"As ye command, Your Highness," Captain Dillon replied, though it was clear from his tone of voice that he hated being asked to serve in such a way.

"Briant, do ye think we can harness the wind if we had a full circle o' thirteen witches?"

"We can but try," Briant answered. "Certainly, a wee bit o' fire willna go astray." And he cast Fèlice a look of admiration as he stepped back to his position at the center of the circle.

The other witches made up their ring of linked hands. With Dillon, Cameron, Rafferty, Landon, and Fèlice joining in, there were now thirteen in the circle, the preferred number for working powerful magic. Once again Nina raised her beautiful silvery voice against the roar of the waves and the wind. The other twelve added their voices to hers. Round and round the chant wove, sucking up power into an invisible whirlwind of pure energy. They felt its tingle on their skin, felt the hairs rise on their body, and tasted its metallic tang on their tongues. It roared about them, drowning out the sound of the storm and the ship, filling their ears and eyes and mouths. They shouted the last words of the chant and flung up their arms. Fèlice saw a cone of blue-white fire spring up about them. Stormy Briant took the power they gave him and spun it into a rope of sizzling white. He seized the wind and knotted his rope about it, and then, shouting aloud in exultation, he rode the storm as if it was a living beast, with tossing mane of cloud and rain, fiery eyes of stabbing lightning, and great hooves of thunder that churned the sea behind them into a white maelstrom.

For six long heartbeats the storm fought Briant. The ship was hammered with wild seas that broke first one way, then the other. Briant was high in the sky, then smashed into the water, flung between wave crest and cloudburst, lightning zigzagging all about him. Then, suddenly, there was a long moment of pure stillness and quiet. High above the main mast, Briant rode the wind, the reins of witch-fire drawn tight in his hands. He was laughing. Everyone stared up at him, amazed and frightened.

"A true storm-rider," Cristina whispered, gazing up at Briant with awe and adoration.

Then the wind shifted. It blew strong and sure, dragging their hair into their eyes. The sails filled. The ship leaped forward. With the waves rolling smoothly under the ship's carved prow, and breaking behind them into a wide white wake, the galleon began to speed towards the Pirate Isles, the rest of the fleet racing behind them.

At the Full Moon

❦

Darkness had fallen. Rats rustled in the straw. A single ray of moonlight pierced the narrow window and fell upon the wall. Its silvery radiance made the shadows seem impenetrable.

Olwynne sat with her hands folded on her lap, waiting.

She had gone past terror and despair to a place of stillness and acceptance. Tonight she was to die. She was utterly sure of this.

Owein had, up to half an hour ago, still gripped her hands and exhorted her not to lose faith. "The Yeomen will get here," he had said fiercely. "We will be freed on time."

Then Dedrie had come and forced Olwynne to drink another of her foul potions, and given her a basin of scented water to wash in, then a loose white nightgown to wear. The skeelie had spoken little, but as she had left the cell she had said, with a meaningful look, "Both moons are at the full tonight. There'll be plenty o' light for us to see by, thank the Truth."

After that Owein had sat slumped and silent. Olwynne could not see him in the darkness, but she could hear his harsh breathing. Rhiannon lay motionless on the far side of the cell. She had dozed off some time ago, and occasionally whimpered in her sleep, as if dreaming bad dreams.

Olwynne knew her time of dreaming was over. For

months her sleep had been stalked by grim visions, of
skeletons and gravestones, murder and betrayal. She had
seen her father struck down countless times in her dreams,
and then once, in waking life. She had seen herself die,
hung by a ribbon of blood, cut down by a slashing scythe.
Now it was time for these dreams to become real.

Ghislaine had once told her that to sleep in a dream was
to die. So Olwynne sat awake, as if to convince herself that
she could in the end avoid the death she herself had foreseen. The potion had made her feel very calm and strange,
almost as if she was floating. Her feet seemed a long way
away from her head. Her hands were heavy and limp and
far too cold. Olwynne breathed slowly and steadily. She
looked at the delicate filigree of black and silver made by
the moonlight falling through straw, her heart aching with
its beauty.

She wished she could have seen Lewen one more time.
She wished she had not had to ensorcel him. If only his
love had been true. If only he had not met Rhiannon. Olwynne could not help thinking that this calamitous turn of
events was all due to the satyricorn girl. If Lewen had not
met her and fallen in love with her, and gone with her to
Fettercairn Castle, and thwarted Lord Malvern in his
dreadful deeds, and caused him to be arrested and brought
to Lucescere, would she be here now, facing her death?
How complex was the tapestry of people's lives, she
thought. Each thread interwoven with another's, so that
one thread could not be snapped and dragged out without
the whole fabric unraveling. If Rhiannon was unraveled
from the whole, would her own history be any different? It
was impossible to tell. Yet try as she might, Olwynne could
not help wishing Rhiannon had never flown into their lives.
Then she might have won Lewen to love honestly, and not
found herself and himself both twisted awry by her ensor-
celment.

She was thinking of this, and trying to ignore the wry
voice that pointed out Lewen had never once looked at her

with the eyes of a lover, when the door was slammed open. Lamplight fell in, turning the delicate construction of moonlight and shadow back into a horrible, damp, rat-ridden cell. Olwynne looked up, her head feeling as if it was filled with too much oxygen, like a pig's-bladder balloon that might float up to nudge the ceiling.

Lord Malvern stood in the doorway, his raven perched on his shoulder. Jem stood to one side, bleary-eyed, unshaven, and stinking of whisky. Piers stood to the other side, holding high the lantern.

"Get the sacrifice," Lord Malvern ordered.

"The red one?"

"Aye. I'm looking forward to seeing MacCuinn blood on my knife."

"But dinna the ghost want the black-haired one? She marked her out in the prison."

"Do ye think she really cares who dies, as long as she gets to live again? No, if I have to cut someone's throat, it may as well be the MacCuinn's daughter, and then I'll truly feel my revenge is complete."

"Och, aye, the red one then," Jem said, and shambled forward, seizing Olwynne by the arm.

She shuddered. Owein roused and turned, his wings rustling the straw. She felt the moment when he came awake and realized the time had come. In an instant he was on his feet, rushing the men in the door, frantic with grief and rage. Jem was waiting for him. He had a heavy iron pike in one hand, and he brought it crashing down on Owein's head. The prionnsa fell and lay still.

Olwynne went down on her knees by his side, and cradled his head with her hands. He was unconscious. She bent and kissed his brow. "Good-bye, Owein," she whispered, and let a tear fall on his cheek, smearing it away with her thumb. She wondered, not for the first time, if he would feel her death. They had a close, uncanny kinship, as so many twins do, and had often felt inexplicable pangs or twinges that were later explained by news the other had been hurt. Since Olwynne had been a quiet, studious child, and Owein a noisy, adventurous one, it was she who had most often felt the phantom pains. It had never been pleasant. It troubled her that Owein would feel her pain as she died, and perhaps more than pain. What did it feel like to be dead? she wondered.

"Look at them, aren't they sweet?" Jem mocked.

Lord Malvern ignored him. He was listening to Piers, who was speaking in a low, urgent undertone. After a moment Lord Malvern waved a negligent hand. "Very well, if it's that important, ye can have her if ye wish," he said.

For a brief dizzying moment, Olwynne thought Piers was pleading for her life, but then, as Lord Malvern continued speaking, she realized with a plunge of her heart that Piers was asking for Rhiannon. He wanted to sacrifice her, to raise his mother from the dead.

"We must raise Falkner and Rory first," Lord Malvern was saying, "but then, certainly, Piers, if ye wish to use the dark one to raise your mother, that would be fine. She's been a thorn in our side from the very beginning, and I'll be glad to be rid o' her. Indeed, if it was no' so fitting that I should sacrifice the MacCuinn's daughter first, I'd use her now, as payback for all the bother she's caused us."

Piers spoke again in the same low voice.

"Aye, I promise," Lord Malvern said angrily. "I gave my word to your father that your mother would be the very next to be resurrected years ago. How was I to ken it would take this long to learn the secret?"

"I beg your pardon, sir," Piers said. "It need be no trouble for ye, my laird. If ye will give me the spell, and the girl, I will go and do it myself." He added hastily, at the frown on Lord Malvern's face, "After we have raised your brother and nephew, o' course, my laird."

"And have ye setting up a circle o' necromancers yourself? I do no' think so," the lord answered with heavy sarcasm. "No, the spell stays with me and me alone."

"We need a circle o' necromancers to do the deed?" Piers said after a moment. "But . . . how, my laird? We have lost . . . we've lost a third o' our circle."

Olwynne turned and looked up at him. She had wondered how he had felt about the callous abandoning of his ill and elderly father by the side of the road in the middle of nowhere. He had hardly spoken since that moment, and she had harbored a hope that he might feel rebellious anger at the lord of Fettercairn, which could, perhaps, be used to turn him against the others. There was nothing in his voice to indicate any such rebellion, however, or even any grief for the loss of his father. This seemed quite horrible to Olwynne.

"I left that up to Ballard," Lord Malvern said, smiling nastily. "He's had a day in Pirate Town. I'm sure he's found someone willing to help slit a throat for a few gold coins, even if they have to don a red cloak and chant a few verses to do it."

It was her throat that was to be slit, Olwynne knew.

"But . . . is that wise, my laird? We were to keep this business quiet, very quiet."

"And so we shall," Lord Malvern answered, and the raven cawed aloud in mocking laughter.

"Are we to stand here gum-flapping all damned night?" Jem snarled. "Do ye no' want me to grab the girl?"

"Aye, Jem, grab the girl," Lord Malvern said sardonically. "Then send Dedrie to look over the boy. We do no' want him to die because ye're a wee heavy-handed with your pike. The other girl needs to be tended too. Piers wants her, and so we need to keep her alive long enough to get home to Fettercairn."

"Fine," Jem responded, and dragged Olwynne to her feet. She did not resist. She took one last look at her brother, lying unconscious in the filthy straw with blood matting his fiery curls, and then let herself be escorted from the cell. The last thing she saw was Rhiannon's eyes, watching silently from the shadows. There was pity and anguish and a desperate regret in the satyricorn girl's eyes, and it broke Olwynne's resolve so she stumbled, tears flowing down her cheeks.

It was a cool, windy night outside, and clouds raced across the faces of the moons. Both were rising out of the sea, and were large and round and golden as new coins, and strangely smooth, as if the pits and hollows on their surface had been wiped away. Olwynne stared up at them as she was hauled across a dark empty courtyard. *This is the last time I will see the moons,* she thought.

They came through a shadowy garden filled with dead trees and a dry husk of a hedge. Weeds flourished where once herbs and vegetables had grown. Olwynne felt thorns snagging her nightgown. Beyond the garden was a grave-yard. It was lit by nine tall candles in iron lanterns. Their flames danced and bowed in the wind, and cast distorted orange shapes upon the grey stones. They cast very little light. The moons did a far better job of illuminating the grave-yard. By their cool, remote light Olwynne could see crooked crosses and angels and tilted slabs of stone covered with worn incisions. To one side was a great gaping hole where a grave had been dug up. The earth was mounded high beside. Laid out on a grave nearby was a skeleton.

Only then did Olwynne begin to sob and fight and beg for mercy. It was no use. Hands dragged her forward, closer and closer to that pale fretwork of bones. The white nightgown was torn from her. Shears snapped at her head, cutting off the great mass of her hair. She was forced to lie upon the skeleton, feeling its sharp bones grinding into her hip, her breast, her throat. Straining every muscle in her body, she sought to tear herself away, but inexorably she was bound to the skeleton with ropes made of her own hair. She was screaming, but it was like a dream. She made no noise, and all her most desperate effort resulted in no effect, no motion. *It is just a dream,* she thought in relief. *Nothing but a dream.*

But then, in the corner of her eye she saw the flash of a

silver knife. All around her were figures clad all in red, chanting out words that had no meaning. The one with the knife reached forward and seized her chin, forcing her head back. The knife slashed down. Olwynne screamed. But there was no sound. She had no throat left to scream with. A moment of redness, of darkness. Then Olwynne was dead.

Lewen woke with a jerk.

He had fallen asleep in his chair, shoved in a corner of his tiny bedroom at the Theurgia. His knife lay on the table before him, amidst a pile of shavings. It was late, and his candle had burned itself out. He could see clearly, though, for moonlight streamed in through the tall, narrow window.

His heart was slamming in his chest. He could hear its echo in his ears. Dazed, uncertain, Lewen got up and went to stand at the window, staring out at the round moons hanging over the witches' wood.

"Rhiannon," he whispered.

His hands were trembling. He pressed them together and tried to control his ragged breathing.

Something had happened. He had the confused impression of a nightmare. Darkness, mist rising from a grave, figures grabbing, a woman laughing aloud in glee. Yet it was not the aftermath of the dream that made his heart race and his hands shake.

It was as if he had been crouched in a gilded cage, its bars pressing close about him, and after weeks and weeks of straining every muscle to break the cage asunder, the bars had suddenly cracked and burst open, and he could stand up and stretch and breathe deeply and, if he wanted, run.

"Rhiannon," Lewen whispered again.

It seemed suddenly unbearable that he did not know where Rhiannon was, or whether she was in danger. He thought again about his nightmare. Lord Malvern had been in it, looming over the dream like the shadow of a black scarecrow. He remembered falling. What if it was Rhiannon who had fallen? What if she was hurt or, even worse, dead?

Lewen could not bear it anymore. He had to follow her, he had to find her. He had to make sure she was safe, because, he realized at last, a life without Rhiannon would be one without joy, adventure, laughter, or passion. It would be a barren field, the soil poisoned, the furrows sown only with thistles.

There was no time for thought, no time to hesitate and lose all on the crux of indecision and utter impossibility. The idea came to him like oil igniting with the touch of a spark. It was an instant conflagration of the brain.

It was an imperative on which he must act.

So Lewen seized his tool belt from his hook and his coat from the chair, and grabbed his knife from the table, and went running out his door and down the stairs, his boot heels clattering on the stone steps and echoing through the cavernous stairwell. Everything was pitch-black. Only long familiarity with the eccentricities of the worn stone prevented him from stumbling or even falling. Through the dark, silent hall he ran, and out through the great double doors, not caring that they banged behind him, as loud as a pistol shot.

It was cold outside, and he was glad he had had the forethought to catch up his coat. He struggled to drag it on as he ran, and thrust his numb hands into his pockets. It seemed impossible that midsummer was only two weeks ago, when the air had been like a warm bath, and he had sweated in his best clothes as he jumped the fire with Olwynne. *Olwynne,* he thought, and a splinter of dream came back to pierce him, momentarily, with horror. He could not grasp it. A splinter no longer, a mere shred of hallucination, a mere inkling of disaster. It made him catch his breath and shudder, and run on even faster, through silver moonlight and dark lace of shadows.

He came to the massive stable block, where he had

kissed Rhiannon good-bye two weeks ago. It had been a
stormy night. Lightning had felled an old oak tree. It still
lay where it had fallen, no one having had the time or the
energy to remove it. Most of its branches had been sawed
away for firewood in this unnatural winter. The hulk of the
tree remained, gnarled and ancient and scorched black
with lightning.

As Lewen stared at it, momentarily daunted, the tower
bell began to strike midnight. On and on it tolled, remind-
ing him of the night Lachlan had been murdered and his
three children stolen away, and of how he himself had
stopped the bell from ringing the very next dawn, saving
Rhiannon from death by hanging.

Lewen's skill did not lie with words. He could not have
explained why the sound of the bell roused him from his
sudden vacillation and spurred him on with fresh vigor
and courage. He would have shrugged, the tips of his ears
turning red, and said uncomfortably, "Time's a-getting
away."

Armed with only the small tools of his whittling kit,
Lewen set to carve himself a winged horse from lightning-
felled oak. He saw the fabulous beast clearly in his mind's
eye, a stallion as tall and strong as his beloved Argent, with
tossing mane and tail, a proudly raised head, crowned with
two spiraling horns, a bright, wise eye, and sardonically
curled lip. From the stallion's great shoulders sprang two
magnificent wings, some of the feathers as long as Lewen
was tall.

He worked under the light of a great ball of witch's light
that he conjured from nowhere. Lewen's powers had never
been strong in fire, and he had never been able to maintain
such a large source of light for so long. Now he did it without thought, needing it, and so making it.

Armed only with his knife, gouges, chisels, sandpaper,
files, and rasps, Lewen made sure the stallion's hide was as
smooth as silk, its feathers as finely grained as any finch's,
its wooden mane as liquid and rippling as the mane of a

real horse. It took him a long time. The moons sank and the sun rose before he had finished, and his hands were cut all over from working in haste in the darkness. He had smeared his blood and sweat and tears of utter grief and frustration into every inch of the magnificent winged stallion that stood before him, one feathered hoof lifted, its head turned to regard him with a quizzical eye, as if it might at any moment lift those mighty wings and soar away.

Lewen could not bear to look at it. He closed his eyes, stepped forward, and laid his hot, filthy cheek against its wooden shoulder, one hand reaching up to caress its hard cheek.

He wished, he hoped, he wanted, with such desperation he thought his heart would simply fail to beat. For a long moment he stood there, in the cold streaky dawn, unable to breathe, tears choking him. Then, unbelievably, he felt a sudden rush of hot breath on his arm. He felt the skin under his hand shiver and twitch and, looking up, gazed straight into a great, dark, living eye.

The stallion bowed his head and nudged him, whickering.

Lewen staggered and almost fell. He could not believe he had done it. To whittle a living horse out of an old hunk of wood—it was too close to being a god. He covered his face with his bloody, filthy hands and muttered, "Thank ye, Eà, thank ye! I ken this is your doing. Thank ye!"

The stallion was nudging him, almost pushing him over. Lewen wiped away the tears on his face and then stumbled into the stable, pumping cold water over his hands, drinking deeply, splashing it over his face. The stallion followed him and pushed him aside to drink from the trough. Lewen stroked his shoulder, his flank, ran his hand over the deep curve of his back, marveling, wondering. Then he turned and hurried into the stable, where the horses snoozed in their stalls, and a stable boy named Jack was yawning and stretching as he stirred up a brazier of coals to make some dancey.

Lewen knew Jack well. It did not take long to beg and borrow some of what he thought he would be needing for a desperate journey across land and ocean. He borrowed Jack's all-weather hooded jacket, some saddlebags, a coil of stout rope, a blanket, and a dagger to replace his knife, which was worn and blunt after the hours of whittling. Then he sent Jack running to fetch him his longbow and arrows, while Lewen drank Jack's cup of hot dancey with true gratitude, and raided the stable hands' kitchen for supplies.

By the time Jack returned, most of the stable hands were awake and standing about the courtyard, staring wide-eyed at the winged horse calmly munching a bucket of warm mash. Lewen poured all the money he had in his pockets into Jack's hand, and then, holding his breath in trepidation, slowly laid the saddlebags upon the stallion's back. The horse did not even flinch. It seemed, as if by making him, Lewen had also tamed him.

Lewen then took another deep breath and climbed up onto the stallion's back, using the trough as a mounting block. The stallion turned and looked at him, and flicked away a fly with his tail.

"A thigearn has no need of bridle and saddle," Lewen whispered to himself and, winding both hands in the thick mane, gently urged the stallion forward. Instantly the horse responded, and Lewen's heart sang at the fluid grace of his movement. Lewen leaned forward, clicked his tongue, and said, *Fly, my beauty* . . .

At once the stallion spread his wings and soared into the sky. All the stable hands shouted in excitement and flung their caps into the air. Lewen gasped aloud, and clenched his hands so tightly on the stallion's mane, the hairs sliced into his already sore and throbbing palms. The ground whirled away. Lewen shut his eyes, raised his face to the wind, and thought, *Rhiannon! I'm coming!*

Sliced Bellfruit

〜❦〜

Rhiannon sat with her head bowed over the unconscious form of the prionnsa, who lay on his side with his head in her lap, his wings folded along his back.

He had been unconscious for hours. Rhiannon had been unable to sleep much because of the pain in her shoulder, so she had sat vigil over him, every now and again making sure he was still alive by lowering her cheek to just above his mouth, so that she could feel his breath in the darkness like the invisible brush of moth wings.

Now the darkness was fading away, and she could see his pale face and the barest outline of the curve of his wing. She sat quietly, willing him to live, for Lewen, for Fèlice, even for his mother, the angry, avenging Banrìgh who had hunted her down on dragon-back and dragged her back to the city to face her own rough justice. Rhiannon did not know Owein. She cared nothing for him personally, but she had seen too much grief these last few months. She wanted to save Owein for those who loved him, and for her own sense of atonement.

The light grew brighter. She saw his red curls were matted in a nasty gash above his temple. They had left a jug of water and a cup nearby. Rhiannon dampened the hem of her shirt and sponged away the worst of the dried blood, then dribbled a little water over his pale lips. His eyelids flickered, and he swallowed. Rhiannon felt some of the constriction in her chest ease.

I'm sorry, Lewen, she thought. *I could not save her.*

Tears welled up in her eyes. She was oppressed by the heaviness of her failure, and by her acute anxiety over Blackthorn and her little bluebird, and by her dreadful fear of the future. The weeks chasing after Lord Malvern had done nothing but sharpen her terror of him. Rhiannon knew he would cut her throat without a twitch of compunction or regret, and leave her to slowly drown in the pool of her own blood.

Does he not fear the dark walkers? she wondered. *So many people he has tortured and killed, so many ghosts left to haunt his land. How can he sleep at night?*

The tears slowly worked their way down her face.

One fell onto Owein's cheek before she could move her hand to wipe it away. He sighed and murmured, and put up a hand to shade his eyes from the light.

"Owein?" she whispered, and then remembered he was a prionnsa. "Your Highness?"

He blinked and rubbed his eyes, then gingerly touched his wound, and winced. Then he looked up at her. Blue grey eyes looked down into dark brown, and shared a broad current of pain.

"She's dead, isn't she?" His voice was hoarse.

Rhiannon nodded. "I think she must be. It's been hours since they took her away."

He closed his eyes. She felt his shoulders shake.

"I'm so sorry," she said, her tears quickening. "I tried, I really did, but I just couldna save ye both. There were too many o' them."

He did not answer or open his eyes, but his chest rose and fell in a gasp of pain.

They sat quietly for a long time, Rhiannon scrubbing away her tears with a furious hand. She hated to show any weakness, yet what she felt and thought always defeated her. Owein heard her sobbing breath and lifted himself away from her, staring at her incredulously.

"Ye're crying."

"No, I'm no'!"

"Aye! Ye are. Ye're crying."

Rhiannon did not answer, but dried her eyes and nose on the sleeve of her shirt, refusing to meet his gaze.

"But why do ye care? I thought ye hated Olwynne."

"I do! But I . . . I promised Lewen. I promised I'd save ye for him. Both o' ye. Lewen loves ye both. He wanted ye back. Ye and your sister. I said I'd get ye back for him." Rhiannon gulped a deep breath.

"But surely ye were glad Olwynne was taken. I mean—"

"She ensorcelled him!" Rhiannon flashed. "He was mine and she stole him away. I was going to save her and take her back and make her take off that spell, so that Lewen would be mine again. Now it'll never be broken. Lewen will never ken . . ."

She gave a little wail and began to cry harder. She put both hands over her eyes and endeavored to bring herself back under control.

After a long moment Owein said very coldly, and with distaste evident in his voice, "If it is true what ye say, and my sister did cast a love spell on Lewen, which, mind ye, I do no' believe for a moment, well then, it would have been blood-magic—all dark magic is—and the spell would be broken with her death."

Rhiannon dropped her hands and stared at him.

"The spell would be broken?"

"Aye." Owein spoke curtly, and stared over her shoulder at the wall.

"Thank the dark walkers!" Rhiannon cried, then at the resentful flash of Owein's eyes, said, "Nay, no' about the spell—though o' course I'm glad it's broken. I'd rather it had been me that had broken it, though. I mean, I wish she'd no' had to die like this . . . it's horrible. No one should die like that. We should die . . . rightly."

Rhiannon was struggling to express what she meant.
Language was still a mystery to her, filled with pitfalls and
embarrassments. She looked at Owein pleadingly, willing
him to understand. He was frowning, angry, and stubborn
in his grief.

She tried again.

"No, the reason I'm so glad is that, if the spell has truly
been broken, well then, Lewen will be coming! He'll be on
his way! Lewen will save us."

In the soft misty dawn upon the hill of the Tomb of Ravens,
eight figures abruptly materialized from thin air.

Gaunt-faced, filthy, and ragged, they all fell to their
knees. Some retched convulsively. Others moaned or wept.
A great black dog howled. A tiny white owl fell from the
sky and clung, trembling, to Isabeau's shoulder. She was
on her hands and knees, gulping great breaths of air, her
red curls in wild disorder all about her face and shoulders.
She put up one hand to pet Buba, and tried to hoot reassuringly at him, only to find her throat too sore and dry.

Donncan staggered to his feet and plunged his hands
into the long, oblong pool, splashing his face with water
again and again. Cailean and Ghislaine joined him, dous-
ing their heads and hands, and swallowing great gulps of
the icy-cold water. Stormstrider composed himself with an
effort, and helped Cloudshadow to her feet, supporting the
Stargazer's fainting steps to the pool so that she too could
drink and revive herself with its coolness. He then offered
his hand to Thunderlily, who had lost so much weight during their ordeal she looked as delicate as a bellfruit seed
spinning on the end of a twig. She took his hand gratefully,
and he helped her to the pool and sank his big hand into the
water for her to use as a cup.

Isabeau and Dide, helping each other, managed to crawl
to the pool and drink also. Neither thought they had slept,

though both believed the other had done so. They were white and haggard in the morning light.

"I had forgotten . . ." Dide said, watching the water trickle through his fingers, ". . . what it is like to drink cool water when you are desperately thirsty."

"It's good," Isabeau croaked.

"Very good," he replied, and smiled.

It was all he could manage. He could not rise. He lay there on the flagstones, his head on his arms, and said, "I think I've aged a hundred years. Are ye sure we're back in our own time, and no' a hundred years hence?"

"We just need to get to Rhyssmadill," Donncan said. "Then we can rest."

Ghislaine cast one despairing look across the mist-wreathed park to the castle, its spires rising, ethereal and sharp from the mist. "It's too far," she cried. "I canna walk so far. I ache all over. My joints . . ."

She was close to tears. All of them were the same. The journey home, which had taken no more than a few seconds, had stretched them to unbearable limits, physically and emotionally. Isabeau had suffered the torture of the rack from Maya's inquisitors in her youth. She could think of no other experience that came close to the agonizing pain of traveling the Old Ways through time. It was all she could do not to weep with utter exhaustion.

Donncan groaned, and moved his shoulders experimentally. Of them all, he was the least affected, being only twenty-four and a strong and athletic young man used to riding hard and camping rough. "I will fly to the castle," he said. "It will no' take me long. I'll bring back help. Wait here. Rest."

As everyone heaved great sighs of relief and gratitude, Isabeau smiled at him, thinking what a great rìgh he would be.

"Will ye send word to Lucescere?" she asked.

"Aye, at once," he said. "Mama must be beside herself with anxiety."

"She'll be so glad to ken ye are home again, safe and sound," Isabeau said, tears starting to her eyes.

He nodded, and shook out his ruffled feathers, and rolled his aching shoulders. "Thank Eà!" he said, and launched himself rather clumsily into the air.

And what about Bronwen, my wife? he thought as he flew towards Rhyssmadill. *Will she be glad to have me home too?*

Elfrida stared up at the silk-hung roof of her bed. She listened.

No voice in her ear. No sly insinuations, no threats, no nasty hints and promises, no laughing out loud in glee. No rummaging through her memories, and turning black ones blacker and gold ones to ash. No constant hissing in her ear, warning her, reviling her, deriding her, mocking her. No gloating, no looting, no lying, no sneering, no harrying, no harassing. No voice. No ghost.

She was free.

Elfrida gasped aloud with laughter. Then she wept, her hands over her face. She gasped and shuddered with tears for a long time, but eventually lay still, listening again, wondering what to do.

The ghost had gone. Had she gone for good? It seemed impossible. Elfrida had been tricked before. She was not the only one Margrit haunted. Sometimes Elfrida had been free for a matter of hours, free to sleep, free to pray, free to try to think of some way out of her predicament. But always Margrit would return, bullying, threatening, deceiving, and conniving, occupying every nook and cranny of Elfrida's mind and soul until Elfrida no longer knew who she was or what she herself wanted.

But it had been six hours of silence now, the hours from midnight to dawn. Elfrida had lain awake the whole time, waiting for the ghost to return, and slowly feeling her body begin to fill with hope as the room filled with light. Six hours of freedom.

The bell began to toll the ending of the curfew. Elfrida rose stiffly from her bed, and bent her aching knees till she was kneeling on the floor. She closed her eyes, folded her hands, and prayed.

She stayed there, praying and weeping, for a very long time, looking for guidance, begging for forgiveness. Her god was cruel, however, and the only sign sent to her was a tall, thin man with hair as pale as a newborn baby's, and eyes as cold as stone. Dressed all in black, he came to her with news.

"Get up off the floor," he said, without any pretense at courtesy. "The time has come to close the trap."

Elfrida looked up, her face all blotchy and wet with tears. "Wh-what?"

"Donncan MacCuinn has been found alive and well. He is at Rhyssmadill, with the Keybearer and the rest o' her party. The Celestine whore is there too."

"Donncan is alive and well?" Elfrida repeated stupidly.

The pastor's brows drew together and he looked down at her in scorn. "Aye. They arrived back this dawn, and sent a homing pigeon with the news. The whole city is celebrating. The Fairgean half-breed is all in a dither, getting herself ready to sail down the river to meet him. She must be stopped."

"But . . . but why?"

"Do no' be so stupid," he said savagely. "We canna allow the MacCuinn to live. Yet if he dies while she is near, she will always be suspect. No, she must be above suspicion and so must ye. We shall keep the half-breed here, and have her send Neil in her place. I will go with him, and I shall make sure Donncan dies, and the suspicion falls on someone we hate. One o' the *uile-bheistean* would be best."

Elfrida was shaking. "But . . . but will it be safe? They

may suspect Neil. I do no' want him in danger. Canna he
stay here, with me?"

"What excuse could ye then make for sending me? I am
no friend to the Keybearer and those other witch-whores,
nor to the MacCuinn. We canna risk him returning here,
with the Yeomen to watch over his every step. No, we must
strike fast—and that means Neil must take me to
Rhyssmadill this very day."

Elfrida tried to remember that she was a NicHilde, and
a banprionnsa, but she was so exhausted and bewildered
that she could not find any strength to draw upon.

"What . . . what are ye going to do?" she quavered.

"No' me. Ye." He smiled. "Now, we do no' want to kill
her, so ye must use a light hand. Drop a little o' this into
her wine or food, using the poison ring, then rinse it out
well afore ye give it back to me. I'll be using a different
powder for the MacCuinn."

His smile stretched wider as he passed her a little fold
of paper containing rough brown powder. Elfrida stared at
it, then held out her trembling hand to take it. She rested it
on the bedside table as she slid open the secret compartment in the big onyx ring she wore, a ring that had once belonged to Margrit, like the golden fan she had disposed of
two weeks ago. Her hands were shaking so much it was
difficult to tip the powder into the ring, but she dared not
spill any with the pastor's cold grey eyes watching her. At
last it was done, and she snapped the secret compartment
closed. All it needed now was a quick wrench sideways
and the poison would spill out.

"Excellent," the pastor said. "Now, we must be quick.
The half-breed is breaking her fast afore heading down the
river. We must no' let her leave Lucescere!"

Bronwen could hardly catch her breath, she was so filled
with tumultuous emotions. Foremost was utter joy and relief that Donncan was alive and unhurt, and they would

soon be together again. But almost as intense was her trepidation. Would Donncan ever forgive her for seizing the Lodestar? Would he demand she give it to him? Would they be able to share it, and raise it together, as they had done as children, or would it demand to be held by one and one alone? She did not know the answers to these questions, and so she paced up and down the breakfast room, drinking cup after cup of angelica tea, and giving terse and distracted answers to all the questions her servants and councillors hurled at her.

"How long will I be gone! Eà's eyes, how should I ken? Pack enough for several weeks, I suppose. Donncan may be hurt . . . he'll need to rest . . ." Her voice quavered.

"Please, Your Majesty, sit down," Neil said, and drew out a chair for her. "Ye must eat. I havena seen ye eat in days." He pressed her down into the chair gently, and waved at one of the servants to serve her some griddle cakes. Bronwen grimaced. The very sight of food made her feel sick. She waved them away, and gulped down more of the tea.

"Porridge," Neil said. "Try some porridge."

The lackey put a bowl before her, and she stirred the gluey mess with her spoon, not wanting to hurt Neil's feelings.

The room was full of people, rushing in and out, shouting to one another, everyone smiling and looking happy for the first time in days. The bells were ringing loudly.

"Will I pack your court dresses, Your Majesty?" the mistress of the wardrobe cried, looking very harassed.

"No! No! We are still in mourning, and Donncan's note said only that they were all exhausted and needed to rest," Bronwen cried back, and pushed her bowl away. "I'll no' be needing much really, just a few plain dresses."

I never thought I'd hear those words out of my mouth, she thought to herself, and laughed out loud.

"Perhaps Her Majesty would prefer a little fruit," Elfrida said, suddenly appearing at Bronwen's shoulder with a silver platter of peeled bellfruit. "I ken it's your favorite."

"Thank ye, I would," Bronwen said, surprised but pleased, and ate one, while her squire poured her another cup of tea. Someone else was at her shoulder with a sheaf of papers to sign before she left, and Elfrida disappeared back into the crowd as Bronwen absentmindedly popped another morsel of fruit into her mouth, and scrawled her name where directed. The fruit was not as sweet as usual, and looked a little bruised, but after the ravages of the snowstorm, fruit had been in short supply, and Bronwen had missed it. She felt her feelings towards Elfrida warming. It had been kind of her to think of it.

She ate a few more slices, her thoughts on Donncan and their coming meeting. She would be so sweet to him, she decided, that he would not think to mind her taking the throne. What else could she have done? She would show him that it had not been hungry ambition that had driven her, but a care for the country. She would tend him so sweetly, smile at him so lovingly, indeed she would . . .

Bronwen put one hand up to her head. She was feeling very sick and faint. "Neil," she said.

He was by her side in an instant. "Your Majesty?"

"I feel . . ."

"Is something wrong, Bronny?"

"I think I'm going to be sick," she said, and was, inelegantly, all over the sleeve of his doublet and the half-empty plate of browning bellfruit.

There was a flurry of dismay and disgust. Bronwen pressed her hand over her mouth. "I'm sorry," she said, and was sick again. Her head was swimming. Her stomach heaved. Someone thrust a silver wine bucket at her, and she grasped it and used it gratefully. It was Elfrida, she noticed, and Elfrida who helped her out the door and up the stairs, and up the stairs, and up the stairs, till at last she reached her own floor, retching every step of the way.

"Could she be . . . ye ken . . ." she heard someone say,

and shut her eyes in utter misery. *No!* she wanted to scream, but her voice was all taken up with gagging. Then Elfrida was laying her down on her own bed, and taking off her shoes, and placing a damp, lavender-scented cloth on her forehead, and giving her water to rinse out her mouth. Bronwen could have wept with gratitude.

A very unpleasant hour passed, and when at last the paroxysm had worn itself out, Bronwen was so weak and miserable that all she wanted to do was sleep. Mirabelle had been called, and she had given Bronwen something that calmed her stomach but made her very drowsy.

"Your Majesty?"

Half-dozing, feeling clean and comfortable again, but very sore and worn out, Bronwen forced open her eyes.

"Aye?"

It was Gwilym the Ugly. Bronwen smiled weakly at him. She had known him since she was little more than a baby.

"Your Majesty, we have decided it would be best to send a delegation to Rhyssmadill as soon as possible, to welcome the Keybearer and the Rìgh home and to hear their story."

Donncan . . . Bronwen thought, and a tear rolled out of the corner of her eye.

"The healers say ye must no' travel, so I thought I would go," Gwilym continued, looking sorry for her, "and His Grace Neil MacFóghnan o' Arran as well. We'll explain to His Majesty all that has happened in his absence, and how very sick ye've been. I'm sure in a day or two he will be well enough to come home to Lucescere."

Two more tears slipped down her cheeks.

"Try and rest, my dear. Ye've been driving yourself too hard. Mirabelle says ye are utterly exhausted. We'll send news as soon as we have it, never ye fear."

She nodded. He bowed and patted her hand, then stumped from the room, making a thump-tap-thump-tap sound as first his boot, and then his wooden leg, hit the floor. She closed her eyes. Then Neil was leaning over her, pressing her hand between both of his own.

"Oh, Bronny! Ye poor darling! Ye rest up now, and I'll make your excuses to Donn. He'll understand, I ken, once he hears how sick ye've been."

"Cuckoo . . ." Bronwen said faintly.

Neil turned back to her. "Aye?"

She shook her head. "Naught. It's naught."

"All right. Go to sleep now. I'll see ye soon."

As Neil hurried out of the room, Bronwen turned her cheek into the pillow and felt the tears flow faster. It would not have been kind, she thought, to charge a man who loved her with words of love for another man, but Eà's eyes, she wished she could have sent Donncan some message, some token of how she felt. Their coldness to each other at their wedding hurt her like whip cuts. She wished she had not been so proud. She wished they had wed, and parted, in loving joyfulness. Bronwen closed her eyes, and after a while the tears stopped and she was asleep.

Frost at Noon

❦

Margrit of Arran lay on her bed in a welter of silks and satins, laughing.

"I want more!" she cried. "And bring me wine, and roast lamb with baby peas, and oysters, and lobster, and fresh bellfruit and strawberries. And hot water with rose oil in it. And a hipbath. And someone to wash my hair for me, and scrub my feet. And bring me a man. Ye! Ye will do for now!"

She pointed at Piers, who took a step backwards, startled.

"Ye are the only one who doesna stink or have one foot in the grave," she said. "Why did I have to be raised by a coterie o' necromancers all auld enough to be my father? Come on! Dinna goggle at me like that. Have ye spent so much time up to your elbows in the bodies o' the dead that ye've forgotten what a real live woman feels like?"

She laughed and rolled about. "Live! A real live woman! Golden goddess, I had forgotten how good it feels to be alive!"

The lord of Fettercairn stood leaning on his cane, scowling, and the others all looked scared and bothered in equal measure. This was not what they had expected.

The spell of resurrection had gone as planned, with the substance of the NicCuinn girl's body going to rebuild that of Margrit of Arran's. Dedrie had ready the antidote to the poison that had killed the sorceress so many years earlier, and had administered it quickly. They had then expected the long-dead sorceress to fall on her knees before them in abject gratitude, for them to accept her thanks gracefully and then get on their way at once, back to Fettercairn Castle and the bones of their own long-dead beloveds. Everyone knew that they must move quickly, for any hesitation and the hounds of vengeance would be upon them.

Margrit of Arran had different plans, however. As far as she was concerned, they were her servants and must do as she bid. She laughed at Lord Malvern for thinking he could outrun the royal navy, and predicted they would see sails upon the horizon by dawn, despite all his weather-witchery. Rather to Lord Malvern's chagrin, she had been right. Despite the tempest that had swept upon them, rattling the rickety stones of the old fort, the white sails of the royal navy had approached swiftly and inexorably, making any quick escape impossible. Margrit had ordered the pirate town to take up arms and, to Lord Malvern's mortification, the pirates had obeyed instantly.

"Oh, but we are auld friends," Margrit had purred, seeing the expression on all their faces. "Did ye no' ken?"

Her ghost, it seemed, had been haunting quite a few inhabitants of Pirate Town, many of whom had served her when she had lived in the old fort, during her exile from Arran. When Lord Malvern had sent his bodyguard into the town to hire cutthroats to assist them in the spell of necromancy, he had in fact been hiring men already worked upon and subjugated by Margrit. So when Lord Malvern had given the signal for his men to fall upon the pirates and kill them, to stop any word of what they had done leaking out, they had found themselves instead outnumbered and surrounded.

Bemused and aghast, Lord Malvern could do nothing but acquiesce to all Margrit's demands, even though he found his heavy purse of gold being rapidly emptied.

"Out! Out!" Margrit screamed. "Go get me my wine

and my oysters! Bring me the richest perfumes, the finest silks! Go on. Else I'll order my pirates to slit ye from ear to ear!"

The huge, hairy, scarred, tattooed, and gap-toothed pirates standing about the room grinned and nudged each other with their elbows, fingering their knives. As the lord of Fettercairn's servants all filed out, looking very despondent, Margrit laughed in joy. She loved it when she outwitted someone, even an impotent old fool like Lord Malvern. His face, when he had realized the graveyard was full of her bullyboys, their weapons concealed in the weeds! It was almost worth having to put up with him now. Lucky he was rich, else she might have grown bored of his blustering hours ago and had him fed to the sharks.

The cream of the jest, she thought, was that all Lord Malvern had required to raise her from the dead was a living soul and a sharp knife. Apart from knowledge of the spell, of course. So he need not have risked employing pirates from the town to make up his circle of nine necromancers. Yet it had suited her purposes to let him think he needed a full circle to enact the spell, and so she had kept him awake night after night, hissing "Make sure ye have the nine" in his ear until he had done just as she wanted.

Margrit smiled and stretched her arms above her head. It was then she noticed that the youngest of the lord's servants had not left the room with the others, but stood waiting, deliciously unsure.

She nodded to him. "Take off your shirt. Slowly. Mmmm, not bad. Turn around. What is your name?"

"Piers, my lady. Piers Harper."

"A harper are ye? I guess that's why your arms are so delightfully well muscled. Come, harper. Let us see if ye can make me sing."

Fèlice gripped the ship's rail with both hands and watched as the Pirate Isles slowly grew from a grey smudge on the horizon to a collection of tall hills, rising steeply from deep frills of white foam.

"I hope we're in time," she whispered. "It's taken us so long to get here!"

"It was the full moon last night," Landon said, sounding as dispirited as she felt. "If they were planning to do anything, it would've been done last night."

"We couldna have gone any faster," Rafferty said. "The sailors canna believe the speed we've made already. We've covered almost six hundred miles in less than two days!"

Rafferty had spent the last forty-eight hours making himself thoroughly at home on the ship, climbing the rigging like an arak even in the worst of weathers, hauling on the ropes and coiling them like an old hand, and sharing his cup of rum and a melancholy song at the day's end with the other sailors. He could not understand why everyone else had been so sick, particularly Cameron, with whom he had always shared a friendly rivalry. Being a year older and a little taller and heavier, Cameron had nearly always bested him, and so Rafferty took great pleasure in asking after him solicitously, and offering to bring him soup, the very mention of which was enough to make Cameron lurch for the bucket, which he was sharing with a very sick and miserable Finn.

It had been a wild, rough journey. Spitting ice and sleet, the spell-wind had stayed at their backs, without swerving or dropping, for two whole days, driving them over the sea at a breakneck pace. Stormy Briant had not dared sleep in case he lost control, and had ordered his former apprentices to lash him to the mast to stop him dozing off. There he stood, facing towards the Pirate Isles, a length of rope knotted about his hands like reins. Occasionally Fèlice could hear him shout or laugh like a madman. He ate nothing, but took a dram of whisky every hour or so, and urinated over the side once or twice a day.

Behind their ship came sixteen other galleons and carracks, all propelled by a full set of sails that strained to hold the power of the wind. They had lost four in the storm, and could only hope the ships had been swept off course and would be able to make their way back to Dùn Gorm.

Ahead of them was sunshine; behind them storm. Basking in the sunshine were the six islands that made up the Pirate Isles. Their coasts were rough and rocky, and far too dangerous to approach. Instead the fleet tacked, to sail around to the mouth of a wide lagoon. As they sailed in through the heads, cannons on either headland began to fire, and the royal fleet fired back. Although some damage was sustained, the ships were all traveling too fast to be easy targets, and none were sunk.

"Great Eà!" Cameron said, his mouth hanging open. "Will ye look at that!"

Sailing out to greet them was a fleet of more than twenty large ships, all flying the black and red flag of the pirates. Already the ships were firing at them. They could see the white puffs of smoke, and then hear a huge bang, and minutes later everyone dived to the deck as a cannonball whizzed through one of the sails, bringing rigging crashing down onto the deck.

"They were ready and waiting for us!" Rafferty cried.

"Lads, get below deck!" Iseult ordered, striding up the deck towards them, her helmet on her head and her hand on her weapons belt. She was very white, and her eyes were red-rimmed. Looking at her face, Fèlice's heart sank like lead.

"But Your Highness!" Rafferty protested.

"Get your skates and be ready to go," Iseult continued.

"Our ice skates?"

Iseult flashed him a look. "Aye! Did ye think they were purely for decoration? Go!"

Rafferty, Cameron, and Landon ran to obey, but Fèlice lingered.

Iseult glared at her. "Ye are no' at court now, lassie, but a soldier on my ship! Do as ye are told!"

"Aye, Your Highness," Fèlice said. "It's just . . . I wanted to ask . . ."

"What?"

"Are we too late?"

Iseult stood stock-still, her hands clenched on her belt. Then she jerked her head, just once. "Too late for Olwynne," she answered, her voice shaking. "She was murdered last night, at midnight. Finn felt her go. I wish . . . I should've . . ." Her voice trailed away. "We are no' too late for Owein, though," she said, after a long moment in which Fèlice fought to hide her tears of shock and horror. "And we are no' too late to make them pay for what they've done."

"No, Your Highness," Fèlice whispered.

Iseult turned and looked at her. "Do ye love my son?" she asked quietly.

Fèlice nodded. It was not a time for lying.

"I wondered what he saw in ye, apart from your pretty face," Iseult said. "I think I'm beginning to see. Do ye wish to help?"

"Aye, Your Highness," Fèlice said, very subdued.

"Good. Wait a moment. I just need to . . ."

Iseult's voice trailed away. Her gaze grew unfocused. Fèlice felt the temperature drop sharply, and shuddered, hugging herself as snow began to spin down from the sky. Iseult raised her hand. Lightning leaped out of the dark-bellied clouds that chased them. The snow whirled more thickly. The shadow of the cloud fell over the sparkling blue waters of the lagoon, turning it all to grey. It grew colder and colder. The water shivered and then lay still, turning paler and paler. The ship slowed precipitately, jerking everyone on board forward.

Fèlice suddenly realized what she was seeing. The water of the lagoon was freezing over, turning into ice.

"I come from the Spine o' the World, ye ken," Iseult said to her, a rueful smile lifting her lips. "It is all ice and snow up there. I grew up knowing naught else."

The ice met the pirate ships and slammed into them like a white fist. Some, hit side on, foundered and began to sink, before being seized in the ice, which stove their boards in and broke the ships apart. Others crashed into it head-first, and were frozen there, immobile for long moments, before the ice began to slowly squeeze and a great whining, groaning noise rose.

The Royal Stag pushed on. Frightened and amazed, Fèlice looked back at the other ships and saw they too were pushing slowly forward into the ice, seemingly unaffected by the dramatic change in the medium on which they floated.

"All the royal fleet has been fitted out for sailing in the northern seas," Iseult said. "Our first great sailing journey was up to Carraig during the last war with the Fairgean. We were sailing in seas which were often so cold they froze over, so all our ships were built to withstand it. I dinna think the pirate ships would be so reinforced, considering they normally sail in the warm seas o' the south."

"I see," Fèlice said. "How clever!"

"Thank ye," Iseult replied. "I canna use my powers for much, no' having been properly trained, but turning water to ice is something I can manage. We always have to work with what we've got."

"True," Fèlice nodded.

"Did ye bring ice skates?"

Fèlice nodded her head, unable to help smiling.

"And can ye use them?"

Fèlice nodded again. "I come from Ravenshaw too," she said smugly.

"What about a bow and arrow? Can ye shoot while ye skate?"

Fèlice's smile faded. She shook her head.

"Never mind. Ye can carry a flaming torch. Try no' to get too near the pirate ships, or they'll shoot ye. Skate in fast, throw your torch, and get out o' there again. Are ye any good at throwing?"

Fèlice was silent, then shook her head miserably.

"At least you're honest. Well, I do no' want ye being shot. Owein would never forgive me. How about ye help arm the catapults? That way ye'll still be helping, but no' getting too close to the main fighting."

Fèlice nodded. "Thank ye," she managed to say.

"No' your fault ye were never taught to throw properly," Iseult said rather caustically. "That has to be laid at your father's door, along with no' teaching ye to shoot."

"My father's rather auld-fashioned," Fèlice said meekly.

"It's amazing ye turned out so well. Come on, lass! Get your skates on! It's time to go and hunt down some pirates!"

Then Iseult was clambering over the side of the ship and down a ladder to the ice, her skates bumping against her back.

The rest of the day passed in a haze of smoke as the pirates desperately shot cannonball after cannonball from their flaming and disintegrating ships. All about the trapped galleons, swift skaters swooped and circled, firing flaming arrows into the rigging or hurling torches into the pitch-soaked boards. The royal fleet had managed to advance into a rough semicircle about the trapped pirate fleet before they could go no farther. From the catapults on their decks they hurled fireballs at the pirates, while their cannons boomed, boomed, boomed ceaselessly. By sundown, the enemy fleet was demolished and the skaters were hunting down those pirates who tried to flee, slipping and sliding all over the ice.

Those left in the pirate town had not been idle all through the long, bloody day. They had busied themselves fortifying their barricades, and bombarding any skater who came too close. Their fire had broken up the ice all along the shore, so no one could approach the town on their skates. The royal forces had to retreat to their ships to regroup and rest, to tend their wounded, take some sustenance, and plan the assault on the town. It was decided to attack again in the early hours of the morning, silently, under the cover of darkness, when hopefully the ice near the shore had had a chance to freeze hard again.

Filthy, exhausted, and coughing from the smoke, Fèlice, Landon, Rafferty, and Cameron all found themselves a spot on the deck, and gulped down some water gratefully.

"Her Highness says the Banprionnsa Olwynne is dead," Fèlice told them hoarsely. "They killed her last night."

"Oh no!" Landon cried.

"What o' the witch they wanted to raise?" Rafferty asked.

"I guess she's alive and up there somewhere," Fèlice said, looking up at the old fort, which, high on its hill, was still touched by the last of the sunlight. "She's a powerful sorceress by all accounts. I dread to think what she plans."

"And the prionnsa?" Cameron asked, coughing.

"Alive still, though who kens for how long?"

"What o' Rhiannon?" Landon asked, his hands clasped together before his chest. "Any news at all?"

"None," Fèlice replied, and suddenly began to cry. She had never seen a battle before.

Rafferty and Cameron both put their arms about her, banging each other by mistake, and scowling at one another over her head. Fèlice wiped her eyes.

"I just hope she and Blackthorn are all right," she said. "I wish I kent where they were!"

Both Rhiannon and Owein were still locked in their damp, smelly, unpleasant little cell. Dedrie had come at one point, to bring them more water and some food, and to look at their wounds, but she had been distracted and in a hurry, and well guarded by a surly-faced Jem and Ballard, so it was impossible to try to escape.

After that, no one had come near them. They had spent all day listening to the distant boom of the cannons, and agonizing over what was happening.

"It's the Yeomen! They've finally come!" Owein cried. "But too late for Olwynne." Impatiently he passed his hand over his eyes.

"It's a miracle they are here at all," Rhiannon said. "Ye dinna see the storm they had to face to get here."

"What's happening? What's going on?"

"I dinna ken," Rhiannon answered irritably. "Stop pacing up and down, ye're stirring up all the dust and sneezing really hurts my shoulder."

"Eà's eyes, I wish I kent what was going on!"

Just then there was a high, joyful trill, and a tiny bluebird swooped down through the bars of the cage. Rhiannon was overjoyed. "Bluey!" she cried. "Where have ye been? I thought ye must've been hurt or killed when they shot me down! Where's Blackthorn? Is she all right?"

The bluebird answered with another trill, and both Owein and Rhiannon looked at each other in relief as they heard, in the simple language of birds, that Blackthorn was alive and unhurt, hiding out in the forest behind the old fort.

"We have some chance o' escape then," Owein said, beginning to pace again. "Oh, Rhiannon, please ask your wee birdie to go and see what is happening. I'll go mad shut up in here and no' knowing what is going on!"

So the bluebird flittered in and out, giving the two captives a very vague and imprecise idea of what was going on. One piece of news cheered Owein up immensely.

"Snow and ice," he cried. "That's my mama! Thank Eà she's here. It'll no' be long now, Rhiannon, and we'll be free!"

Rhiannon did not have the same high opinion of the Dowager Banrìgh as Owein, but she nodded her head and smiled, and then bent her head to the bird. "Find Lewen," she whispered. "Find Lewen and bring him here."

Lewen was flying through the twilight, the sky ahead of him filled with long lines of grey rain like battalions of soldiers. He had his hood up over his head and his shoulders hunched against the sharp wind, but he was gladder than he had been for weeks. Beneath him, the stallion's great shoulder muscles moved rhythmically, as the magnificent wings shaped the wind and bade it serve him. Lewen could not believe how swiftly the land rolled by beneath them, like a dark green eiderdown stitched together with thin shining rills of water. Already they had traversed half the distance to the sea. Tomorrow he would be flying over water. The day after that, if all went well, he would see the sharp peaks of the Pirate Isles rising out of the ocean.

Keep safe, Rhiannon, he thought. *I'm coming . . .*

Uncovering the Cage

Bronwen lay on a chaise longue in the sunshine, feeling as limp as a scullery maid's rag. They had carried her out here at her urgent request, as she could not stand being incarcerated in her stuffy room any longer. They had brought her to one of her favorite spots, a deep green pool in the forest, just far enough beyond the hedges of the garden that she could see nothing but the curve of one golden dome above the trees. Here she could lie, and listen to the birds and the wind in the trees, and soak up the warmth of the sunshine.

They had set up a little table nearby, with a jug of iced water and a glass, some smelling salts, a pile of the latest broadsheets that made Bronwen's head ache to look at, and a plate of fruit and sweetmeats for which she had absolutely no appetite. Joey stood beside her, holding a parasol to shade her face from the brightness of the sun, and Maura crouched in a chair next to her, for once sitting idle, and looking very ill and wretched. Her breath wheezed in her chest, and every few breaths she coughed, a deep guttural cough that sounded as if her lungs were full of mud.

"Oh, Maura, please go to bed," Bronwen said faintly. "Your coughing is making my head ache!"

"I dinna . . . cough, cough . . . want to . . . cough . . . leave ye."

"Ye're sick. Go to bed. I'll send Mirabelle to tend ye."

"Nay, thank ye!"

Bronwen raised herself on one elbow. "Why no'? She is the head healer now. It is her job."

"Bogfaeries have own remedies," Maura said, her voice hoarse with coughing. "Besides, me no like that one, with her poxy face. She never smiles."

"It's no' her fault she's pockmarked," Bronwen said. "I'm sure she's a very good healer, else she'd no' be head o' the Healers' Guild."

"Like that other one? Who took our Donn? She mighty fine." Maura paused to cough throatily into her handkerchief.

"Ye shouldna judge Mirabelle just because she was Johanna's assistant," Bronwen said, and then a terrible thought occurred to her. So terrible was it, and yet so obvious, that she sat utterly frozen for a moment, looking back over the past few days and seeing its pattern tumble into an entirely new configuration.

"Joey," she said after a long moment.

"Aye, Your Majesty?"

"I have a fancy for some o' Mirabelle's special angelica tea. Could ye please go and ask the butler to make me a pot, and bring it out to me here?"

Joey hesitated. "I was told I shouldna leave ye alone," he said.

"I'm no' alone. Maura is here. She can look after me. Please. I do think it will make me feel better."

"Aye, Your Majesty. I'll go now." He propped the parasol against the chair, carefully wedging it with a stone so it would not fall and subject Bronwen to the harsh glare of the sunlight, and then he went running back towards the palace at top speed.

"Maura," Bronwen said. Her voice was slow and thick and difficult to force out through her numb lips. "When did ye start feeling sick?"

The bogfaery coughed violently before answering, and then stared for a moment at her handkerchief. "Day or two ago. Maybe more. I been so sad and heartsick since winged one die, it's hard to tell."

"Have ye eaten anything unusual?" Bronwen asked.

Maura was surprised. "No, no. I eat as usual. In kitchen with other maids mostly. That boy o' yours, he been kind, he bring me soup and bread at night, when I sit up a-waiting for ye. I do get tired these days. No' as young as I was."

"Joey's been bringing ye soup?"

"Aye, soup and a nice drop o' hot elderberry wine. I done changed my mind about that boy. Me thought him very quick and sly when first Cuckoo brought him, but he been kind, and saves my legs."

The bogfaery's voice was broken continually by coughs and the clearing of her throat.

"Maura, will ye please go to bed? For me?"

The bogfaery protested, and Bronwen said, her voice strengthening with the urgency of her emotions, "Maura! Ye are making me feel ill listening to ye. Go . . . to . . . bed! And on your way, will ye send Dolan to me?"

"Och, Dolan no' feeling too good either," Maura said. "Did ye no' hear? Half the palace guard are down with the same thing as ye. Sick as cats, they are."

"Barlow too?"

"Och, aye. They think some kind o' rot got into the grain, perhaps, because o' the weather. They been up all night, coughing up their guts, poor boys."

Some kind o' rot, all right, Bronwen thought grimly. She wondered what to do. She was so weak she could barely walk. Her breath shortened in her chest. She found it hard to breathe. *It's all just coincidence. Just my stupid suspicious imaginings. Mirabelle taught me when I was just a lass. She couldna possibly be a traitor. She couldna possibly be poisoning me . . .*

"Your Majesty, how do ye feel?" Mirabelle's shadow fell upon her.

Bronwen jumped violently. She put one hand to her

heart. "Terrible," she said in a whining voice. "Like I've been beaten with clubs."

"Let me give ye some more medicine," Mirabelle said, measuring out a dose from one of her big brown bottles. "Joey says ye've asked for some more tea. It'll be here in just a moment. I'm so glad ye've been enjoying my special brew. I made it up just for ye."

I bet ye did, Bronwen thought as she accepted the cup of medicine. She held it to her lips, and noticed how fixedly Mirabelle watched her until she had drunk down the medicine and given her back the empty cup.

"Ye'll have a nice sleep now, and when ye wake ye'll feel much better, I promise," Mirabelle said, and went quietly away, her green healer's robe almost invisible among the shifting hues of the garden.

Bronwen leaned over, thrust her fingers as far as she could down her throat, and vomited up the sickly sweet medicine. Maura watched her in dismay. "Ye sick again! I get healer!"

"Dinna be a fool," Bronwen said savagely. "Get me my mother! And then, Maura, I want ye to get away from here. Go find yourself a nice inn in the city. The Nisse and Nixie would be best. Get a faery healer and get them to purge ye. Do ye hear me?"

Maura stared at her, then turned and looked with frightened eyes up the path, where Mirabelle had gone.

"I canna . . . cough, cough . . . leave ye . . ."

"Aye, ye can. Please, Maura. I'd never forgive myself if anything happened . . . please . . ."

Maura nodded. "What else me do first?"

"I just want my mother. Tell her to send Joey off on some other errand, so we have a chance to talk in private. Then get yourself somewhere safe, and find someone to help ye. Wait! There's money in my bedchamber, ye ken where it is. Take a purse o' coins, and try and get away with no one seeing ye."

"No one notices servants," Maura said. "I'll be fine."

She bent and embraced Bronwen fervently, patting her arms with her tiny, wrinkled paws. Then she hurried away, leaving Bronwen alone. Despite the warm, golden sunshine, Bronwen felt very cold.

Was it Mirabelle who killed my uncle, then? she wondered. *But no. It couldna have been. Mirabelle was at the healers' hall. She was drugged like the others. Though Gwilym did say she was the first to recover . . .*

Bronwen dropped her face into her hands. Was she wrong in suspecting Mirabelle of being involved in this plot to undermine the throne? What proof did she have? A tea that tasted delicious but left one with a desperate craving for more and an inability to sleep? More medicine, to help her sleep, that left her feeling as though her head was stuffed with wool and her limbs weighed down with lead. Mirabelle's constant presence in the palace, even at night, fully dressed, with her pockets filled with potions? And the way Bronwen always felt uncomfortable around her . . .

These were not proofs. Mirabelle was one of those heavy, lumpish, envious women who always made those that had been more fortunate in the lottery of life feel awkward. It was no fault of hers, and no fault of Bronwen's. It was just the way things were. And Maura's dreadful cough, and the sickness decimating the palace guard, they too could just be coincidences, and not an attempt to isolate Bronwen and leave her vulnerable.

Though she did feel very vulnerable.

Her aunt Isabeau had once said to her, "Always trust your intuition. It is the witch-sense, prickling at ye. Listen to it."

Wishing desperately that Isabeau was here now to help and advise her, Bronwen got to her feet, holding on to the chaise longue for support. She looked up the path, wanting her mother desperately. She was all alone in the garden. This felt all wrong. Bronwen was never left alone without servants or guards of some kind. Her sense of fear almost overwhelmed her. She had to lower her head and breathe deeply, as she had been taught during her days at the Theurgia, before she could force the panic back down.

"How are ye yourself, Your Majesty?" Elfrida's voice cut across her thoughts. Bronwen looked up. Elfrida stood before her, carrying a tray with a teapot and cup. "Ye look very ill," Elfrida said. "Have ye been sick again? Sit down, my dear. Shall I call Mirabelle?"

"No!"

Elfrida raised an eyebrow.

"I'm sorry. I'm fine, really. I stood up and got all dizzy. I'll sit down again. I'll be fine."

"I heard ye wanted some tea. Joey has been waylaid by your mother, to run some chores for her, so I thought I would bring it out to ye myself. Where is your little bog-faery? Ye shouldna be alone."

Bronwen was sending up a fervent prayer of thanks at the news her mother had got the message, and so she was stumped for an answer for a moment. "Oh. I . . . I sent her to get me a book from my room."

"Ye shouldna be out here all alone, when ye're so sick and dizzy. Ye could faint or be sick again. Here, let me pour ye some tea."

"No, no. I'm fine. Maybe a wee drop o' water. Thank ye. Please, no need to fuss. I'll be right in a moment." Bronwen drank a mouthful of water to stop herself gabbling, then passed the glass back to Elfrida. She found her gaze riveted by Elfrida's bare fingers. No onyx ring with the seal of the Thistle upon it. Bronwen was oddly disturbed by this. She remembered the silver tray of sliced bellfruit, and began to wonder. Elfrida sat down next to her, spreading out her black skirt, setting her feet side by side and her hands in her lap. Bronwen suddenly realized one of the weird dissonances about Elfrida today was the lack of the pastor behind her, like the thin elongated shadow of early evening. It made Elfrida seem warmer, pinker, more human.

"Has it no' grown hot today, with the Dowager Banrìgh

gone and all her frost and snow with her?" Elfrida said, fanning herself with her hand.

"Aye, it's almost like summer again," Bronwen said, lying back with a sigh. "Poor Mistress Dorcas. That's the mistress o' the wardrobe, ye ken. She'll have packed away all the summer clothes and dug out all the winter clothes, and now suddenly it's summer again. She will be in a tizz." A thought suddenly occurred to her. "What a shame I'm in mourning! My fan is all white, and I have no wish to dye it black. It's made from the feathers o' the white bhanais bird, ye ken, the one in the maze. It's very rare. If it's going to get all sultry again, I'll order a new one. Made of black silk, perhaps, with sticks o' jet."

It made Bronwen feel much better to be sitting in the garden, chatting about fashion, even though she knew it was only a diversion to stop Elfrida suspecting anything was wrong. Any moment now, Maya would come, and Bronwen could make some excuse to get rid of Elfrida. Bronwen wanted her mother desperately. Maya had the sharpest, most cunning mind of anyone she knew. She would know what to do.

Elfrida moved back her chair so she was not sitting in direct sunlight, and waved her hand up and down again. It was warm. Bronwen noticed small beads of sweat along Elfrida's upper lip.

"Where is your fan?" she asked idly, having another sip of cool water. "I remember admiring it at the wedding. It was heavy gold, and very ornate. Some kind o' antique, was it?"

She glanced up at Elfrida, and was surprised to find her pasty-white and breathing heavily. "Och, aye, my fan," she said. "Mmm, it broke. I threw it out."

"But surely it must have been very valuable! It was gold!"

"Happen so, but . . . it was broken. Couldna be fixed."

"What a shame. It was lovely, if ye like that heavy, ornate style. No' your usual thing, though, I would have thought. What a shame it broke. How did it happen? It looked sturdy enough."

Bronwen was talking more to keep the conversational ball rolling than for any other reason, but she found herself in a strange position of gradually revealing something to herself while she spoke, as if her words were heavy sheets over a shrieking creature in a cage, and with each word, another cover was whisked away, until at last Bronwen could see the ugly, terrible thing that lay beneath. Her voice faltered. Her breath stopped in her throat. She took a long sip of water, gazing out at the garden, carefully not looking at Elfrida.

"It was nothing special," Elfrida was saying. "It belonged to my mother-in-law. Ye're right, it's no' really my style to carry a gaudy thing like that. I'll have another made, something lighter to carry."

"We'll all need new fans if it gets much hotter," Bronwen managed to say. She still could not look at Elfrida. Incredulity was burning through her veins. Surely it was impossible! Elfrida the murderer? Elfrida the secret assassin? Cuckoo's mother!

This sickness has affected my brain, she thought. *I'm imagining vile things, horrible things, about people I've kent for years. It's no' true, none o' it is true.*

Yet her mind continued to worry at the problem, turning little jigsaw pieces of oddness around and finding they were making a shape. Elfrida and Mirabelle in the corridors in the dark hours of the night. Mirabelle saying to the banprionnsa, "Now is no' the time to be giving in to doubts and weaknesses." What had she meant by that? Why not now? The angelica tea. Elfrida giving her the bellfruit. The dreadful sickness that had followed. The golden fan, with its thick embossed sticks, that Elfrida had clutched so tightly all through that long, terrible night that Lachlan was murdered, and then tossed aside so carelessly later. The fan's sticks had been wide enough to conceal a thin blowpipe and some barbs. It had belonged to Margrit of Arran,

who by all accounts had had no hesitation in poisoning her
enemies. Margrit of Arran, whose ghost had haunted the
lord of Fettercairn, and led him to the spell of resurrection.
Margrit of Arran, whose ring Elfrida had been wearing,
and was no longer. Margrit of Arran, whom the lord of Fettercairn sought to raise from the dead, using the blood of
Bronwen's cousin, Olwynne. Margrit of Arran, called the
Thistle.

"Where is your ring?" Bronwen asked abruptly. She
saw the ugly flush that suddenly rose up Elfrida's face.

"My . . . my ring?"

"Aye, the black one."

"Why, I . . . I dinna ken. It'll be somewhere. In my jew-
elry case, no doubt."

"But ye have worn it every day o' late. Why no' now?"

Elfrida was seriously discomposed. "I dinna ken . . . I
dinna like it any more . . . it is too heavy . . ."

Bronwen saw the sudden hunching of Elfrida's shoulders, the flash of suspicion in her eyes. She tried to think
of something innocuous to say, something that would de-
flect Elfrida, but she could think of nothing. Her breath
was coming fast in her throat, and she clutched the arms of
her chaise longue desperately. *Cuckoo's mother!*

"Ye've guessed it, haven't ye?" Elfrida said. She sat up
and pressed her hands over her face for a moment. "It was
Margrit speaking through me the other day, wasn't it?
Telling that young fool to take care when touching the
Thistle. She was angry. I tried to hold her back, but she will
never take care. He is lucky she did not kill him there and
then. If he had been drinking or eating, she would've, I'm
sure."

"The ring . . ."

"Aye. Like the fan, it's got a trick to it. A little twist and
out falls the poison, into your cup or your plate . . ."

"The bellfruit . . ."

"Aye."

Bronwen was silent, sick with horror.

Elfrida sighed. "I did try to withstand her, ye ken," she said conversationally. "But she was in my ear all the time, whispering dreadful things about me, and my past, telling me that Iain cared more for his rìgh than for me, and now his son Donncan was doing the same, stealing Neil away from me. It never stopped. I heard her voice everywhere in the Tower of Mists, telling me I was ugly, stupid, powerless, a dupe. She said she would make sure Neil was hurt or crippled in some way if I did no' do what she said. For years and years she burrowed her way inside me, and took up residence there, waiting, waiting, for her chance. Sometimes she seemed to sleep, or she went somewhere else, I do no' ken where. She wanted me to find the spell o' resurrection for her, but I resisted, really I did. I would no' come here to Lucescere, I stayed in Arran and tried to keep her hidden."

She took a ragged breath. "I thought . . . I thought Father Francis would help me. Drive her spirit away, somehow. I prayed every day, seven times a day, I begged him for help. But he is the Fealde's creature. He saw how Margrit's hunger for revenge would help the Fealde's dreams o' conquering and converting the western lands. He said we must do what she said, and made me come here to Lucescere, bringing her with me like some foul fetus in my belly . . ."

Slowly the tide of horror within Bronwen subsided, and she was able to speak. "Ye killed Uncle Lachlan? Ye spat the poisoned barb at him?"

"Aye. It was the work o' only a moment. No one saw. By the time they thought to search the room, I had the blowpipe and barbs safely concealed inside the sticks o' the fan again. I sat there all night, holding the fan, while they searched my room and all my luggage." She laughed.

"Is she . . . is she in ye now?"

"No. She's gone. I'd say she's got her way and lives again. She has no need o' me anymore. Or at least, no need o' my body, to be hers, my arms and legs, my mouth . . ."

Bronwen swallowed. "So . . . Olwynne . . ."

"Dead, would be my guess."

Tears welled up in Bronwen's eyes. She and Olwynne had never been close, but she was still her cousin, and it seemed a dreadful way to die.

Elfrida had been unscrewing the lid of a small brown bottle she had taken from her pocket. She got to her feet and stood, looking down at Bronwen. "I'm sorry about this. It'll wreck all our plans to have ye dead. It would have been much easier to keep ye alive and marry ye to Neil, and win the throne without war. But ye do see I canna let ye live now, don't ye?"

Bronwen stared at her, then suddenly heaved herself up, seeking to escape. But Elfrida put her knee into her chest, and her free hand on Bronwen's forehead, forcing the bottle between her teeth. Bronwen fought desperately, but she was weak and dizzy still from her illness, and Elfrida was surprisingly strong. Inexorably the contents of the bottle were poured into her mouth, while Elfrida held her hand clamped down over Bronwen's nose, cutting off her airways so she could not breathe. Try as she might, she could not free herself. Involuntarily she swallowed, gasping for air.

Bronwen recognized the heavy, sickly sweet taste of Mirabelle's poppy tincture. *Two fingers, no more,* the healer had said, and Bronwen had just swallowed an entire bottle full.

She gagged, but Elfrida had her face tilted up and her jaw clamped shut. Choking, unable to breathe, Bronwen struggled weakly, but the banprionnsa was too strong for her. "It will no' take long," Elfrida said in a tone of regret.

Then she disappeared.

One moment she was looming over Bronwen, forcing her back into the chaise longue, suffocating her, poisoning her. The next she was gone. Bronwen coughed and coughed, and struggled to sit up. Then she screamed and shrank back. A black rat was sitting on her chest, squeaking in dismay, its red eyes bulging. Bronwen swept it away with her arm, and it fell and twisted midair before scurrying into the undergrowth.

Bronwen heaved a great breath and then rolled over, and once again forced herself to vomit. Again and again she retched weakly into the grass.

Someone sat down beside her and passed her a glass of water. Thankfully Bronwen rinsed out her mouth, and then drank a mouthful. Her throat was exceedingly sore.

"I always thought Elfrida was a bit o' a rat," Maya said thoughtfully, stroking back Bronwen's damp hair. "The way she was always scurrying about, spying on people, sniffing out foul smells. I never liked her."

"Ye did that? Ye . . . changed her?"

Maya nodded. "O' course. What else was I meant to do? She was killing ye."

There was no remorse in Maya's voice. Bronwen shivered. She had always found this Talent of her mother's the most frightening thing about her. Any story about the days of Maya's rule were full of the people she had transformed. Lachlan and his two elder brothers had been turned into blackbirds, and Maya had set her hawk to hunt them down. Isabeau and Iseult's father had been changed into a horse, and Maya had ridden him for years. Tabithas the Keybearer had been turned into a wolf, and Margrit of Arran's chamberlain had been turned into a toad. It had been Maya's most secret and devastating weapon, and quite possibly her cruelest. Bronwen did not like to be reminded about this aspect of her mother's character. She preferred to think of Maya as the mute and scarred witch's servant who had once been the most beautiful and powerful woman in the land. Yet it was impossible to pretend ignorance when someone you had known all your life was transformed into a rat right before your eyes.

"What . . . what will happen to her?"

"Plenty o' cats about," Maya said indifferently. She

examined Bronwen closely. "Ye look terrible. How do ye feel? Did ye get all the poison out?"

"I hope so."

"It'd be better if we could purge ye," Maya said. "Only, for obvious reasons, we do no' want to go to the healers' college asking for a purge. Did they teach ye anything at that school o' yours about how to rid the body o' poison?"

"It was no' really on the curriculum," Bronwen said shakily, "at least no' for me. I was never going to be a healer. Oh, I wish Aunty Beau was here."

"So do I," Maya said. "If only to change into a terrier and hunt down that rat for me. I dislike loose ends."

"Canna ye do that?"

"I canna change myself, only others," Maya said. "I could turn ye into a cat or a dog, if ye want to do the deed."

Bronwen realized incredulously that her mother was not joking. "No, thanks," she said with a shudder.

"Come, let's get ye mopped up and ye can tell me the whole story. Maura told me only that ye suspected Mirabelle o' dosing everyone with something, and making them sick. I take it that ye discovered that Elfrida was in on the plot too?"

Bronwen told her mother the whole story while Maya quickly and efficiently cleaned her and the chair up, and washed away any sign of vomit on the grass with the tea in the teapot.

"She meant to marry me off to Neil," Bronwen said. "As if I would ever marry Cuckoo!"

"Ye might o'," Maya said. "If Donncan was dead, and ye were all alone, and Neil there to support ye and comfort ye. He was doing a pretty good job o' it already."

"Donncan," Bronwen breathed. "That pastor o' Elfrida's is on his way to meet him. He must be planning to kill him!"

"I'd say so," Maya said, using the last of the water to dab away any marks on Bronwen's gown. "Elfrida probably gave the poison ring to Neil so that he could tip something foul into Donncan's wine."

"No! No' Neil!"

"Why no'? There's no doubt he wanted ye, and he'd be a fool no' to want the crown too."

"But . . . but Donncan was his best friend! They grew up together, almost like brothers."

"Naught like a woman to come between friends," Maya said. "Or brothers, for that matter."

Bronwen leaped to her feet, and had to grip tight to the chair as her vision disappeared in a sparkling haze. "I have to . . . I have to warn him . . . I have to stop Neil . . ."

"How?"

"I'll send a message . . . I'll . . ." She stopped as she realized the difficulties. There was no one she could trust. If Mirabelle was one of the conspirators, who else could be? Bronwen's secretary, recommended to her by Neil? Her page Joey? The new Lord Steward? All of them Neil's men. And if she went to the pigeon loft by herself, to send a homing pigeon to Rhyssmadill, what guarantee would she have that the pigeon made it in time? She had no way of knowing how far the tentacles of conspiracy had writhed through the palace. Any of the servants or guards could be in Elfrida's pay. And if Bronwen did anything at all out of the ordinary, she would mark herself out and put herself in danger. Maya had bought her time and safety by transforming Elfrida into a rat, but not for long. The banprionnsa would soon be missed, and Mirabelle was by nature suspicious.

Bronwen pressed her shaking hands together. "I must go myself," she said. "There is no other way to make sure Donncan is kept safe. I'll swim. If I change into my seashape I'll get down the river faster than any boat. Mama, ye must help me."

"How?" Maya asked.

"Ye escaped Lucescere once. Tell me how ye did it."

Maya nodded. "All right. We do no' have much time.

Mirabelle must no' realize that ye are all alone. I sent that pageboy o' yours off on a wild-goose chase, but he'll soon realize and be back. Let us think o' the best way o' doing this. And let us do it quickly!"

THE WHIRLIGIG
OF TIME

*"And thus the whirligig of time brings
in his revenges."*

—SHAKESPEARE
Twelfth Night, 1601

Escaping Lucescere

◁◦◦▷

It was growing cool as the sun dipped down towards the trees.

Bronwen looked back at her mother and smiled. She lay in Bronwen's bed, pale-cheeked, her long black hair spread out over the pillow, wearing Bronwen's face and one of her nightgowns.

Bronwen could not believe how effective was Maya's glamourie. It was like looking at herself in the mirror. Except Bronwen no longer looked like herself. She looked like an old bogfaery, with a wrinkled black-skinned face, shining eyes like black beads, and a hunched back under her simple grey gown and apron. She carried a basket over one arm, with a cloth hanging over the top. Inside the basket was hidden a large waterproof bag that belonged to her mother and had been hurriedly packed with some clothes and food. It would take two or more days of hard swimming for Bronwen to reach Rhyssmadill, and she would need to stop and rest and eat at some point.

She opened the door, and almost fell over Joey, who was sitting right outside. He looked shiny-eyed and red-nosed, and she wondered if he had been reprimanded for leaving her alone in the gardens for so long.

"What ye do, boy, underfoot all the time?" Bronwen grumbled in what she hoped was a fair copy of Maura's voice and manner.

"Naught, ma'am. Just waiting to see if Her Majesty needs me."

"Her Majesty is going to sleep now, so dinna ye go on disturbing her," Bronwen scolded as she shut the door firmly behind her. She went out into the corridor, past two guards she had never seen before in her life. She nodded to them, as she imagined Maura would, and went away down the hall as quickly as she could without arousing suspicion. The glamourie would not last long, Maya had warned her. She could not linger.

It was hard to remember to walk with little steps, as if she was only three feet high, and to moan and sigh and shuffle as Maura usually did. A glamourie was only an illusion. Bronwen had not been turned into a bogfaery, only made to look like one. If she walked under a low-hanging branch she would still hit her head, even though it looked like she had inches to spare. If she walked like a young, long-legged woman, so would her semblance. Maya had warned her that many glamouries were unmasked by a failure to act as one looked.

The guards had barely glanced at her, and Bronwen breathed a little easier. But then she began the descent down the stairs, and came full upon Mirabelle, in urgent consultation with two palace guards.

"What do ye mean, ye canna find her! She must be here somewhere. Ask around, find out who saw her last."

"Aye, ma'am," the guards said and hurried away.

Bronwen could hardly breathe for terror. If Mirabelle had the gift of clear-seeing, as many witches did, she would see straight through the glamourie and Bronwen would be unmasked. She decided she must act just as usual, and so she came stiffly down the stairs, sighing with every step, with one hand on her hip as if it ached, nodded to Mirabelle and said gruffly, "Evening, Mistress Mirabelle," and went on past her.

The healer barely noticed her. She jerked her head in response and stood staring off into space, her hands clenched together. She was still there when Bronwen went around the corner and down the next flight of stairs, fighting the urge to run.

It would have taken Bronwen hours to get to the loch if she had gone the usual way—down the avenue, out the palace gates, past the scrutiny of the soldiers, through the bustling city streets to the gate, hurrying to get there before the sunset curfew, past another set of guards, over the bridge and down the long, winding road to the jetties and warehouses on the loch shore. Lucescere was built on an island between two rivers that poured down into the loch over a two-hundred-foot cliff, and so it was not an easy city to slip out of unnoticed.

Instead, Bronwen made her way, disregarded by any of the guards and servants, out through the front hall and into the garden. It was true, she realized, what Maura had said. No one noticed a little old maidservant.

The garden was filled with warm evening light. It struck through the frost-blighted trees and storm-stripped branches like a benediction. Clutching her basket, she went through the witches' wood to the maze at the heart of the garden, and found her way easily through its twists and turns till she was at the Pool of Two Moons. Here she shed her servants' garb, tucking it in behind a hedge even though she did not expect anyone to look for her here. As far as she was aware, the only people who knew that Maya had once escaped out through this pool were Lachlan, who was dead, Isabeau, who was far away, and herself.

The pool was brimming over, filled with all the rain and sleet and snow of the last fortnight's wild weather. Bronwen took her mother's waterproof bag out of the basket, slung it on her back, and then dived, naked, into the pool.

The water was icy, but Bronwen hardly noticed. The Fairgean were used to swimming in seas filled with icebergs. She dived down, transforming by instinct into her seashape, her nostrils clamping shut, her gills fluttering.

There was no bottom to the Pool of Two Moons, she discovered. It narrowed down into a vertical tunnel through
which she dived, rock scraping her shoulders. Down,
down, she dived, and slid through into some kind of underground stream that took her, undulating at high speed, racing through deep channels until at last she was spat out into
the Ban-Bharrach River.

Storm-swollen, the river swept her along, head bobbing
up and down. She had no time to catch a breath. If it had
not been for her gills, she would have drowned, she was
sure. She saw the great frill of sun-struck spray ahead of
her, where the river dived over the edge of the cliff and fell
down, down, down. The setting sun had turned it into a
shimmering rainbow. Bronwen managed a deep breath,
brought her arms over her head, and did a swan dive over
the edge.

Two hundred feet she fell. If she had not known her
mother had taken this fall and survived, she might have
crumpled, sure her end was near. But she kept her body
poised, did not try to breathe through her lungs, and rode
the waterfall all its great length down to the loch below.

It took her deep below the surface. Bronwen waited till
the pressure eased, and then struck up for the surface,
swimming diagonally to gain as much distance as possible
from the turmoil where the falls hit the loch. She could
stay underwater at least three minutes, and she used every
second of it, swimming out far into the loch. Then she
broke the surface, gasping for breath. Once her pulse had
steadied, she began to swim, using the swift undulating
long-distance stroke of the Fairgean.

Bronwen swam most of the night, taking advantage of
the darkness and the emptiness of the river to put as much
distance between her and Lucescere as possible.

Several times she stopped to rest, hanging onto the anchor rope of one of the river barges bobbing up and down
near the shore. Once she crawled ashore and lay panting
on the ground, her chest hurting, her limbs trembling. It

was hard to slip back into the water and go on, when all she wanted to do was slip there into sleep, naked and cold, on the stones. Only her desperate fear for Donncan drove her on.

By the time it was light enough for Bronwen to see, she was a long way up the river. Moving very quietly, she climbed up the ladder at the stern of one of the river barges and concealed herself among the sacks and barrels stored on its broad deck. From the waterproof satchel she had carried on her back, she pulled out one of her mother's old dresses and dragged it on over her wet, shivering body, then ate ravenously. She had packed the food they had brought for her dinner—cold roast pheasant, soft white bread and cheese, a fish pie, and a selection of small fruit pies. Eaten at dawn, on the back of a stinking old barge, surrounded by boxes and barrels, after a long night's swimming, it was the most delicious meal Bronwen had ever eaten. She hoped her mother had not gone too hungry.

By the time she had finished eating, and wrapped herself in an old shawl to sleep, the bargemen had roused and were stumping about the boat, their pipes lit, and big mugs of strong black tea in their hands. Bronwen lay tense, fearing discovery, but the men did not think to examine their wares. Before long the barge was being poled smoothly along the river and Bronwen was lulled into sleep.

She woke midafternoon, stiff and sore and most uncomfortable. She eased her cramped muscles as well as she could in her stuffy little nest, and peeked out through the boxes.

The bargemen were still poling the boat along, working together at a steady, comfortable rhythm. The river was busy with all sorts of craft, and the air rang with shouts and cries, the rattle of chains, the slap of rope and sail, and the subtle lapping of the water under the hull. White birds hovered overhead, screeching raucously as they dived for the fish heads being tossed overboard from another craft. There was a slight tang of salt to the air. By raising her head slightly over the edge of the boxes, Bronwen was able to see that the river had widened out into a loch of considerable size. Her pulse quickened with excitement. The bargemen had made good time. They were on Lochbane, the last of the Jewels of Rionnagan.

The bargemen dropped anchor at sunset, and fried themselves up a mess of onions, bacon, sausages, and potatoes that tortured Bronwen with its appetizing aroma. She was just wishing that she had saved herself more to eat than the remnant of cheese and bread, now quite hard, when a huge, brown, callused hand suddenly appeared over the top of her nest, holding a sizzling, heavily loaded plate.

"Figured ye must be hungry," a rough voice said.

Startled, Bronwen looked up and saw a square, leathery face with a grizzled chin and mild brown eyes with heavy pouches underneath.

"Ye're welcome to clamber out and eat with us, if ye wish to stretch your legs," the voice went on. "Ye must be all cramped up in there."

"I am indeed. Thank ye." Bronwen recovered her composure in an instant, and let the old bargeman help her out of her hiding place. She could only hobble over to the bench seat where the other old bargeman sat, sucking on his pipe and eyeing her curiously, but after a few minutes the blood began to circulate freely through her veins again, and she was able to tuck into her dinner with great gusto.

The bargemen did not ask her any questions, though they must have wondered what she was doing hiding on their boat. Considering she was dressed in a servant's gown, Bronwen thought they must think she was an indentured apprentice fleeing a cruel master. That was the story she intended to tell if they asked. They did not speak, though, apart from a few comments about the weather, and whether she had enjoyed her meal.

"I did indeed," Bronwen replied, wiping the plate clean with a hunk of dark bread.

"If ye want to bunk down for the night, we can offer ye a bit more space over there," one said, pointing at a stretch of deck with his pipe.

"No, thank ye," Bronwen said. "I'm very grateful for your kindness, but I'll be moving along once it's dark."

They raised their eyebrows, glanced at the river gleaming under a twilight sky, and then shrugged. The shore was a considerable distance away. Bronwen wondered if they guessed she was part-Fairgean. In her mother's shabby old dress, high-necked and long-sleeved, her gills and fins were well hidden.

They made her a mug of tea, which she enjoyed as much as she had their fried sausages, and then, once it was fully dark, Bronwen thanked them again and said her farewells.

"If ye wouldna mind just shutting your eyes for a bit?" she asked.

They looked at each other, shrugged again, and covered their eyes with their huge, horny hands. Not confident that they would not peek, Bronwen retreated behind the barrels, stripped off her dress and shawl, and thrust them back into the waterproof bag, pulling its strings tight. Then, naked once more, Bronwen dived into the river, leaving hardly a ripple behind her.

She found her second night of swimming much easier than the first. The day of rest and two solid meals had helped her regain much of her strength, and she had had time to get over the horror of Elfrida's attempt to murder her. As she swam, her thoughts were focused on Donncan. Where had he been all this time, and what had happened to him? Would he be pleased to see her? What if he did not believe her? What if he chose to trust in Neil rather than her? What if she was too late?

Within two hours, Bronwen had come to the Berhtfane

and was having to swim more slowly, being careful to
avoid the many boats, barges, and ships moored all along
the wharves and jetties. The harbor glittered with the lights
of the city. Dùn Gorm was a great port town, taking up
nearly all of the eastern shore of the bay. To the west, all
was dark, except for the castle, which was alive with lights.
Bronwen fixed her gaze upon it, hoping desperately that
she was in time. She had swum faster than any boat could
travel. Surely, surely, she had beaten the party from
Lucescere?

There were many pleasure boats out on the harbor that
night, filled with people laughing and talking, listening to
musicians, and even, on some of the larger boats, dancing.
Bronwen had to take great care not to be seen. She dived
deep and swam underwater, heading straight across the
harbor towards the castle. When she finally surfaced,
everything was much quieter and darker. The castle on its
tall rock loomed overhead. She was in its shadow.

A boat was being rowed across the harbour towards her,
lights hanging on its bow and stern. She heard the low
rumble of voices. Bronwen tried to steady her breathing,
her gills fluttering madly in her throat. Then she dived
again, not daring to make even the tiniest splash, and surfaced right beside the boat, seizing a small metal bar at the
back and hanging on to it gratefully. She could hear the
voices of the passengers clearly.

"No' long now," Gwilym the Ugly said. "We made excellent time. I must admit, I will no' be able to truly relax
and rejoice until I see the Rìgh with my own eyes."

"Should we be calling him the Rìgh, when it is his
lovely wife who wields the Lodestar?" Father Francis said.
Bronwen gritted her teeth. If she had had her mother's
powers, she would have no compunction transforming him
into something slimy and horrible. A snake or a toad.

"But o' course," Gwilym said, surprised, "they will
share the Lodestar and the throne together, surely?"

"Can the Lodestar be shared?"

"I dinna ken," Gwilym said, sounding troubled. "They raised it together as children, to defeat the Fairgean king. Surely they shall do so again. They are both o' MacCuinn blood."

"What one is prepared to do as a boy is far different from what one will tolerate as a man," Father Francis said.

"True," Neil said. "I canna expect Donn will be happy about it. I mean, it was meant to be his."

I couldna leave it lying there on the floor amidst all the rubbish, Bronwen thought to herself, and put her free hand up to touch the bag hanging over her shoulder. She had brought the Lodestar with her, of course.

"Well, they will sort it out," Gwilym said. "The Banrìgh has carried herself well these past two weeks, in very difficult conditions. I ken her husband the Rìgh will be grateful."

Floating in the dark, chilly water just a few feet below the one-legged sorcerer, Bronwen smiled and thought, *I hope ye are right, Gwilym.*

There was a broad landing platform at the base of the steep cliff, with a massive iron door set into the rock. Lanterns cast a bright orange light out onto the water. Bronwen stayed in the shadows, as much from modesty as a desire not to reveal herself too soon, as the boat grated against the platform and the crew leaped out to secure it.

A plank was shoved across, and the party of men from Lucescere all stepped ashore. Apart from Gwilym, Neil, and Father Francis, there was the Lord Chancellor, a very frail old man with shaky hands and a shiny bald head surrounded by a halo of white hair, and his secretary, Lord Morgan, an old friend of Neil's from the Theurgia.

"Why, Father, I see ye have a new ring," Lord Morgan suddenly said. "Is that no' Lady Elfrida's?"

There was a pause, and then the pastor said smoothly, "Ah, yes. Her Grace gave it to me afore we left, as a token o' her appreciation. I believe it is very auld."

"Why, that's the thistle ring," Neil said in surprise. "It's a family heirloom."

"Is it?" the pastor replied. "I dinna realize it had any value. Your mother said your father dinna care for it, and I may as well have it, as a reminder o' Arran. I am leaving your mother's service, ye see, my laird, and returning to Tirsoilleir just as soon as our task here is finished."

"I see," Neil said. "Well, it is true my father does no' care for the ring. It was his mother's. I'd have a care, Father Francis. My grandmother's things often tend to contain a nasty surprise."

His voice sounded odd. Without being able to see his face, Bronwen found it hard to tell what he was thinking. She thought there was chagrin and anger in his voice, yet also relief at the idea the pastor was leaving his mother's service.

One of the servants had pulled a rusty chain by the door, and they heard the bell clanging loudly far above their heads in the castle. Bronwen had been to Rhyssmadill many times before. She knew it would take some time before someone descended the two-hundred-odd steps to open the river door, and then an even longer time for the party to climb the steps up into the main part of the castle. Gwilym would find the steps difficult with his wooden leg, and Cameron, the Lord Chancellor, was so old and doddery it would surely take him ages.

Bronwen floated in the darkness, thinking furiously. Her best chance, she thought, was to try to get to Donncan before the others, so she could have a chance to explain and warn him. Surely that would be better than climbing out onto the platform now, naked and dripping wet, in front of all those eyes? And if she waited for them to start the climb, then got out, dressed and tidied herself, before ringing the bell, she would be ten minutes behind them at least. More than time enough to tip a little poison into Donncan's glass.

If Bronwen could find the secret underwater entrance to

the castle, however, she would have a chance to get in front of the men and reach Donncan before them. Bronwen, Donncan, and Neil had all explored the underground caves, years ago, after giving their nursemaid the slip one day. Bronwen felt sure she knew how to find the entrance again. So she took a deep breath, and dived.

Poisoned Wine

Deep, deep, she dived, right down to the very roots of the rock on which Rhyssmadill was built. It was pitch-black. Even with her eyes wide open and staring, she could see nothing. Bronwen had only her sensitive, long-fingered hands to guide her. The entrance was not far from the river gate, she knew, but several minutes passed and she was forced to come up, gasping for air.

On her third dive, she found it, a narrow crack in the rock that led her through a long underwater tunnel. Bronwen's ears were thundering, and she was sick and dizzy from lack of oxygen when her head at last broke through the water.

She could see nothing, and hear nothing but her own tortured breath and the constant lapping of the water about her. Holding her hands out in front of her, Bronwen swam slowly forward, wondering how she could ever have thought this was a good idea. Her hands found a stone ledge, and she pulled herself up on it, and then rummaged through her bag until her fingers found the smooth round-ness of the Lodestar. At once light sprang up in its depths. Gratefully she pulled it free of the swaddle of clothes, and stuck the scepter through the rungs of the rusty old ladder that disappeared up the wall into darkness. By its light she dressed herself hurriedly and then thrust the scepter into the bag, drawing its strings tight just below the Lodestar so its radiance still lit her way. With the bag slung over her shoulders, Bronwen began the long climb up the ladder.

Rhyssmadill had been first built by Brann the Raven, many centuries before, and this secret entrance was only one of the castle's many mysteries. Years ago, when Bronwen had been a child, the Fairgean had used this hidden entrance to invade Rhyssmadill and attack Lachlan and his people while they celebrated Beltane. It was one of Bronwen's most dreadful memories. Now, climbing the ladder in the fitful light of the swinging Lodestar, Bronwen could not help an oppressive feeling of dread. Her blood hammered in her ears, and her breath came unevenly. *Donncan*, she thought, and fixed her will and desire upon him.

At last Bronwen reached the top of the ladder, and found a wooden cover had been pulled across the well opening. It took the last of her strength to heave the heavy cover to one side. Giddiness overcame her. She lay half-fainting in the dark courtyard, the starry sky spinning above her. At last the giddiness ebbed away. She managed to sit up and unhitch her bag so she could hug the Lodestar to her, drawing strength from it. She did not know how much time had passed. Too much, she feared. Hampered by the heavy, damp skirts, she began to run.

Where would they be? In the grand receiving room? In the great hall? Or in the solar? Perhaps even in Donncan's bedroom, if he was sick or injured.

With her Lodestar pressed close to her heart, Bronwen sent out her thoughts as she had been taught at the Theurgia. She was sick with apprehension, and wished, not for the first time since her uncle's murder, that she had not wasted so much time at the witches' school in frivolity and fun. Her heart leaped. She could feel Donncan! He was alive, he was smiling, she could hear him speak.

"Gwilym! Neil! How glad I am to see ye! Come in, come in. Tell me all the news. Can I offer ye some wine?"

No, Donncan! Bronwen screamed with all her mind-force. *Do no' drink the wine!*

Panting, sobbing, she ran up the stairs towards the solar. Rhyssmadill was a huge castle, seven stories high in parts, with many towers and balconies. It was a steep climb from the well in the courtyard to the Rìgh's solar at the very height of the tower. She passed a number of servants on the way, pushing past them, too distraught to even try to explain. Even in her drab servant's gown, they recognized her, and cried out, "My lady! Your Majesty! What do ye do here?"

The guards, recognizing something was wrong, hurried after her, their pikes held at the ready.

By the time she reached the top floor, Bronwen was gasping for breath and bent half double over the stitch in her side. There were guards outside the solar, and they sprang to attention and flung open the door for her.

Bronwen stumbled inside, trying to catch her breath.

The room was round, and richly furnished with cushioned chairs, embroidered curtains, and many tall paintings in ornate gilt frames. A fire was lit in the massive grate, and a party of people were all drawn up in front of it, laughing and talking. Bronwen saw only her husband, standing with one booted foot on the iron grate, a glass of wine in his hand. Beside him stood the pastor like a man of bone and shadows, the reflection of the fire flickering in his hooded eyes, a tiny smile on his lips as Donncan lifted his cup to his lips.

Bronwen could not speak. Her breath sobbing in her throat, she heaved up the Lodestar and pointed it at her husband. *Stop* . . . she thought.

Donncan froze midmotion, his cup at his mouth. Bronwen walked forward, so slowly it felt as if she was wading through mud to her waist. Around her she saw the expressions of those caught frozen in place. Consternation, shock, anger, suspicion. She saw Thunderlily with one hand stretched out to her in painful surprise and joy, and said *Poison* . . . She saw Isabeau's face alter as the Keybearer heard the mind-thought too, and saw Dide's eyes suddenly open wide.

Bronwen reached her husband. Frozen in place, only his eyes were alive with anger and hurt. All he saw, she knew, was his newly wedded wife walking towards him with the Lodestar in her hand, immobilizing him and all his friends like bees caught in a spider's web. All sorts of dreadful suspicions were flashing through his mind. She could see them all in his eyes. He struggled to move, to force a hand up against her, but he could not.

Her breath ragged and uneven, her breast heaving painfully, Bronwen took the cup from his lips. She turned and offered it to the pastor.

He stood as still as Donncan, only his eyes darting about under his hooded eyelids.

Bronwen was still too short of breath to speak. She urged the cup on him, and he shook his head slowly, trying to smile.

"What is this?" he asked, licking his dry lips. "Some kind o' game?"

Bronwen managed a snort of laughter. "No game," she answered. Everyone was beginning to be able to move again. Their eyelids flickered, their hands reached out towards her. Bronwen turned to Neil. "What about ye?" she asked, her breath wheezing in her chest. "Will ye drink it?"

Neil looked utterly flabbergasted. "Bronny . . . Your Majesty . . . what is it?"

"Will ye drink it?" She held the cup to his mouth.

He pushed it away violently. "What's going on? What are ye doing here? Ye were sick . . ."

She nodded. "Aye, I was. Very, very sick."

"Bronny, what do ye mean? What's wrong?" He turned apologetically to Donncan. "I dinna ken what she means. She's been sick. We were just telling ye that was why she couldna come . . ."

Donncan could not move or speak. He was still frozen

in place. Bronwen felt his eyes on her, scorching her with his suspicions. The Lodestar felt very heavy in her hand.

"But I did come," Bronwen said. "Despite ye."

She was feeling very odd and giddy again. The world wavered before her. She forced herself to stand upright, to hold the cup of wine steady. She looked pleadingly at her husband.

"It's poisoned," she said. "They poisoned me too. That's why I was sick. All o' us at the palace, sick."

The pastor said, "I think the illness has turned her mind. She's raving. Look at her! She's wet through. She's been in the river. What madness, to swim at night in the river when she's clearly unwell."

As he spoke, he moved forward a step, then pretended to stumble. His arm sent the cup in Bronwen's hand flying. In utter dismay, she saw the cup fly up and then tumble down to the ground, the wine spilling in a wild flurry of crimson.

Stop . . . Bronwen cried silently again and felt the Lodestar blaze up in response. Once again the whirligig of time spun slower. The cup hovered in midair, the wine frozen in its dark curlicues, all the faces in the firelit circle caught mid-cry.

Bronwen took a deep breath, then she walked to the table, picked up another cup and, with the Lodestar caught in the crook of her elbow, held the cup with both hands so it caught the wine as it once again began to gently fall. It splashed into the cup she held, and then Donncan's cup fell to the ground with a clatter and rolled away under a chair.

"If it isn't poisoned, ye willna mind drinking it," she said to the pastor, and offered it to him again challengingly.

"Drink it," Isabeau said, her voice very low and dangerous. "Bronny's right. If it's no' poisoned, ye shouldna mind drinking it."

The pastor's eyes darted this way, then that.

A dagger suddenly glinted in Dide's hand. "I guess he doesna want to drink," he said. "Shall I make him?"

"Go on, Father Francis, drink it," Bronwen said. "Else admit to treason and conspiracy to murder, and face the gallows."

The guards were all standing with their weapons drawn and pointing straight at the pastor. Neil looked white and sick, but he said nothing, his hands hanging by his side.

"On what evidence?" the pastor said, his voice shaking.

"I can have the contents o' this cup analyzed," Bronwen said, her voice coming more strongly. "And if we look at the ring that ye wear, I am sure we will find traces o' the poison in there as well. And we'll search the healer Mirabelle's rooms, and Lady Elfrida's too."

Neil started forward a step, and the guards at once had their spear points at his throat. The pastor cast a quick look around the room, then suddenly he seized the cup from Bronwen's hand. She cried aloud in surprise and flinched back, but he did not throw it at her, or toss it in the fire, as she had expected. He laughed, lifted it to her, and hissed, "Blaygird half-breed, may ye burn in hell!"

Then he drank down the poisoned wine.

It was not a pleasant death. It seemed to go on for a very long time, and although Isabeau and Ghislaine tried to ease his agony for him, the pastor was beyond help. At last his thrashing and screaming ended, and Ghislaine was able to throw a rug over his purplish countenance, hiding the dreadful engorged eyes and tongue and foam-flecked skin.

Bronwen could not help weeping. Thunderlily wept with her, the two girls pressed close together, crying in each other's arms. When at last it was all over, and the shocked and horrified murmurs were filling the room, Bronwen gently extracted herself from Thunderlily's arms and went to Donncan.

Although he was no longer under her power he stood as still and silent as before, staring at her with narrowed eyes.

She offered him the Lodestar.

"I couldna leave it just lying on the floor," she said.

He took it from her, still angry and suspicious.

Tears stung her eyes. "Oh, Donncan, I am so glad ye're home!" she cried, and flung her arms about his neck.

For a bare instant he did not respond, then suddenly his arms enfolded her and he was squeezing all the breath out of her, and then she lifted her face, and he lowered his, and they were kissing, deeply, passionately, breathlessly.

"Oh, Bronny!" he murmured into her hair. "Thank Eà! I've missed ye!"

"And me ye," she sobbed. "Ye can never ken how much."

"I'm so glad ye're here."

"I'm so glad I got here in time. I was so afraid . . ."

"Here in the nick o' time."

"I never meant to raise the Lodestar against ye."

"I ken, I ken."

"I dinna want to steal it from ye. It called to me though, Donn, it called and I had to answer."

He was silent. She felt him looking over her head, to where he held the Lodestar still in his hand, pressed against her back. "Canna we share it?" she whispered. "We raised it together when we were bairns, and look what we did! Canna we hold it and the land together? Work together as friends and allies?"

"O'course we can," Donncan replied, and bent his head to kiss her again. "And lovers too, I hope," he whispered in her ear.

She smiled her slow, beguiling smile.

It was very late. Isabeau and Dide lay together in their bed, firelight casting soft, ever-changing shadows all over the room. They lay close, but not together, both naked under the warmth of the counterpane, both feeling oddly self-conscious. Isabeau's hair, freshly washed and plaited, lay neatly along the pillow. Dide's eyes were wide open, staring up at the shape-shifting shadows.

"Dide?"

"Aye?"

"Dide, Dide . . . do ye care? Do ye mind? Ye must . . . ye must *hate* me!"

"I do no' hate ye."

His words did not satisfy her. "But do ye mind? Does it . . . does it make ye feel different, to ken that I could do such a thing?"

He stroked her hair away from her face and said nothing.

"Dide?"

"I do feel different," he said at last.

She tensed. "Has it changed things?" she asked in a small voice. "Do ye feel differently about *me*?"

He glanced at her. "I dinna ken," he said at last. "I mean . . . I'm still struggling to understand it all. What happened, how I felt. I was afraid, Beau, terribly, terribly afraid."

"That's natural . . ." she began, but he hurried on.

"No, I mean, I was afraid that all ye witches are wrong and that death is *the* end o' it all. I was afraid I'd die and discover that there is no soul after all, and we are just machines clothed in flesh that run down and stop like an unwound clock, and then our tale is over. It was no' death itself I was afraid o', but what I would discover after."

Isabeau was silent.

"But I dreamt while I was dead," he said softly. "Is it possible? Could I truly dream? Was I dead or just asleep? If it was no' for this . . ." He put up his hand and traced the scar on his throat. "I would think it all a dream, a joke, a trick."

"Do ye remember aught? Were ye aware?"

He snorted in bitter laughter. "Always the witch, wanting to ken everything."

"Well, did ye?"

"Only fragments," he whispered. "But I canna help feeling I should remember. What they told me, it was terribly, terribly important . . . but I canna remember."

"Who were they that spoke?"

He put out one hand and traced the line of her cheek. "Ye will mock me."

"I? The Keybearer o' the Coven? Dide, I am hungry for aught ye can tell me. Please."

He shrugged. "I can no' remember. They seemed like beings o' light . . . yet their faces were shadowed. Their voices were great and terrible. I could no' look at them. They said . . ."

"What?"

"Maybe they did no' tell me, maybe they showed me . . . but Beau! It was proof. I ken it was proof. I wish I could remember."

"Proof? O' what?"

He made a helpless gesture with his hand. "O' the rightness o' it all, perhaps. O' Eà."

Tears prickled Isabeau's eyes.

"I wish I could remember."

She touched his heart, and then the pulse at his throat, and then the point between his brows where, witches believed, the third eye was hidden. "Ye remember," she said softly. "In here."

He sighed.

She nestled closer to him.

"Beau?"

"Mmm?" she said sleepily.

"Since . . . it happened . . . I'm hearing things all the time," Dide said. "What people are thinking, all the time. My head aches, it is so full o' noise, my ears are ringing with it. I canna stand it, it's intolerable."

Isabeau lifted her head so she could stare at him.

"There's more," he said. "I . . . I ken how to do things."

"Like what?"

He gestured towards the fire and it went out abruptly, plunging them into darkness. A few seconds later it flared up again, a raging inferno that tore at the wood with hungry jaws and threatened to leap free of the hearth.

Isabeau calmed it with a thought.

"I've always had a few witch-tricks," Dide said, "but no' like that."

Isabeau was quiet.

"Am I Brann?" Dide whispered. "Have I become him?"

She reached out and stroked back his hair from his eyes. "Nay," she said. "Ye are still your own sweet self. I'd say, though, that the whole experience o' dying and being reborn has . . . opened some doors in ye. Knocked aside the veils. Ye have always had potential, Dide, ye just were never ready to take the journey towards realizing them. Ye canna expect to come through such an experience and remain unchanged."

"What should I do? I . . . I dread sleeping. I'm afraid he waits for me there, in the dream world, wanting to possess me."

Isabeau nodded. She could understand that fear.

"I can block your third eye, for a time at least," she said. "It will make things easier. And Ghislaine can dream-walk with ye, and find the door that has been opened and shut it. I think ye will have to come to the Theurgia, though, Dide, and learn as much as ye can about controlling and using these new powers."

He did not answer. Dide had never submitted to the discipline of the Coven. He had always been a free spirit, a wandering jongleur, spying in his rìgh's service. All these years Isabeau had tried to draw him into the Coven and he had always resisted. She did not want to press him now, their love still feeling so fragile.

"There are other things we can do," she said quietly. "I have been thinking . . . the first thing we should do is gather together a circle o' sorcerers and go to Brann's grave and exorcise him. He has lingered too long, it is time he went on to the spirit world and was born again, to learn his lessons anew.

"Then we need to hide or destroy the page on which he wrote the spell o' resurrection. I have been very troubled in my heart about this. *The Book o' Shadows* is our most sacred text, the Coven's grimoire. But that spell is wrong, it is evil, and it has the potential to do harm again. It canna be allowed to lurk inside *The Book o' Shadows* like . . . like . . ."

"A sand-scorpion," Dide suggested.

She smiled. "Aye, or a swarthyweb spider. No, it must be destroyed."

He nodded, the tension in his face relaxing just a little.

"Dide, *leannan,* the best thing ye can do . . . to keep yourself safe, I mean . . . is fill your life with love and joy and good things. Evil spirits can only possess ye if ye have room in your heart for them." As she spoke, Isabeau began to draw small circles on the smooth skin of her chest, slowly moving her hand lower. She bent her head and kissed his shoulder. He stirred and turned to her.

"Love," he whispered.

"Aye," she whispered back. "Drive away the darkness, the fear, all the bad things, with the good things, the things that matter."

As her mouth and hand moved lower, he smiled and tangled his fingers in her hair. "Now that is a very good thing indeed," he murmured, and closed his eyes.

Safe Passage

Margrit paced up and down the shabby old room. She was smiling, an expression Piers had already come to fear.

"That red-haired auld hag!" she laughed out loud. "She thinks she can defeat me with her pitiful little ice storm? Hah! What is your laird doing? I thought he had a Talent with weather? Tell him to strike the hag down with a bolt o' lightning!"

"Their witches are too strong," Piers said, and immediately regretted it.

"Too strong!" she shrieked. "She's no' even fully trained. She doesna even have a full circle o' power! They're apprentices, half o' them."

"It's more than we have," Piers said.

"Ye were meant to come with a circle o' necromancers. And what do I find? An auld mad laird, a village skeelie, some stupid servants, and a pathetic, impotent harper who canna even sing the song o' love properly." Her voice rang with scorn. "Two days we've been holed up in this freezing, drafty auld fort, and ye have the temerity to come and tell me we're out o' gunpowder!"

Piers wisely did not tell her they were out of firewood too.

Margrit stopped at the window embrasure, the snowy wind blowing back her grey-streaked dark hair. She was

wearing a heavy fur-trimmed mantle over a rich velvet
dress, yet still she shivered and rubbed her gloved hands
together. It was bitterly cold. The fire in the hearth glow-
ered sullenly, spitting occasionally as snow fell down the
chimney. Outside nothing could be seen but the white driving snow. There was no glass in any of the fort's windows,
and Piers had helped Jem and Ballard nail up rough shutters to try to keep out the worst of the cold. It was little use.
The wind was so wild, it wrenched their makeshift shutters
off the nails, or caused them to bang so ceaselessly that
Margrit had been driven mad with irritation, and threatened to hammer nails into all their heads if they did not
stop the noise immediately.

"I never liked this rat's hole anyway," Margrit said suddenly. She turned away from the window and came to
warm her hands at the low fire. "It was never a fitting residence for I, Margrit o' Arran. Ye say Fettercairn Castle is
very large, and rich?"

"Aye, my lady," Piers said with misgiving.

"And strong. It's never been defeated, is that no' right?"

"Only once, and that was by guile and trickery," Piers
replied.

"Och, aye, by the MacCuinn, the time he killed your
laird's brother. I remember the story. Well, it sounds a lot
more salubrious than this stinking hole. We shall go there."

"How?" Piers asked, and looked out at the howling
storm.

"We will negotiate," Margrit said, smiling sweetly. "Either the auld hag gives us a ship and safe passage out o'
here, or she watches her precious laddie being disembow-
eled on the battlements. Slowly."

Piers took a deep shaking breath. "That could work."

"O' course it'll work. Is this whole stupid battle no' all
about her trying to free her bonny son? I'll give him back,
almost in one piece, if she gives us safe passage out o'
here. Then, once we are safely back at Fettercairn Castle,
we can make plans for the future."

"My laird wants to sacrifice the MacCuinn lad to raise his brother," Piers reminded her.

She snorted. "Lord Malvern's had his revenge in slitting the sister's throat. Tell him no' to be greedy. We'll be able to find a nice young man to do the job when we are back in Ravenshaw. Has he thought beyond that point? What does he plan to do once his brother and nephew are alive again?"

"I do no' ken," Piers answered.

"Well, I can think o' a few pretty tricks o' my own. How auld was the boy?"

"Six," Piers said reluctantly.

"A little young, to be sure, but he'll grow. And they're malleable at that age. I'll be able to teach him. Och, aye, it's the best plan. Now send someone down to the town with a message. Tell Iseult o' the Snows that if she doesna bring me some warmer weather, and a promise o' safe passage, by dawn tomorrow, I'll be gutting her son myself. With pleasure."

"Aye, my lady," Piers replied, and thankfully bowed himself out of the room.

Down in the pirate town, Iseult and her companions were sitting at a big table before a roaring fire, with rough diagrams of the town and the old fort laid out before them. They were planning an assault on the fort in the morning.

It was the evening of the second day after Olwynne's death. The days had each been spent in bitter, brutal fighting, winning and securing the pirate town, and then attempting to take the fort. Although it was half in ruins, the fort was in a virtually unassailable position, high on its hill with only one road leading up to it. Quite a few of the pirates had managed to retreat to it before the road was barricaded, and the fort's old but still effective cannons had been turned on the town, reducing much of it to rubble. It was difficult for Iseult's forces to retaliate, as the cannons on their ships were not powerful enough to do much damage to the fort. So they had used magic, pounding the old ruin with hailstones as large as fists, rattling it with gusts of wind powerful enough to tear off much of the roof, and sizzling it with bolt after bolt of lightning.

This was exhausting work for the witches, particularly since both Margrit and Lord Malvern had powerful magic of their own. The sorceress had sent mists filled with illusions to mock them and terrify them and weaken their resolve. Mists filled with snakes and tentacles and dreadful creeping beasts; mists filled with rank after rank of warriors that marched upon them mercilessly; mists filled with the voices of the dead and the desired, pleading, mocking, seducing.

The lord of Fettercairn had turned their own weather back on them whenever he could, and had managed to kill a whole company of soldiers by hitting a barrel of gunpowder with lightning. The lord's methods were more brutal, but Margrit's far more subtle and cruel, undermining everyone's faith and resolve, and making many a hardened soldier weep with yearning for a lost loved one.

Iseult had not wept. The grief she felt for her murdered husband and daughter was deep and bitter, and she was still riven with anxiety over her two sons, but she was determined not to lose herself in the blackness of despair again. Iseult's mother sank into sleep whenever life grew too hard for her to bear, and Iseult had always mocked and resented her for that weakness. She was all too aware that the wildness of her grief had only made things worse after Lachlan's death. If she had not conjured ice and snow, if she had not called the dragon's name to chase after Rhiannon, instead of begging it for help to find her children, if she had not sulked in her room for two long weeks, instead of using her powers to find Lord Malvern, perhaps Olwynne at least would still be alive. So Iseult was keeping her emotions firmly under control, and focusing all her energies on sav-

ing Owein, and defeating Lord Malvern and Margrit of
Arran.

"I do no' want to blow the whole fort up!" she said now
in exasperation. "Owein is still locked up in there somewhere. I think a stealthy attack to find him and liberate him
is a far better idea, Captain Tobias! Then we can blow them
up, as often as ye like!"

"My lady, we do no' even ken if your son still lives," the
captain said.

"He still lives," Finn said. "I can feel him clearly. He
and Rhiannon are in a dark cell somewhere to the right."

"Rhiannon!" Fèlice cried in joy. "Rhiannon is there?"

Finn nodded and smiled at her. She had spent the past
two days on one of the ice-bound ships and had only come
to join the soldiers after the town had been won. She was
looking wan and puffy-eyed, and had a big cloak wrapped
around her against the cold. Goblin, her familiar, was
curled up as close to the fire as it could get without singe-
ing its fur.

"Aye, she's there. I feel her strong as a bell. She's been
injured, but no' seriously."

"Finn, will ye lead a covert expedition to free them?"
Iseult asked. "Only ye can do it. Ye could climb the cliff,
like ye did when ye freed Killian the Listener from the
Black Tower."

"O'course I will," Finn said.

Jay had been listening quietly, frowning. Now he leaned
forward and seized his wife's hand. "Nay, Finn. It's too
dangerous. Ye canna do it."

"Rubbish!" Finn said, and waved him away irritably.

"Finn, I mean it."

"Flaming dragon balls, man, will ye no' be quiet!"

"Nay, I will no'! It's the life o' my baby ye're putting in
danger just as much as your own. I won't allow it."

"Who are ye to be telling me what to do?" Finn demanded, but without too much conviction.

"Finn! Are ye trying to tell me ye're pregnant?" Iseult cried.

"I'm no' trying to tell ye aught. It's Jay that's let the cat out o' the bag, no' me. Typical male. Canna stop their tongues from flapping."

Iseult was out of her chair in an instant, and hugging first Finn, then Jay, smiling for the first time in days. "A wee babe! What wonderful news. Och, no wonder ye've been so sick."

"I'm always sick on boats," Finn said, her color rising in her embarrassment. "Jay says I'm like a cat, I hate being on water. It's got naught to do with the babe."

Everyone else crowded around them too, congratulating and teasing them.

"No wonder Finn's been so cross," Dillon said, hugging and kissing her. "Ye'll have to take things more slowly now, my wild cat."

"No, I will no'." She scowled. "Why should I? It's a babe, no' a disease."

"Just ye wait until ye're nine months along, and then I'd like to see ye scaling walls and walking tightropes," Iseult said. Suddenly her face altered. "Oh, Eà! O'course, Jay is right. Ye canna be climbing the cliff in your condition."

"What a drayload o' dragon dung. O'course I can. Why, my belly's no' that big yet. It willna get in the way."

"But what if ye slipped and fell? Jay would never forgive me. *Isabeau* would never forgive me. Do ye ken how rare it is for a babe to be born o' two sorcerers?"

"That was why we were rather surprised ourselves when we found out," Jay said dryly. "Neither o' us ever thought it was possible."

"Oh, it's possible. Just no' common," Iseult said. "Why dinna ye tell me earlier? I would never have let ye go in pursuit o' Owein and Olwynne if I kent."

"That's why we dinna tell ye," Finn replied.

Iseult was troubled. "Oh, Finn, ye should've. I ken it must've been a shock to ye, to discover ye were with babe, but ye should no' be putting yourself or the babe at risk now that ye ken."

"I remember that ye were pregnant with Donncan when we marched on Lucescere," Finn pointed out, scowling. "We had to walk for miles, and climb mountains, and cross raging rivers, no' to mention fight once we got there. I remember how much I admired ye for it."

"But I was pregnant with twins, remember," Iseult replied softly. "One o' which I lost. I would no' wish ye to lose your babe, Finn. It's no' an easy grief to get over." Her voice broke, and she dashed one hand over her eyes and turned away, shoulders hunched against her pain. Iseult had lost both her daughters now, and it was a grief she thought she could never recover from.

Finn's eyes widened. Though she did not reply, she no longer argued with Iseult. Goblin got up, stretched languidly, and came to jump into her lap, and Finn sat quietly in the firelight, petting her familiar, her face thoughtful.

"Dillon, ye will have to be the one to lead the party up the cliff," Iseult said, once she had regained control of her voice. "It'll have to be under the cover o' darkness. Do ye think ye can do it?"

"O'course, my lady," he replied, frowning, his hand caressing the hilt of his sword. "Finn is no' the only one able to scale a cliff."

"I will come and show ye the best place to approach," Finn said sweetly, and he flashed a look at her, half-resentful, half-amused.

"Finn, if ye could mark where Owein is on the map?"

"My lady . . ." Fèlice said hesitantly.

"Aye?" Iseult turned to her, an eyebrow raised.

"The laird o' Fettercairn used to be a Seeker o' the Anti-Witchcraft League, remember? He can track people, just like . . . Finn can." Fèlice hesitated a little before saying the sorceress's name, knowing that she was a banprionnsa by birth. Having been brought up in the exquisite politeness of the court of the MacBranns, Fèlice found it difficult not to call Finn by her true name and title. Finn hated being called "my lady" or "Your Grace," though, and had made her feelings known quite strongly on the first day of their sea journey together. Fèlice still found it difficult to address her by name, however, and quite often avoided the issue by not addressing her at all.

At Fèlice's words, Iseult frowned and bit her thumbnail. "That's true. I had forgotten that. Rhiannon said she felt he knew she was coming several times, and lay in wait for her. They will be expecting some kind o' assault. I do no' want to send ye into a trap, Dillon."

"How profound is his Talent?" Finn asked. "Does he always ken, without effort, or must he focus his thoughts upon a particular person?"

"Apparently he was a powerful Seeker," Fèlice said. "But I do no' ken any more than that."

"Lewen and I once eavesdropped on him without him realizing," Nina said. "We could no' do that to ye, Finn."

"No," she answered. "Nor to any true witch. If I remember rightly, Laird Malvern was kicked out o' witches' school while still an apprentice. I imagine he has a raw ability, untempered by much training. In which case, he can probably only focus on one or two people at a time, and only on people he knows, or if he has something o' theirs to hold. We could perhaps trick him . . ."

"By sending a decoy," Captain Dillon said, a spark lighting in his hooded eyes.

"Aye. Nina would be best. He kens her, and has reason to fear her powers, after their confrontation at Fettercairn Castle."

"While I could lead a small, well-concealed party up the cliff at another spot."

"It's worth a try," Iseult said. "Right. Let us think about the best timing. Together, or at different times? Which would be best?"

Just then there was a loud, cawing sound, and then a cry

from the sentry. Captain Dillon got up and strode to the door, opening it a crack, shielding his body with the wall.

"What is it?" he called.

"Raven's brought some kind o' message," the sentry replied in a low voice. There was a pause, and then a small scroll of paper was passed in to Dillon, a little damp from the snow. They could hear the mocking cry of the raven as it soared back up to the fort.

Dillon read the message, frowning, and then passed it to Iseult. She read it quickly, then sat down, the message pressed to her heart, her face very white.

"What does it say?" Nina asked anxiously.

"They want safe passage out o' here," Dillon said. "Another attempt to take the fort and they'll kill the prionnsa. Slowly, and with great enjoyment, it says. They want a ship, armed and provisioned, and fair weather. If we give them all that, they'll give us back Prionnsa Owein, alive. If we do no', we'll get him back in pieces, it said."

There was an outcry from all around the crowded room. Everyone began to debate the message and its implications, and what was the best course of action. Some thought they should storm the fort at once, and wrest Owein back. Others pressed for caution. Some thought pessimistically that they were bound to get the prionnsa back in pieces no matter what promises they gave. The hubbub was deafening.

Only Iseult did not speak.

Nina went and knelt by her chair, putting her arms about her. "What are we to do?" she asked gently.

Iseult looked up at her. "Whatever they want, o' course," she said. "I'll do naught to risk Owein's life! I have already lost my darling girl, do ye think I want to lose Owein too? Nay, nay, Margrit will have her ship if I have to hand her onto it myself. Once we have Owein back safely, then we'll think about how to deal with Laird Malvern and the Thistle." She smiled down at the paper in her hand. "Slowly, and with great enjoyment," she quoted softly.

"Ye want revenge?" Nina asked, frowning.

"He waited twenty-odd years for his revenge, and said it was a dish best eaten cold. Well, this is one dish I plan to eat hot!"

An Everything Thing

❦

Owein and Rhiannon spent another miserable night, huddled together in their freezing-cold cell. Even with Rhiannon's cloak and blanket wrapped about them both, and Owein's great wings folded over them, they could not keep out the cold. Their jug of water froze solid, and icicles hung from the bars. As the early-morning sun struck through the icicles, it turned them into daggers of blinding brightness.

"I suppose this is one way to get to ken ye better," Owein said to her with an ironic smile. "Since ye're in love with my best friend and all."

"And him with me," Rhiannon retorted fiercely.

"Aye, and him with ye," Owein replied placatingly, rubbing his hands together and blowing on them.

"Well, and are ye no' in love with my best friend too?" Rhiannon demanded.

Owein looked at her in surprise.

"Fèlice," Rhiannon said.

"She's your best friend?"

"The bestest and truest friend a girl could have," Rhiannon replied, remembering how Fèlice had kept coming to visit her in prison when no one else would, and how she had been there at Rhiannon's hanging, screaming "Spare her!" at the top of her voice.

There was a long pause, and then Owein said softly, not looking at Rhiannon, "She is a sweetheart, isn't she?"

Rhiannon nodded, and wriggled her fingers in her gloves and her toes in her boots, wishing she could conjure fire like Fèlice could. Owein had tried, and had managed a small blaze for several hours, but once all the straw had been consumed and there was nothing left to burn, he had had to let it lapse. Keeping a fire burning without fuel took immense power, he explained despondently, and Owein had never been much of a witch.

"So do ye love her or no'?" Rhiannon said, when Owein said nothing more.

"Why? Do ye think she loves me?" he demanded.

"I asked first."

Owein grunted with amusement. "I dinna ken," he answered after a moment. "Maybe."

"Ye either do or ye dinna," Rhiannon said scathingly. "Love is no' a maybe thing. It's an all or nothing thing. It's an everything thing."

Owein nodded. "Ye're right," he said, very low, not laughing at Rhiannon's awkwardness with words. "I guess I'm just . . ."

"Afeared?"

He jerked his shoulders. "I guess so."

"And Fèlice such a little thing, and ye so big and strong," she teased. "She's very scary, I ken!"

He scowled, and then laughed. "Oh, well, love is scary," he said. "It's one o' those big, scary things, isn't it?"

"Like death," Rhiannon said.

Owein was immediately sobered. "Aye, like death," he echoed.

There was a short silence. "Ye're no' very tactful, are ye?" he burst out.

"What's tactful?"

Again he gave that little snort of amusement. "I guess it's hard to be tactful if ye don't even ken what it is."

"So what is it?"

"No' saying things that may upset other people," he said.

"Oh," Rhiannon said.

"Aye, 'oh,'" he mimicked.

She shrugged. "Well, how am I meant to ken? It makes no sense, half the things people get upset about."

"Well, do ye no' think I might get upset to be reminded about death and dying?" he said. "After all, I may well die tomorrow."

"So may we all," Rhiannon replied.

"True. But it's me whose sister was murdered by these madmen only a few days ago, and me they plan to disembowel on the battlements tomorrow!"

Rhiannon winced and put her hands over her ears. "No need to shout. I'm right here," she said. "And I ken how ye must feel about tomorrow. I've had the hangman's noose about my neck, remember? I ken what it is like to be staring the dark walkers right in the face. But I canna see how it makes it better to no' talk about it. We both may die tomorrow, if we do no' die o' the cold first! Are we no' better thinking about it, and talking about it, and saying aught that should be said first?"

There was a long silence. Owein's breath came with difficulty. Then he nodded once, a sharp jerk of the head. "Ye're right," he said. "Wisely and bravely, that's the way to do it."

"Aye," she said a little uncertainly.

He flashed a smile at her. "It's our family motto. *Sapienter et Audacter.* I said it to Olwynne afore . . . afore . . ."

"I wish I had a family motto," Rhiannon said rather wistfully. "I guess I'll never find out now who my father was, or where I really belong."

"I wouldna be surprised if ye were related to the Mac-Ahern clan somehow," Owein said. "They are the thigearns, ye ken, the ones to first tame a flying horse. It is a rare Talent indeed, the ability to charm horses, particularly ones with wings. Their motto is *Nunquam obliviscar,* which means 'I shall never forget.'"

"I shall never forget," Rhiannon repeated, and smiled. "It's a good motto."

Owein nodded. "Aye. I'll never forget Olwynne, and how she died. And I'll never forget how ye came and tried to save us. I have no' really had a chance to say thank ye, but I'd like to. Ye were very brave."

"But I failed," Rhiannon said. "I wish I had no'."

"Me too," Owein replied, and they fell silent.

"If . . . if it all goes horribly wrong in the morning, and they do . . . ye ken . . ."

"Aye?" Rhiannon turned so she could see his face.

"Will ye tell Fèlice . . . will ye tell her I . . ."

"Ye what?"

"Will ye tell her I love her?" Owein said, color sweeping up his fair skin.

Rhiannon nodded. "For sure." She gave a quick smile. "I shall never forget."

Again there was that long brooding silence. Rhiannon touched Owein with her elbow. "He'll come, ye ken. He'll be here on time, and he willna fail."

"Who? Lewen?"

Rhiannon nodded.

"I wish I had your faith."

"He'll be here, and we had best be ready for him," she said. "Because he'll need our help."

"Right," Owein said. "I'll keep my eyes peeled."

Rhiannon stared at him in utter shock and bemusement, and then suddenly began to laugh. She laughed so hard she almost choked. After a second or two, Owein began to laugh too.

"Ye'll keep your eyes peeled," Rhiannon cried. "Eyes peeled! What a stupid language ye all speak. Eyes peeled!"

They laughed and laughed and laughed, and when at last they could laugh no more, they sat smiling in the dimness of the dawn. Laughter, Rhiannon realized, drove the dark walkers back into their cracks and holes like nothing else ever could.

I shall never forget, she thought to herself.

The sunlight had crept across to warm their toes when the bluebird came swooping in through the bars, twittering Danger! Danger!

Then the door of the cell crashed open. Jem stood there, scowling, his unshaven face more repellent than ever.

"Time to see how much your mama loves ye!" he sneered.

Owein and Rhiannon were already standing, and at the gesture of Jem's dagger, they went out together, shoulder to shoulder, both wondering if they dared try to wrest his dagger away from him.

Ballard was waiting outside, though, with four huge, bearded pirates. One had a rough blue tattoo of an anchor on one forearm, and the words "hate" and "kill" tattooed on his knuckles. Another had lost an eye, which had been sewn clumsily shut, and the third had bright ginger hair and was missing half an ear. The last was the biggest, towering over them all, and he wore huge golden hoops in his ears and had a pet rat perched on his shoulder.

"Is this the prionnsa?" Ginger demanded. "Dinna look like much."

"Best no' try to fly away, bird-boy, or we'll cut your pretty wings off," One-Eye said. He was missing most of his teeth, and the few he had left were black and crooked.

"Your mama's promised us a ship," Anchor said. "She thinks she can save your hide, but we ken better, don't we, laddies?" He roared with laughter, and Rhiannon and Owein flinched back from the smell of his breath, as much as from the implication of what he said.

"At least it's stopped snowing," Rat said eagerly. "That's good, in't?"

Squinting their eyes against the bright sunshine, Owein and Rhiannon made their way across the snow-heaped courtyard and down through a maze of dilapidated halls and stairways until they were prodded out onto the gatehouse's battlements. Lord Malvern was waiting for them there, leaning on his cane, the raven on his shoulder. Margrit was pacing up and down, dressed in a heavy velvet mantle edged with fur, while Dedrie stood nearby, clutching her basket. Irving and Piers waited beside her, next to a large mound of luggage.

The six small islands of the Pirate Isles curved around before them, making an irregular circle about the lagoon, which glittered blue in the sunshine. The water was so clear they could easily see the black hulks of the wrecked pirates' fleet littering the seabed. There were a little over a dozen ships still floating, all flying the green and gold flag of the MacCuinn clan. One had been moored at the remains of the jetty, and soldiers were busy carrying boxes and barrels on board. All the MacCuinn flags were being removed and hastily replaced with red pirate flags.

Margrit was frowning. "Did I no' tell ye that stupid witch would do everything we told her to? Look, sunshine! The snow's all melting! The storm's blown off. We'll be out o' here and on our way to Fettercairn afore we ken it."

"As soon as she has her son back, she'll attack our ship and sink us," Lord Malvern said dourly.

Margrit laughed. "Ye do no' ken I'd really be so stupid as to just hand him over, do ye? No, no, the MacCuinn lad comes with us, and my little black-haired witch too." She smiled radiantly at Rhiannon. "How lovely to finally meet ye, in the flesh, as it were."

At the sound of her voice, Rhiannon felt a deep cold take hold of her, despite the warm sunshine. She had felt a deep, instinctive fear of Margrit from the moment she had first seen her ghost intrude upon the circle of necromancers at the Tower of Ravens so many months earlier. Margrit had haunted her sleep ever since, mocking her, threatening her. Rhiannon would make the perfect sacrifice, she had said, being so like Margrit as a young woman—beautiful, dark-haired, with strong magical powers and a ruthless heart. Rhiannon had utterly rejected this. *I am nothing like you!* she had shouted again and again into the darkness, but Margrit's ghost had only laughed. Now, seeing how Rhiannon shivered and grew pale, Margrit laughed again.

She likes people to fear her, Rhiannon thought.

"But how are we to manage that?" Lord Malvern said. "They are waiting for us to hand him over."

"He will be our shield," Margrit said, and beckoned him over. Owein did not move, and one of the pirates pushed him forward roughly. Margrit took hold of his arm, bringing her dagger up to press against his throat.

"Mmmm, very nice," she said, running her hand up and down his arm muscles. "I wish I had kent ye were in our dungeon. What a very pretty young man you are. And with your mother's red hair. I've always had a soft spot for red hair. They say it's a sign o' a passionate nature. Are ye passionate, my fine young cock?"

Owein gritted his teeth and said nothing. She stroked his cheek, then slipped her hand down his chest until it was hovering just above his belt buckle. As Owein went fiery red, she sighed and said regretfully, "No doubt they are watching us through a spyglass. We do no' want to rouse your dear mama into a rage, do we, by seducing her dear boy in front o' her. Plenty o' time for that once we are on board our ship. Come, my pretty one, ye lead the way. That way they'll have to shoot through ye to get to me, and somehow I do no' think Iseult would like that."

They went down the stairs and into the gatehouse. Two of the pirates hauled on the ropes that brought up the portcullis, and then the gate was cautiously opened. The yard beyond was empty. Guarded on one side by the tall walls of the fort, and with a sharp drop to the side and front, the only access to the yard was by the road, which fell away steeply to one side.

Ballard scouted forward to check all was clear. At his wave, they all came out into the wide-open area before the gatehouse, everyone looking about them suspiciously. There was no sign of any ambush.

Rhiannon looked over the edge of the wall and down to the pirates' town. The ship with the pirate flag was docked well away from all the other ships, and the royal army was gathered together at the far end of the wharf. Rhiannon could see the Dowager Banrìgh, her red head like a beacon in the sunshine, with Nina and Iven Yellowbeard and Roden at the very back of the crowd, the little boy standing still and quiet for once, holding Lulu's hand. She could see Captain Dillon standing by the Dowager Banrìgh, tension in every line of his body; and Finn the Cat, wrapped in a big cloak despite the warmth, and Jay the Fiddler. Then, to her joy and surprise, Rhiannon recognized the thin, stooped figure of Landon standing next to two big, brown-haired boys in royal livery who could only be Cameron and Rafferty. There was another boy standing with them. Rhiannon stared and frowned, and stared some more, then suddenly grinned. Fèlice! In boys' clothes and all her hair cropped off. She should have guessed Fèlice would refuse to stay quietly at home and wait.

Jem pushed her forward, and Rhiannon went reluctantly. The sight of her friends had given her new hope. She took a deep breath, enjoying the freshness of the air after the foul smell of the cell, and moved her shoulder experimentally. It hurt, but not nearly as much as it had three days ago. Rhiannon thought she could fight, if she had to.

They were all moving in a tightly clustered group, Owein held right at the front, Margrit and Lord Malvern close behind him, with Dedrie treading on their heels in her fright. There were about a dozen pirates in all, with cutlasses or daggers in their hands, and they came behind, looking about them suspiciously.

Suddenly a winged horse soared up from behind the shelter of the wall. It was the color of old oak, with mane and tail like black rain, and poised on its back was Lewen. He rode with no saddle or rein, like a true thigearn, keeping his balance only with the grip of his knees. In his hands he held a longbow with an arrow nocked.

The first arrow whistled past Owein's ear and buried itself in Margrit's eye. The second split the first down the center, driving deep into the sorceress's brain. Without uttering a single cry or moan, Margrit fell back. Owein at once spread his wings and soared away. A great yell of joy rose from the crowd on the jetty.

One after another Lewen's arrows found their mark, quicker than thought. Jem fell next, and Rhiannon bent and seized his dagger, scrambling away from the pirates, who all dropped like stones about her, except for the largest of them all, who squeaked with fear and flung up his hands in surrender, his rat burrowing under his wild hair in terror.

Irving's father had died by flinging himself in front of Lord Malvern and taking an arrow meant for him. Irving the Second had no such instinct. He grabbed the lord about the neck and dragged him in front of him, using him as a shield. Lewen did not hesitate. He shot an arrow with such force it drove straight through Lord Malvern's right shoulder and pierced Irving in the heart. The seneschal cried out in surprise and horror, and staggered back, causing Lord Malvern to fall upon him, driving the arrow deeper into his breast.

Impaled upon his seneschal, Lord Malvern clutched the feathered end of the arrow protruding from his shoulder and stared up at Lewen in utter horror. "No!" he cried.

Lewen had no time to waste on him. Ballard was taking careful aim with his own bow and arrow. Lewen wheeled his horse about, just as Rhiannon's dagger found its mark in the big bodyguard's body. Ballard stiffened in shock, and his arrow flew awry. As Lewen soared away safely, Ballard looked down at the dagger, cupped both hands about it, and then toppled forward, driving it deep into his own body.

Rhiannon managed a gasping breath, and looked about her frantically. Apart from the big pirate, who was cowering with his hands over his head, there was no one left

standing but Dedrie, who had managed to drag Lord
Malvern off Irving's body and was staunching his wound
with her kerchief. Together they began to stagger back into
the fort.

The lord's raven had soared up into the sky after Lewen
and was now attacking him savagely, beating about his
head, pecking at his face, screeching in rage. Lewen had
both his hands up over his head and was twisting about in
his effort to avoid the bird. Any moment now he would slip
and fall, hurtling hundreds of feet to his death.

Rhiannon took two great strides forward, seized the bow
that had fallen from Ballard's hand and grabbed some arrows from the quiver still attached to his back. She raised the
bow high and took careful aim. If, by ill chance, she should
miss the raven, it would be her lover she would be killing.

Rhiannon's arrow flew true. High up into the air it
soared, and pierced the raven straight through the breast. It
fell in a welter of black feathers, and thudded into the
ground just in front of Lord Malvern.

"No!" he screamed. He dropped stiffly to his knees,
picking up the raven and cradling it to his breast, sobbing.
"Donal, Donal," he cried, and pressed his cheek into the
black, lifeless feathers.

"My laird, my laird, run!" Dedrie screeched. Then, seeing the shadow of the winged horse growing bigger with
every second as Lewen dropped towards them, she left him
and scuttled towards the door of the fort.

"No, ye don't!" Rhiannon cried, and tackled her with a
flying leap.

Dedrie hit the ground with a thump. Rhiannon sat
astride her then, as Dedrie tried to heave her off, grabbed
her head with both hands and knocked it hard against the
ground. Dedrie lay still.

The winged stallion's massive hooves came down
lightly upon the ground, and then Lewen's boots.

"Ye still banging people's heads on the ground?" he
said.

"Indeed I am," Rhiannon replied, then she scrambled up from Dedrie's prone body and ran to throw herself into his arms. They closed strongly about her. For a long moment they stood, embracing fiercely, rocking in each other's arms, then mutely Rhiannon raised her face and Lewen's mouth came down on hers.

A clatter of hooves, an indignant neigh, and then the emphatic shoving of a black muzzle separated them. Rhiannon looked around, caught between tears and laughter, to find Blackthorn behind her, dancing a little in her impatience. Rhiannon put her arms about her horse's neck, pressing her damp face into the silky black shoulder. Beside them, Lord Malvern rocked and wept, crooning to the dead raven in his arms, utterly oblivious to anything else. Lewen quietly took a coil of rope from his saddlebags and bound it about the old man. Lord Malvern looked up, briefly, his face misshapen with grief, then bent his grey head over the dead bird again.

"So ye're a thigearn now?" Rhiannon said when at last she found her voice. "Where on earth did ye find yourself a winged horse?"

"I made him," Lewen said, almost apologetically. "I could no' think how else to get here."

"Ye carved him?"

"From the oak tree that fell the night ye left."

"He's beautiful."

"Thank ye. I've called him Lightning."

"Blackthorn likes him too," Rhiannon said with an impish smile as the two horses touched noses, then whickered softly. "Do ye think . . . ?"

"Maybe one day," Lewen answered, grinning. "Who kens?"

Then, as the bluebird swooped around them, singing ecstatically, he stepped forward and slid his arms about Rhiannon again, his mouth finding hers. "I love ye," he whispered unsteadily when at last he came up for breath.

"Och, I ken," Rhiannon answered.

Bodies of Speech

Rhiannon and Lewen had only a few moments before Captain Dillon and the Yeomen were running towards them, faces grim. They took in the sight of the heaped bodies incredulously, then looked at the lord of Fettercairn, who rocked back and forth, keening over the body of his raven.

"Take him into custody," Captain Dillon said, and let his hand fall from his sword hilt, grateful that Joyeux was to be deprived of her feast. "And the skeelie too."

Lord Malvern clutched the bird closer and scuttled away as the soldiers approached him. "No!" he screamed. "Let me go! I'll give ye anything, anything ye want. I ken the secret o' life and death, ye ken. Help me escape and I will share them with ye. Is there no' someone ye love who is dead and cold in the ground? I will raise them for ye!"

Captain Dillon's face was hard as granite. His past was littered with dead loved ones. He turned away, saying quietly, "Gag and bind him, and throw him in the hold. The laird has an appointment with the hangman."

"Mercy! Mercy!" Lord Malvern screamed.

"I'll show ye the same mercy ye showed my lady Olwynne," Captain Dillon said, and strode away as the soldiers roughly wrested away the dead raven, bound and gagged him, and dragged him away. Lord Malvern fought them every step of the way, his face turned back to stare at the limp bundle of black feathers, tears pouring down his agonized face.

"To think that, in the end, the only thing he really loved was that blaygird bird," Lewen said.

"Should we no' let him have it?" Rhiannon said unhappily. "We canna just leave it lying there on the ground."

Lewen drew her to him, and kissed her. "Ye ken, ye try so hard to be fierce, but I do believe ye have the softest heart o' anyone I ken."

Rhiannon scowled. "What dragon dung!" she said scornfully.

Lewen laughed. "I see two weeks in Finn the Cat's company has improved your vocabulary immensely."

She grinned. "I do like her . . . what do ye call them? Her bodies o' speech."

"Her figures o' speech," Lewen corrected, and then saw her eyes gleaming with laughter. "Minx," he said.

They watched as the big pirate with the pet rat surrendered, meekly, and Dedrie was securely bound and carried away by two of the soldiers. Rhiannon called another back and gave him the dead raven. "Give it to the laird," she said gruffly.

The soldier grimaced with distaste, but took the bird and carried it away with him.

"Alone at last," Lewen said. "We have much to say, I hardly ken where to start. Tell me first. How are ye yourself? Are ye hurt?"

She touched her bloodstained shoulder. "A scratch, no more. And ye? How is your head?"

"Still ringing," he replied with a grin. He drew her to him again, and kissed her lingeringly. "I do no' ken what to say," he murmured at last. "I am so sorry."

The words were inadequate.

Between them lay an ocean of emotion—Rhiannon's anger and heartache at Lewen's betrayal of her, his own guilt and confusion, as well as the grief and horror he felt at Olwynne's death, even though it meant he had been freed from her love spell. Rhiannon had never been one for words, though. The look in his eyes, the warmth of his hands on her body, and the mesmerizing touch of his mouth were enough for her. She smiled and lifted her mouth to his again.

His hands were sliding under her shirt, pressing her closer and closer to him, his breath coming short, when Rafferty and Cameron came racing up the road in high excitement, Landon laboring along behind. Reluctantly Lewen let her go and stepped back, his color high, his expression rueful.

Once again their chance to talk and kiss privately was lost, as the boys dragged them back down to the burned and ruined pirate town, where Iseult waited to thank and congratulate them both.

All was noise and confusion. Owein was having his head rather inexpertly bandaged by a rosy-cheeked and shining-eyed Fèlice, while Iseult tried hard not to weep with relief and desperate sorrow. Captain Dillon was overseeing the rounding-up of all the prisoners and their safe incarceration in the hold of his ship. The sailors were readying the ships to sail at high speed, since everyone was most anxious to get back home to see what had happened in their absence. A company of soldiers had been sent up to bury the dead, and to exhume Olwynne's bones, to take back to Lucescere for burial in the MacCuinn crypt. Still more soldiers were loading up the ships with all the pirate loot taken as the spoils of war, while the pirate town was systematically burned to the ground behind them.

Roden was leaping around in high excitement, Lulu scampering beside him. He threw himself into Rhiannon's arms, embracing her joyfully, only to realize that she was hurt. So then Rhiannon was being bandaged up as well, and fussed over by Nina and Iven, and Lewen could do nothing but stand by, a hand on the back of both winged horses, while everyone marveled and exclaimed over the miracle of Lightning.

Lewen was feeling very hot in the cheeks, torn between pride and embarrassment at the clamor everyone made over the winged horse he had created out of a lightning-felled oak. He still did not understand himself how he had managed such a miracle, and he felt, uncomfortably, that it was due more to the grace of Eà than to his own puny powers.

He was relieved when Rafferty touched him gently on the shoulder and said, "My lady Iseult would like to speak to you, when you have a moment. Rhiannon, too."

Lewen could not help noticing the diffidence of Iseult's summons. He was used to a far more peremptory command. He nodded and caught Rhiannon by the elbow, steering her out of the noisy crowd. They followed Rafferty to an inn close to the jetty, one of the few buildings till standing in the fire-scorched pirate town.

Iseult was sitting by the unlit hearth, staring without seeing into the ashes. She was still dressed in her old-fashioned leather armor, stained and battle-scarred, though her helmet lay discarded on a nearby table. She had loosened her hair, and it flowed down her back, its fiery color faded almost as much as the embers in the grate. Her eyes, though, were as brilliantly blue as the summer sky, and for the first time in weeks, Lewen's breath did not hang frostily before his mouth as he approached her.

She smiled at him wearily. "I'm sorry to drag ye away from the celebrations," she said softly, indicating with a graceful gesture of her hand that they sit. "I just wanted to thank you—and apologize to you."

"No need," Lewen stammered as he sat down on the very edge of his chair.

Her smile widened. "I know how much I owe to ye both," she said. "If it was no' for ye, Owein would still be in that blaygird sorceress's hands. Margrit would never have let him go, I ken that. We would have had to fight, and more among us would have lost their lives, even if Owein had survived. I still find it hard to believe . . . the sight of

you soaring over the cliff, striking Margrit down, your
hands moving so fast they were a blur! Oh, Lewen! You
have been a true friend to the MacCuinns. Thank ye!"

Lewen swallowed a lump in his throat. "I . . . I'm glad I
could help."

"I am sorry I bid you stay behind," Iseult said. "I ken I
hurt ye."

He shrugged. "I wouldna have whittled Lightning if ye
hadn't."

Iseult laughed. "Then I am glad! The Spinners move in
mysterious ways. Obviously it was meant to be."

He found it hard to say the next words. "I only wish I
could've . . . been in time . . . got here earlier . . . Olwynne . . ."

Iseult put up one hand and pressed it against her eyes.
"Yes," she said. "I know. I too wish . . . oh, I wish so many
things! And all of them useless. Lachlan is dead, nothing
will bring him back, Olwynne . . . my little Olwynne! So
bright, so beautiful, so brilliant! I still cannot believe she is
dead. I've been thinking . . . I canna help thinking . . . why
canna we use the spell o' resurrection to bring her back?
Could we no' have saved her somehow? But who would I
sacrifice for her? Who could I kill without causing some
other mother the dreadful grief I feel now? I could no' do it."

Rhiannon moved restlessly.

Iseult glanced her way. "Ye think none would grieve to
lose ye?" she said, rather sharply. "Ye're wrong! There are
many who love ye, satyricorn girl, and many who would
grieve if you were lost. And I know ye did your best. I
know ye came close to saving her. Owein told me. So
thank ye for trying. I ken ye did no' love Olwynne. I ken
she did ye wrong. Owein told me it all. I am truly grateful
and . . ." She paused and fought a little battle with herself,
then said, more sharply than before, "I'm sorry too. I also
did ye wrong. If it was no' for Lewen, ye would've been
hanged, and that would have been a heavy burden on my

conscience, now I know the truth. I'm sorry. I hope ye will forgive me."

Rhiannon frowned, and did not know how to answer. The truth was, she had not forgiven Iseult. She had imagined she would carry a grudge against the Dowager Banrìgh forever. She was surprised to find herself moved by Iseult's words. Rhiannon would have mistrusted glibness, but the difficulty Iseult had in speaking the words made them seem more true.

When she did not speak, Iseult sighed and drew herself straighter in her chair. "When we are back in Lucescere, I will speak to Donncan . . . and to Bronwen . . . to the Rìgh and Banrìgh . . . I am sure they will reward you handsomely."

"I did not do what I did in hope of reward," Rhiannon said stiffly.

"No." Iseult's face softened. "Ye did it for love, did you no'? Lewen is a very lucky man, to be loved so much." Her voice wobbled.

"I am," he said. "Very lucky."

He put out one hand and covered Rhiannon's, clenched on the arm of her chair. She flashed a quick glance at him, and he smiled at her. After a moment, against her will, she found her mouth softening and the corners turning up. He grinned at her encouragingly, gave her hand a little pat, then tucked it up in his own big, warm hand and drew it into his lap. She could not help but smile more naturally.

"I'm sorry about Olwynne too," she said then, on impulse. "I really did try."

Iseult nodded. "Thank ye. It is no' your fault they killed her. All o' us tried, all o' us failed. I could spend the rest o' my life thinking if only, if only, and try as hard as I can, I canna help it running through my head almost continually. But I am determined not to wallow in my grief. That, more than anything else, is the true cause o' Olwynne's death. I was so overwhelmed by my grief for Lachlan, I did no' act fast enough . . . or well enough . . . and so now Olwynne is dead too."

"It's no one's fault but Laird Malvern's," Rhiannon said emphatically. "He wielded the knife! If ye're going to blame anyone, blame him!"

"Believe me, I do," Iseult said coldly.

"What will happen to him? And to Dedrie?"

"They will hang," Iseult answered. "And they should be grateful. If I had my way, they'd be staked out for the White Gods!"

By the look on Iseult's face, Rhiannon guessed her gods were as dark and fearsome as the dark walkers of the satyricorn. She made a little superstitious movement against harm, and Lewen took her free hand and tucked it up with the other.

"My lady," he said. "You spoke of the Rìgh. Does that mean . . . do ye have news?"

Iseult's face brightened. "Indeed I do! As soon as the weather calmed, a messenger bird flew in. It's a miracle it survived the storm. Donncan is safe in Rhyssmadill—and, can you believe it! If it wasn't for Bronwen, he could've been killed too, poisoned by the Fealde's man!" She told them about Bronwen's desperate swim to Donncan's side, and it was clear from her voice that she was amazed and impressed by the Banrìgh's courage and fortitude. "Who would have believed she had the wit, or the spunk?" Iseult marveled. "And Beau says she and Donncan are just as a newlywed couple should be, with eyes and hands for no one but each other." She sighed, and then shrugged and smiled, dabbing at her eyes with her sodden scrap of a handkerchief.

"But here's news!" she cried. "Beau and Dide are to marry! After all these years! I can hardly believe it. And he is to join the Coven, so I daresay we shall be seeing a lot more o' him. I am so glad."

Lewen and Rhiannon both exclaimed in surprise and pleasure, and then Lewen said, a little of his diffidence returning, "My lady, ye ken that I . . . that Rhiannon and I . . . we shall want to jump the fire too, just as soon as we can."

Iseult looked at him in silence for a long moment, then slowly nodded her head. "I ken Olwynne ensorcelled ye," she said, low and stilted. "I ken it was no' true love that led ye to jump the fire with her. But if ye and Rhiannon could wait a while . . . just a while . . . I do no' want all to ken . . ." Her voice trailed away.

Lewen glanced at Rhiannon. It was half a question, half a plea. Rhiannon had to wrestle with her jealousy and pride. She wanted everyone to know that Lewen was hers, and had always been hers. So she tossed her head and said, "It'll have to be a while, anyway. I have lots I want to do. I want to go see this Theurgia everyone keeps talking about and see if I want to go there, and then I want to go back to Fettercairn Castle . . ."

"But why?" Lewen exclaimed.

"Rory. The little ghost-boy. He is still there, all alone, except for the ghosts of all those other murdered boys. I promised to help him, though I do no' ken how."

Iseult smiled at her. "Isabeau can help you there. She will ken what to do."

"I would like Rory to be at rest," Rhiannon said. Much to her shame, tears prickled her eyes. She scowled and willed them away.

"I would no' be surprised if Donncan and Bronwen give ye the castle for your own," Iseult said.

Rhiannon gaped at her. "Me? Fettercairn Castle? Why?"

"By all accounts, it is in a most strategic position," Iseult said. "Donncan will want someone loyal to him and Bronwen to man it, and ye and Lewen have proved your loyalty over and over again. If ye plan to marry, as ye say ye are, well, then, it would be a fitting wedding present, do ye no' think so? Besides, Isabeau will want the Tower of Ravens to be rebuilt, and I canna think o' anyone better suited than ye and Lewen to head it . . ."

"Me?" Both Rhiannon and Lewen spoke at once, then glanced at each other and laughed.

"In time," Iseult said, smiling. "Ye are still only very young. Yet I would be very surprised if you are no' awarded your sorcerer's rings for what you have done these last few weeks—especially ye, Lewen! Whittling a living horse out o' a lump o' old wood! It's extraordinary!"

"I do no' think I could ever do it again," Lewen admitted, looking worried.

"Your winged horse is testament enough to the fact ye have done it once . . ." Iseult began.

"Twice!" Rhiannon cried. "Do no' forget Bluey!"

The little bluebird had been perched all this time on the back of Rhiannon's chair, sharpening its beak on a cuttlefish it had found down on the seashore. At the sound of its name, it looked up and chirped and ruffled up its wings, then returned to the cuttlefish.

Iseult was properly amazed, and Lewen and Rhiannon had to tell her the whole story. Then Lewen asked, rather shyly, "What about ye, my lady? What do ye plan to do now?"

She looked pensive. "I will join the Coven, I think," she said. "I have much to learn. And then, if all goes well, I will go back to the snows. I have missed them dreadfully all these years. The Tower of Roses and Thorns needs a First Sorceress—it is the only witches' tower to survive Maya's Burning intact, and yet few witches have been willing to leave Lucescere and go up there to the mountain heights. So much knowledge there, in the library, just waiting to be found!"

Just then, the door to the inn opened and a stream of happy, bright-faced people poured in, looking for food and drink. Owein was in the lead, his arm about Fèlice's waist, with Rafferty, Cameron, and Landon on their heels, and Nina and Iven following behind with Roden swinging between them. All were talking and laughing, though there was a shadow on Owein's face that no amount of relief and

pleasure at his safe deliverance could banish. Owein had
lost his twin sister, and had not yet had time or leisure to
truly realize the implications of that loss. Lewen knew his
friend would find it very hard in the upcoming months, and
promised him silently that he would be there for him. They
exchanged a quick glance of troubled understanding, before Owein turned away and called for ale.

At the sight of Rhiannon, Fèlice ran forward, her hands
held out, her face shining. The two girls embraced eagerly,
though Rhiannon could not help wincing and pulling away
at the fresh pain in her shoulder. They had much to tell
each other, and sat exchanging stories for quite some time,
while everyone else ate and drank and talked around them.

"But your hair, your bonny hair," Rhiannon said. "How
could ye cut it all off!"

Fèlice tossed her head. "It took only a second, I assure
ye, and I've no' missed it at all! I feel much lighter and
freer without it. Besides, I'll wager ye that it'll be all the
rage the day after I get back! All the lassies will be cutting
their hair off too, I promise ye."

Rhiannon grinned. "I only make bets when I can be sure
o' winning them," she said. "Oh, Fèlice, it's so good to see
ye!"

"I was so worried about ye," Fèlice said. "Is everything . . . is everything all right now?" She searched Rhiannon's face.

Rhiannon smiled broadly. "It's better than all right."

"I'm so glad," Fèlice said and squeezed her hand. Then
she leaned forward and whispered, with a quick sideways
glance at Owein, "I think everything's all right for me too."

"I ken it is," Rhiannon replied, and cast Owein a laughing glance.

By noon, the ships were ready to leave the Pirate Isles behind them.

"It is too far for ye to fly back to Dùn Gorm," Iseult

said. "Let us tether your horses on the deck, and ye can travel back with us."

"No, thank ye," Lewen said firmly. "Lightning would no' like that at all."

"Nor Blackthorn," Rhiannon said.

"Are ye sure?"

"Sure we're sure," Lewen said. "Leave us some supplies, and we'll rest up here for tonight and fly home in the morning."

"We'll beat ye home," Rhiannon said challengingly.

Owein grinned at his friend. "Cunning dog," he said in a low voice, knowing how crowded and noisy the ship would be, and how difficult it would be for him to get Fèlice alone, as he so wanted to do.

Lewen smiled. "Have a pleasant trip. See ye at Rhyssmadill!"

They stood together on the jetty and waved until the ships were sailing out of the lagoon, then Lewen turned and seized Rhiannon fiercely. "Now where shall we go?" he demanded, bending to kiss her throat. "The pirate town's a ruin, so that leaves the fort or the forest."

Rhiannon laughed at him. "Can we try the fort?" she asked plaintively. "I would so like to make love in a bed, with pillows and sheets, just for something new."

Lewen laughed. "That's another thing I love about ye, Rhiannon," he said. "There's never any pretense at coyness."

"I'm no' quite sure what that means," Rhiannon said, "but I'm guessing it's a compliment."

"It is, believe me, it is."

"Well, let's go and check out the auld fort," Rhiannon said. "I can tell ye they have one very cold and uncomfortable cell, but other than that, I ken naught."

She swung herself up onto Blackthorn's back, smoothing the mare's silky black hide with a loving hand.

"Race ye?" she asked with a wicked grin, then dug her

heels into the mare's sides so that Blackthorn leaped straight up into the air, wings snapping open.

Laughing and cursing, Lewen leaped onto Lightning's back and bent low, urging his stallion to follow. The big bay spread his dark wings and soared in pursuit. Darting ahead of them, caroling in joy, flew the bluebird.

Higher and higher, the two winged horses climbed, until the sea lay below them like a discarded gown, and the misty horizon curved. Then slowly, enjoying the tilt of the earth on its axis, they circled down, in search of a place where they could love each other in peace.

AFTERWORD

"Thence we came forth to see the stars again"

—DANTE ALIGHIERI
Divina Commedia, 1314–1320

Goblin

~~~⌄~~~

The grand dining room of the Theurgia was humming with talk and laughter as the morning meal was brought in by a long line of servants.

Rhiannon sat at a long trestle table with Fèlice, both dressed in the sober black robes of apprentice-witches, giggling and pretending to ignore the winks and waves of Owein and Lewen at the boys' table alongside. It had been almost three weeks since Olwynne's death, and although Owein still grieved for his murdered twin, he was by nature buoyant and optimistic, and even more determined than ever to enjoy his life to the full.

"Fèlice!" he cried. "Do ye want to go to the Nisse and Nixie tonight? Maya the Mesmerizing is singing again!"

"Maybe," she called back. "Is fuzzle-gin on the menu?"

"For ye, anything!" he called back.

"In that case, it's a date," she called back. "As long as ye can organize a few extra boys for Maisie and Edithe."

Owein groaned. "Do I have to?"

"Aye," she said sweetly. "Else I simply canna come."

"Lewen, we need sacrifices, willing or unwilling," Owein said. "Who do we know?"

Lewen bit back a grin. "Got a score to settle with anyone?" he asked. "How about that boy that dared ask Fèlice to dance last night?"

"I like the way your mind works," Owein replied. Then

he scowled. "As long as he doesna try to ask Fèlice to dance again."

"I'm sure he wouldna dare, after the black looks he got from ye last night," Lewen said. "Besides, once we let Edithe know he's there to squire her . . ."

"I'll tell her he's an up-and-coming lord with great prospects at court," Owein said triumphantly. "She won't let him out o' her sight!"

Just then the peace of the morning was disrupted by screams. Lewen and Owen at once leaped to their feet, pulses suddenly hammering painfully. It was not as easy to forget the past as they had thought.

But the screams were caused by the sight of a tiny elven cat resolutely dragging a huge black rat up the aisle. The rat was dead, and three times the size of the little cat.

Goblin dragged the dead rat all the way up to the high table, where Finn and Jay were breakfasting with the other sorcerers. Isabeau and Iseult sat side by side, like mirror images in their white sorceress robes, their eyebrows shooting up in surprise.

Finn put her hand over her mouth. "Goblin!" she cried weakly. "Must ye?"

Goblin laid the dead rat down on her shoe, then sat back, purring loudly.

Iseult and Isabeau looked at each other. "I wonder . . ." the Keybearer said.

"We will never know," Iseult replied.

Glossary

acolytes: students of witchcraft who have not yet passed their Second Test of Powers; usually aged between eight and sixteen.

ahdayeh: a series of exercises used as meditation in motion. Derived from the Khan'cohban art of fighting.

apprentice-witch: a student of witchcraft who has passed the Second Test of Powers, usually undertaken at the age of sixteen.

arak: a small, monkey-like creature.

Arran: south-east land of Eileanan, ruled by the MacFóghnan clan.

Aslinn: deeply forested land, ruled by the MacAislin clan.

banprionnsa: princess or duchess.

banrigh: queen.

Beltane: May Day; the first day of summer.

Ben Eyrie: third highest mountain in Eileanan; part of the Broken Ring of Dubhslain.

blaygird: evil, awful.

Blèssem: rich farmland south of Rionnagan, ruled by the MacThanach clan.

Blue Guards: the Yeomen of the Guard, the Rìgh's own elite company of soldiers. They act as his personal bodyguard, both on the battlefield and in peacetime.

Brann the Raven: one of the First Coven of Witches.

Known for probing the darker mysteries of magic, and for fascination with machinery and technology.

Broken Ring of Dubhslain: mountains that curve in a crescent around the highlands of Ravenshaw.

Bronwen NicCuinn: daughter of former Rìgh Jaspar Mac-Cuinn and Maya the Ensorcellor; she was named Banrìgh of Eileanan by her father on his deathbed but ruled for just six hours as a newborn baby, before Lachlan the Winged wrested the throne from her.

Candlemas: the end of winter and beginning of spring.

Carraig: land of the sea-witches, the northernmost land of Eileanan, ruled by the MacSeinn clan.

Celestines: race of faery creatures, renowned for empathic abilities and knowledge of stars and prophecy.

Clachan: southernmost land of Eileanan, a province of Rionnagan ruled by the MacCuinn clan.

claymore: a heavy, two-edged sword, often as tall as a man.

cluricaun: small woodland faery.

Connor: a Yeoman of the Guard. Was once a beggar-boy in Lucescere and member of the League of the Healing Hand.

corrigan: mountain faery with the power of assuming the look of a boulder. The most powerful can cast other illusions.

Coven of Witches: the central ruling body for witches in Eileanan, led by the Keybearer and a council of twelve other sorcerers and sorceresses called the Circle. The Coven administers all rites and rituals in the worship of the universal life-force witches call Eà, runs schools and hospitals, and advises the Crown.

Craft: applications of the One Power through spells, incantations, and magical objects.

The Cripple: leader of the rebellion against the rule of Jaspar and Maya.

Cuinn Lionheart: leader of the First Coven of Witches; his descendants are called MacCuinn.

Cunning: applications of the One Power through will and desire.

cunning man: village wise man or warlock.

cursehags: wicked faery race, prone to curses and evil spells. Known for their filthy personal habits.

Dai-dein: father.

Day of Betrayal: the day Jaspar the Ensorcelled turned on the witches, exiling or executing them, and burning the Witch Towers.

Dedrie: healer at Fettercairn Castle; was formerly nurse-maid to Rory, the young son of Lord Falkner MacFerris.

Dide the Juggler: a jongleur who was rewarded for his part in Lachlan the Winged's successful rebellion by being made Didier Laverock, Earl of Caerlaverock. Is often called the Rìgh's minstrel.

Dillon of the Joyous Sword: Captain of the Yeomen of the Guard. Was once a beggar-boy and Captain of the League of the Healing Hand.

Donncan Feargus MacCuinn: eldest son of Lachlan Mac-Cuinn and Iseult NicFaghan. Has wings like a bird and can fly. Was named for Lachlan's two brothers, who were transformed into blackbirds by Maya the Ensorcellor.

Dughall MacBrann: the Prionnsa of Ravenshaw and cousin to the Rìgh.

Eà: the Great Life Spirit, mother and father of all.

Eileanan: largest island in the archipelago called the Far Islands.

Elemental Powers: the forces of air, earth, fire, water and spirit, which together make up the One Power.

Enit Silverthroat: grandmother of Dide and Nina; died at the Battle of Bonnyblair.

equinox: a time when day and night are of equal length, occurring twice a year.

Fairge; Fairgean: faery creatures who need both sea and land to live.

Falkner MacFerris: former lord of Fettercairn Castle.

Fettercairn Castle: a fortress guarding the pass into the highlands of Ravenshaw, and the Tower of Ravens. Owned by the MacFerris clan.

Finn the Cat: nickname of Fionnghal NicRuraich.

Fionnghal NicRuraich: eldest daughter of Anghus Mac-Ruraich of Rurach; was once a beggar-girl in Lucescere and Lieutenant of the League of the Healing Hand.

First Coven of Witches: thirteen witches who fled persecution in their own land, invoking an ancient spell that folded the fabric of the universe and brought them and all their followers to Eileanan in a journey called the Great Crossing. The eleven great clans of Eileanan are all descended from the First Coven, with the MacCuinn clan being the greatest of the eleven. The thirteen witches were Cuinn Lionheart, his son Owein of the Longbow, Ahearn Horse-laird, Aislinna the Dreamer, Berhtilde the Bright Warrior-Maid, Fóghnan the Thistle, Rùraich the Searcher, Seinneadair the Singer, Sian the Storm-Rider, Tuathanach the Farmer, Brann the Raven, Faodhagan the Red and his twin sister, Sorcha the Bright (now called the Murderess).

Gearradh: goddess of death; of the Three Spinners, Gearradh is she who cuts the thread.

gillie: personal servant.

gillie-coise: bodyguard.

Gladrielle the Blue: the smaller of the two moons, lavender blue in color.

gravenings: ravenous creatures that nest and swarm together, steal lambs and chickens from farmers, and have been known to steal babies and young children. Will eat anything they can carry away in their claws. Collective noun is "screech."

Greycloaks: the Rìgh's army, so called because of their camouflaging cloaks.

Hogmanay: New Year's Eve; an important celebration in the culture of Eileanan.

Horned Ones: another name for the satyricorns, a race of fierce horned faeries.

Irving: seneschal at Fettercairn Castle.

Isabeau the Shapechanger: Keybearer of the Coven; twin sister of the Banrìgh Iseult NicFaghan.

Iseult of the Snows: twin sister of Isabeau NicFaghan; Banrìgh of Eileanan by marriage to Lachlan the Winged.

Iven Yellowbeard: a jongleur and courier in the service of Lachlan the Winged; was formerly a Yeoman of the Guard; married to Nina the Nightingale and father to Roden.

Jaspar MacCuinn: former Rìgh of Eileanan, often called Jaspar the Ensorcelled. Was married to Maya the Ensorcellor.

Jay the Fiddler: a minstrel in the service of Lachlan the Winged. Was once a beggar-boy in Lucescere and member of the League of the Healing Hand.

Johanna: a healer. Was once a beggar-girl in Lucescere and member of the League of the Healing Hand.

jongleur: a traveling minstrel, juggler, conjurer.

journeywitch: a traveling witch who performs rites for villages that do not have a witch, and seeks out children with magical powers who can be taken on as acolytes.

Keybearer: the leader of the Coven of Witches.

Khan'cohbans: a faery race of warlike, snow-skimming nomads who live on the high mountains of the Spine of the World.

Lachlan the Winged: Rìgh of Eileanan.

League of the Healing Hand: a band of beggar children who were instrumental in helping Lachlan the Winged win his throne.

leannan: sweetheart.

Lewen: an apprentice-witch and squire to Lachlan; son of Lilanthe of the Forest and Niall the Bear.

Lilanthe of the Forest: a tree-shifter; married to Niall the Bear, and mother to Lewen and Meriel.

loch; lochan (pl): lake.

Lucescere: ancient city built on an island above the Shining Waters; the traditional home of the MacCuinns and the Tower of Two Moons.

Mac: son of

MacAhern: one of the eleven great clans; descendants of Ahearn Horse-laird.

MacBrann: one of the eleven great clans; descendants of Brann the Raven.

MacCuinn: one of the eleven great clans, descendants of Cuinn Lionheart.

Magnysson the Red: the larger of the two moons, crimson red in color, commonly thought of as a symbol of war and conflict. Old tales describe him as a thwarted lover, chasing his lost love, Gladrielle, across the sky.

Malvern MacFerris: lord of Fettercairn Castle; brother of former lord Falkner MacFerris.

Maya the Ensorcellor: former Banrìgh of Eileanan, wife of Jaspar and mother of Bronwen; now known as Maya the Mute.

moonbane: a hallucinogenic drug distilled from the moonflower plant.

necromancy: the forbidden art of resurrecting the dead.

Niall the Bear: formerly a Yeoman of the Guard; now married to Lilanthe of the Forest, and father to Lewen and Meriel.

Nic: daughter of.

Nila: King of the Fairgean; half brother of Maya the Ensorcellor.

Nina the Nightingale: jongleur and sorceress of the Coven;

sister to Didier Laverock, earl of Caerlaverock, and grand-daughter of Enit Silverthroat.
nisse: small woodland faery.

Olwynne NicCuinn: daughter of Lachlan MacCuinn and Iseult NicFaghan; twin sister of Owein.
One Power: the life-energy that is contained in all things. Witches draw upon the One Power to perform their acts of magic. The One Power contains all the elemental forces of air, earth, water, fire, and spirit, and witches are usually more powerful in one force than others.
Owein MacCuinn: second son of Lachlan MacCuinn and Iseult NicFaghan; twin brother of Olwynne. Has wings like a bird.

prionnsa; prionnsachan (pl): prince, duke.

Ravenscraig: estate of the MacBrann clan. Once their hunting castle, but they moved their home there after Rhyssmadill fell into ruin.
Ravenshaw: deeply forested land west of Rionnagan, ruled by the MacBrann clan, descendants of Brann, one of the First Coven of Witches.
Razor's Edge: dangerous path through the mountains of the Broken Ring of Dubhslain, only used in times of great need.
Red Guards: soldiers in service to Maya the Ensorcellor during her reign as Banrìgh.
Rhiannon: a half-satyricorn; daughter of One-Horn and a captured human.
Rhyssmadill: the Rìgh's castle by the sea, once owned by the MacBrann clan.
rìgh; rìghrean (pl): king.
Rionnagan: together with Clachan and Blèssem, the richest lands in Eileanan. Ruled by MacCuinns, descendants of Cuinn Lionheart, leader of the First Coven of Witches.

Roden: son of Nina the Nightingale and Iven Yellowbeard; Viscount Laverock of Caerlaverock.

Rory: deceased son of Lord Falkner MacFerris of Fettercairn and Lady Evaline NicKinney.

Rurach: wild mountainous land lying between Tìreich and Siantan, and ruled by the MacRuraich clan.

saber-leopard: savage feline with curved fangs that lives in the remote mountain areas.

sacred woods: ash, hazel, oak, rowan, fir, hawthorn, and yew.

Samhain: first day of winter; festival for the souls of the dead. Best time of year to see the future.

satyricorn: a race of fierce horned faeries.

scrying: to perceive through crystal gazing or other focus. Most witches can scry if the object to be perceived is well known to them.

Seekers: a force created by former Rìgh Jaspar the Ensorcelled to find those with magical abilities so they could be tried and executed.

seelie: tall, shy race of faeries known for their physical beauty and magical skills.

seneschal: steward.

sennachie: genealogist and record-keeper of the clan chief's house.

sgian dubh: small knife worn in the boot.

Siantan: northwest land of Eileanan, famous for its weather witches. Ruled by the MacSian clan.

skeelie: a village witch or wise woman.

Skill: a common application of magic, such as lighting a candle or dowsing for water.

Spinners: goddesses of fate. Include the spinner Sniomhar, the goddess of birth; the weaver Breabadair, goddess of life; and she who cuts the thread, Gearradh, goddess of death.

Talent: the combination of a witch's strengths in the different forces often manifest as a particularly powerful Talent; for example, Lewen's Talent is in working with wood and Nina's is in singing.

Test of Elements: once witches are fully accepted into the coven at the age of twenty-four, they learn Skills in the element in which they are strongest, i.e., air, earth, fire, water, or spirit. The First Test of any element wins them a ring, which is worn on the right hand. If they pass the Third Test in any one element, the witch is called a sorcerer or sorceress, and wears a ring on his or her left hand. It is very rare for any witch to win a sorceress ring in more than one element.

Test of Powers: a witch is first tested on his or her eighth birthday, and if any magical powers are detected, he or she becomes an acolyte. On their sixteenth birthday, witches undertake the Second Test of Powers, in which they must make a moonstone ring and witch's dagger. If they pass, they are permitted to become an apprentice. On their twenty-fourth birthday, witches undertake the Third Test of Powers, in which they must remake their dagger and cut and polish a staff. If successfully completed, the apprentice is admitted into the Coven of Witches. Apprentices wear black robes; witches wear white robes.

Theurgia: a school for acolytes and apprentice-witches at the Tower of Two Moons in Lucescere.

thigearn: horse-lairds who ride flying horses.

Tìreich: land of the horse-lairds. Most westerly country of Eileanan, ruled by the MacAhern clan.

Tìrlethan: land of the Twins; ruled by the MacFaghan clan.

Tìrsoilleir: the Bright Land or the Forbidden Land. Northeast land of Eileanan, ruled by the MacHilde clan.

Tòmas the Healer: boy with healing powers, who saved the lives of thousands of soldiers during the Bright Wars; died saving Lachlan's life at the Battle of Bonnyblair.

The Towers of the Witches: thirteen towers built as centers of learning and witchcraft in the twelve lands of Eileanan. Most are now ruined, but the Tower of Two Moons in

Lucescere has been restored as the home of the Coven of Witches and its school, the Theurgia. The Coven hope to rebuild the thirteen High Towers but also to encourage towns and regions to build their own towers.

tree-changer: woodland faery that can shift shape from tree to humanlike creature. A half-breed is called a *tree-shifter* and can sometimes look almost human.

trictrac: a form of backgammon.

uile-bheist; uile-bheistean (pl): monster

Yedda: sea-witches.

Yeomen of the Guard: Also known as the Blue Guards. The Rìgh's own personal bodyguard, responsible for his safety.

Kate Forsyth lives in Sydney, Australia, with her husband, Greg; their three children, Benjamin, Timothy, and Eleanor; a little black cat called Shadow, and thousands of books. She has wanted to be a writer for as long as she can remember and has certainly been writing stories from the time she learned to hold a pen. Being allowed to read, write, and daydream as much as she likes and call it working is the most wonderful life imaginable and so she thanks you all for making it possible.

You can read more about Kate on her Web site at www.kateforsyth.com.au or send a message to her at kforsyth@ozemail.com.au.

THE ULTIMATE IN
SCIENCE FICTION AND FANTASY!

From magical tales of distant worlds to stories of
technological advances beyond the grasp of man, Penguin has
everything you need to stretch your imagination to its limits.

penguin.com

ACE
Get the latest information on favorites like
William Gibson, T.A. Barron, Brian Jacques,
Ursula K. LeGuin, Sharon Shinn, and Charlaine Harris,
as well as updates on the best new authors.

ROC
Escape with Harry Turtledove, Anne Bishop,
S.M. Stirling, Simon R. Green, Chris Bunch, Jim Butcher,
E.E. Knight, and many others—plus news on the
latest and hottest in science fiction and fantasy.

DAW
Mercedes Lackey, Kristen Britain, Tanya Huff,
Tad Williams, C.J. Cherryh, and many more—
DAW has something to satisfy the cravings of any
science fiction and fantasy lover.
Also visit dawbooks.com.

*Get the best of science fiction and fantasy
at your fingertips!*